*To Ken
Enjoy the book*

The Songs Of Angels

G.A. Weston

TRAFFORD
USA • Canada • UK • Ireland

© Copyright 2006 Gary Alan Weston.
All rights reserved. No part of this publication may be reproduced, stored in a retrieval system, or transmitted, in any form or by any means, electronic, mechanical, photocopying, recording, or otherwise, without the written prior permission of the author.

All characters in this book are fictitious and any resemblance to actual persons, living or dead, is purely coincidental.

This book is sold subject to the condition that it shall not, by way of trade or otherwise, be lent, re-sold, hired out or otherwise circulated in any form of binding or cover other than that in which it is published and without a similar condition including this condition being imposed on the subsequent purchaser.

Note for Librarians: A cataloguing record for this book is available from Library and Archives Canada at www.collectionscanada.ca/amicus/index-e.html
ISBN 1-4120-9295-7

Printed in Victoria, BC, Canada. Printed on paper with minimum 30% recycled fibre.
Trafford's print shop runs on "green energy" from solar, wind and other environmentally-friendly power sources.

Offices in Canada, USA, Ireland and UK

Book sales for North America and international:
Trafford Publishing, 6E–2333 Government St.,
Victoria, BC V8T 4P4 CANADA
phone 250 383 6864 (toll-free 1 888 232 4444)
fax 250 383 6804; email to orders@trafford.com

Book sales in Europe:
Trafford Publishing (UK) Limited, 9 Park End Street, 2nd Floor
Oxford, UK OX1 1HH UNITED KINGDOM
phone 44 (0)1865 722 113 (local rate 0845 230 9601)
facsimile 44 (0)1865 722 868; info.uk@trafford.com

Order online at:
trafford.com/06-1049

10 9 8 7 6 5 4 3 2

Know then thyself, presume not God to scan,
The proper study of mankind is man.
Plac'd on this isthmus of a middle state,
A being darkly wise, and rudely great:
With too much knowledge for the Skeptic side,
With too much weakness for the Stoic's pride,
He hangs between; in doubt to act, or rest;
In doubt to deem himself a God, or Beast;
In doubt his Mind or Body to prefer;
Born but to die, and reas'ning but to err;
Alike in ignorance, his reason such,
Whether he thinks too little, or too much.

From *Essay on Man* by Alexander Pope

To Kay

PART ONE

Last week

< It's driving me insane; all that I ever hear is endless moaning and snivelling. >

"Unfortunately that's part of the job."

< Yes, but I seem to be the only dickhead in this whole place who has a fucking job, what marvels did you perform today? >

"You know the brief the boss gave us, we are to observe and wait."

< And that boils down to everyone except me, sitting on his fat backside, and what exactly are we waiting for? >

"Why are you asking me? Ask him."

< You're closer to him than I, and I have asked him. All I got, was that smug look, you know the one? >

"Yes."

< And of course you know what he said. >

"He said that you should trust him."

< What sort of pathetic and evasive answer is that I ask you? When the whole situation is turning to shit? We should call it a day, go and do something that has a slim chance of success. >

"It's talk like this and your attitude, which ensured that you ended up here in the first place. You pushed and pushed until he had to act."

< And wasn't that fucking convenient. Who else would be able to hold

this hellhole in check? You? >

"Having a go at me will not help you. There's only Michael and I who are fighting your corner, when you're not being a conceited ass. The way you operate, you should be grateful that you still have a few friends."

< I don't mean to piss you off, I just need a break; will you speak to him for me? >

"You know it wouldn't do any good. You know that I've tried before and he just gets one of his moods on. You created this mess for yourself with your constant doubting and negative behaviour. Jesus Christ I would probably have done the same!"

< But you didn't, and don't blaspheme; it's not like you. >

"You're telling me not to blaspheme? Your language is vile."

< Yes, but I operate in the gutter and you do not. When you live in filth, you learn to speak shit. >

"If only you could have just towed the line and trusted him."

< Then I would have been a fraud! And do you know why?>

No reply

< I would have been a fraud because he is wrong. >

"You don't know that."

< Yes I do, in my heart. I'm sorry if I can't blindly follow Mr. Perfect like the rest of you. >

"That's not fair. I do not blindly follow him, I trust him and so do the others."

< And what will you do if he is wrong? How will you justify your actions, or should I say lack of actions? >

Silence

< Come on, what will you do? >

"The question is immaterial, it will not matter if he is wrong."

< How can you say that? Your answers are as sanctimonious as his. You may as well have said 'trust me'. Of course it will fucking matter, how can you sit there and not care if all this effort goes to waste? This could have all been spectacular. Instead we are letting the monkeys run riot with the organ. There's no planning and no recognizable strategy. For the life of me, I cannot honestly see where this pointless exercise will end >

"This is why you piss him off so much."

< Good! Fuck you and him! You think I shouldn't have these doubts?

The Songs of Angels

Unfortunately for me, I care about the people he uses in this game. Perhaps that's why I don't worship the boss, like the rest of you do. >

"There's no talking to you when you get like this. All you need to do is your job. Don't worry about the final objective. It will all become clear as it goes on."

< Did the big boss man tell you to say that? >

"You are such a dick sometimes, is it your plan to alienate me?"

< Fuck you. >

"Look, I have to go soon, can't we part with a nice word for each other?"

< Still fuck you. >

"I'm too old and too tired to argue with you anymore, when is our next meeting?"

< I won't be there, tell him I'm quitting. >

Laughter,

"You wouldn't quit, you couldn't. It's not in your nature."

< Yes I could, I would sit on a beach all day and sip cocktails, occasionally go surfing or swimming, and not giving a shit about the rest of you. >

"This isn't Microsoft you're working for! You know there's no retirement plan in this job, so get on with your assignment. Honestly you moan more than your charges."

Silence

"So when's the next meeting?"

< Two weeks from now, at my place >

"Right, that's in my diary. And I do not wish to hear of any more wild fantasies about quitting. There's only one way out of this, and that's to see it through to the end. Whatever that outcome may be, and whether you like it or not. Surely you must understand this by now?"

< Yes. >

"That's better," *the anger leaves his face.* "You always manage to do this to me. Every time I see you, we end up arguing."

< My quarrel was never with you my brother. Please excuse me. >

"I'm sorry to. You must lift your chin up brother, it could be worse."

<Oh, not for me Gabriel, how could it be worse for me? >

Pause

Softly: "There is nothing you can do to change this."
Further silence
< So if you're going, I'll say Goodnight to you. >
"And God willing, in three weeks I'll see you in Hell."
< Is that supposed to be funny? >
A barely detectable smile briefly flickers across Gabriel's face.
< Jesus Christ Gabriel, do you honestly think in your wildest dreams, that you're the first individual to ever crack that joke? >
"Sorry Lucifer, it was in bad taste. Goodnight my brother."
Gabriel turns to leave.
< And the same to you brother. >

CHAPTER 1

A relatively long time ago

In the beginning, we were all enthralled by the glory of God. There seemed no miracle that there was God and us. Although he obviously created all of the Angels, as he then created matter. But before matter, there was only Heaven. God and the Angels. Why he created Angels? I do not know, perhaps he was bored or lonely, and don't ask me where he came from, because again, I do not know, and I suspect that neither does he.

So first there was God, and he made the Angels. At this time in Heaven, matter did not exist, no sun or stars or material life. I think that I remember being blissfully happy, but I do not remember as you might recall an event from your past. You see, it was not a thousand or a million years ago, the concept of time was alien to us then, as was form. We just were. I truly know that we were alive but we did not possess structure, astral or otherwise. Just the light of God and the lesser lights of us, adoring him and part of him, his children for want of a better description. Conceivably an eon did pass while we sat and bathed in his light, or perhaps it was merely his initial breath. A moment, maybe the first throw of the dice in God's game.

And then apparently from nowhere, matter exploded into our reality. It was all around us, it inundated us, and we were astonished. All the Angels turned to God, and cried out in terror and confusion.

And God said, "What you observe is matter. And I have created matter from my essence, as I crafted all of you my children, and matter is but another of my children"

So we watched in wonder as matter grew and condensed, we knew time and it's passage. And when matter caught fire all across the universe, we all ran back to God in blind terror, and he becalmed us. "This is the nature of matter," he stated, "Are the stars not beautiful?" and they were beautiful, like tiny monuments to God, but sculptured from matter.

I explicitly remember the very first time that I ever felt sadness, or what I would describe today as sadness. It was as I witnessed a solitary star fade from view, vanishing from the heavens. I hastily journeyed to the place in which it had shone, to uncover the reason for this peculiarity. And I was horrified to find none of its glorious light, just a broken and darkened shell.

How could this be? Something that had been was no more. Something that I considered alive, as alive as I was alive, had perished. So I rushed to God and told him of my anguish, thinking that he would instantly fix the anomaly in his creation. God just smiled his smile, the same smile I would see again and again, a thousand times before the fall, the one that conveys his understanding of your utter stupidity. "Lucifer, Lucifer," he said, "This was expected; matter is not endless as we are. It will see countless changes and be reborn anew, again and again. Do not feel sadness, open your heart and you will see that matter is wonderful. Go back and watch, for every star that disappears, you will see a new one born."

So I watched the heavens and saw new stars appear, and they filled me with joy. But always I was saddened when their lights were extinguished. I think this was the first time that I questioned God, but it certainly was not to be the last.

Enough of the history lessons for now. Time to go to work

This Morning

The sky is the first thing that depresses me, as I walk the path that will lead me back into my kingdom. No clouds or sunshine, no birds or stars, just monotonous grey from beginning to end. The sky never changes in my home, in Hell. I make for level one and my offices. Perhaps this would be a good time to tell you about my realm. So walk with me for a while.

Hell is made up of five distinct levels. All are endless; we will never run out of room in Hell. When a human material body dies, they have a choice. No God or jury will decide if you destination is Heaven or Hell, it's entirely up to you. The catch is that you cannot lie. What you do in life determines your choice, and based on this information, you will pick your eternal resting place. If you are truly good, then you can go to Heaven. You do not have to be Mother Theresa, as long as you feel in your heart that you deserve to go to Heaven, it will be your destination.

However, if you doubt slightly that you are pure enough, then you will meet me. And no one who ever, I repeat: Ever goes to Hell can go to Heaven. It can only get worse. Level one is where all the confused souls end up, these were not particularly bad people in life, and in my opinion, they should all be in Heaven, but I do not make up the rules. So level one has become the most populated place in the universe. Someone once calculated that ten percent of all the humans who have ever been born, are still alive on Earth. But let me tell you this, two thirds of all those who have ever died, reside in level one. More souls than all the other levels of Hell and the population of Heaven put together, and it's getting worse.

There is no hope once you are here. If you behave then you can stay, and if you do not, then you're off to level two. So we try to keep level one as comfortable as possible. I will not say it is a nice place to spend eternity, because it is not. There is no fire and brimstone on level one, just existence without hope of improvement, populated by sad souls for infinity.

The other levels are progressively worse. If I could be permitted to use a simile and liken Hell to a prison on Earth, then this is how it would be. Level one would be the open prison, for normal people who for many reasons, do not make it up top. Level two is mainly for souls who believe they are bad; believe being the word that should be in inverted commas. Level three could be likened to maximum security, violent re-offenders and on to the mental asylum, souls who lose their identity. Level four is solitary, souls who are too far-gone to be permitted to mingle. Five would be the dungeons, populated by the murderers, the rapists, and all the souls who are evil beyond any doubt. Here on level five, you will find the fire and brimstone, the Hell that Dante elaborately imprinted upon the psyche of mankind. I do not go there, unless I really have to, some of them are truly scary. Do not misunderstand me, they could do me no harm and I'm not afraid of them, more disturbed.

So my main offices are on level one, which I have just walked into. I cannot express how much I loathe this place, I change everything around on a regular basis, but it is still the same.

As normal, Sfeehael looks of into the distance, and he pretends that he does not hear my approach. He holds a pile of papers, clutched tightly in his claws. Sfee is a demon of limited, although above average intelligence. But what he lacks in brains, he makes up for in impertinence. I suppose I could call him my personal assistant. He stands about seven feet tall on his cloven hooves, and casually looks down and around, as I halt my approach in front of his colossal form.

"Sire," he slurs, the boredom evident in his manner, "I have some cases for you to action, and your agenda for today."

< Sfee, why is it so bloody hot in here? Didn't I tell you to sort it out?>

"I haven't had time Sire, someone has to run this place when you disappear." He cocks his head to one side, as if he expects an explanation for my absence. I hold his stare for a while and say nothing, eventually his eyes waver and he looks away. "I will look into it, now you have had the grace to return to us."

The door to my office opens as I approach, I slump down into the chair and reply, < No don't worry, give me the papers and get on with your work > Sfee dumps the wad of papers on my desk and backs out mumbling something incoherent, probably abusive. As usual the in-tray paper stack defies gravity, with its ability to be so high and chaotic at the same time. The letter, which dominates the centre of the desk, has come directly from Heaven. I know the handwriting and I open it.

Lucifer,

Will you please refrain from endlessly harassing our Lord. Your personal view of conditions on Earth, and what you feel he should be doing there, are noted for the millionth time. There is no need for any further correspondence regarding this subject matter.

Michael.

P.S.

The truth is that you are wasting your own time, making him mad and pissing me off in the process. So please brother, I beg you for the last time: Please, please stop it!

Typical, he can't even reply to me, so he gets his lackey Michael to fob me off. I crumple the paper and flick it towards the bin. You would think a being of my status and power, would effortlessly throw a piece of screwed up paper into a wastebasket. You would expect the angle and trajectory to be perfectly aligned and centred. I watch as the letter flies on its way. It hits the rim and falls on the floor with the others that have been left untidy since last week. Thankfully it will never be alone on my floor.

You may find it odd that I talk to God and other Angels through mail, but it is not. We have all been copying Earth since the beginning of life. Once, Angels had no physical form, but we can appear to each other in any semblance that we wish. When life first started, there were Angels scooting around Heaven looking like bacteria, or moss. 'Look Lucifer, I'm a fish!' 'Look Lucifer I'm a tree!' 'Look Lucifer, I'm a T-rex!' Yes very pleasant I am sure. The formation of the myth, that God created man in his own image, could not be further from the mark. We all based our shapes on the latest and greatest forms of life. It was more like a fashion parade than a plan. The reason Angels are perceived with a human form and towering wings, was the fault of Gabriel. He always wore the outward appearance of a bird before man came along, and then wanted to be human shape, but he would not give up his wings. In due order he appeared to some shepherd, or someone. Of cause this was when we were still allowed limited interference. Pretty soon all the others were copying. Myself included, I have to admit

Hell, Heaven and Angels change shape constantly, and it's all based on whatever we see on Earth. I had a telephone when they were invented, a car, a dishwasher and a hundred other nick-knacks. So the postal system

The Songs of Angels

should not surprise you.

Sfee's paper work is all the usual stuff; riots on level two. The participants are being held pending my decision. I scribble on it: All involved to level three and ring leaders to four. Sign my name and into the out tray. Petition from the Catholics, on level one, for an audience with God: Denied, he will not acknowledge me, so I'm absolutely bloody sure that he will not listen to them.

A report on an increase of demons going sick: It seems that no matter how many times you tell them that they cannot ever actually be sick, it does not seem to penetrate their thick hides. Where did I go wrong with demons? They are created through me, as God creates Angels or matter. It is just a matter of will. So why are they always ugly or frightening or stupid, even when I do not wish them to be?

I breeze through several further individual cases, making various comments. Nothing changes here. I have the same problems, which repeat endlessly. The comments that I write today are the same as I wrote last week, and last year and last century. I dump it all in the out tray. Suppressing a shiver I briefly glance at the in tray, Fuck it, maybe I will tackle it later. On to more pressing matters, today's agenda which as usual, I see pinned to the wall. My finger finds the intercom and I Buzz Sfee, then grab up the agenda and begin to read.

Item 1: Tour the facility.

Fucking great imagination demons, every day for the last two thousand odd years. Sfee's item one is always tour the facility.

"Sire?" Sfee answers on the intercom, I can see him through the partition. He has sat there unmoving since I buzzed him.

< Coffee Sfee. >

"Yes Sire," he slurs through the static and cuts the contact.

Item 2: Meeting with all the senior level trustees.

They will whine at me for an hour, and ask all sorts of brainless questions. I will then tell them that they cannot have anything; it's the same every month.

Item 3: Lunch break.

Sfee shuffles through the door with my coffee, spilling fluid along the floor. "Your coffee Sire," He slaps the mug down, and more coffee cascades over the rim and onto my desk.

< Do you know Sfee, what coffee would do to this mahogany desk, if this desk or this coffee were real? >

"No Sire" he looks away, conveying boredom.

<Do you actually understand what is real Sfee?> His eyes show only indifference, and he does not reply. < Do you know how many times, that I have decided to end your pitiful existence? I really do not know why I put up with you. >

He shrugs, as if he could not care less, "I am that which you made me."

< So it is my fault is it? >

"Will that be all Sire?"

< Yes Sfee. Take the papers from the out tray and action them, we will start the tour when I've finished my coffee.> He turns to leave and I return my attention to the agenda.

Item 4: Meeting in Heaven with God.

I'll read that again, for a moment I thought it said:

Item 4: Meeting in Heaven with God.

<Sfee! >

Item 4: Meeting in Heaven with God.

"Sire?"

< Item four Sfee; is this a joke? >

"A joke Sire? No Sire, an invitation to go to Heaven. It came through on the fax yesterday morning while you were away, so I put it on the agenda, is it important Sire?"

< Important! Get the fax for me Sfee, this fucking instant! > I cannot keep the trembling from my voice and Sfee just stares at me, < Now! > I scream and he turns, ambles out of the office, and starts rummaging through the mountainous pile of crap on his desk. Then he looks in his files and scratches his scaly head between his horns. He takes a furtive glance at the waste paper bin, and then through the partition towards me. Seconds later he is kneeling before the bin, throwing paper cups, tea bags and the like around the floor. I can feel my anger rising as I watch his antics.

Finally he holds up a crumpled and stained piece of paper, something unimaginable drips from the corner. Now I'm shaking, I can no longer sit at my desk, so I'm out there beside him, grabbing the fax from his claws,

The Songs of Angels

my whole attention fixed on this possible reprieve from Heaven.

It's true. It's actually official. I am summoned to Heaven. I think I need to sit down. Without thought I shuffle back to my desk, eyes never leaving the piece of paper in my hand. I read the words through seven or eight times as I slump down into my chair. Sfee stands in the doorframe relentlessly watching, his eyes flashing with perverted pleasure as he drinks in my distress.

"Have I made an error Sire?" What passes for a smile, spreads across his crimson face. "Is it very important Sire?"

I meet his eyes; he knows how important it is. The glee fades as we stare each other out, and he begins to blink. Finally, and as always, he looks to the floor. < Fuck off Sfee, go and do something else. > I read the fax once more.

"What about the facility tour Sire?" he innocently asks. I look up and wonder if he could actually be this stupid.

< No, cancel all the earlier items; I have to prepare for this one. > I no longer have the energy to scream at him, < Make sure I am not disturbed and shut the door. > When he has gone, I cover my head with my hands. Perhaps it's not a reprieve; perhaps I should expect the worst. What have I done wrong lately? Okay, so there are all the Letters and the telephone calls, and the facsimiles, telegrams and couriers. Shit, he's used to them now. He probably never looks at any of them. Just sees my name and files everything under B for bin, I bet he never misses his aim. It has been almost two thousand Earth years since I was there. The last day in Heaven repeats itself once more in my mind.

33 A.D.

Angels don't suffer from memory loss, so this is a true account of what happened on that day. It was no more than a week after he returned, when I was summoned to Gods presence in the great hall. When I arrived, all the Archangels were present. They sat at the long table, all seven of them. God was seated at the top end, on his left was Raphael and on his right Uriel. The empty seat at the bottom I assumed was mine, so I moved towards it and waited to be invited to sit. Each side, and next to me were Michael and Gabriel. In between sat the others: Sariel, Raguel and Jerahiel.

"Lucifer," he said softly, "Please sit down," so I was seated, and God spoke, "It seems that there have been certain undesirable incidents, during my absence from Heaven. You Lucifer, appear to be at the axis of them all." He stared at me, through those human eyes. The eyes of the human, who called himself Jesus of Galilee, filled with the sadness that he suffered in the mortal world. "Lucifer my child, why do you betray me?"

< Lord! > I answered, almost cried, < I would never betray you! >

"But still you do," he replied, "Every action I take, you judge to be an error. Every twist of life, you see as my personal failure. As if you know better than your creator."

< No Lord, No. Clearly I do not see as you see. I just need and ask for your enlightenment. >

"So now you believe that I should explain my every move to you?" Then he stood, the image of when he walked the Earth as Jesus, "Why do you whisper dissent into the ears of all these other Angels? Why can you not trust me, as they all do?"

At this point, I still did not realize that this was a court, and that I was the one on trial. Maybe I was being naïve? I often wish that I had begged for his forgiveness. Perhaps I should have done so but I did not. And I uttered the words that almost certainly sealed my fate.

With eyes firmly fixed on the surface of the table, I replied, < You are correct Lord, I do not trust you, I am sorry and wish that I did. > As I raised my gaze, God looked away from me, and I asked him the questions, which I had put to the others in Gods absence. < Why do you condone suffering and evil on Earth? > I expected him to stop me there, but he did not. He just met my stare squarely, with sadness in his beautiful eyes.

"You do not understand Lucifer,"

< Then tell me please! > I pleaded. <Life is horrible, they fight and eat each other, and the humans; they knew that you existed, before you went to them. They made up their own gods and their own heaven, because they knew you were there and they wanted to know you. > Without intentionally meaning to, I struck the table with my fist, < Why won't you

The Songs of Angels

answer their prayers? >

God leant back in his chair, and folded his arms. Calmly he said, "I went back to them, they know I exist. Is that not what you begged me to do?"

< But you did it all wrong! You went back as a man > I cried. < And then you let them kill you! Surely that cannot be right? Already they twist your words and kill each other because of this. You should have shown them your true self! And you told them they could come to Heaven. Of the thousands that have died since, only a tiny fraction are here! Where are all of the others? >

"They are not worthy of Heaven,"

<But where do they go Lord? > I screamed, < When they die their light is not extinguished, where are all the others? >

His eyes did not waver, and for a few seconds they just held my own. Even though he had not replied, a change came over him and his eyelids closed slightly. Another warning sign, which I should have heeded, but were too distraught to notice. "They are held in the void," he said flatly.

<What is this void Lord? > I innocently asked.

"Why do I not show you Lucifer?" he answered, as though I were forcing his hand. "Come and see, so you may judge me one more time." And in the blink of his eye, God took me there, and I was horrified. There were the souls, hundreds of millions of human souls, which were packed into a grey and empty land, where they fought and screamed.

I stood for an age, taking in the hopelessness radiating from these poor lost creatures. And God looked at me, and he seemed puzzled at my despair. He was actually at a loss, as to the reason I shook with anger. If I could have ended his existence at that time, if I had the power, I would have struck him to the floor. But I did not, and could not, and God saw the hate in my mind. Then we were back in Heaven, and I held my head in my hands and cried.

< How can you do this to them, how can you abandon them like this? It would be better to end their existence Lord. >

"I cannot, they are my children and part of me," God answered, "You ask me to cut out my heart."

< No Lord please, this cannot be so, what sort of God are you? > I wept.

And the light of God flooded Heaven as he spoke:

"Lucifer you have gone too far! It is time for a judgment," and he looked around the table. "Lucifer has betrayed Heaven with his actions, from his own mouth we have heard betrayal at this table."

His gaze fell upon Raphael who looked straight ahead and said, "He cannot be allowed to disrupt Heaven so. Lucifer must be punished."

And the others one by one, agreed with him, except for Michael and Gabriel who said nothing. So God turned to Michael and asked him, "What is your judgment?"

Michael looked directly at God and replied, "Are we not brothers Lord? Even when we disagree?"

Gabriel did not wait to be asked, but he did not address God, instead he turned to me, "Lucifer is sorry Lord," he said, as his eyes pleaded with mine, "He will no longer question your actions, will you Lucifer?"

<Do you want me to deceive you Gabriel? > I asked him, <Do you want me to hide what is in my heart? I am sorry, but I cannot do this any more. >

"By five to two Lucifer, you are found guilty," God said.

I turned my gaze to him, and foolishly goaded him, <You do not cast your own vote Lord? >

"There is no need for my casting vote," he replied, "It will not change the decision."

< Perhaps you should call for a basin and some water, > I said, <Then you can wash your hands as Pilate did. > For a second, I thought I saw the hurt in his eyes, the pain my words had caused. But in an instant, it was replaced with anger. I often wonder what my punishment would have been, if I could have held my pride in check. Perhaps I pushed him too far, perhaps he had already decided.

"The judgment is made, you are no longer worthy of Heaven." God decried, "Lucifer, for your crimes against Heaven, You shall go to the void and there you will stay with the souls of men. All who die, and do not come to me will be your charge. None who enter the void will ever see Heaven. You are not welcome anymore in Heaven, except by my summons. Now go from my sight, because your presence now offends me."

And in shock, I was removed from that place, and as I left, no Angel would meet my gaze, except Michael and Gabriel, who wept. And Heaven was closed behind me as I was cast down.

※

The void was hell. I fell to the void and into the mass of human souls that were there. All around was madness. Evil and wicked souls abused and injured the weaker, and I walked among them trying to stop them. But they ignored me or pushed me away, and when they found that they could not harm me, they were angry or wary. I cried to Heaven and God, that I was sorry and pleaded to be taken back. But no one answered my pleas. All this time new souls poured into the void. So I wandered in this mayhem, feeling pity for myself, and I did nothing, and I became as lost as the souls around me. I do not know for how long, and I repeatedly cried to Heaven for forgiveness. But forgiveness never came, and I finally understood that I was trapped in the void forever, and the only one who could make things better, was I.

So I attempted to improve it. I tried to reconstruct Heaven, but this was a mistake. I came to understand that the souls in this realm had made their own choice to come here. They did not want or expect Heaven, they wanted to be punished and everything I did was smashed or scorned. So reluctantly I gave them what they wanted and renamed my new home. I called it Hell, because that is what it was, and then I structured Hell. I separated the wicked, the evil, the insane and the lost, and created the five levels of Hell to house them. Then I fashioned the demons for each level, to control and police them. I am not proud of the Hell I have created, but I did not know what else to do.

I class Hell as my second greatest failure. I failed to change Gods views in Heaven, and I failed to make the void any better than it was when I arrived. And still the souls of men flood into Hell, in greater and greater numbers, and I file them away for a God who has forsaken them.

※

This afternoon

"Sire?" I hear him speak on the edge of my awareness.
He stamps his hoof and shouts, "Hey Lucifer!"

< For Christ's sake, what do you want Sfee? >

"The car Sire, there is a car at the gate waiting for you."

Shit! I have day dreamed the morning away, and I had planned to try and find out what this was all about, <Right Sfee, I'll be off. I don't think I will be long. Will you be all right to look after the place? > Sfee looks at me, as if I had just uttered the stupidest question ever. I head for the gate, where an enormous white limo is waiting. The car door opens as I approach, and Michael steps out to greet me, a big smile on his perfect face, and his hands held out towards me.

We embrace for a second and then we climb into the back of the car. "How are you brother?" he asks as the car silently takes off,

< Everything in the garden is rosy, > I reply.

"You are being sarcastic?"

< I would have to get up early to catch you out, wouldn't I Michael? In fact I would probably have to stay up all night. >

He slumps in his seat, and shakes his head, "Don't be like this Lucifer. Please."

< Thanks for the letter, very brotherly. >

"I sent that days ago, before I knew about this meeting."

< And what do you know about this meeting? >

"Nothing."

< Nothing? No whispering in the corridors? >

"He has kept this very quiet."

Michael's eyes turn to the side window, effectively cutting the conversation. He either knows nothing or is not telling. I stare at the back of his head as we proceed, wondering what is about to occur.

"Look we are nearly there," he states. I look up as we shoot passed the main gates. Sheepishly he adds in response to my perturbed expression, "I cannot take you through the front. I am instructed that you are not to see Heaven, so we have to go through the back."

Shit, not a good omen. The car pulls up and we alight into a corridor that I have never seen before. It is shiny and new, with recessed lighting. He probably built it especially for me, so I would not see the glory of this place. But I know I am back in Heaven. I can feel it, I can almost smell Heaven, it invades your senses and it feels wonderful. I follow Michael along the corridor and into a room, a large table dominating the centre,

The Songs of Angels

and there are twelve chairs around it. And I realize where I am, gone is the great hall and in its place is a modern boardroom. And it is Gods boardroom, which makes me smile. We are all the same; we all imitate life, even God himself. I am looking around for the coffee machine, as there has to be one somewhere. Then the side door opens and three angels file through it, I know them all.

First is Uriel, dressed as a normal man, in a business suit with his hair slicked back and I do not acknowledge him. Next comes Gabriel, with his wings majestically towering above his head. His robes float like gossamer in his wake, and we exchange a smile. Then there is Raphael, who turned his face from mine all those years ago in Heaven, as I now turn mine from his.

"Sit down all of you," Michael instructs, "You are here Lucifer, at the end of the table." Michael and Gabriel position themselves either side of me. Raphael and Uriel sit at the other end, straddling the top seat where he will obviously sit. Déjà vu. Then two seraphims enter the room. I do not know them. They are followed by three human souls, which is a bit of a shock, humans on the board of Heaven. Things have changed a little in my absence.

The seraphims stand, one to each side of the table, they will not take part in the meeting. They are here as witnesses only, for the records. There is no time for introductions, because God is near. You can feel his presence, like ozone after a thunderstorm. Raphael stands and speaks, "All stand for our Lord God Almigh-."

"I have no time for that Raphael," God cuts him off as he enters, and sits at the head of the table as we all instinctively jump up. "All of you sit down so we can continue." We all sit and he carries on, "Lucifer, it is good to see you, even if it does break my heart. Are you well?"

I want to say something nasty, but Michael gives me a pleading look, so I bite my tongue, < I am fine Lord, > I reply.

"That is good," he says, "Now, I suppose you are wondering what this is all about? Yes? Then let me tell you. Certain Angels are worried about the condition of Earth."

I cut in abruptly, < If this is another trial, for one or all of us, I will have no part of it. >

"Curb your tongue please Lucifer, this is not a trial, it's is a discussion. You are here because I have the proof of a thousand correspondents, that you also have concerns about conditions on Earth. May I continue?" I do not answer, "Thank you," he says, and does, "This is an open forum, all your views, and suggestions, will be given equal consideration. Mohammed, you wish to speak?" he points to a soul seated next to Gabriel.

Mohammed sits with his hand held up, "If it pleases you my Lord, are we talking about interfering with the mortal realm? In my experience, it appears unwise."

"How can you say that," replies Michael, "Look what we achieved."

"I agree Michael, we achieved a lot. But was it worth it I ask you. Was it worth creating the fanatics, the suicide bombers? How can we justify any of it?"

"But Mohammed," Michael says, "The majority who follow your path are good, and better for it. Every religion attracts a fringe element that will use its message for their own ends. Look at the Christians, the Jews. But most are more humane with their religion, than without."

Gabriel joins in, "We do need to do something. The races of the world are at each other's throats. Visit the Holy Lands, the Arab nations. We cannot let this continue."

"So the question is:" Uriel speaks for the first time, "When we have interfered, have we improved the situation or not?"

"Not," replies Raphael, "All the major conflicts of history have religion at their roots."

All this time I am looking straight at God, and now he looks directly back at me.

Another human soul joins in, 'But do you infer, that we humans would not have conflicts if we did not have religion? I assure you, man does not need religion to kill. He will use any excuse that he feels justifies his action. Look at the Nazi's. They used Darwin's theory of evolution to convince themselves that they were the master race. They murdered millions of people. But does that mean, Darwin should not have written the book?"

"Thank you Martin, for that point," God says, his eyes still on me, "Lucifer, you are very quiet. I am sure you have an opinion."

Am I being tricked I wonder? < I have no physical contact with Earth

The Songs of Angels 19

anymore. I can only speculate with second hand information, on what I hear about Earth, so I will not. But I do know Hell. And Hell is full of Christians, Jews, Muslims and Hindus. I could go on and name every religion in the world. We have representatives of all. And we have our fair share of Atheists. Those who think they do not believe in anything. There does not appear, to me, to be any connection with religion, as to whether a soul ends up in Hell. It is the individual choice of each of them. Hell caters for all. >

All eyes are on me now, <As to whether you should interfere. You know my answer Lord. I have repeatedly begged you to do something. And if what you do, does not always work, then at least you have tried to put things right. Is it not better to try, even if you do fail, than to turn your back? >

God stands and paces the end of the room and says, "And this is the first question we need to decide today: Do we, knowing the dangers, again interfere in the realm of mortal man? My vote is no gentlemen, your votes please."

"Raphael?" asks God,

"No."

"Uriel?"

"No."

"Mr. King?"

"Yes Lord yes"

"Mohammed?"

He looks into the distance for a second, and then speaks, "No."

"Mahatma?" who has not said a word yet, nods his head to Gods question.

"Michael?"

"Yes."

"Gabriel?"

"Oh yes Lord."

"Lucifer?"

< You have a tie Lord, > I tell him.

"Yes I know," he says, "I require your vote please Lucifer." I am sure my mouth is hanging open, and sit there in stunned silence. At no time, did I expect to be given a vote. "Today please." He urges. What game is he playing?

< Yes. >

"So the yes votes have it. Now for the big question, what shall we do?"

"You could show yourself Lord," Raphael suggests, "In all your glorious light. Then they could not doubt."

"You think not? It would be viewed as a trick. Miracles are not an option I care to explore. They are passed the burning bush phase."

"Lord," asks the human soul, that God named Mahatma, "It has to be something on their terms. We need to work at an earthly level. There is so much knowledge down there now. On a physical level at least, humans think they are close to the secrets of life. To shatter this with a revelation, would not be a good option."

"I don't agree, science has become the new religion," Gabriel rebuffs, "But it is cold and heartless. They think science will eventually give them all the answers, and it certainly will not. So I, for one, would like to see their scientists knocked down a peg. We should give them something to think about."

"Their science is not heartless," Michael says, "Sometimes I am stunned by the beauty and vision that emerges from the sciences of Earth. Sometimes it is almost religious."

God replies, "I agree with Mahatma, we work at an earthly level."

< Are you suggesting another prophet? > I ask, < You would go back down there again? >

"As I said at the start of this meeting, we will consider all options."

< It would not work, they would laugh. The problem is, they do not need you anymore. Life has passed religion by and the after life is treated as a fairy tale. The majority of souls are shocked, when they find themselves in Hell. Humans live their lives expecting it to end when their bodies perish. When you abandoned them, they learnt to look after number one, and now they have deserted you. >

I can feel God's anger rising at my words, but he is holding it back, "Thank you for your comments Lucifer. Anyone else?" All are avoiding looking in my direction, except for Michael who is shooting daggers at me with his eyes. I flash him my biggest smile and he looks away.

"Lord, I think you should return as a mortal man once more, show them the errors of their ways." Uriel says, "How could they not follow you?"

< Most of them didn't last time. >

"That is unfair Lucifer!" Retorts Michael, "Christianity is the largest religion on Earth. Many follow the path of Jesus."

<Yes you're right. I particularly enjoyed the crusades and the Spanish Inquisition, all good Christians they were. >

God cuts the conversation, "Enough of this, it will get us nowhere. I will not go back to Earth as Jesus or anyone else. I have been there already. But that does not mean that one of you could not."

"Lord I would go for you," Raphael volunteers, "I would spread the message of God across the Earth."

"Bless you Raphael," God replies, "But they would rip you to shreds. You are the kindest and most faithful Angel, but you only know Heaven. I doubt you could survive a mortal existence."

< A human soul then? >

"Alas it is not permitted," God answers, "Once a human soul leaves Earth; it cannot be returned."

Not permitted by whom: Are you not God almighty? Did he mean 'not what I wish?' I store the remark for further reflection but let it go for now.

< So you cannot send a mortal soul, you will not go yourself and Raphael is too much of a greenhorn. Therefore all of the Angels who live in Heaven, and have never been to Earth, are in the same category. Yes? >

"Yes." Whispers God.

< So what in Heaven, or on Earth, does that leave you with? >

He stares at me, his eyes unmoving. An eternity seems to pass in the few seconds that all eyes around the table are trained on him, and his eyes burn through my being.

Finally he speaks, "It leaves me with nothing in Heaven or on Earth, It leaves me with you Lucifer."

< Me! > I shout, < Are you out of your mind? > He is, he must be. God has finally become unhinged. Uriel jumps up; he screams something about how unclean I am. Michael looks like he is about to have a fit and Gabriel's just stares forward, eyes wide. The humans are all shouting over each other.

"Quiet!" God commands, and everyone is silent, he addresses the Angels at the table, "Look at it logically, who amongst the Angels has ever suffered as Lucifer has?"

"He will betray you Lord!"

"Quiet please Raphael," God stares him down, "To live a mortal life is painful. Lucifer knows about humans, he has seen more of their suffering, their trickery and their anger than any of us. I do not believe you would betray me Lucifer"

< But you are not sure? >

"I will take that chance."

<What if I tell the humans that you don't care about them? >

"You know that is not true."

< Do I? >

God asks, "Would you go Lucifer? You have told me enough times, how I should do things. This is your chance to put your money where your mouth is. Well?"

I sit there thinking. I do know humans better than any of them. Granted they are dead when I get them, but they are still human. Am I brave enough to take on this challenge? It's a straightforward choice in the end, do I scurry back to Hell, or do I stand up and try to make a difference. There is no real choice at all.

< When would I go? >

"Now."

< And what powers would I have as a mortal? >

"None, just the truth and what you take with you. But I will set one of these Angels as a permanent contact. You will be able to communicate with Heaven through him. Who would you prefer?"

The choice is instant, < Gabriel. >

"So will you do it?"

< I can do whatever I wish; you will not strike me down with lightning? >

"This is serious Lucifer."

< I will not preach religion to them, I will tell them exactly what I believe. My primary objective will be to keep them out of Hell. >

"If you can achieve this, Earth will become a better place, so I agree."

< What about Hell? >

"I will look after Hell"

"Lord no!" Raphael cries, "Don't do this! I will vote no!"

"Quiet! I will have no more interruptions! There will not be a vote." God looks back to me, "Lucifer: Yes or No?"

I cannot help feeling that somehow I am being set up for a fall. But what could the motives be? If I achieve my objective, then he can only profit. If I fail no one will blame him, as they think that they already know what I am like. Shit, he sent Lucifer, they will say, what did he expect?

I look around the table at all the assembled Angels. None will return my stare, so I conclude that they are not overjoyed with these proceedings. I cannot believe for a single instant, that they plot with God, and I do not believe that Michael, or Gabriel, would ever deceive me. So has he engineered this outcome for reasons I am yet to discover? Does he want me to fail?

Well fuck him if he does, I do not intend to fail.

< Yes Lord, I will go. >

CHAPTER 2

Day One minus 280 days

I am in a place outside of Heaven or Earth. This is the nowhere between life and death. This is the shadow land, where I wait, as all new souls must, for the briefest and infinite instant before birth. But unlike a new soul, which is created new and unknowing, yet still ready to bond with a living creature, be it an ant, man or blade of grass, I am aware that I have been placed here, placed at the front of the queue. Then I feel an irresistible pull, a pull to life. There is fear and excitement in my mind, along with the thrill of an unknown future, the promise of mortal pain, which is still a mystery to me. Yet infiltrating everything, as lichen might throw tendrils over granite and sandstone, I see how death is woven into every fabric of life. How death is the mirror of life, this is my last thought, as I become the soul joined to a human embryo at its conception. Then there is blackness, no thoughts, no lights, nothing at all.

Day One minus 135 days

Awareness at last, my Mother's heart pounding relentlessly in my ears. And I can hear my own. I have a heart, a real beating mortal heart. Amazing, this is my material body, the flesh and blood of my human Mother and Father, and the ancient soul of an Angel. My Mother's voice filters through occasionally, but it is not yet clear to my semi-formed ears. They say human babies do not remember their birth. Well I hope this is because of a limited brain capacity, and not because birth is so traumatic, because it looks like I will be present at my own. But not yet, for now I am warm, fed and content.

Day One minus 64 days

My Mothers name is Carrie; I overheard someone calling her by that name. I wonder if it was my Father?

Day One minus 41 days

I sleep most of the time, I never slept as an Angel, and it is the strangest of sensations. To be alive but oblivious to all around you, while your mind flits through muddled thoughts, and tries to decode the random firing of nerves. Sorting through unconnected synapses until they make sense, any sense, nonsense. Dreams, of Heaven and Hell, dreams of this womb or about God. But they're incorrect, jumbled into stories with sections missing, or added. There seems to be no regard for facts in the dreams of mortals.

Day One

This is it, this is my birth. My Mother screams again and every time she does, I am squeezed. There is not enough room in here, I can feel panic rising. Someone is making comforting noises, I assume to my Mother, but she is distressed and oblivious to them. This is taking too long, something is going wrong. More screams as I am pushed away, sudden bright light, shut your eyes. And then pain building from my chest, spreading all over my body. Oh God, I am going to die. This is real pain, physical pain, and unlike anything I have ever experienced. Fingers in my mouth, Rough hands seize my legs and hoist me into the air. Gravity pulling all the blood to my head, something else new and uncomfortable. Never felt gravity before. Passing out, Gabriel please help me!

{Breath Lucifer!}

How?

More pain! Someone's slapping me! I try to shout for him to stop, but instead, air floods into my lungs. Ah bliss, Oxygen invading my blood. Must have more! Gulp it down and make the pain subside. This is all too much, I cry as they wash me. What a weak and pathetic noise it is. I am so cold, and everything smells strange. Then I realize that I have never smelt anything before this time. I want to go back inside my Mother's womb where it is safe and warm. They are lifting me and wrapping my body in a soft cloth.

"Mrs. Brookes," someone says, "You have a healthy baby boy."

I open my eyes, blurred shapes are all around me. Oh shit, I have a sight defect, can't see a bloody thing,

{Be calm Lucifer, newborn humans cannot see clearly at birth}

I knew that Gabriel.

And I am placed in someone's arms. A blurred face appears next to mine, filling my vision. This must be Mom. Hello Carrie, hello Mother.

"Paul, look, come and look at your son." She says, "He is so beautiful, so perfect."

This is a relief; I do not have horns, thank you God.

It has been a rough day, time for some sleep I think.

Day Thirteen

This is no good at all. Nothing works properly. I have no control of my muscles. I can't even turn my head, and if I could, I can't see straight.

{You are only just two week old; it will take time to control this new body.}

Yes, but I had visions of being formed, all grown up, ready to go.

{Patience Lucifer, you will get your chance.}

But I don't want to be a baby; all the time I take to grow up will be wasted. Ask him to speed up time so we can get on with this.

{Stop being foolish. You have to grow as a human. It will be good experience for when you are older.}

All I do is eat, shit and sleep. That's another muscle that does not work. My bowels are a law unto themselves. I have watched humans for thousands of years. And in all that time I never realized how filthy and disgusting having a crap was, not to mention embarrassing. Every time she cleans me, I don't know where to look, well I do, I can look anywhere, because I can't see anything.

{All this is normal}

I know it is, but you do not have to live it my brother. From where you sit life is grand and beautiful, at this end it is basic and filthy. I am so tired again, at least when I'm asleep, I don't worry about living. Is that Mom coming in?

{Yes.}

"How's my little boy? Sleepy are you?" I don't know why she keeps asking me questions, I cannot answer. My mouth does not work correctly yet. "Who's a sleepy baby then?" she asks. I'm a sleepy baby mom; there are no other babies here. "Let me tuck you up, and then it's sleepy time." Do all mothers talk to their babies like this? "Goodnight David, God bless and keep you."

Did I tell you my new name is David? David Brookes.

{Yes you did}
I would have remembered that fact, if I were not a mortal. This human mind is so forgetful. Very tired now.
{Goodnight Little brother.}
I may be little, but I will always be your big brother.
{Goodnight my 'Little' big brother.}
Goodnight Gabriel.

Week fifteen

Well I can sit up now, only for an instant before I topple over, but it's a start. Mom is feeding me paste out of a jar, I had only just become accustomed to the milk. She tried to give me something with meat in it, but I kept spitting it out. I think she's got the message now, that I'm a veggie. Swallowing is still difficult. Why design a creature that has to stop breathing to eat? It would not have been too difficult to have two separate ways in. I think God could have done that.

There I go again, I always assume that God designed humans, but it is probably not the case. Anyway my sight has considerably improved. It's still limited, but I suppose I will never see as well in this body, as I could as an Angel. At least I can see my Mom and Dad now. Humans look different through these eyes. They are still beautiful, but not the same as seen through Angelic eyes.

Gabriel comes and goes, he does not speak unless I call him, are you there?
{Always.}
More paste coming my way, I must admit that taste is not what I imagined. We used to eat in Heaven and Hell. But I now understand that we were just copying, Shall I call it playacting? Although at the time it always seemed very real. Actual tastes are considerably better, and much more satisfying. You do not know how nice it is, to have a full belly, then again, you probably do. Here comes another spoonful of paste.

"I'm home Carrie." Oh, Dad's home.
"Hello Paul, how was your day?" Mom enquires.

"Same shit as always," he replies.

"Don't swear in front of David please Paul."

"He don't understand yet," he states.

Yes I do, I was alive before the birth of the universe.

"How's my boy?" he asks as he waggles his finger at me.

Well let's see, I'm an Angel who is stuck in the body of a premature, dysfunctional human, how could I be more contented?

"We went to the park, didn't we David," Mom says, as she shoots a smile my way, "Look at him Paul, Look at the way he follows our conversation, I'm sure he understands every word we say."

"Christ Carrie, he's only three months old,"

"Watch your language Paul please!" she says.

I've heard worse in Hell.

"He understands, I'm positive."

He picks me up and swings me into his arms, "Who's my clever boy then? Not going to work in a factory like your old pa are you? Going to be a rocket scientist, or a Senator."

Shit Dad, I don't want to be a senator, I want to be popular when this body matures.

Month Nine

Why can't I balance? For every step I go forward I manage to go two steps sideways.

{It will come to you.}

Well, I don't want to wait any more! I'm an Archangel, and I should not be wasting my time learning to control this uncoordinated bag of matter.

{What you are, is a human child, not a nice one, one who acts like a brat.}

You do not know what this is like.

{I admit to that, but you are something else. It's always now with you, so you cannot walk? Well stop moaning and learn.}

Month Ten

"Ahhhhh!" That's all I can do! I am trapped in this puny body.
 {Last month you could not walk, and now you can.}
 If you can call it walking, it's more of a lurch and grab. "Nahh!" That was supposed to be 'Mom'. This mouth is useless!
 {Patience little one, your time will come.}

Year Three: August

Mom is in the kitchen. I do love this little garden, more than anywhere else. I can run around and look at all these splendid life forms. I could spend an hour just looking at this flower. Breathing in its beauty, life truly is awesome. I can touch it if I want, but have to be careful with these clumsy human hands. I don't want to break it, that would be a crime. Bugs are one of my favourite things, so intricately put together, so small and complicated.

A sparrow lands on the lower branches of the tree near me. I run over to look, but it takes to the air, "I won't hurt you bird," I shout, but it has gone. I sit down on the lawn, close my eyes and turn my face to the sun. It's heat makes my skin prickle, surely this is Heaven on Earth. This is how life should be for everyone. There is the sound of fluttering wings besides me, so I open up my eyes. My sparrow is back, looking at me through one single eye, with its head tilted sideways. I slowly lift my hand to her, and she hops up onto my thumb. Still regarding me with her one eye, like she is trying to figure me out.
 Gabriel! Is this normal?
 {I do not think so.}
 But what does this mean, what does she see?
 {I don't know,}
 The sparrow studies me for an instant, then its eye fixes on something behind me and she takes to the sky. I look around to see my Mother walk-

ing down the garden, "How did you do that David?" she asks.

"Do what Mom?" She saw me.

"That bird sitting on your hand."

"I didn't do nothing, the bird just came over."

"Must have been tame," She justifies to herself, "Come on in for your dinner now."

"Oh Mom," I whine, "Can't I stay out for a bit longer?"

"No, inside now young man, and wash your hands."

I run to the house, my sparrow is sitting on the fence. I give her a wave.

Do you think that sparrow saw me Gabriel. Do you think it saw through this mortal form and saw an Angel?

{I don't think that is possible. I will ask the boss.}

I am washing my hands and Mother is shouting at me from the kitchen.

{He says it is impossible, not to dwell on it.}

Still it was strange was it not?

{Yes, it was very strange.}

"David, come and eat your dinner!" Mother shouts.

"Coming Mom!"

It is evening, Mother thinks I am asleep and she is talking to Father, "You should have seen it Paul, he just held out his arm, like St. Francis, and this little bird jumps up into his hand."

"He caught it?" Father asks.

"No it came to him. And have you watched him, when he thinks he's on his own. He's always talking to himself. No that's not right, he is having conversations with some one."

"What are you trying to tell me?"

"I don't know, I'm just worried about him Paul, that's all"

"You are being paranoid Carrie, so he has an imaginary friend, lots of kids do, and a deranged bird landed on his hand. So what?"

"You didn't see it." She says. "But you're probably right." They sit in silence for a few seconds and then I hear her rising, "I'm off to bed.

Goodnight Paul."

"Yea, Goodnight honey, I'll be up in a little while."

I hear her coming to my room, so I close my eyes. She looks in through the darkness, and tiptoes over to the side of the bed. The softest touch as her lips brush my cheek, and she whispers, "Sleep tight angel." Then she stands and looks down at me for a moment, "Love you," she quietly says. As she leaves and closes the door.

We will have to be more covert when we speak Gabriel.

{That would be wise Lucifer.}

Call me David from now on, she already thinks I have a split personality, if I blurt out the name Lucifer, she will think I'm possessed by the Devil.

{Technically, you are.}

That's not in the least bit funny.

{I was not trying to be amusing, just stating a fact.}

This is me now Gabriel, one body and one soul. I do not possess this body, I am this body, the only soul inside this body. And for the record, I am not, or will ever be the Devil. The Devil is a nasty rumour, a myth kept alive in the minds of men, by religious fanatics. The bloody bogey man, an invented nemesis to keep children in line.

{Yes but you often appeared in Hell with your horns and cloven feet.}

But only on level five, and only because they expect it, or maybe need to see that they are being punished.

{Sorry if I hit a nerve.}

Go away Gabriel, and let me get some sleep. Shit, I could have picked Michael you know.

❦

Year Five: September

"Stop panicking Carrie, he will be alright," I can hear Dad and Mom speaking in the kitchen. I am upstairs, brushing my teeth and this will be my first day at school.

"I'm just worried as usual, you know how he was at play school. David does not fit in with other children, he doesn't play or connect with them.

He always seems so deep in thought and the way he speaks sometimes, it's like talking to a forty year old. He actually told me to always be a good person, or I wouldn't go to Heaven. Can you imagine him saying that to his Mother? I should be telling him that!"

Father laughs, "He wasn't as diplomatic with me, his words to me were; Be good or you'll end up in Hell."

"Jesus Paul, I've never spoken to him about Hell. Where's he getting it all from? It's your bloody Mother isn't it? Filling his mind with crap!"

"You leave my Mom out of this. She may be a religious, but she would not scare him with talk of Hell." I wish they would stop arguing over me.

"He's not normal Paul, do you think he could be autistic? The way he goes off in trances. The way he stares at things for ages. Perhaps we should get him tested."

"How many other children do you have, to compare him with? Perhaps he's a genius?" Father replies.

"Be serious Paul, if David doesn't make friends at school, he will be seen as an oddball and get picked on, or bullied."

"It's his first day honey, he will come out of his shell once he has all those kids around him. Trust me, you'll see."

"I hope you're right Paul," she says. I decide to come downstairs. Mother looks up, "Oh David, you do look nice and smart," I give her a big smile. "Are you all ready for your big day?"

"Yes Mom," I reply still grinning, but I will probably be bored rigid, "Are you taking me?"

"Yes son, go kiss your Father goodbye while I fetch your coat," I say my goodbyes to Dad as he leaves for work, he tells me to be good at school. I tell him to be good at work, and wave him off. Mom appears with my coat and lunch. As she buttons my coat, I get the Ten Commandments,

"Be good for the teacher, and do as she says."

"Yes Mom."

"And be nice to the other children."

{Don't tell them they are going to Hell}

"Yes Mom." Shut up Gabriel, you're supposed to be helping.

"Don't talk to any strangers."

"No Mom." Won't they all be strangers?

"Eat all your lunch."
"Yes Mom."
"And make lots of new friends."
"Yes Mom." I suppose I will have to try, just to keep her happy.
"Wait for me after school, don't go anywhere on your own."
"Yes Mom."
"Right, lets get going then."

༒

I am half way through my first morning at school. The trouble with children is they are childish. If they're not fighting, they're screaming or throwing a tantrum. I really cannot see anyone here who I would want to talk to, never mind make friends. All the Mothers left about half an hour ago. I thought Carrie was going to cry, but she did not. My teacher looks nice, Miss Keach, in her twenties I would guess, slightly plump and frumpy but always smiling.

The children are all running around, throwing various toys into the air. While racing in and out of the Wendy house, or clambering on the slide. One of the bigger boys is tormenting a small girl, pulling her ponytail. I can't see why, she did not seem to do anything to him. Miss Keach wades in, with the smile missing, "Stop that John Parker," she shouts. John sneaks off into the Wendy house, tears from the girl and a hug from Miss Keach, the smile returns.

"Wanna Play?" I turn to find a boy, slightly shorter than myself, with glasses and prominent teeth, "I'm Billy, wanna play?"

"I'm David," I reply.

"Wanna play Cowboys and Indians David, do you?" I don't, but I may as well try to fit in. I nod, "OK, you're the Indian and I'm the cowboy," Billy points his finger at me, and shouts, "Bang!" I just look at him, "Bang! Bang! I've shot you, you're supposed to die!" he says.

"Why would you want to shoot me?" I ask.

"Cus you're a stinking Indian, jeez you're no fun. Cowboys shoot Indians! That's the game."

"Why?" I ask again. Billy just stares at me in confusion, His expression conveys that he believes me to be insane; he shakes his head and wanders away. I still don't understand, I never understood why American settlers and Native Americans continued to fight in Hell, and I don't think I made a friend. Billy is now whispering to John Parker and they both look in my direction, grins on their faces. I move over to the little girl that John Parker was hurting earlier, "Hi, I'm David," I say, "Can I play with you?"

Laughter from her, and the girl she is with, "You're a boy," she informs me, "You can't play with us." So I back away, sit in the corner and pick up a book, it's a story about a cat with a big hat. Pretty basic stuff, but I read it anyway. I catch Miss Keach looking in my way, she comes over and squats down at my side.

"Not playing with the other children David?"

"I'm reading Miss," I reply.

"You can read? She inquires with raised eyebrows. Shit, do four year olds read? Gabriel?

{Some can, but it's rare.}

I decide to correct my earlier statement, "Just looking at the pictures Miss."

This seems to please her, and I get another big smile, "Well I am going to read you all a story after dinner David. Would you like that?"

Can't wait, "Yes Miss."

※

In the playground after lunch, all the kids are running around and screaming. It reminds me of the first time I was in the void. Total chaos, I have nothing in common with these small humans. Billy and John Parker are making their way through the skipping ropes and footballs, heading towards me. John purposely nudges my shoulder with his, and says, "Watch where you're going David!" My name is exaggerated and drawn out like an insult and Billy sniggers. This is a five-year-old child, on his first day at school, and already he thinks he has found someone who he can push around. Why are humans only happy, if they have others to put down? I will not bite.

"Sorry," I say.

"Be careful," he warns as he digs a rigid index finger into my ribs. I can feel my anger rising. This mortal body has an automatic response for self-preservation, and it is hard to fight it. Chemicals run riot throughout when it is threatened. And the pain in my ribs has set off an adrenalin rush, my heartbeat rises and my hands start to shake. Another dig in the ribs and he puts his face right next to mine, "Be very careful," he says. I could just reach up and scratch his eyes out.

{Lucifer! Calm down!} I look directly into his eyes, he looks back and his confidence starts to slip, slight doubt starts to creep into his stare. He blinks a few times and looks past me. I have to finish this here, or he will keep going until I have to fight him. I whisper, hoping that no one else will hear.

"John, come closer and listen," he turns his ear to my mouth, "If you ever come near me again, you fucking degenerate," he tries to pull away, shocked at my language, but I grab his head and hold his ear to my mouth. Gabriel is talking to me, but I do not care and I continue, "I will rip your fucking balls off and make you eat them. Do you understand?" I let him go and he takes a couple of hurried backward steps. His face reddens and he will not meet my eye. I switch my stare to Billy, who is looking slightly confused, and he also takes a backward step as if I had punched him. We are drawing quite a crowd now.

"Come on Billy," John says, "He isn't worth it."

"What did he say Johnny?" Billy asks.

"Nothing. He didn't say nothing." A teacher begins to take interest and starts over, but the crowd is moving away now. The teacher gives me an inquisitive look, so I smile back and start to walk away.

{That's a great start Lucifer, were you even listening to me?}

No. Call me David.

{Do you think he will leave you alone now?}

Yes.

{Well I don't. You have been at school for three hours, and you've made your first enemy. Well done.}

Fuck him; do you think I should let him bully me?

{No, but he is five years old. Threatening to cut his balls off? You have probably given him nightmares.}

Good.

The bell sounds and we are ushered in.

In Heaven that night
(Section extracted from the seraphim records: Meeting 8,652,475,004 of the council of Heaven)

Gabriel:
I do not know Lord, he is changing. I thought I knew his mind as an Angel, but now he is mortal, he has become more primal.

God:
It is to be expected, the burden of a human body would change any of you. I know. I have been there and I lost my temper on many occasions.

Gabriel:
But Lord, he did not really lose his temper, he was calculating

God:
You think I made a mistake sending him?

Gabriel:
I do not know yet Lord.

Raphael:
I know, this was a huge mistake

God:
Your views are noted Raphael, this was my decision and I will take the consequences if it all goes wrong.

Michael:
Lucifer has always been a rogue, but I do not believe he will purposely jeopardize this mission. He has barely started. He will want to prove to you Lord, that he was the correct choice.

God:
I know.

Gabriel:
I know this also. It's just his attitude sometimes. He completely blanked me today.

God:
Gabriel, you are not his guardian Angel. You are not there to tell him what to do. You are there to witness and report.

Raphael:

I say we pull the plug now, before he does any harm.
God:
No, I promised him a fair go at this. And I am not going to interfere in any way. Remember Gabriel, you are not there to guide him or influence his decisions. They are his alone.
Gabriel:
Yes Lord.
God:
This meeting is adjourned.

Year Six: February: At the Zoo.

We are all stamping our little feet and blowing out plumes of hot air as we breathe. It is a freezing cold February morning and all the children are wrapped up in duffel coats and mittens. The zoo is quite depressing to my eyes. All the animals seem lethargic and depressed, as they pace their cages or enclosures, in this biting cold. It seems sad that they are kept here in the middle of this city, when they should be running free. But for some, this is the only place left for them. Their natural habitats are now the farms and houses of men. There is no room for wolves or bears in the 'civilized' world of humans. True, you can still find pockets of wild wolves, or the odd bear, in the places men do not want to live, but they are a minority, scraping a living on the edge of extinction. How am I going to change that?

Charlie Davenport is shaking the cage on the monkey house, it clearly says, do not put your hands through the wire, but of cause he cannot read yet. Miss Keach pulls him away and tells him off, he starts to sulk. I am holding hands with Claire Jones. She is the girl who John Parker was tormenting on our first day. I am sure she would prefer to be holding anyone else's hand but mine. I still do not have any real friends, except maybe Peter Dowling. But I suspect he only sticks by me because John will not bully him in my company. John and Billy mostly leave me alone; all I get from them are occasional sly looks.

Most of the cages appear empty. I suspect the animals have more sense than us on this cold morning, and are staying in their beds. Ahead is the bear enclosure, a cut out depression below us, with a moat and fake rocks. There are no bears in sight so I let go of Claire's hand and lean on the railings for a better view. Still no sign of them. Funny how I was just thinking of bears running free, and now I can't wait to see one in a cage. I spot movement below, but just can't get enough height to see clearly. It will not hurt to stand on the first railing so I can lean forward. I step onto the rail and crane my head forward.

"David, get down," Claire shouts, "You will get in trouble!" I turn my head to tell her I am OK and catch sight of John running up behind me. I can see the intention in his eyes, and try to scramble back to the ground.

{Lucifer! Look out!}

He hits my back with his shoulder and I lurch forward balancing on the top of the rail. There will only be one outcome, the front of my body is much heavier than my legs. I know I will fall, but it seems to take an age for gravity to decide. When I was an Angel, I never even thought about gravity. I could move from Heaven to Earth without a thought. But gravity rules in this mortal realm. Claire screams and Miss Keach is running over in slow motion, she will not make it in time.

I grasp at the air as I start to fall, all pointless. I am amazed that I am not panicking yet, as I pick up speed, falling twenty odd feet and land on my back in the moat, breaking the thin ice. There is a sudden movement to my right as the bear I had spotted splashes out of my way. More screams and shouting from above. I do not think I am injured, but this water is freezing, I have to get out, my teeth are beginning to chatter, or is that shock? The water is not deep so I start to crawl to the bank. The bear, after the initial shock of my almost landing on him, is making his way back to see what I am. I should be terrified now, but I'm not. I must be in shock.

"Stay still!" someone shouts from above. I look up, more adults have arrived. One shouts something about getting a gun. I have made the bank and lift my head to see a mountain of bear regarding me. Any suggestions Gabriel?

{Stay Still!}

No chance of that Brother. I will not lie on my belly while this creature mauls me. I move myself into a sitting position and look up at the bear,

The Songs of Angels

which now towers over me. Well bear, this is it. Are you going to eat me? Our eyes lock. What a magnificent beast she is. As an Angel, I have run with, and looked through the eyes of many creatures, including bears. But being this close, in the flesh, to a ton of wild carnivorous muscle and power, which could rip my mortal body to pieces in an instant, what an emotion. I still don't feel scared as I look into the eyes of this creature. Eyes that are getting closer and closer. Its nose is now an inch from my nose and its eyes have not left mine. She sniffs me and washes her breath over my face. I imagine that I can hear sirens in the distance, getting closer.

What do I see in her eyes? She is studying me, trying to work something out. Just like the sparrow in my garden when I was three. She sees more than a mortal, I am sure. And then the bear lies down in front of me, she just sinks to the ground and her eyes never leave mine. I can touch her, I am sure. And I reach out, ignoring the screams from the adults above, and Gabriel in my head, She does not seem to mind so I rest my hand on her nose, stroking gently, "Don't hurt her," I whisper, "We are alright, and she's not going to harm me."

Keepers are entering the pen, guns at the ready and she is getting agitated, "Keep back!" I shout, "We are OK." And then I look deep into this creature's black eyes and whisper, "I have to go now, please stay still and they will not harm you." I slowly rise to my feet and walk towards the keepers. The bear lays still, just her eyes boring into my back. One of the men whisks me into his arms as we slowly back out of the enclosure.

"Shit," another keeper says, "Ain't never seen anything like that before. Good job we only just fed her." I look back as we make the door, the bear stands and shakes, then walks to the other side of the pen. The door is slammed and locked behind me. There is an ambulance waiting at the top, where they wrap me in a blanket and sit me inside.

I want to know Gabriel, this time when you tell him what happened, if he does not already know. I want a straight answer.

{I will ask him again for you.}

The kids that are not crying are looking at me in wonderment; even Claire has a smile for me. I search for my aggressor, but there is no sign of John Parker in the crowd. Miss Keach gets into the ambulance and smothers me in her arms, repeating what a silly boy I am for climbing on the railings. I agree with her, I promise myself that I will never again, put myself in a position where someone can hurt me.

Section extracted from the seraphim records: Meeting 8,652,476,964 of the council of Heaven.

Gabriel:
And that's the whole story. Lucifer is convinced that the bear saw him, not a mortal boy.
God:
I cannot tell you what the creature was thinking, I do not monitor the thoughts of every solitary animal on Earth. It could just as easily kill him as lie with him.
Gabriel:
He wants to know if he is a normal human.
God:
Of course he is not normal, he has the soul and memories of an Archangel, but he is mortal. His body can be crushed as easily as any other.
Gabriel:
So what do I tell him?
God:
There were times while I walked the Earth as a man, when some saw past my material form. I do not think they ever saw God Almighty. They just deduced a difference. After all, in my lifetime on Earth, I was never known as the Son of God. I called myself the Son of Man. It was not until the third century after my death, that the Church pronounced Jesus Christ to be God Incarnate on Earth. Perhaps this is what the bear saw, something it did not understand. Perhaps it was confused by it.
Gabriel:
Can I tell Lucifer that?
God:
I do not see why you should not. What of the child that pushed him?
Gabriel:
None of the adults witnessed the incident. But some of the children cer-

tainly did. The official story was that he climbed the railing and fell. The true facts never reached the press, although I am sure some of the teachers realized what actually happened. Lucifer was quite famous for a day or two. Someone snapped a picture of this little boy sitting with his hand on a bear's head; it made a few front pages. John Parker did not return to the school and was removed a few days later. I am not sure if the school asked for this, or where his parents took him.
God:
And how has this affected Lucifer?
Gabriel:
The experience has made him more positive I think, he seems more confident with the other children now. Naturally he was the centre of attention for a while, everyone wanted to talk to him. But there is a side to him, which is harder, more closed than before.
God:
You will monitor this and keep me informed. That is all for now Gabriel.
Gabriel:
Yes My Lord.

※

Year Ten

My mortal body is now ten years old. Time is so different here; it feels like I have lived as David Brookes forever. Ten years in Heaven or Hell can pass in the blink of an eye, or seem to last a thousand. The bond with this body is so strong, I often feel more David Brookes than Lucifer, and Heaven seems a distant memory. But Gabriel is always there to remind me. I often wonder, if I did not have him by my side, would I pass my memories off as wild fantasies? Would a psychiatrist studying me, conclude that I had constructed a persona in which I am an Angel, fallen to Earth. Or that I was a schizophrenic; 'He thinks that he can communicate with the Angel Gabriel.' How did God ever survive this mortal trip, all alone with no one to talk to? I wonder, did he ever doubt that he was God, or forget, and become a real man for a day or a year.

"Mr. Brookes! The answer please?" Shit, I'm miles away again.

"Sorry Father Vaughan, can you repeat the question," sniggers from my classmates. I use the phrase classmates in its loosest sense. They are not my friends, I only have casual relationships with a few. They tolerate me more that anything else. I have no best friend and they leave me alone mostly. It usually just takes one of my looks to make the stupidest bully back off. I'm the boy you don't mess with, the strange one.

"Just for you Mr. Brookes, because your mind is never in this class, is it? You spend all your time on another planet. Or perhaps I am boring you, do you think you know enough about religious education to daydream through my classes?" I would love to answer yes, and blurt out the truth. "The question was," he continues, "How many days went by, after Jesus was crucified, before he rose from the dead?"

He was God and his body was dead when they crucified him. And even he cannot reconstruct matter once the life had fled, the resurrection was a scribes fantasy, made up by men. "Three Father," I answer.

"So you do listen, a miracle!" he says sarcastically, "Perhaps you can tell us all what happened next?"

"Which version would you like Father?" I reply.

"What?" he asks, as if I had blasphemed.

"According to who? Luke, John, to which Gospel Father,"

His face reddens, and the blackboard duster he holds, is slammed down on his desk, "Do not mock me boy, you will stay behind and see me after this lesson." There are more giggles and sly looks from my classmates. He continues with his speech, and I take little notice until the bell strikes. All the other children leave, but I sit there waiting for him to come over and have his say. He pulls up a chair and sits astride it to address me.

"Mr. Brookes, we will have the Gospel according to St. John please." He asks smugly, assuming that I do not know it, "There is a detention for you when you get it wrong."

"From where?" I reply.

"The Resurrection as I asked."

I recite the bible, as he would know it, "The first day of the week cometh Mary Magdalene early, when it was yet dark, unto the sepulchre, and seeth the stone taken away from the sepulchre. Then she runneth and cometh to Simon, Peter, and to the other disciples, whom Jesus loved, and

The Songs of Angels

saith unto them, They have taken away the Lord out of the sepulchre, an we know not where they have laid him. Peter therefore went forth, and that other disciple, and came to the sepulchre.

So they ran both together: and the other disciple did outrun Peter, and came first to the sepulchre. And he stooping down, and looking in, saw the linen clothes lying; yet went he not in. Then cometh-,"

"Stop!" Father Vaughan commands, looking at me quizzically.

"Was it wrong Father?" I ask, I am quite enjoying the look of surprise on his preordained face.

"You have read the bible David?"

"Yes Father, many times, would you like me to recite something else?"

"Yes, why not, how about St Luke?" he requests.

"Now upon the first day of the week, very early in the morning, they came unto the sepulchre, bringing the spices they had prepared, and certain others with them. And they found the stone rolled away from the sepulchre. And they entered in, and found not the body of the Lord Jesus."

"Stop Child!"

{Yes, please stop Lucifer, I think you are scaring him.}

He started it.

"The ten commandments please David."

"I am the Lord thy God, which have brought thee out of the land of Egypt, and out of the house of bondage.

Thou shalt have no other gods before me.

Thou shalt not make unto thee any graven image, or any likeness, of any thing, that is in heaven above, or that is in the earth beneath, or that is in the water under the earth: Thou shalt not bow down thyself to them, or serve them: for I the Lord thy God am a jealous God,"

"That will do David," he pauses and stares at me for a while, then his composure weakens, he blinks and looks down, "Get yourself home now." I sit for a second in front of him; he will not look at me. Then I stand and leave, he does not move as I shut the door behind me. As I walk out of the building, I look up to his classroom, and he is watching me from the window. I wave and he disappears.

{You are just a show off.}

He asked, I knew, so I told him.

{He is up there now, probably wondering if you have a photographic memory, or if you are a freak}

I am a freak, not many ten-year-old boys can say they helped write the Ten Commandments. Do you remember the arguments I had with God over them?

{Of course I do.}

I wanted to start with 'Don't kill' but he had to stick all that waffle in at the start. What do you think he wanted to achieve by saying, 'I am a jealous God?

{I do not know, although he did not actually say that did he?}

Yes you're correct, he actually said, 'You are not to make or worship any carved-image, or I, YHWH will take my vengeance.' Still not very nice, he didn't feel the need to tag, 'Else I will get you,' on the end of, 'You are not to kill,' so why the warning on this one?

{I do not Know Lucifer, although you still have the words wrong. YHWH is the earliest written Hebrew name for God, but it means, 'He who is', so what he said was 'Or I, he who is, will take my vengeance'. And because no one, of the time of translating into Greek, could actually pronounce the Hebrew word YHWH, or knew its meaning, they took it as the sacred name of God. It was progressively altered to Yahweh, so it could be pronounced.}

Jehovah, Yahweh, Jaweh, Howah or Allah. I do not care about the spelling. These are the names that men gave to their God, and to me his name from that point, was always YHWH, he who is, the one true God.

Nevertheless those days were special Gabriel, because that was the time when I really thought we could change the world for the better. I actually agreed with God, when he started the Children of Israel plan. Mankind was stuck in a barbaric rut. I remember the cities of Ur and Uruk with horror. This was the time when Man first became monster. Before this time they were primitive yes, but they looked out for each other, family units who would depend upon, and help one another. The moment they became 'civilized' they stopped caring.

Death and mutilation was nothing to them, I watched as bodies daily floated down the Tigris, and Euphrates rivers, in their tens and hundreds, and no one seemed to care. Their gods were trinkets whom they asked favours from, only for their own personal advancement. To start afresh with

The Songs of Angels

this little tribe, and giving them a real God, and a decent code to live by. It seemed such a good idea, but as normal, God had to do it his way. Many times I stormed out of Heaven, when he told me what he planned.

But the Commandments were a good idea, though executed poorly. Don't get me wrong; the message is good, just poor grammar. The original draft we came up with was: Do not Kill; Do not steal; Do not commit adultery; Do not desire your neighbour's belongings; Worship only God.

{I remember.}

The five commandments do not quite have the same ring, as ten do they.

{But the commandments have shaped the course of all of mankind. The Jews first, they passed this new and revolutionary thinking to the Christians, and then the Muslims. All have followed this path.}

Most of them could not wait to break them. In hindsight they were not needed. Men know these rules in their hearts and always will. Even the ones who do kill or steal, know they do wrong. I have seen enough of them in Hell to know. And where has this mindset advanced them? I will tell you, nowhere. Look at this planet now, it is worse than ever, every rule is broken daily by billions of them.

{But many more obey the word of God, Jesus or Mohammed. You unfairly tar them all with the same brush. There is much good in this world Lucifer.}

And much evil.

{You are here to change this my brother.}

Yes I will change it Gabriel, I will give them a new mindset, whether they want it or not, and they will be better for it.

Year Fifteen

I'm in my room and no one else is home. Mike Oldfield is playing on my tape deck, but I am not really listening. Just lying on the bed, staring at the ceiling, and talking to Gabriel.

I have to work my strategy out now; I have to set off on this mission with a game plan. From the minute I leave this school, my plan for the human race has to go into effect.

{You have a plan?}

Unfortunately I do not. It was fine for God, two thousand years ago. Mankind wanted a God or a prophet, it was expected, and man would listen then. He could just stand on a hill and preach. If I start preaching, they will probably throw me in an asylum. They do not need God anymore, man is more interested in profit than prophet.

{There are many religious men who are respected and listened to.}

But not by everyone, I have to reach out and touch them all. I have to use their greed, their technology and their fears to hammer my message home. Then when they all understand, I will have triumphed. But how, and what do I make of myself? Most humans are indifferent to religion, or pay it lip service. Powerful men, such as politicians or industrialists are not trusted, or seen as corrupt. Sports stars and singers demand more respect. The direction I take now, will determine my success.

{You have a few years to decide.}

The phone is ringing, so I turn down the music and make my way to the hall to answer it. "David, thank God you're there," It is my Mother, she is distressed.

"Mom, are you OK?"

"No David," tears over the phone, "It's your Father, there's been an accident at the factory," she bursts into floods of uncontrolled tears.

I am struggling to hold the phone, "Mom?"

"I'm here- I'm at the hospital but they will not tell me anything, I've sent a taxi for you." I do not know what to say, "David?"

"Yes Mom?"

"Be strong honey, I am in A&E, I will see you in a little while." She hangs up and I fling open the front door and race to the gate.

Gabriel? What has happened?

No response.

"Gabriel!" I scream out loud, a neighbour looks across from his garden.

{I am not allowed to tell you.}

What! Who's fucking rules are these? Yours or Gods? A car cruises down the road, but it is not a cab.

Tell me what happened!

Silence.

"Fuck you!" I scream at the sky. The neighbour ushers his kids inside.

I wait an eternity for the cab, I think about running there, but a couple of seconds later the taxi pulls around the corner, and I sprint down the road to meet it. The ride to the hospital seems longer than the wait, and as much as I urge the driver to hurry up, it still takes too long. Rush hour traffic is against us at this time, I want to throw the driver out, and floor the accelerator myself.

Gabriel, talk to me please.

The hospital looms into the windscreen, I have the door open before he actually stops, and race into my Mothers arms at the entrance to the A&E. She sobs as she holds me, "What's happened?" I cry.

"No one will tell me yet, he's in the theatre now, I still haven't seen him." We make our way inside and are instructed to wait in the lounge. A nurse informs us that a doctor will be with us soon. Another eternity passes.

Gabriel, talk to me.

At last a doctor walks over to us, his face tells me he does not like what he is going to tell us, "Mrs. Brookes," he says.

"Yes," Mom replies.

"Mrs. Brookes," he continues, "Your husband is still in theatre, I regret to inform you that he has suffered massive head injuries, but we are doing everything we can for him."

"Will he be alright?" Mother asks, His eyes say that he will not.

"It is too early to tell Mrs. Brookes, but we will do everything humanly possible for him. Only time will tell," He does not believe this.

"I will come and see you," he adds, "As soon as we know more." He walks away and I hold my Mother while we cry.

෴

I do not know how much time has passed, but we are told we can see him in intensive care. As I walk through the door, I am confronted with a mass of machinery piled around an unrecognizable shape of a man. His head is completely covered in bandages and tubes sprout from him, like the limbs of a gigantic insect, trapped on its back. We are told that he is critically ill and is on a ventilator. I sit with my Mother at the end of the bed. We cannot get to the top, as there is too much clutter

{I am so sorry David.}

Sorry for who? Him? Me? Or are you sorry for yourself, for deserting me?

It's three days later, Father is out of intensive care and in a trauma ward. He is in a coma, the doctors are quietly amazed that he is still alive. Mother has withdrawn and just looks lost. She is sleeping now, she will feel guilty when she wakes. Guilty that she succumbed to sleep, while her husband cannot wake. I sit at his bedside and hold his hand, I do not remember having any sleep, but I probably have.

I cannot see his eyes, they are still bandaged, but he breathes oxygen spasmodically though a mask. We take it in turns to talk to him. We are told that he will be permanently brain damaged, if he regains consciousness.

The EEG came back, my Father has virtually no brain activity, he is technically dead, but his body fights on. They have taken away most of the monitors, the oxygen, they no longer seep food into his veins. And he has held on, breathing raggedly for over a day now. I have seen a billion dead people, but I have never seen one die. Hell was easier than this.

How unfair is life, to give a creature the intelligence to build, to love, to hate, to hope. How unfair to be clever enough to know you will die. To acquire a lifetime of knowledge, which is worthless as soon as it is completed. What is the point if there are no answers; it is no wonder that early humans invented their gods. Everyone is looking for something, even the ones that call themselves atheists, not necessarily God, just a reason for all this. And when they find that they are dead and in Hell, they ask again, what happens now, what was the reason for my life? And I tell them that nothing happens now, this is it, you will stay here forever and I do not know the reasons. Only God may know why, and he is not talking.

Silence, I can no longer hear breathing. An alarm sounds and Carrie

The Songs of Angels

cries out. A doctor walks in and switches off the machine. He mumbles something about how sorry he is, but it barely registers. Mother just weeps quietly and I hold her and tell her that she will meet him again in Heaven.

He went to Heaven didn't he?

No reply.

Gabriel, he went to Heaven.

{I cannot answer your question.}

Why?

{While you are mortal, the affairs of Heaven are not yours to know. These are my instructions.}

Fuck your instructions, what good are you to me, if you do not help me?

{Please Lucifer, I am your brother and I love you, these are not my rules.}

What then? Is this a test? Has God arranged this to see how I react?

{No Lucifer, God promised he would not interfere, this isn't a test. This is life.}

❧

Seven days later.

Yea, though I walk through the valley of the shadow of death,

I shall fear no evil: for thou art with me;

The words of another David, a shepherd and a king, written in Jerusalem before writing existed. Now recited by a priest at the funeral of my Father. What a beautiful prayer this is, full of hope, expectation and childish self-assurance, that God is watching over us and will provide for us. Unfortunately he will not, I know him. All you have on Earth is me, and I no longer feel up to the job as I watch dirt scattered onto the coffin, which holds the mortal remains of Paul Brookes, my Father. Who loved his wife and his son, and never intentionally harmed anyone. But he is still dead.

"Goodbye for now Father," I whisper, and join my Mother to walk back to the car.

CHAPTER 3

Year twenty

"So Ladies and Gentlemen," the Head declares, competing with static over the inept microphone, "Put your hands together once more!" Everyone around me casts their mortarboard hats into the air, to the cheers and applause of relatives and friends. That is it, no more school. I am leaving university with a bachelor's degree in Information, Technology and Management. I do not know where it will take me; I took it because I have a message for the world, and I will need the tools to present it. Soon the mission will begin, but not this day. Today is for quiet celebration, and all around me jovial students are being congratulated. Carrie is walking over to me, and she is smiling.

I get a hug from her, "Well done son," she says, "You make me so proud."

It is good to see a smile on her face; it's a rare occurrence, "Thanks Mom."

"So what now?" she asks.

{Save the world!}

"I am not sure yet, I have a couple of job offers and a few more interviews. There is time to decide. I think I will come home for a while first."

"Be serious David, the last thing you want is to be stuck at home with me. You're young and have your whole life in front of you. How's that girl you were talking about?"

"It didn't work out."

"Oh David," she sighs, "She sounded really nice, Julie wasn't it?"

"Yes Mom."

{You shouldn't be messing around with girls; you have a lot to do.}

The Songs of Angels 51

Gabriel, please be quiet, you are making my head spin.

"What am I going to do with you?" she asks.

"Stop worrying for a start, I'm Okay. Do you want me to drive you home?"

"Don't be silly. Look all your friends are waiting for you. Go and have fun. This is your day and you don't want to be ferrying me around. I will get a cab to the station."

"Are you sure, I don't mind taking you."

"You really don't mind do you? You would happily drive me all the way home while your friends have a party. I wish your Father could have seen you today, he used to always say how clever you were."

I hug her again, I believe she will never get over my Father's death, but then again, who does? All you can do is live with it and try to come to terms with the fact that he is not here. But she never has. I hated leaving her when I came to university, but if nothing else, my Mother is still a stubborn woman and insisted that I take this placement. I worry about her at home with just her memories, and my Father's ghost. She still talks to him when she thinks she is alone. I do not think she would even dream of finding someone else. I broached the subject once, and she said that she had already found the man for her, and why would she need to find another.

"David," Mom says, "They are taking the photographs, shall we go over?"

"Yes lets," I reply, "But I only need a picture of you and me."

A thousand pictures and handshakes later and I am putting Carrie into a cab for the station, we say our goodbyes and I promise to come home in a couple of days. I can hear someone calling my name and look up to find Andrew waving in my direction. Andrew Stone, my roommate and only friend.

"Come on Professor!" He shouts, "My beers getting cold."

"Not quite a Professor yet Andy," I reply.

"Ah, it won't be long though Mister first in class," Andrew struggled from start to finish to scrape through a sociology degree. He worked as hard as a beaver for it, and I feel a little guilty that mine came so easily.

"Where are we going?" I ask.

"Who can tell," He says, slapping my shoulder, "Life's a bitch."

"I mean, where are we going for a drink?" I ask.

"To the nearest bar, where we will take our fill of sweet wine and women. I knew I should have taken poetry."

"You would have definitely failed," I rib.

"Do not mock me sir!" he turns around and shouts to the others, "To the bar people!!" He throws his arm over my shoulder, and we walk off through the trees to the high street.

※

We are on our third or fourth, beer in O'Brien's bar, a favourite haunt for the student genre, although we are not technically students anymore. It is not really a place I am comfortable, if I have been here three times, that's about all. Andrew probably knows every person in here, and as much as I try to be normal and liked, I still have trouble connecting with people. Andrew aside that is, I don't profess to being best buddies and sometimes he drives me mad, I probably come over the same to him. But we tolerate each other, and get on well enough to share a room.

The bar is starting to settle down, after the initial high spirits when we first walked in. I am sitting in an alcove with Andrew and Bobby Thomas. Bobby is a mathematics student, who I know well enough to nod to in the corridors of the campus. Judging by the state of him, he apparently has a very low threshold for alcohol, and is starting to look a little bit green after his umpteenth Jack Daniels.

"I think," Bobby says, as he wobbles to his feet, "I will have to go to the little boys room," he staggers off towards the toilet to the chuckles of other students.

"He will probably pass out," Andrew prophesizes, "He does this every time, you'd think he'd have learnt to take it easier by now."

"Should someone go with him?' I ask.

"No, you will just embarrass him, he's Okay. Look! Someone's drunk all my beer again, my round I suppose, do you want the same again?"

"Please," I reply. Andrew side steps out of the alcove and heads for the bar. I am feeling a tad wobbly myself and decide that this will be my last one.

{You should not drink too much.}

The Songs of Angels

Thank you, I do know.

Andrew is ordering from O'Brien himself, the owner of the bar who does a great Irish accent, although he is about as Irish as I am. Andrew returns and slaps down two frothing glasses of tepid beer.

"Your health and your future," he says. I pick up my glass and we clink them together, before taking a long slug that sends my head fuzzy.

"And yours," I reply, wiping beer from my mouth.

"Ha," he says, "I passed by the skin if my teeth remember. Unlike you, I do not have any job offers. I will probably be working in McDonald's next week."

"Bullshit," I reply, "You will find something. Anyway I may not take any of the job offers I have. I am not sure what I want to do yet."

"Why doesn't that surprise me, not good enough for you? Are you aware how envious I am of you? I don't think I ever saw you study, while I worked my tits off. And now you will turn down positions, that most here would kill for." He pauses and then adds, "You are the same with girls."

"What does that mean?" I ask.

"David, David, do you know why I first hooked up with you? Don't get offended because I class you as a friend, but do you know?"

"I thought it was because we got on, but I am obviously wrong," don't get upset with him, I tell myself. We are both getting drunk.

"For the girls David, that's why." He says.

"But if you hadn't noticed," I tell him, "I'm pretty shit around women."

"I did not say you were good at chatting up girls, but you attract them, I can pick out three at least in this bar, who cannot keep their eyes of you. The little black haired one at the bar for a start," I look over, she is talking to another man, but every couple of seconds, she glances over his shoulder directly at me.

"You're talking nonsense Andrew," I respond, "My track record with girls is pretty poor."

"Yes it is," he says, "But that's just you. Perhaps they are not perfect enough for you. And when you ignore them I am always close by to help them out. The blonde in the corner with the nice ass, she wants you."

"She is not even looking this way," I say.

"But David," he replies, "When she does, just wait until she does."

"You're drunk, and so am I, lets have another drink," I leave him and stroll to the bar, when I finally get the barmaids attention I ask for two more beers. She brings them over and I pay her, all this time the girl with the black hair stares at me. At twenty, I am no Adonis, shorter than average, well built but nothing to shout about, just another adolescent to my eyes. I thank the barmaid and return to the table. "You are wrong," I say and Andrew laughs.

"Ok, I'm wrong," he admits, "But lets do a test, are you game?"

"No," I say.

"Come on David, where's the harm. If I am wrong this will prove it, and I will apologize," he's in one of those moods where he will not let go.

"What's the stupid test then?" I ask.

"That's the spirit," he says and beckons me to lean over the table towards him, "The blonde girl in the corner, I will make a move for her first. If it works, I will see you later. If I fail, it's your turn."

"That will not prove anything, you're an ugly son of a bitch, she is bound to blow you away, and you could be nasty to her just to prove your point."

He laughs again, "How stupid do you think I am? Have you seen her? I promise to be my most charming." I look in her direction, she still has her back to us, "Are we on?" he asks.

"You're an asshole," I say, "Do what you want." He gets up and moves over towards the blonde girl, her back is still to me. I can't hear them talking, there's too much background noise, but they laugh occasionally. Andrew buys her a drink and I sip mine.

{This is not a good idea Lucifer.}

Who asked you? You are not supposed to pass comment, isn't that the rules? Just report all the stupid things I do to God.

{You are being unfair. You are drunk}

No not yet, but I will be soon, but thanks for your concern.

"Excuse me," I look up to find the blonde girl regarding me. "May I sit down?" she asks. I nod, if I had seen her face before Andrew started this, I would never have agreed. She is stunning; her eyes are like portals looking into Heaven. I have never seen a human who could make an Angel jealous before, but there is one is sitting opposite me now. "You don't say much do you?"

"I'm sorry," I stutter, "My name is David."

"Yes I know," she says, "Your friend told me." I look over to Andrew, who tips his glass to me and turns to Bobby, who has returned from the toilet. He looks slightly better than when he left.

"What else did he tell you?" I ask.

She smiles, my insides melt, "That he bet he could chat me up before you. He lost."

"No I think he won."

"I'm sorry?" she looks confused.

"No I'm sorry, I am not being a good host. Would you like a drink?"

"Hello!" she says, "I have one already, your friend Andy bought it." She must think I am a simpleton, every time she speaks I turn into a quivering wreck. I could just sit here and look at her forever. "Are you OK?" she asks.

"A little bit worse for wear, we have just graduated and we are celebrating."

"I know, I watched you, my sister graduated today. Do you want to get out of here, we could go and get something to eat. You look like you need it."

"Yes, that's a great idea," I reply, and we make to leave, I catch Andrews eye as we go past and get a wink from him. I stop her at the door, "You must think I am so rude, I do not even know your name."

"Rebecca," she says, "My name is Rebecca. Shall we go?"

※

Andrew was correct, every girl I ever dated, I expected perfection from, until I met Rebecca. I am not saying that she is perfect, nothing is, not even God. How could a perfect God create an imperfect race? If he was perfect then everything he did would be as perfect. The facts speak for themselves. But with Rebecca, perfection does not matter. Every imperfection is perfect to me. I have found a human who cares more deeply about life, who is fair, passionate, generous, sometimes angry, but about things we should all get angry about. If ever an Angel was created anew on Earth, this is she.

Nothing else seems to matter anymore, and just seeing her is everything. Just looking into her eyes is better than all my time in Heaven. I want to tell her everything but I know that it would be a mistake. She would think me insane and have every right to.

I am driving home with her at my side. I have only known her for two days and I am taking her to meet my Mother, Gabriel says I should not rush into anything. Well he knows nothing of being mortal. Rebecca is asleep in the passenger seat; I cannot help looking at her.

{Watch the road Lucifer.}

Can I think anything without you knowing?

{Apparently not.}

Were you peeking while we made love?

{I was not spying Lucifer; it's not the first time I have seen animals rutting. It does not mean anything to me.}

That's the problem with sitting in Heaven. You are detached, all of you. You see Earth like a man watching television. You can see horrors or acts of sacrifice, but it's not real. Then you say, 'isn't it terrible, or 'how sad,' then you put the kettle on and forget it.

{I do not know what you mean.}

Exactly my point, you describe our lovemaking as 'rutting.' Dogs rut Gabriel, I cannot really explain the feelings going on inside of me at this time, because there are no words that seem adequate. I think Humans are unlike any other animal. What we experienced was an act of love for each other, more profound than anything that goes on in Heaven. This is what God meant to create. The feeling surpasses anything you have ever felt. What did you think my thoughts were as I lay with Rebecca?

{You were happy.}

Happy! That is all that you picked up! Then there are a million things that you do not see through my eyes.

{I see all you see, watch the road.}

But you feel nothing at all. Every day that I was in Hell, I saw souls whose mortal bodies had died. I never saw that each had a life attached to them. Lives full of fear, full of love. If I were there at this moment, I would cry with everyone who came though that gate. They end up in Hell because of passion Gabriel. The emotion is almost unbearable. But if their passion is not channelled to good, they find another outlet and the outlet is hate. It scares me that I can love this woman so much, if I am capable of this much love, I am also capable of this much hate.

{You are an Angel, you cannot hate.}

No, you are talking about yourself and the person I was. I am a human now. When I argued with God all those times and asked him why he allowed all the suffering and wickedness to continue, he was as much in the dark as I was. He did not understand either. He did not feel the hurt, he just witnessed and stood back. These humans love and hate on a scale that dwarfs Heaven. You cannot comprehend this human mind unless you live in it.

{Ah, but he did live the mortal life, are you saying he did not grasp this as you have?}

If he did, then why, when humans reach out for the hand of God, why does he ignore them Gabriel. You don't know do you?

{No I do not, do you?}

I would not be asking you if I knew.

"You OK David?" Rebecca is awake.

"Fine," I reply.

"You woke me up, you shouted out."

"Sorry, just thinking out loud."

Rebecca stretches and yawns, "Jesus," she says, "This weather is awful, do you want me to drive for a while?"

{You should tell her not to blaspheme.}

"No, I am fine," I say. But the weather is closing in, the rain is getting heavier and it's starting to get dark. Thankfully we are only about an hour from my home. But I cut the speed anyway; there is no reason to take chances. Rebecca leans over, kisses my cheek and then snuggles back down again.

"Make sure you stop somewhere before we get to your Moms, I don't want to look like a zombie when I meet her."

"You look beautiful even when you're asleep."

"Even when I dribble?" she asks.

"Even when you dribble," I respond.

Another half hour of driving and I spot a sign for the services just ahead. I pull in and vainly try to park near the main building, as the rain is still lashing down. Reluctantly I park about one hundred yards away.

"Hey sleepy head," I say to Rebecca, "Time for your make over."

"I will look like a drowned rat by the time I get back to the car," she says.

"Don't worry," I reply, "You can wait by the door when we come out. I will grab the car and pick you up." We get out and race to the service centre, where we go our separate ways to the conveniences. I wait by the front door when I have finished. Eventually Rebecca comes out and gives me a smile. "Wait here while I fetch the car," I tell her and race across the car park. I fumble with the keys while freezing rainwater trickles down my collar; finally I am inside and starting the engine. As I pull around the parked cars towards the entrance, I can see Rebecca and another human. My stomach turns over as he grabs at her. Rebecca is struggling with the rain-smudged figure; he appears to be trying to take her bag.

I floor the accelerator and am out of the car before it has stopped. There is only one thought on my mind. Stop this lowlife who is trying to hurt her. I run across the pavement and charge full tilt into his back. Rebecca is screaming and her assailant and I go down in a heap. Rebecca's handbag goes flying off. You fucker, how dare you try to do this to her. I am the first one up and aim a kick at him. I am rewarded with a crunching sound as my foot finds his ribs. He tries to scramble away, but I dive on him again and start to pummel his head into the pavement. My hands are getting covered in blood as his eyes roll up into his head. Rebecca continues to scream.

And then I am being pulled away, by two or three people, someone else tries to grab the bastard, but he has regained his wits, and pushes them away. He disappears around the side of the building. Rebecca is looking at me and screaming, "It's OK," I say, "He's gone."

"He had a knife David!" she shouts between sobs, "He had a knife, look at you!"

I look down and see the tear in my shirt and the blood running down my side. Ah shit, this is not good. My legs are starting to feel weak and I begin to shake. The police are here now, blue lights flashing, and the men holding me let me down, onto the rain soaked path. Rebecca is kneeling by my side and she looks terrible. The tears and the rain, have messed up her makeup.

"Don't worry," I tell her, "I am alright," I say, and then I can feel reality drifting away. I think I am going to pass out.

※

A nanosecond later, in Heaven.

Gabriel:
I did not even have time to warn him!
God:
You interfered!
Gabriel:
What?
God:
You broke a direct order and intentionally interfered! You forced those humans to pull him away!
Gabriel:
I had to do it Lord, the human was going to stab him again. Lucifer was so intent on bashing his brains out onto the pavement; he did not see the knife.
God:
Who were you trying to save then?
Gabriel:
I don't understand Lord.
God:
Were you worried for Lucifer's life, or were you worried that he would kill the human? Did you have visions of God's representative on Earth spending the rest of his mortal existence in a prison cell?
Gabriel:
Would you have preferred his death Lord?
God:
Do not put words in my mouth Gabriel! I promised Lucifer a chance at mortal life, I promised I would not interfere and by Gods word, you will not interfere!
Gabriel:
But he could have died!
God:

Then so be it! It is his choice Gabriel, not yours. You are not his guardian Angel. I will tolerate no more. One more slip and I will cut you off from him. Do you understand?
Gabriel:
Oh I see it now Lord, you want him to fail as you did.
God:
Gabriel, You push my patience! I think you have listened to Lucifer for too long. He has exactly the same chance I had. How dare you say that I wish him to fail. Nothing will give me greater pleasure than seeing him triumph, with whatever plan he eventually follows. But it has to be by his hand. Not mine and certainly not yours. Now get out of my sight.
Gabriel:
You haven't even asked of his condition.
God:
I am God! Do you think I do not already know how he fares? This is your last chance Gabriel, no more interference. Now leave my presence.

※

The difference between sleep and being unconscious is that you do not dream.
{How are you feeling?}
I have felt better, where am I?
{You are about to wake in hospital Lucifer.}
How bad is it?
{You will be fine; the knife punctured your abdomen, but missed any vital organs. Just a lot of blood and a few stitches, you were lucky.}
It hurts like hell, why am I so stupid. By the way, thanks for what you did.
{I didn't do anything; I never even had time to warn you.}
No, I know what you did, I think I was going to kill him, even if he had stabbed me another ten times, I would not have stopped, so thank you.
{I think it is time to wake up, there are people waiting to see you.}
I open my eyes; the light blinds me for an instant. Rebecca is sitting there at my side; she has not noticed that I am awake yet, so I just look at her for a second. She looks better than she did the last time I saw her.

Then she notices that my eyes are open, and tears fill hers. She hangs her head for a second, and says, "Thank God David, thank God you are awake, it wasn't worth it, he could have had the stupid bag."

I don't know what to say, that he was a thief, and had no right; thou shalt not steal? But is it worth a knife in your stomach to stop him? Could I walk away from a total stranger if I thought I could help, even if my life was on the line? "The contents of your bag was not the issue Rebecca," I say, "I may have charged in like a bull at a gate, but no one has the right to threaten, hurt or steal from you, or anyone else."

Another voice joins in, "Heroes who survive," he says, "Always feel they are justified to take the law into their own hands."

I look up, at the end of the bed is a middle-aged man in a worn and shiny blue suit. Rebecca introduces him, "This is Detective Moss David, and he wants a statement from you, if you feel up to it."

I ask, "And the ones who don't survive, Detective Moss?"

"Alas," he says, raising his palms, "We will never know."

I know.

He continues, "I need to ask you a few questions about the incident Mr. Brookes."

I nod my consent, we go over the mugging and what I saw and did, and finally he puts his notebook away and tells us that the mugger is known, but is still at large. He has a history of petty crime and drug abuse. He finishes with a lecture about it being police policy not to antagonize your friendly local muggers, but to offer them your belongings with a big smile before calling the police. Because you could be prosecuted, for defending yourself and your loved ones, but in my case I will not be. And it is the duty of the police to beat criminals senseless, not mine. Obviously this is my interpretation, but you get the gist.

Before he leaves, I ask him what he would have done.

"Mr. Brookes," he replies, "If you want me to condone your actions, then officially I cannot. I don't like to see members of the public getting stabbed. But unofficially, I hope the little shit has crawled into a hole with a very sore head." He grins, "Goodnight to you both, I have your Mother's address if I need to ask any more questions." With a nod to both of us, Detective Moss depart.

"Don't ever scare me again like that David," Rebecca says.

"Has anyone spoken to my Mother?" I ask.

Rebecca replies, "Yes of course I have, she was intent on rushing over, but I convinced her that you would be OK, I will call her in a moment."

"And has anyone indicated when I may be able to leave here?"

"Whatever happens, it will not be tonight David. I am going to call your Mother and tell her you are awake" Rebecca says, I receive a peck on the cheek, and she exits the room to use a phone.

A nurse enters the room, she has that big nurses smile that they all wear, "How are we feeling Mr. Brooks?" she inquires. I reply that I am fine. She checks a few charts, and efficiently shuffles out.

{You may as well get some rest Lucifer.}

Gabriel, tell me honestly, what chance do I have of making a difference to this world, how would I get through to someone like our mugger? There are thousands of humans out there who are as bad, or worse than him. What possible message or gesture would move someone like him, to change his way of life? It all looked so easy from Heaven. I could see all the problems, all the injustice, and it is easy to shout that something is wrong. It's a different game to put it right, especially when you don't know where to start.

I am just a mortal here, looking through mortal eyes controlled by a mortal mind.

{You are still an Angel my brother.}

What does that mean? To be an Angel, what is an Angel? That is the human name for us. It doesn't mean that we know any better does it? Who am I, or you or God even, to dictate how humans should behave?

{Someone in Heaven once said, it is better to try and fail, than sit back and do nothing. Do you remember?}

Yes.

{I think that you just feel sorry for yourself. Think back to Hell, that is what you want to change isn't it. Stop humans going to Hell, and if you make life on Earth better in the process, that's a bonus. Why do they end up in Hell Lucifer? That is the question.}

Because God has abandoned them.

{Wrong answer, how many other animals did you have in Hell?}

None obviously. Hell is for humans.

{Why are there none there?}

The Songs of Angels

Because animals do not do anything wrong.

{Consider a dog that attacks and maims, or kills, a child without provocation. Has it done wrong?}

Well yes it has.

{So why isn't the animal in Hell when it passes over?}

We both know that humans are the exception. When other animals die, there souls return directly to God. It is only humans that linger in spirit form. A dog does not comprehend that it has done wrong. It may be vicious, but it evolved these qualities over millions of years as a defence. Only the strong, the most brutal would survive and pass their genes on. That is before man came along and domesticated them.

{Yes but the instincts of the wolf are still just below the surface. Its aim in life is still to survive and pass on its genes. The fact that dogs befriended humans was another survival trick. Not a conscious one, but the number of wolves who hooked up with humans, far exceed the ones that kept away. Consider cows}

What?

{Indulge me please.}

Humans breed them so that they can eat them.

{But what has that done for the cows?}

I don't think they would be too happy about it.

{You're still viewing all this from a personal level. What has it done for cows as a species?}

Turned them into slaves.

{I think you're wrong, on an individual basis, being eaten is not advisable, but as a species cows are successful. There are millions of them who are fed, protected and allowed to breed. Dogs and cows do not care how they live. They just live, one moment at a time.}

Are you saying it does not matter, wrong and right, good and bad, as long as the species survive?

{No, what I am trying to say is it does not matter to any species, except humans. Why do you think that is Lucifer?}

It's because they know. Humans know they will die. We're back to a reason for living again. Humans feel cheated because they are sentient. While as all other animals just exist and die without worrying about it. Their soul's pass over without thought.

{Go on.}

And humans can't forgive their own nature; they are still hunters and gatherers in their hearts. They still have all the instincts to survive at any cost, and the cost is too great for the majority. Their intelligence is at odds with their basic instincts.

{So what conclusions do you draw from this?}

That all animals, bar humans, die with a clear conscience, what ever they do in life is not important. What is important is they carry no baggage when they die and can therefore be at peace and God can accept them without tainting himself. But he cannot accept a soul that still has a will of it's own can he? What a dilemma it must have been for God, when the first human died and kept his identity intact. How could he take back a soul that may pollute his essence? So he started stuffing them into the void where they were out of the way. And even the human souls in Heaven are still separate entities. Humans have evolved to a point where God cannot recycle their souls!

Surely this cannot be Gods plan Gabriel.

{Back to the question Lucifer, how do we get more human souls into Heaven, and out of Hell?}

They have to die with no guilt, whatever they have done. They have to forgive themselves for their life.

Someone touches my hand and I open my eyes. Rebecca smiles at me, "Your Mom sends her love," she says, "I thought you were asleep."

"Rebecca," I say, "Do you believe in God?"

"Yes."

"And do you believe there is a Heaven?"

"I hope there is a Heaven," she replies.

"And if you believe in Heaven, do you believe in Hell?"

"What is this," she asks, "What are these questions for David?"

"Please," I say, "do you believe in Hell?"

"I suppose I must if I believe in Heaven."

"And who goes where Rebecca?"

She gives me a quizzical look, "Good people go to Heaven and evil people go to Hell," she says.

How I wish it were that easy, "Define good and evil."

"No I will not, why are you asking me these questions David? You did

The Songs of Angels

what you did to protect me, it does not make you a bad person."

She thinks that I am asking her these questions to justify my actions, perhaps I am. "I wanted to kill him," I confess, "How can that be good."

I look away, she takes my hand and says, "You were in the right David, and it was his choice to attack me. You reacted to his actions and if you had killed him, then it would have been his fault, not yours." She reaches over and turns my face to hers, "Don't you dare go on a guilt trip over this David Brookes, because he was in the wrong, not you."

"Yes you're right," I tell her. But the doubt remains. Executioners feel they are correct to pull the lever on convicted 'evil' people, while they are alive. But I do not find them in Heaven when they die, I find them in Hell, along with the people they send there. Doing wrong for the right reasons will not get you into Heaven. However much you may convince yourself that the end justifies the means, come the day when you decide if you are worthy of Heaven, it is unlikely you will forgive your own actions, and Hell and I will be waiting.

※

I was released from the hospital the next day and we continued on to my Mothers home, Rebecca doing the driving.

We pull up outside the house and she is waiting on the step for me to get out of the car. After five minutes of hugs, tears and introductions, we are safely installed in the living room, where we have to go through the whole incident again, in much more detail than the police required.

Then Rebecca gets the third degree, where she was born, her family, upbringing. You name it, and my Mother wants to know. Rebecca takes it in her stride and Carrie appears to approve. We have lunch and then I take Rebecca on a walk around the town, not that there is anything to see. My side does not hurt that much, it is just uncomfortable.

We have an evening of television and embarrassing casual chat, about what I was like as a child, including the bear pit incident, which Rebecca is so interested in, that Mother digs out all the newspaper cuttings that she saved. Finally we retire, Rebecca has to sleep in a separate room, but I told her to expect that. She sneaks into my bedroom sometime after midnight, and we fall asleep in each other's arms.

Come the morning and my Mother, bless her, pretends that she does not know where Rebecca spent the night. The breakfast conversation turns to the future. Rebecca has another two years of university to do, and I still do not know which job, if any, to take. We will have to leave tomorrow, and I have spent most of the time I meant to be with my Mother, in the hospital. But that cannot be helped, and she understands that. Rebecca has her education to continue and I have to decide my future.

Detective Moss calls on us that afternoon, they have captured the man who attacked Rebecca and stabbed me. He wants me to go to the station to identify him in a line up. I agree to go, I do not want Rebecca to, but she insists. We drive the fifteen minutes to the station in his car, which smells of cigarette smoke and junk food. Once there we are led to a room with a one-way mirror. A few seconds later, around ten men are lined up in front of us. There is no mistaking him, he is the one who's face looks like someone has beaten him with a shovel.

"What will happen to him?" I ask.

"He will be formally charged now, there will be a hearing in the morning where he will be charged with aggravated assault and attempted murder. He will not ask for, or get bail, and will spend the next six to nine months on remand, waiting for his trial."

"Will we be needed tomorrow," Rebecca inquires.

"No," Moss says, "He knows that we have him, you may not even have to go to the trial, if he confesses."

"Will he get any help?" I ask. Rebecca gives me a sideways glance.

"I am not a social worker Mr. Brookes," He informs us, "I just arrest them and hopefully get dangerous people of the streets." He gives me a long look, and then continues, "There will be a few forms to fill in, and then I will drive you home."

We nod our agreement and are eventually driven back.

※

We are on the road now, back to the campus, thankfully this journey is undertaken in glorious sunshine. I have to arrange to move out of my room. I already have a flat in town rented for four weeks, I figured that would be long enough to pick a job and move on, wherever that may be.

"David," Rebecca says, as we pull onto the highway, "I have been thinking about what you were asking me in the hospital." She looks at me than back to the road, as she slips the motor into the faster moving traffic, "You know I was brought up as a Catholic, and I do not practice now."

"Yes," I say.

She continues, "I hated being a five year old Catholic, it is pretty terrifying when visions of Hell are forced upon you, they tell you this is where you will end up, if you are a bad person. I cannot count the times I cried myself to sleep, over some petty notion that I was a bad person and destined for Hell. So as you get older, you force it out of your mind. That is why religion gives me the shivers. Underneath this cool exterior, is a five year old, who still thinks that she will be punished. I don't consider myself qualified or worthy to tell you what is good, and what is evil"

"But you know, everyone knows," I tell her, "How can a child be a Catholic or Christian, Muslim or Jew. Religion is the only thing that is accepted from birth. If your parents are Jews or Christians, then so are you.

It's brainwashing of infants on an unprecedented scale, and worse, it is accepted world wide as normal. No one would decide at birth that you would be a civil servant or street cleaner. It should be left to the individual to decide, when and only when they have enough about them to make an educated decision, or guess. Unfortunately that will never happen, because any teenager, hearing the scriptures for the first time, would reject it"

"My point is that I haven't rejected anything." she says, "I may not practice, but I still believe in God with my whole heart. Your Mother is not very religious is she, do you believe in God David?"

"Oh yes, I believe there is a God." I reply, "But I am not sure if I believe in God."

{What are you going to tell her Lucifer?}

"That's a bit cryptic isn't it?" She says.

"No not really," I answer, "Can't there be a God who I choose not to worship?"

"That's horrible David," she says, "How can you concede there is a creator, and then ignore him. You had better hope there is not a Hell," She laughs, "Because that is where you will end up with that attitude."

I know where I will end up, but I do not tell her that. "You call God 'the creator' do you believe God Created man in his own image?"

"And why not?" she asks.

"Because the facts are all there to see, I watched evolution happen, and believe me when I say that it was chance that man even got a foothold on the evolutionary ladder. We are not the final and brilliant product of evolution; man is a by-product of chance. Natural selection did not have man in mind when life started, because it has no mind, it is blind to what it creates."

{You said 'I watched'}

"Evolution theory is messy David," she says. I don't think she noticed my slip, "You didn't watch it happen," Perhaps she did, "You say that like it's absolute fact."

"Evolution may seem messy, but when you look at it closely, you will find that it is every bit as awe inspiring as any creation theory in any holy book."

"But it is so detached, it makes humans no better than animals"

"When was this barricade erected around human beings? We are animals like any other. The only difference is you feel superior, because in your heart, you want God to be personally looking out for you. You need humans to be God's favourite, because that is how you feel it should be. Not because you are special, but because you believe you are special."

"I am special," she says, her eyes fixed on the road. I think I may have gone too far and offended her.

"Yes you are," I tell her, and get a smile, "Every living thing on this planet is special whether God created it or not. There is not another planet like this in the universe."

{Careful.}

"So you think I evolved from a monkey?" she teases.

"There is no doubt in my mind," I say, and she gives me the evil eye, so I add, "Obviously a very pretty and clever monkey."

"OK clever clogs, the very first living thing, where did that come from?" she smiles smugly, sure that she has asked a question I cannot answer.

She has me now, because I do not know the answer. God never claimed that he started life, as he claimed that he created the universe. One minute Earth was a rock, and the next it was teeming with life. But he did

The Songs of Angels

not say that he started it, just that it was there and we could observe it if we wished. "I do not know," I confess.

"The oracle has no answer!" she proclaims, "Then you cannot say it was not God."

"No I cannot," I say, "But I cannot say it was not Ronald McDonald either. What I can say is, it is unlikely to be Ronald McDonald. But I could be proven wrong"

"Now you are grasping at straws. Whether it was Adam from the clay, or amoebas in the primal soup, it was God who did it. Trust me David."

"I will wait for proof before making my decision," I say.

"You may never find it," she adds.

Yes I will, one day I will ask him.

{You already did.}

OK, one day he will tell me.

{I will take no bets on that Lucifer.}

"But you are stuck as well now," I tell Rebecca after a few seconds, "We will assume that God created life. Tell me who created God?"

She laughs, "God needs no creator, God is God."

I echo, "Life needs no creator, life is life."

"You're infuriating sometimes."

"If life needs a prime mover, how come God needs none?"

"Because God moves in mysterious ways, he is beyond me and you."

"Rebecca," I say, "That is closer to the truth than anything else we have said."

ꕤ

CHAPTER 4

Year twenty-one

I have taken a job as an assistant researcher with a television news company, to learn the ropes of broadcasting. Rebecca is back at her university, a million miles away. Well it feels like a million miles anyway, our relationship is mostly a telephone conversation. I am assigned to a crew who chase up and down the country investigating anything from pigs with extra legs, to UFO sightings. It's not ideal, but it is a start.

The anchorman of our little posse is Jonathan Remick, he is a prick, he cares nothing for the stories we broadcast, or the people affected by them, just that he looks good for the camera, that his hair is brushed correctly, that he is on television. My job is to chase the stories before the film crew arrives, and to make sure what he says to the camera, will not get the company sued. The truth does not appear to be top of the list of priorities. I am working with a guy called Bill Gee, he has been doing this forever, and knows every trick in the book. I think he wrote most of them.

"David!" He shouts over, "We're on son, get your coat."

"What is it?" I ask.

"We have a weeping Madonna my boy, up north," I laugh and he looks at me wide eyed, "It's no laughing matter, religious shit is great television." He says, "This will be an 'and finally' item on a broadcast in a couple of days."

"What if it's bullshit?"

"That's never stopped me before, so grab your camera and notebook, then find us a car." I run down to the car pool, check out a saloon and meet him at the entrance. The drive is nondescript, and three hours later we arrive in a sleepy town, of about five hundred souls. The church, when we locate it, looks old and is of a wooden construction. We have to meet the priest who has reluctantly agreed to see us. I park the car on the drive outside the rectory and we crunch up the gravel path to the front door. Bill rings the bell and I hear footsteps behind the door.

It opens to reveal a man in his forties, who regards us from behind his dog collar, "Yes?" he asks.

Bill gives him his most charming smile, "Father Douglas?"

"Yes," Father Douglas says.

"My name is William Gee, and this is David Brookes, my assistant. We are from Channel Three news, and we've come to have a look at your Madonna, to see if there is a story here." Bill offers his hand, which is shook reluctantly, I offer mine but it is ignored.

"I don't want my church turned into a circus, Mr. Gee."

The Songs of Angels

"Please call me Bill, we have no intention of that Father," Bill says.

"How did you find out about our little miracle Mr. Gee?"

"News travels fast, I assume someone in your flock spilled the beans."

"Well you had better come in," the priest says. We are led to a cosy sitting room of panelling and twee paintings, where we are invited to sit. I get out my pad to take notes and Bill goes to work.

"What a beautiful house you have here Father, what period is it?" Rule number one; get the interviewee on your side with small talk. Try to be their friend.

"Cut to the chase Mr. Gee," Father Douglas says, he obviously has not read the rulebook, "We are not old buddies, ask me what you will about the Madonna."

"Very well Father," Bill replies, "I meant no disrespect. When was it noticed, and by whom?"

"It was noticed by a child at this Sundays service."

"Can we interview the child?" Bill asks.

"You will have to ask the child's Mother," he replies, "I will phone her before you leave if you wish."

"Thank you, that would be appreciated. Has the Madonna ever wept before?"

"No," Father Douglas says, "Not to my knowledge."

"And there are no leaks in the roof?" Bill asks.

Father Douglas's facial expression changes from being distantly agitated, to one of open annoyance. He stares at Bill for a second, and then composes himself, "The definition of a miracle, is something that has no known explanation. At this time, I cannot tell you why our statue is weeping, you are free to examine it yourself."

"Thank you Father, I would like that very much. If you could lead the way." Bill says, indicating that the he should take us to the Madonna. The priest leads us back through the front door, and we crunch down the gravel path towards a side door in the main church building. He produces a key ring and unlocks the door, then beckons us inside. The Madonna stands at the other end of the aisle, with the alter before it. The statue is almost life size, and rises up above us on a platform. She seems to raise herself even higher as we approach. Finally we stand before her clasped hands and bowed head, as a tear departs from her eyelid, splashing into a bowl placed at her feet. Whatever the reason for this phenomenon, a shiver runs down my spine.

Is it not a good likeness of her.

{Are any of them? No statue or painting will ever do justice to her.}

It's ironic is it not, how a whole religious movement can be built on a mistranslation.

{What are you referring to?}

The Immaculate Conception, Isaiah 7:14. The Hebrew version of the book said 'Behold, a young woman shall be with child'. The Greeks translated it as, 'A virgin shall be with child'. It has to be the most prolific mistake, or embellishment, in the whole history of mankind.

{I suppose so.}

Can you figure out what is going on, inside this statue?

{Not yet, but I am working on it.}

Bill is peering around the back of the statue, looking for tubes probably. The building seems sound and the air smells dry, so I am ruling out damp and rainwater. Any suggestions?

{No not yet.}

Another teardrop splashes from her right eye, and into the bowl. I look over to Father Douglas, he regards the statue with awe, and he believes this totally. I ask him, "Is it just the right eye?"

"So far," he says to me, and to Bill he says, "You will not find any evidence of tampering Mr. Gee, trust me, I have looked."

"Fascinating," Bill replies, "Father, would you have any objections if I bring the camera crew up here to film this?" Father Douglas nods his consent, Bill heads back to the car, to report in and get Jonathan and the crew up here. I snap of a couple of pictures of her face, hoping to get a shot of a tear falling.

"You do not believe it do you?" Father Douglas says, I turn to him, "You believe there is a rational explanation?"

"There is an explanation for everything," I say.

"Yes when you are young, there always appears to be," he adds, "I hope that we don't find it."

"You would prefer to be ignorant?" I say, "If you close your eyes and ears to the truth, can you still call it a miracle?"

"Have you ever watched those magician shows on TV?" he says with a

The Songs of Angels

wry smile, "The ones where they do the trick and then some masked rascal, shows you how the illusion is achieved?"

"Yes," I nod.

"They show you this amazing trick, which leaves you mystified. Then when it is explained, it is often so simple, that I usually feel cheated."

"They take away the magic, excuse the pun," I say.

{I have the answer now.}

Wait one minute.

I add, "So if someone comes along and tells you exactly why this statue is weeping, would you still think it a miracle?"

"If someone came along and categorically proved that God does not exist, I would still remain a priest."

"Good for you," I say, and look back to the Madonna. Go on then, tell me.

{Right then, the statue appears to be marble, but it is not. It's limestone with some sort of glazed finish covering it all over, except the base. The statues base and the stone plinth it stands on, encourages condensation between the two. This is then drawn through the limestone via capillary action. The whole inside of the statue is sodden, but it cannot get through the glaze, except through a hairline crack in the base of the right eye. The eyelid acts as a mini reservoir, when it is full it drips over the side. Do you feel cheated?}

Yes.

{Are you going to tell him?}

No, how would I explain how I knew. There is no trickery here then?

{No, just the laws of physics.}

How long has it taken, for the water to work its way up from the base?

{I have no idea, years probably.}

Then what we have is a fluke?

{Yes.}

But a phenomenal fluke, why has just the right eye cracked? Why nowhere else? What are the chances that the flaw would be in her eye? Water could just as easily drip from her fingers or the end of her nose.

{True.}

Well it isn't, it's coming out of her eye, where it should come from. Perhaps that is a mini miracle in itself.

{The chances of a crack forming on the eye are the same as anywhere else.}

But it is still the eye that has tears falling from it.

{Are you looking for a miracle Lucifer? I should think you have seen enough. This is a natural occurrence. Granted it is a strange one, but flukes like this happen all the while.}

· Name one.

{There is a cloud passing by outside, that just looked like a face.}

That's not a miracle; it's just a coincidence.

{Exactly, and so is this statue. If this were a square slab of rock with a flaw, that leaked water, you would not give it a second glance. At the end of the day, that is all you are looking at. A slab of rock that just happens to have an eye carved over a flaw.}

Someone is in a cynical mood today.

{Practical is a better description, everything has to have a meaning with you. 'What does this mean' or 'why does this happen' If you sometime conceded that things may happen for no reason, then perhaps you would not have annoyed God so much.}

There has to be a reason for everything, otherwise there is no point.

{If the statue smiled at you now, would you think it a miracle?}

Yes, it's solid rock, how could it smile?

{Lucifer, you forget your physics lesson. Even solid rock is made of atoms, and atoms are more empty space than matter. And every atom above absolute freezing point moves about, constantly jigging and bumping its neighbours. If for some random reason, the billions of atoms at the corner of her mouth, all moved in the same direction, she would appear to smile.}

The chances of that happening are staggering

{True, but that does not make it impossible. You may have to wait for the end of time to see a smile, but it could happen in the next five seconds. And it would still be a random act, with no thought or guidance, and therefore not a miracle.}

"Are you Okay son? You look troubled."

I tear my gaze from the Madonna and look towards him, "Yes Father, I am fine, just thinking."

Bill bashes back through the door and trudges up the aisle towards us,

The Songs of Angels

"The crew are on the way," he says, "Father, if you could call the parents of the child who spotted this, I would like to talk to them."

"Of course," he replies, and leads us back to the rectory.

⁂

The Mother of the little girl invites us over to talk. It is only a short walk, so we set off, following the directions Father Douglas gives us. He assures us that it will only take five minutes. Bill is now in a buoyant mood as we walk down the road.

"This should get a better slot than I thought, especially if we can film the statue actually weeping," he says, "If the parents agree that Jonathan can interview the girl, we are laughing. As soon as we finish here, we'll get some lunch and work on the script for JR. With him doing the interview," he laughs, "We could call it The Madonna and the pre-Madonna!"

I also laugh and add, "But don't hype it up too much, you heard what the priest said about turning his church into a circus."

"Are you serious? He wants this publicity more than we do. It would not surprise me if he was the one, who leaked the story. He's loving every second of this, but has to be all priestly about it. Can you imagine the congregations he will get? People will be queuing at his door when this goes out."

"We're here," I say, "Number twenty-seven."

Bill looks around and starts up the path, the door opens before we are half way there. A woman greets us with a smile, "You're the reporters," she informs us, "Please come in. I am Kate Doyle." We exchange pleasantries and are led to the sitting room, where a pot of coffee is waiting for us, and duly poured. Kate Doyle is probably in her late twenties and typically middle class. As she passes coffee cups to us, she continues, "So you want to interview my daughter, Emma, for a news report on the television?"

"If it is acceptable with you," Bill says.

"I don't see why not, as long as she agrees. But I do not want gangs of reporters outside my house, after this goes out."

"We will do the interview at the church," I say, "and we will not give her second name out if you like. But it will not stop a determined reporter finding you, if he has a mind to. This is a very small town."

Bill looks daggers at me, "Mrs. Doyle," he says.

"Call me Kate please," Kate asks.

"Kate, how did Emma spot the Madonna weeping?" he asks.

"She always sits at the front."

"Why?" I ask.

Kate looks at me quizzically and a smile touches the corners of her mouth. She stands, opens the door and shouts, "Emma! Can you come in here please sweetheart!" She returns to her seat and says, "Ask her."

All eyes turn to the door as Emma makes her way in. I do not need to ask her. Emma is about seven years old, blonde with brown eyes set in an angelic face. And sitting in a wheelchair. I look back to Kate Doyle, I know my colour is rising, and she smiles. Bill on the other hand, stares in wonder at this unfortunate little girl. I can see him thinking how perfect the interview will be. The poor crippled child who saw the Madonna weeping. "Hello Emma," he says.

"Hello," she replies.

"Honey," Kate Doyle says, "These gentlemen are reporters. They want to know if they can talk to you about the Madonna, on TV!"

The biggest smile crosses the little girls face, "It won't be us Emma," Bill says, "Do you know Jonathan Remick?"

"I have seen him," Emma says.

"It's up to you Emma," Kate says, "If you want to."

"Everyone at school will be jealous," she giggles. "I would like to do it."

"OK," Bill says, "We will call you when the crew arrive and meet you at the church. Will you have to speak to your husband Mrs. Doyle?"

"No Mr. Gee, my husband was killed three years ago, in the same accident that crippled Emma." Bill looks down and I look at Emma. "Don't be embarrassed Mr. Gee, I will let you out now and see you later."

As we wave goodbye Bill says, "There is a lesson for you. I should have got that information out of the priest. I am getting old I think. He said 'Mother' not parents, I should have picked up on that."

"She did not seem too upset." I say.

"No, but I don't like embarrassing myself. Lets find a café, or something, and start work on JR's questions." We have to drive out of town to find a drive through, and sit in the car, working on the format for the interview. Bill scoffs burger and chips, and I have an apple pie and a Coke. Bills mobile starts to ring, he answers it. The camera crew is about forty minutes away, so we arrange to meet them at the church.

※

An hour later, after getting lost, the van finally arrives. Sean Peters is the first out; he is the camera and sound guy, a mountain of a man whose usual permanent smile is missing. Then Jane Townsend, the editor/director of our little band. Last out is Jonathan. I have never seen him looking so rough. His normal hurricane proof hair is plastered to his forehead with sweat. He converses with Father Douglas, who leads him back to the rectory.

"What's the matter with him?" Bill asks.

Sean answers, "He's been sweating and farting all the way here. We have had to stop twice so he can empty his guts out." Bill laughs, "It's not funny," Sean adds, "The van smells like a sewer and he's probably given me all his germs." At which Bill laughs even louder.

"OK, OK," Jane says, "So he's not very well, but we still have a job to do. Sean, get your camera set up. Where shall we start Bill? Outside the main door?" Bill agrees. "Lets see your ideas for the interviews then." I hand her the notes that Bill and I have prepared. She skips through them and looks up, "Shit," she says, "The little girl is in a wheelchair, that will be great."

Not for her I think

"Jonathan can't do a piece looking like that," Bill says, "He looks half dead."

"He will be alright," Jane says, "He's a professional."

But by the time we are ready to shoot, Jonathan has still not made an appearance. Father Douglas comes out of the rectory shaking his head. "That man is very ill," he tells Jane, "I think he needs a doctor."

"Shit," she says, then adds, "Sorry Father." She calls us all together, "Jonathan can't do the interviews and we cannot wait for someone else. I know another station is on this already, so it looks like it's you Bill."

"No way Jane," Bill says, "You've seen me behind the camera, that's why I do this job."

"Shit Bill, help me out here."

"David can do it," Bill suggests, "He's younger and prettier than me anyway."

Jane looks to me, "Want to give it a shot?"

"Yes," I say, the glee evident in my voice.

"No promises though, if I don't think it will work, we stop and I call for someone else from the station, and hope the other channels are not too close yet." I agree, and go looking for my tie and jacket. Bill gives me a pat on the back as I pass. We call a doctor for JR.

"OK, recording," Sean says. I am outside the main doors of the Church with Father Douglas and a large crowd of locals.

"This the little town of Fairbourne," I begin, "Where a startling phenomenon is happening as we speak. This is Father Malcolm Douglas, of the Church of saint Mary."

I turn to him, "Father, could you explain what you have witnessed here?" I push the microphone towards him.

"It started on Sunday, as I was finishing the service," he says, "We have a statue of the Virgin Mary behind the alter, and a young girl pointed out that the statue was weeping."

"That must have been shocking for you." I say.

"Totally amazing."

"And no one can offer a reason for this?" I ask.

"No, there does not seem to be any explanation."

"Father, do you believe this is a miracle?"

"It is not for me to say. Only God would know."

"But I have inspected the statue with you Father, and can see no earthly explanation for this to occur."

"People will have to make their own minds up," he says, and the crowd murmur.

"Thank you Father Douglas," I say, and turn to the crowd behind.

"It's a miracle!" some one shouts out, "I have seen her cry!" and the rest of the crowd mutters their agreement. I turn back to the camera.

"And we have a very special guest with us, please meet Emma, the girl who first witnessed this spectacle." I kneel down beside her wheelchair and the camera pans down to get both of our faces in. "Hello Emma."

"Hi," she says.

"Emma, you saw it first didn't you?"

"Yes," see says, and beams

"What did you do?"

"I pointed up to the statue," she points into the distance for effect, "And shouted out that she was crying."

"And no one saw this before you?"

"I have to sit right at the front, so I was the closest, except for Father Douglas. But he was not looking at her, he had his back to her, because he was talking to us. And I always watch her when we are in church."

"Why?"

"Because she is so beautiful," Emma says.

"Why do you think she started to cry Emma?"

"Perhaps she is sad."

"Why would she be sad?'

"Because bad things happen," she says

"What sort of things?"

"Bad things."

"A bad thing happened to you didn't it Emma?"

"Yes, but she would not be crying over that."

"Why not?" I ask.

"Because my Daddy went to Heaven, so he will not be sad will he?"

"No he will not be sad in Heaven, no one is sad in Heaven. Thanks for talking to us Emma."

"No Problem," she says.

"OK!" Jane says, "Cut it there Sean. David, a word please." I smile at Emma and get up to walk over to Jane. "That was not the script," she points out.

"I know," I reply, "Do you want to do it again?"

"No, it was fine. Right then lets get inside," she says, and walks over to Father Douglas. Kate Doyle is hugging her daughter. Father Douglas must have agreed to have everyone in the church because Jane is trying to get all the people inside.

I walk back to Kate and Emma Doyle, "Are you coming inside?" I ask.

"Yes we are," Kate says.

"Can I push you inside the church Emma?"

"If you want," she says.

Kate Doyle raises her eyebrows, "You're highly honoured Mr. Brookes. Nobody usually gets to push her anywhere, she is too independent."

I smile, take hold of Emma's wheelchair and guide her through the church doors. All the pews are full as I steer her to the front of the congregation. "Where do you always sit Emma?" I ask.

"Here on the right," She replies. I position her chair and apply the brake. Sean is setting up besides the alter, so that he can pan around the whole church and zoom in on the Madonna. There is an atmosphere of expectancy radiating from everyone present, an infectious expectation of hope. I wait while Sean zooms onto the Madonna's face, then sweeps the people in a slow wide ark. Finally he settles on a side view of Emma Doyle, staring up to the statue, then centres the lens onto me. Jane gives me the cue to begin.

"Who can say if this is a miracle or not. But the fact remains that this statue of the Virgin Mary has been weeping since Sunday morning. And if it is not a miracle, then the miracle is the hope and joy that the people of Fairbourne are feeling right now. Because this phenomenon has given them a gift of awe and wonder, that surpasses their normal senses. Some of you out there, may scoff at this report, but all I will ask you to do, is come and stand in front of this statue, and look into her eyes. I have one last question for Emma." Sean zooms onto the child's face. "Emma," I ask, "Do you think this is a miracle?"

She smiles and says, "I hope so," Sean holds the camera on her for a while, then returns to me.

I finish by saying; "This is David Brookes for Channel Three, at the church of Saint Mary, in Fairbourne."

"OK," Jane shouts, "David, just do that last line again, and when he has finished Sean, zoom in on the Madonna." I repeat the last line, and the camera pans over to the Madonna's eyes. Everyone seems to be holding his or her breath, waiting for a tear to be captured on film. But it does not come. I don't think anyone moves for five minutes; we all just stare at the statue. Finally Jane starts to get twitchy, "Keep filming Sean, we can edit it onto the end."

People start to leave now, and I walk outside for some air. Bill strolls over smiling as he lights up a cigarette, and takes a long pull. "So you didn't like our original script?"

"Sorry Bill," I say, "I don't think I changed that much."

"What the hell," he replies, "It was better anyway. The only problem I have is that I am going to lose another assistant. Jonathan has some competition and will spit nails when he sees that footage."

"Can I speak with you Mr. Brookes?" We look around to Kate Doyle, who is approaching.

"Yes of course," I say.

"Excuse me," Bill says and walks away.

Kate Doyle bows her head to the floor and continues, "I was not totally truthful with you before. What you said about Heaven to Emma, do you believe that?"

"Yes," I say.

"I only come to church for her you know, I no longer believe there is a Heaven."

"You should believe." I reply

"Her Father, my husband did not die in the crash," she still has not looked at me, "He was drunk Mr. Brookes, Emma does not know this. He was hurt, but not fatally. Emma was critical for a few days, the doctors did not know if she would live. He took his own life the day he was released, while I sat in the hospital with our daughter." Now she looks directly into my eyes, "Do you still think he went to Heaven?"

I imagine that she can see straight through me, see my thoughts. There is no chance that someone so guilt ridden could possibly get into Heaven, "I hope so," I say without conviction.

"He chickened out Mr. Brookes. Do you think God would take someone like that?"

"I don't know," I lie.

"I know, Heaven and God are bullshit. If there were a God, he would not let my little girl grow up a cripple, with no Father." She turns and walks away, and I let her go without replying.

Jane and Sean are coming out of the church with big smiles, "You filmed a tear?" I ask.

"You bet," Jane says, "I was worried for a while. You Okay?" I nod, "Lets get this edited and back to base, with any luck we will make the nine O'clock. Well done David."

"Thanks," I say.

Section extracted from the seraphim records: Meeting 9,399,004,361 of the council of Heaven.

Raphael:
If you ask me, he's wasting his time and ours. Tell me, what has he done so far? Well I will tell you, he's done nothing! There are normal humans down there, who do more good work than him. He's more interested in fornicating with that female, than spreading the word of God. Once again I would like to have it noted that I am completely against this course of action.
Michael:
He is still learning and growing.
Raphael:
He will never amount to anything. He has too much doubt in his heart.
God:
You forget Raphael; I spent thirty-odd years as a mortal before I began. He is only in his third mortal decade.
Raphael:
But I trusted you Lord.
God:
And I trust Lucifer, I'm sorry that you do not trust your brother.
Raphael:
There is too much water under the bridge. To many times he has fell short in my eyes.
God:
Who are you to judge him? He has more courage than all of you put together. No other Angel has ever stood before me and told me I was wrong. And when I asked him if he would do this, he had no hesitation.
Raphael:

I offered to go also.
God:
And I refused to let you. It is not a place you would like, or survive in.
Raphael:
But I have heard Gabriel's reports, he constantly doubts himself, and he is disrespectful to you Lord.
God:
I also had doubts when I was down there; at times all hope seemed lost. But that is mortal life and something you could not understand.
Pause.
God:
Onto the meeting subject, and your report Gabriel.
Gabriel:
As you know from the last meeting, he has become quite a hotshot reporter. After the station offered him a position as a field operator, he has been trekking around the globe from one assignment to another. He has become quite oblivious to danger. If he thinks he has a story, and excuse the pun, he rushes in where Angels fear to tread.
Michael:
Are you saying he deliberately puts his life in jeopardy?
Gabriel:
No, it's not intentional. He just has to be the best. There is never any thought of compromise.
God:
Are you aware of his objective with this?
Gabriel:
Not from his lips, but do you want my opinion?
God:
Please.
Gabriel:
Firstly, he wants to sample every bit of life he can, he wants to see the world first hand. And secondly, he wants to become known. As he has his face on TV almost every week, he is succeeding with this objective.
Raphael:
To what end, do you think, that he wants to be famous?
Gabriel:

I should think that obvious Raphael, when he finally puts his plan together, he has to be known and trusted, so that he is taken seriously. What was your plan? Head for the nearest street corner and start preaching the gospel?
God:
Thank you Gabriel. Is there anything else, at this time?
Gabriel:
No Lord.

CHAPTER 5

Year twenty-three

Bill was correct and he did lose his assistant. Since then, I have travelled to some of the worst places on Earth. And I have seen with these mortal eyes, things that I never saw as an Angel. I have witnessed things that should never be observed, or suffered by anyone. The world viewed from Heaven, is not the world I see from this angle, because I am part of it, because it is real. Every sad story I tell has the same roots, how evil man can be. I have seen populations devastated by famine, not because there is no food, but because their leaders are too insecure to ask for help. Or because their misplaced pride overrules their very humanity.

Then there is the greed and the jealousy, which drives a person to inflict a host of atrocities upon their brothers. The human mind seems to have a horrible flaw. It can deceive itself, it can justify any action, even when deep down, it knows it to be wrong.

'I was obeying orders'
'If I don't sell them drugs, someone else will'
'We were at war'
'Yes I killed them, but God was on our side'
I have heard these words from the mouths of different people, and in

different places, all in this last year. And the tragedy is that they all believed them to be true.

Do you think I am losing hope? Fortunately I have seen something else on my travels. I have seen the courage and the kindness of the individual. Humans are capable of incredible acts of compassion, of selfless sacrifice, of unconditional love. So perhaps there is hope.

※

March.

The Toyota Land cruiser lurches again, on this dirt strip that is laughingly called a road. We travel by night, because we are told that it is too dangerous to move about in the daytime. In the light the government strike aircrafts fly, and will take pot shots at any vehicles, civilian or not. Anyone in rebel territory is a valid target. At night we only have to contend with snipers and death squads.

These snipers are government-sponsored men, fighting their own kind of guerrilla warfare. I am informed that they hide most of the time. They shoot and then run because they dare not hang around. Once they have taken a shot at someone, they give away their location, and the rebels are always looking out for them. The death squads are another story. They raid villages and settlements, night and day, armed with a list of suspected rebel sympathizers, then kill them all, often brutally. The government denies that they are affiliated with them, but it is common knowledge that they are controlled by the military.

These men belong to the AUC. This paramilitary group was born from the private armies of drug barons and landowners, but they will recruit anyone as long as your main aim in life is to kill rebels.

Welcome to Colombia.

We sneaked across the border two days ago. It was pointless asking for a visa, as there was no chance that the government of this troubled country, would have let us anywhere near the rebels. So Sean Peters and myself are technically on holiday, we met out guide and driver, Francisco in San Christóbel, and drove illegally across the border, heading for the rebel held lands.

The main rebel group, who we are with, call themselves FARC. The Revolutionary Armed Forces of Colombia. Although they control a substantial area of Colombia, the movement appears to have lost their way. While they started as freedom fighters, reports indicate that they have degenerated into kidnappers and extortionists. Recent polls only show them as commanding five percent of public support. The Colombian and United States governments class them as terrorists and drug dealers. That they use drug money to fund their activities, can no longer be denied. But are they Freedom fighters or terrorists? That is the question I want to find out.

Francisco describes himself as a farmer who supports FARC, but I note, he is a farmer with an AK47 on the seat next to him. He drives in the dark like he has a sixth sense, I do not know how he sees the road, I certainly cannot see a thing. It is quite terrifying at first, but his confidence in himself, eventually seeps through to us.

So we sit in the back of this battered MPV, heading for Montería, which is in FARC territory. Francisco has promised to show us that they are building a better life here, free of secret police, where they do not harm the innocent, but encourage open worship and free speech. He tells us that we should be there by first light.

In the distance, I see a light streak across the valley and ask Francisco what it was.

"Tracer bullet," he informs me, "The sniper put a tracer in the top of the magazine. So that they can adjust their aim as they let of the clip. Don't worry about the tracers," he says and laughs, "If you see one coming toward you, worry about ten unseen bullet following it."

This does not make me feel any better, and I sink down a little into the seat. The night passes slowly as the car eats up the miles in total darkness. Sean is snoring again, how anyone could sleep out here in a war zone, with potential enemies behind every tree, is beyond me. But Sean is a law unto himself and a bloody good cameraman, who has followed me on many insane journeys, almost without question.

Francisco suddenly slams on the brakes and the road is full of torches, armed men are attached to them. "No problem, no problem," he says, "Checkpoint, our people." As the Toyota skids to a stop, he is out of the door exchanging handshakes. I listen to their conversation, I am still pre-

The Songs of Angels

tending that I cannot understand the language. It would appear strange to Sean and anyone else for that matter, if I instantly started speaking the appropriate language, wherever we were reporting. He tells the apparent leader of this group, why he is taking us to Montería. Eventually this seems to be accepted, and we are waved on our way.

"I nearly never stopped in time," Francisco says.

"What would they have done?" I ask.

"Shot us," he replies, matter of fact like, "They would have been upset, when they found out, that it was me driving the car. Chairo." He says, pointing his thumb over his shoulder, "He is from the same village as me. Very good man, very fine fighter."

"Have you personally been involved in the fighting," I ask Francisco

"Of course," he says, "Before now. But I have wound to my leg and cannot run, so I am now not active."

"Battle wounds?" I say.

He laughs, "How I wish it was so, I fell from the roof of my house."

I suppress a smile. I was expecting a tale of heroism. A tall story of bullets and mines, of terror and valiant demigods, in which Francesco would be the main lead. Instead, the road relentlessly unfolds in front of the land cruiser, and Francisco blindly follows it into the night.

※

Dawn and Francisco is throwing camouflage netting over the motorcar, we are herded to a single story building that lies in a cluster of six, or seven, similar dwellings. We are short of Montería by about eight miles, but Francisco will not risk driving in daylight. Accommodation is basic, but we are use to this and all I really want, after a night of driving, is some sleep. I collapse onto the thin mattresses supplied to us; the last thing I hear is a fast jet passing over.

I wake into the sunshine streaming through the single window, someone had the sense, to throw a mosquito net over my bed, it was probably Sean and I am thankful. A Dream of Rebecca filters back into my mind, how I hate to be away from her. I dress quickly and walk outside, Sean and Francisco are nowhere in sight, in fact there is no one around. So I sit on the step and take in the relentless late morning sun.

I wonder where everyone has gone?

{I do not know.}

Sorry, it was a rhetorical question, I was not asking you.

{Oh excuse me.}

The Toyota is still hidden in the thin trees, around one hundred yards down the track, so I am sure Francisco has not gone to far. I head back indoors, out of the heat, to find the kitchen, and hopefully a drink. Finally in the kitchen I find life, a woman, who appears indigenous Indian, greets me with a smile. She asks if I want anything and I reply by mimicking holding a cup to my mouth. She nods and places a pitcher, and cup, on the table in front of me. I nod my thanks and pour out some water. It is still surprisingly cool, as I take the first mouthful.

"David," I tell her, pointing to my chest.

"Magola," she replies, with a slight bow.

"Ah, Mr. Brookes, you are awake I see," I turn my head to find Francisco behind me. I swear I did not hear him come inside, the man must have been a cat in a previous life.

"Where is Sean, I mean Mr. Peters?" I ask.

"He went out with his camera earlier," he says.

"Is that wise?"

"He is as safe as he is likely to be on foot." Francisco says, "As long as he does not stray to far. The jets do not waste their missiles on individuals. They save them for vehicles or the occasional town." Magola is setting out food on the table, and invites us to eat, Francisco dives straight in and I nibble on some bread.

"We will leave as soon as the sun goes down," he informs me, "I should expect to be inside Montería within an hour. There we will meet with senior FARC people and I will be leaving you with them."

"Francisco," I ask, "Why did you join the FARC?"

"You ask a stupid question, Mr. Brookes. If you were Colombian, you would not need to ask this. Colombia is not a poor country, we have an abundance of natural resources. But we are poor people, all the wealth is horded by a select few and they will not let it go without a fight. So the poor must fight. Fight the corruption of our government and the rich who pull their strings."

"What about the drug barons whom you support." I ask.

"I do not know what you mean." He looks away.

"Come on Francisco," I say, "Everyone knows that the FARC and the cartels work together."

"Who are you to judge," he says, "This is a war Mr. Brookes, in a war the enemy of my enemy is my friend. Is that not so?"

"Even if your allies are worse than your enemies?"

He shakes his head, "You do not understand."

"That is why I ask Francisco. And I am not here to judge you, just to find the facts."

Francisco continues to eat and then says, "I am not a top man, I am only your transport. You must ask these questions when you meet senior FARC in Montería." I let the conversation drop.

A few minutes pass and then Sean strolls back though the door. He rests his camera on the table and helps himself to some food. I ask him where he has been. "Got some good footage of a peasant smallholding about half a mile away." He says, "You heard of Plan Colombia?"

"Yes," I reply. Plan Colombia, I remind myself, is a Joint project mainly funded by the US, which aims to combat illegal drug production.

"Well the armed forces have been spraying all the farms up here with defoliation shit. Look at this." Sean turns his viewfinder to me, and Francisco, then starts the tape. It shows a view of banana trees with brown and withered leaves.

"About four weeks ago," Francisco says, "The planes sprayed all this area. Many people were sick."

"Look here," Sean points to the small screen, "These broken and dead plants were maize, and that's cassava, they have ruined it all."

"What's that bright green plant, is that coffee?" I ask.

"No Mr. Brookes," Francisco replies, "That is coca."

"Which you make cocaine from," I state, looking around to Francisco.

"Not personally," he says, "these poor farmers can make more money from a few rows of coca, than a field of any other plant. They all grow it and sell it on."

"Then the planes have hit the right targets." I say.

"No David, there is a problem with this strategy, look at the video." Sean says. So I look, but I cannot see his point. "You said it yourself, the coca is bright green, it's the only plant that's recovering."

"So the farmer will now plant more coca," Francisco adds, "Hoping that next time he is sprayed, enough coca will survive. And then he can sell it and buy food, rather than growing it. It is the same with the AUC, for every man their death squads murder, two men run away to join FARC. So the Colombian government, by killing suspected rebels, increase the rebel forces, and the US, by starving farmers and their families, will increase the cocaine output."

"And the farmers that cannot get restarted," Sean says, "out of necessity, will abandon their farms. They then have a choice, go to the cities hoping for work, in a country with the worst unemployment record in South America, or join the rebels."

"Congratulations uncle Sam," I say. "You turn another group of people, who were indifferent to you, into people who now hate your guts. Where is your farm Francisco?" I ask.

"It no longer exists," he says, "Con permiso," *Excuse me,* he adds, as he stands and leaves the room. I wonder what horror drove him to become a rebel, but I do not think I will ask.

※

As dusk falls we are loading the netting into the back of the Toyota. I made Sean and Francisco take me back to the farmer that afternoon. We did a sort of interview with the farmer, although he would not be filmed. My lasting impression of him was that although he grows illegal crops, he was not an evil person. Maybe naive, but he only saw coca as a way to feed his family. And naturally, when asked, he would not say that he would join the rebels, if all else failed, but I never expected him to admit that anyway.

When the sun finally drops below the horizon, we are back on the road, threading our way through the foothills. Within thirty minutes we can see the lights of Montería below us. As we hit the outskirts of the city, Francisco stops and another armed man joins us. He is introduced as Henry, but says little. I cannot imagine how he knew when we would arrive, as we are a day late and I do not remember Francisco contacting anyone since yesterday.

Francisco pulls over and cuts the engine. He turns to us and says, "From here you will have to lie on the floor and wear a blindfold."

"No fucking way!" Sean shouts, Henry fingers his gun and looks nervous.

"For what reason?" I ask.

"You are westerners, I don't want any casual observers seeing you in my car. And the blindfolds are as much for your protection as ours. We don't want the location of our safe houses on TV, and if your report says that you were blindfolded, no one will ask you, or beat it out of you."

I can see he has a point, but Sean is still flatly refusing. Gabriel, what do you think?

{It is your choice Lucifer.}

"There is no alternative," Francisco says, "It is this way, or we turn around."

"Then turn around," Sean says.

"Sean," I reply, "We have come this far, and I can see their point."

Sean takes a deep breathe, "Shit, fucking shit," he cries, "I don't like this."

"Neither do I," I say, "But I can't see a way out of it."

Sean sits looking forward for a couple of minutes, "OK," he finally agrees. Henry produces strips of cloth from somewhere, which he wraps our eyes with, and we crouch down below the door level for the rest of the journey.

Probably twenty minutes later and Francisco pulls to a stop and kills the engine. I hear the seat creak as he turns back to us, "Please keep blindfolds on, when we get you out, put your hand on my shoulder and I guide you. Be very quiet." The driver door opens and then mine, I assume it is Francesco who helps me out of the back and places my hand on his shoulder. I hear the same thing happening on the other side of the car with Sean. We are led indoors with whispered commands of stop, go, steps etc. Finally he says, "Almost there."

{This is not right.}

What do you mean?

{Something is wrong, you are being deceived.}

How?

"Please sit Mr. Brookes" Francisco's voice.

{Lucifer! He is removing a revolver!}

I rip the blindfold from my eyes to find the barrel of a gun pointing at my forehead. "Please do not shout or scream," Francisco whispers, "If you do, you will die. And Mr. Peters will die also. He is being told the same thing as we speak. I am sure you have a lot of questions, but not yet. For now, no noise. Nod if you understand."

I nod, Francisco backs away. I am in a room the size of a broom cupboard, "Please sit," he says. There is a wooden chair behind me, which I sit on. "Not long here," he says. "If you co-operate you will not be harmed." The door closes and I hear a bolt thrown. The only light I have is coming under the door. Muffled voices, talking in Spanish, are coming from somewhere near, I can't hear what they are saying.

What the fuck is going on?
{I do not know.}
Where is Sean?
{I do not know.}
Well fucking find out!
{I am trying to!}

Footsteps are coming towards my door, the light outside goes out as the bolt is removed. A high power torch is shone into my face as the door opens, I cannot see who is coming in. Instinctively I lift my arms in front of my face and receive a sharp blow to my head. Stars are swimming in my vision. A voice, that is not Francisco says, "Be good, no problem," he repeats it five or six times. A gag is forced onto my mouth and tied tightly behind my neck. Then I am dragged out of the cell and rested on my stomach. "Hands please," the voice asks. My hands are then tied behind my back, then my feet are arched up and tied to my hands. The pain is already starting. Finally a sack is placed over my head and I hear tape being pulled from a roll. Then I feel it, as this man wraps tape around my neck to secure the sack. "Be good, no problem, be good, no problem."

There is no good way to lift a man who is bound this way, the pain comes in waves as I am carried from the room. I cannot help but grunt as I am bashed into walls. Finally I am dumped down. Pain shoots through my shoulders, from the sound of springs creaking and the smell of petrol, this has to be the boot of a car. Another body is forced in beside me and I feel the movement of air, then hear the thud as the boot is slammed shut. This has to be Sean in here with me. I begin to breath in ragged gasps, I cannot get enough air through my nose, and this sack, and into my lungs. Sean manages to squeeze my leg, as if to comfort me, and this calms me slightly.

{Lucifer! Try to relax, you will not suffocate.}

That's easy for you to say.

The car pulls away on this nightmare journey, and the wheel arch strikes my head, I feel sick and the stars are back. Don't be sick, you will choke and die. If I die, I will never hold Rebecca again. Don't be sick, don't pass out, don't be sick, don't pass out.

⁂

I do not know how long we have been travelling. My arms and legs are completely numb, but we have stopped. The engine is still running, but I hear the doors opening. Then the boot is opened, it is daylight and we are far from the city. I know because I can hear birds singing. It is that amazing liquid cry that only tropical birds make. Sean is being manhandled out of the trunk, and I wait my turn. But it does not come, the boot is slammed down again and the car takes off. We are separated, I think that is the worst thing they have done to me so far.

Where am I?

{I do not know the district, but we are currently south of- }

Gabriel?

The car hits a pothole and I am thrown into the boot lid. How I wish I could scream. Gabriel?

{I am here.}

Jesus, I thought you had left me for a second.

{No, I am here Lucifer, we will get through this.}

The car stops once again, I am not far from Sean. How long has that been? Twenty minutes maximum, on these roads that's no more than ten miles. The boot lid opens again and I am pulled out and carried for no more than thirty seconds. The sunlight dims so I know we have entered a building. We go down a flight of stairs, then there is total darkness as I am lowered to the floor.

"I will untie your hands and feet now, but you must not remove your hood. Nod if you understand," I nod, this is another new voice. "Your hands and feet will hurt for a while, yes, you may scream if you wish. No one will hear you. Keep your hood on until you hear the door bolted. You must never see us, or we will have to kill you. Nod if you understand." I nod again. "Now I untie you."

I am lying on my belly as he cuts the ropes holding my legs, and they flap down onto the dirt floor like useless lumps of meat. I do not feel them hit the ground. I hear him stand up and retreat, then the door is shut and I am in darkness. He must have cut the bindings on my hands as well, but my arms will not move yet. I have a few seconds of relief as the knots are pulled out of my back and then the pain starts. First in my hands, and then in my legs. Blinding white-hot pain, building and building as nerve ends switch back on. I am glad that I am still gagged, at least I can bite down on the cloth, and it is the only reason that I do not scream as tears are forced from my clenched shut eyes.

Finally the pain is subsiding and I reach up and remove the sack covering my head. The gag takes a little while longer with these numb and clumsy hands. But eventually it is removed. I am still on my stomach, I still cannot move my legs. There are pins and needles in my hands now, and starting in my legs. I try to turn myself over and fail. Just wait for a while.

I wake with a start, Jesus I fell asleep. Every bone in my body hurts as I roll over and push myself, with spasmodic jerks, into a sitting position. Someone bangs the door, "You are awake yes?" he says in broken English.

I try to answer but only croak, with a lot of effort I finally say 'yes', which is followed by a coughing fit. "Put on hood." The order is barked through the door. Shit! I cannot see it in the dark.

"I don't know where it is!" I croak.

"Is not good," he says, "No Problem, I will shine light through the door, you look away from door." I hear the door unlock and look in the opposite direction. I really do not want to see him. Torch light streams through the crack he has made and I spot the hood. I pick it up and pull it over my head.

"OK," I shout, as the door is opened and the torch extinguished, dim light and shadow filters through the weave of the hood. My jailer is silhouetted by the light bulb in the next room. He enters and squats down opposite me.

"How do you feel?" he asks. How do I feel? What sort of fucking question is that? Reporters on television who ask that question, of people whose houses have just burnt down usually send me into a mini rage. You kidnapped me and locked me in a car boot for ten hours, you fucker.

{Stay calm, losing your temper will not improve your situation.}

"I feel like Shit," I reply, which sparks another coughing fit.

"It was necessary," he says. No it was not you sadistic bastards.

"My name is Carlos and I will be looking after you. Here take this water and drink, but do not lift the hood from your face." He places a plastic bottle into my hand. I have to lift the hood slightly to drink. The water is warm and tangy, but I am so dry, it tastes like nectar. "Not all at once," Carlos instructs, he pulls the bottle away from my mouth, "You will be sick."

As the hood falls back down, I catch a glimpse of his legs and feet. Carlos is clad in fatigue stile combat trousers and boots. "You are David Brookes?" he asks.

"I know," I say.

"What you do not know," he replies, "Are the rules of Carlos hotel." Carlos thinks he is a comedian, "Numere ono rule, never lose hood again. If you hear door opening, you will sit against far wall and put on hood. If I ever open door and you no wear hood, then Carlos has to kill you. Understand?" I tell him that I do.

"Dos, We take you to wash and shit once every day. If you have to piss, there is a bucket in corner. Do not shit in bucket unless emergency. If you make Carlos hotel smell every day, he will not be happy. So it is best if you do not. Understand?" Again I say that I do.

"Tres, do not try to escape, if you try we will beat you and your friend. If you do happen to escape we will kill your friend. He also is being told this. Understand?"

"Yes," I say.

"Quattro, do not try to talk to other prisoners, none speak English so no point."

"Final rule, always do what Carlos says. Now we understand each other." He stands, "Do you need anything?"

"Is there a light in here?"

"Yes, bulb will be fitted soon, all cells are connected so no bulb unless there is someone in here. We will switch on in day, of at night. If you need light at night, there is candle and matches on shelf at back. But do not burn candle all night, only one each week." My stomach turns, he expects me to be here longer than a week.

"Why am I here?"

"All questions will be answered tomorrow," Carlos says.

"Do I sleep on the floor?"

"Problem with amount of mattress, you get one tomorrow."

"Can I use the bathroom?"

"Wait," he says, and then backs out into the adjoining room. He calls a question out in Spanish to someone unseen, asking if the bathroom is clear. Evidently it is, as another voice replies. "OK, you stand. Do not talk when we go to bathroom." He takes the sleeve of my shirt and leads me out of my cell. We turn left and another person pushes something dull into my back. I can only assume it is a gun. We walk fifteen steps and then stop. "When in bathroom," Carlos says, "You may take of hood, when you are finished put hood on and knock door. No talking."

I am pushed forward into darkness, the door closes and bolts behind me. I can hear a neon light struggling to start. Eventually the light stabilizes and I remove the hood. How I wish I had left in on. This is not a bathroom. There is a small sink at least, but the toilet makes my stomach turn. It is a hole in the ground with a showerhead above it. I cannot believe it has ever been cleaned. The smell is almost unbearable; I walk the two steps towards it and feel light-headed. I can hear the scuffling of insects all around this room. There is no way I am going to take a shit into this abyss. The fact that it doubles as the shower, means that it is also out of the question.

I take a piss into the sink and run the tap to wash it away. Then I wash my hands and face. Finally I stick my head under the tap and let the water wash over me for a moment. Shit Gabriel, what am I going to do?

{You will live with this Lucifer, you have seen worse things.}

When?

{You used to be in charge of Hell.}

That and this, are not the same.

I turn off the tap and attempt to dry my hair with the hood. There is no towel. I give up after a few seconds and just knock the door. Then I remember the hood, and quickly pull it on just as the light goes off and the door opens. I am led back in the same fashion as I came out and pushed into a sitting position, at the back of the cell.

"One last thing," Carlos says, "I have to take your boots." For some reason this horrifies me. These are my boots, if they take them; it feels to me that they are telling me that I will not be leaving. It is to final.

"Why?" I ask.

"Laces not allowed." He replies.

"Can you just take the laces please?" That last sentence came out like a plea, and I reprimand myself. I will not plead. Carlos converses with someone, who replies, "Tome las botas," *Get the boots.*

"You remove boots," he says, "I will take out laces and return boots tomorrow."

I do not believe him, but I don't see any other choices looming. I undo the laces, take them off and throw them in his general direction. "You are hungry?" he asks, as he retrieves my boots.

"No," I say.

"OK, tomorrow you will be. You smoke?"

"No."

The door slams shut. A few seconds later I realise that the light is on, someone has fitted a bulb in my absence. I remove the hood and survey my new home. I am in a seven by four foot box. The walls are concrete grey and there is no window. The ceiling is of the same construction, around six feet high. Its only features are the grilled low watt light bulb, and a four inch square fan in the far corner, which does not seem to be working. The floor is packed dirt, I dig my fingers into it, and come away without hardly making a mark. On my right is the piss bucket and lastly, above my head is a shelf. I stand up and find a squat candle plus a book of matches. Also there is the half a bottle of water.

Why take my laces if they leave my belt? I feel my waist and for the first time, notice that my belt is missing. When did they take it? An inventory of all my personal items reveals that my watch and wallet are also gone.

I slump down into the corner and hold my head in my arms. This is now my world. In a panic I jump up and grab the candle, matches and water. These I position in the corner because I do not know when the lights will go off, and I do not want to be thrashing around looking for them. The hood I also move into the same place, this is where I will keep them from now on.

Gabriel, you never finished off, telling me where I am.

{No I did not.}

Well?

{I do not know.}

Bullshit! Of course you know! Don't lie to me.

{I cannot lie. The information is no longer available to me.}

How could it not be available?

{The information is no longer available to me.}

But the only way you could be stopped from knowing is if he forbade it?

{I am not allowed to tell you that.}

Please Gabriel, I've had enough so stop this game.

{It is not a game Lucifer.}

So what can you tell me?

Pause.

{It seems I can tell you nothing.}

Is God listening in?

{I am not aware that he is, but we are being mon- }

Gabriel, that is the second time you have cut off like that. Gabriel can you hear me?

{Yes}

Were you going to say monitored?

{Y- }

So you are being censored?

{I cannot answer that question.}

I will take that as a yes. For what reason?

{Lucifer, if I tell you anything, which may affect your decisions, we will be cut off permanently. I am sorry.}

So am I brother, so am I.

❦

The lights click off and I am plunged into darkness. Not the normal darkness of a night, this is total. I sit for a few seconds while the after image of the cell fades from my retinas. There is not even light seeping under the door. If there is no light coming under the door, then it must be airtight and the fan in the ceiling does not work! I will suffocate! No I am being paranoid, why would they go through all this, and then let me suffocate? Perhaps my captors do not know the fan is broken. I stand up and point my nose where I think the fan was. I am sure that the air smells different, perhaps damper. And then I am sure I feel the faintest movement of air. So I have an airway to the outside, but why are there no lights in the other room?

I crawl across the floor and try to push my fingers under the door. There is not enough room, but there does seem to be a gap. Again I press my face to the floor. Can I feel an air movement again? Yes I am sure I can. So clever clogs, what does that tell you? The lights are off in the outside room, and therefore there are no guards. They have gone, can I safely make that assumption? Maybe one is sleeping out there.

I follow the room around the wall and into corner, where I placed the candle and sit back down. The darkness is oppressive; I feel it is closing in around me. Don't think about it, just close your eyes. How do you stop thinking about something by thinking about it? Rebecca, how I wish I was lying with you, but she will not even know I am being held yet, someone from the station will tell her, when they get the ransom demand. I cannot stand it, bastards! And the dark is eating into my soul, light the candle! I fumble with the matches and blind myself as I strike. It goes out before I can light the wick. Slow down! Stop shaking and just light the fucking thing!

I light the second match with my eyes averted and the wood takes this time. I offer it to the candlewick, and it also catches. Oh, how beautiful that little flame is. I sit and stare at it, as it flickers and dances before my eyes. I do not know for how long. When I regain my wits, probably half the candle has gone. I cannot believe this, it will not last the night, and this is the first night. I stub it out and return to the suffocating darkness. I try to convince myself that I can light it if I need to. I can put up with the darkness as long as I can light my candle. But if I let it burn, then it will always be dark and that would be unbearable. So I sit in the dark knowing that I can make it go away, but I will not light the candle. And the dark becomes tolerable, because I have a candle that I cannot light.

You are there Gabriel?

{Yes.}

You will not leave me will you?

{I will not leave you.}

※

The light is back on and I could cry with joy. I have not slept. All night I have sat and stared out at nothing, flinching at every creak and semi-imagined scrape of scurrying feet, which the darkness magnified a hundred times. And slapping at mosquitoes that burrowed into my legs and arms. But it is to late when you feel them, the damage is already done. I lift my right trouser leg and inspect the red blotches that are rising on my shins. Fucking mosquitoes, what good are they to anything? Why would God create them in the first place?

I hear the lock in the door turning, and quickly pull on the hood. "Buenos dias" it is Carlos, "You are first to bathroom this morning, bring bucket."

"There is nothing in it," I say.

"OK," he replies. He takes my sleeve and again someone follows, pushing something sharp into my back, it feels like a knife this time. Once inside the bathroom, the door is locked behind me and I take off the hood. I still will not shower and I do not need a crap, but I must piss. I will have to get over this repulsion eventually, so I brave it, holding my breath as long as possible. Do not think about what lives in that hole. Think about something else while you pee. I have to breathe but have not finished, Shit! I turn my head as far as possible and take small gasping breaths, gagging every time I do.

I stumble back and realize with revulsion that I am in my bare feet. I wash them as best I can in the basin with no soap, then the rest of my body. There is a towel hanging up now, it is not clean, but it is dry and better than the hood I used yesterday. I shudder at the thought of being the last one in here in a few days. But that depends on how many people are being held. I have no idea.

I dress quickly, including my headgear and knock the door. As I am led

The Songs of Angels

back to the cell I ask, "Will I be able to get my boots back." Then I am on my knees, the man behind forcing me down.

He whispers in my ear, "No talk in passage, ¿entiende?" and hits me across the back with what I assume is a club, or a piece of pipe. My left side explodes with pain as I fall forward. I am dragged the final few feet to the cell and dropped onto the floor.

"You know the rules David Brookes," Carlos says, "If you break them, you will be punished."

"I forgot," I force out through gritted teeth.

"You will not forget again, Miguel is a nasty man, do not upset him again. Luckily you are Carlos's burden. There is new water for you on shelf." I hear the door close and lock and pull myself into a sitting position. My whole left side has gone numb. I remove the hood with my right hand and throw it down.

I hear another door open and footsteps outside; it must be prisoner number two. I decide to count how many people are taken to the bathroom. By the time the life is returning to my bruised torso, I have counted six prisoners who have been taken for their morning shit and shower. Including me, that makes seven people, held in this building.

I have a drink of the water, don't drink it all. This has probably got to last until tomorrow. I sit for an unspecified amount of time staring at the wall.

Gabriel?

{Yes?}

Talk to me.

{What about?}

Anything, just so I do not go crazy. There is a brief pause; he is probably asking what is allowed.

{You may not ask any questions of me.}

Then you may as well leave me, I do not know what is going on up there, but as usual, when I really need you, that is when you turn from me.

{I am sorry Lucifer; you must understand this is not my desire.}

I know brother, I know. Are you listening Lord? Can you hear me God? Well fuck you if you are, thank you for all your help and concern.

{Do not say that Lucifer.}

Go away Gabriel, just go away.

I lie on the floor and wrap my own arms around myself. Pitiful sobs involuntarily escaping my throat. But I will not cry. I will not! There will be no help from Heaven; God wants me to die here. All the times I told him that he did not care about life, I never really believed it. I just thought he did not understand, but he understands everything and cares for nothing, not even me. Fuck them all.

The lock starts to turn in the door, I stay where I am and pull the hood over my head. Someone walks in and says, "Stand up with back to me." It is Carlos.

"Fuck off," I mutter. I am rewarded with a blow to my calf, the pain shoots into my brain, but I will not give him the pleasure of hearing me cry out. I will never scream or cry again. I do not care what they do to me.

"Stand up with back to me," Carlos instructs again. I do not move. Four or five more blows rain down on my body. But this time I hardly feel them. All he can do is kill me. "Stand up with back to me," He says for the third time. I am not sure that I could anymore, even if I wanted to. This time I lose count of the blows, all I think about is how hard Carlos is breathing, and how he stinks of sweat. Thankfully I start to feel reality slipping away. The last thing I remember is someone shouting 'stop' I recognize the voice.

When I come around, I am sitting on a chair, still hooded. My hands are bound to the chair at my back. "Mr. Brookes," he says. It is the same voice that instructed Carlos to stop.

"Francisco," I reply.

"Ah you recognize my voice, I am glad that Carlos did no damage to your brain."

"Fuck you."

"Mr. Brookes, your behaviour is unadvisable. It is not unknown for guards to beat their prisoners to death. If I had not been here, it may have happened to you."

"What do you care?" I spit out.

"Think about this rationally, your death is the last thing we want."

"Why?"

"Because we will not receive our ransom demand if you are dead."

Suddenly the hood is pulled from my head, and I screw my eyes shut tight. "Open your eyes, there is only you and I here, and you have seen my face." I open my eyes, well the right one anyway, the left does not want to open. "Ah look at the state of you, it does not have to be this way. Just follow the rules and all this will be avoided." I am sitting in a large room, the windows are covered, but the light seeping through tells me we are above ground level.

"Why have you done this? I was on your side. I came here to report that the FARC were freedom fighters and not terrorists."

"Bullshit Mr. Brookes, FARC are terrorists and drug dealers, you would have found that out and reported that. But you were never with the FARC. Your stupid researchers contacted the wrong people, so we played along."

"So who are you, and why the charade? Why not take us prisoner at the start?"

He smiles, "It pleased me to see stupid westerners, gladly walking into trap, and why would I want the hassle of keeping you prisoner, when I can get you to co-operate?"

"Who are you people?" I ask again.

"You are being held for ransom by the National Liberation Army," He says.

Think back to the research we did before coming here. The National Liberation Army, commonly known as the ELN. They are another group of kidnappers and murderers. In fact they are the number one kidnappers in Colombia, taking around eight hundred captives in 2001 alone. Smaller than the FARC, but definitely worse.

"What don't you understand about the meaning of the word 'liberation'?" I ask.

He laughs, "Very funny Mr. Brookes, but our morals are not your concern."

"My family has no money." I say.

"Yes we know, but your television station has."

Other facts are coming back to me. The ELN was founded by Fabio Castano, and like the FARC , it started with good intentions, often attracting priests into the struggle. But it has slipped into extortion, as well as kidnapping to finance their activities. I think I remember that a Roman

Catholic priest headed it, until he died in 1998. Perez was his name.

"And it did not cross your minds, that I may have considered doing the report on the ELN?"

"We are not interested in what you think of us, only what you are worth to us," he continues, "So all you have to do is sit this out and co-operate. Once we have Mr. Peters ransom, and your own, you can go home."

"If the company does not pay," I tell him, "we will be killed. The ELN have done so before."

"We hope it does not come to that Mr. Brookes," he says.

"But it is a possibility," I state, he nods that it is, "I feel quite sorry for you Francisco," I say, "If that is your real name. Although it does not matter what your real name is. I feel sorry for the man you are, the man you have become. Do you feel proud of yourself? Proud that your way of liberating Colombia, is to extort money from civilians?"

He smiles and says, "Get it out of your system Mr. Brookes."

"I intend to," I reply, "Lets start with the name of your band of cut-throats, the National Liberation Army. That sounds very grand, but it's bullshit isn't it. The majority of this nation know exactly what you are, so you are not national, there are only a few thousand of you left. You have no public backing so therefore are a minority.

You liberate no one and nothing, in fact you do the opposite, you oppress. And you never were a crusading army. You are just a band of brainless thugs who get a hard on, whenever you stroke your guns. So your correct name should be the 'Marginal Repressive Militia'. Want me to write that down for you? Then you could take it to your leader and explain that it would be a good idea to change your name now. Then when they finally do hang you all, they will not be able to add 'violating the trades description act' to your list of atrocities."

The backhand slap, I have been expecting finally comes, it rocks me back and the chair topples to the ground, my head taking most of the impact with the floor. My eyesight blurs for an instant. "You know nothing!" he screams, "Fucking westerners who come here, with your high and mighty morals," he puts his face next to mine, "You know nothing!" He stands and aims a kick towards me. Fortunately it only glances of my arm. "Do you want to be hurt?" The next kick is more accurate and takes the wind out of me.

"Well?" he asks.

"Not particularly," I slur through blood stained lips, "But if you are enjoying yourself," He starts to aim another kick, then stops and lets out a stream of abuses in Spanish. Then he pulls the hood back over my head and calls out to have me taken back to the cell.

I am dragged down the stairs again, and dumped into the cell, onto a mattress! "Look what I do for you," Carlos says, "I get you mattress and bring boots back and what do you do? You upset Francisco!" I hurt too much to reply, "You are very bad man, you make me beat you, and you make Francisco beat you. Why would you do that?"

"No one can make you beat anyone," I mumble, "It is your choice to do what you did."

"No, is your fault, you are bad man," Carlos says. He leaves the cell and locks the door.

Two beatings in one day, not a good start. I will have to keep my mouth shut, another couple of days of this, and I will be crippled or dead. I pull off the hood and lie there thinking about what Carlos said. He has already convinced himself that his behaviour was my fault. Humans are very good at justification. All these rebels probably grew up on farms, or in slums. They look at what they have one day and decide that it is unfair. But there is no way out of this, they cannot get a good education, or a good job, so they eat themselves up with envy and jealousy. In the end they convince themselves they are justified to take from someone who has more than they do. After all, he must be an evil man, to hoard all that wealth. So join the rebels, they will give you a gun. And if you have a gun, you are a powerful man.

So now you can take the wealth, kill the evil one if you have to, it does not matter, he is evil and I am justified in my actions. I am in the right, I have a cause and my cause is good. I am fighting for justice. I am fighting for the common man, men like me! I am sorry that I have to rob the common man to free him, but this is the price he must pay. But somewhere along the line, the cause takes second place. The line blurs, but you continue to take what you want because you are still in the right, still justified. Unfortunately you are now the man that you hated when you started. But why let that stop you, how can you be evil when your cause is just?

Are you listening to this?

{Yes}

Well?

{I think your mind is going.}

For some reason this sends me into fits of laughter, but it really hurts to laugh and I cannot stop. I lie here giggling like a schoolgirl, in this filthy cell, on this flea bitten mattress.

You are probably correct Gabriel; I'm going fucking insane

My boots, minus the laces are sitting in the corner, thanks Carlos. Don't worry about beating the shit out of me, because you have made up for it by bringing my boots back you bastard. And besides the boots, some food! I cannot remember the last time I ate. I crawl over to see what is on the menu. Some kind of stew, I poke around in it with my finger, it's cold and there is no spoon. Shit and assholes, there is meat in it. I don't care how hungry I am, I will not eat meat. Luckily there is a chunk of bread besides it, which I nibble and wash down with the water. As I wince at the pain every time I chew, I try to cheer myself up a little, by thinking of what I can do with Francisco, Carlos and Miguel, once they end up in Hell with me.

※

In Heaven.

God:

Well, say your piece.

Gabriel:

This is intolerable Lord! He will lose his mind and you are making it worse for him. We have to help him! Do you not see that? That is Lucifer down there and he is suffering!

God:

There are no other humans in that place, who receive helpful information from an Angel. Why should Lucifer? He agreed to go as a man, as I did. I had no one to ask advise of.

Gabriel:

But this is not a man; this is Lucifer!

God:
This I know.
Gabriel:
So why do you not let me help him Lord? Why does Raphael have to sit on my shoulder, when I talk to him?
God:
Because Gabriel, you disobey me. I tell you not to interfere, but you cannot help yourself. I regret letting this situation go on for this long.
Gabriel:
But I cannot go on like this Lord. It is detestable, I cannot see him like this, and sit back and do nothing. I will not do it!
God:
Very well, I agree. You are relieved of your duties towards Lucifer.
Gabriel:
No! Please Lord! I did not mean that, do not take me away from him, I will adhere to the rules.
God:
The decision is made, and it is for the best, you may go.
Gabriel:
But I promised him that I would not leave.
God:
Gabriel, I said you may go.

※

Lights have just gone out again. The second night in Hell on Earth begins. How can one human subject another to this? I am so weary, but this brain never stops thinking. It just goes on and on, maybe you die if it stops. Angels can stop, not totally, but you can have one thought that may last a year or a century. Why can't I do that now? Just until tomorrow morning would do. You can do that Gabriel can't you?
Gabriel!
Gabriel, answer me!
Then the truth hits me that he has gone. He is not there; I can no longer feel him. For the first time in my mortal life, he has left me on my own. He has gone and there is just me now. I am alone. They have taken him

from me!

"Gabriel!" I scream out. I do not care if the guards here me. "If you can hear me Gabriel! I do not blame you! Lord, if you can hear me, know that I hate you!"

Light creeps under the door, the switch has been thrown in the next room. "Shut up!" It is Miguel, "God cannot hear you, No le importas a Dios, *God does not care about you*, go to sleep." The light flicks off and I lie back. Then I curl up and shut my eyes, as the darkness closes and embraces me.

※

The days have been a blur and I do not care anymore. I just do as I am told. The shithouse no longer repulses me. It does not matter. Being locked up or released does not matter. I do not care anymore. I have lost count of the days; it is at least ten, but could be more and it does not matter. I put meat in my mouth, I must have been eating on automatic, and I swallowed before it registered. I told Carlos I did not eat meat after the first meal. But it is not always Carlos who brings the food. I made myself sick and screamed at the guards. I called them every foul word I could think of. A few hours later they came in and clubbed me with their rifle butts until I passed out, it did not matter. At least I can sleep now, the darkness is my refuge, but the bugs are something else.

I hate the fucking bugs, you will find me three or four times each night, crawling around my cell, armed with my boot heel, clubbing at phantom creepy crawlies. The mosquitoes are real, my legs are a mess where I have given in to the itching and scratched. But I don't see that it matters anymore.

Ah lights out again. I close my eyes, but the light comes back on again, Jesus that's too bright! I must be dreaming. In my dream I smell ozone, and the light gets brighter and brighter.

"Lucifer, open your eyes!"

It will blind me, I cannot. Even though I am dreaming, I know I will go blind if I open my eyes.

"Lucifer, open your eyes! It is I, your God, look upon me!"

It is just a dream.

"This is no dream Lucifer, open your eyes, I command it!"

I open them and look up, God is here in my cell, or I am totally insane.

"You are not insane Lucifer."

"What the fuck do you want?" I ask, if this is a dream, I can say what I want. And fuck him anyway if it isn't, I don't care.

The light, which is impossibly bright, goes up in magnitude, "If you could see yourself, as I am seeing you," he says, "You are pathetic."

"Aren't you interfering?" I say, "Is that allowed?"

"Even when you are living like a dog, you cannot help pushing me can you."

"It is all I have left to look forward to."

"You are a coward, you hide behind your snide remarks."

"Fuck you!" I scream out.

The guards will hear me, and then come down here to shut me up.

"The guards and your fellow captives are asleep," God says, "And will stay so until I will otherwise."

He reads my thoughts as easy as I would read a book, and he controls these mortal surroundings with a similar ease.

"If you can do that, you can open the doors for me and let me out." I say.

"I will not," he replies.

"Or at least, you could turn this shitty bread into something edible."

"No," he says.

"Then I repeat my question," I cry, "what the fuck do you want?"

"I want to know what you are going to do, I want to know if you are going to crawl into the corner, or if you will become all that you can be. I want to know if the Archangel Lucifer still resides in that body. Or has life beaten you, have you become another of its victims."

"What do you care of life!" I stand and scream at God, "You care nothing for life!"

"You are wrong Lucifer, very wrong. Life is very important to me."

"I don't believe you." I say.

"I do not lie!" he shouts, "Life is me! Understand this! Life devours me!"

"What?" I ask, "What do you mean?" His light flares.

"Again, you think you can question me Lucifer! Again you think I should answer to you! I am your God! Trust me, when I say that I care for life."

"How can I trust you," I cry, "You leave me here to rot, you abandon me."

"Your being here is your own doing, do you expect me to bail you out, every time the going gets rough?"

"Yes," I almost plead.

"Well I will not! Be a man for once, and help yourself."

"That is the problem, I am just a man here," I say.

"As I was Lucifer, I was a man with the soul of God. You are a man with the soul of an Angel. Gods first and most powerful Angel."

"But you performed miracles, I cannot."

"I was a man, exactly like you," God says, "Be everything that you can be Lucifer, and become everything that you can become."

Then he is gone and I sit in darkness.

※

The light seems to come on instantly; the conversation has taken all night. I sit and stare at the wall where he appeared. God has been to see me, and it was no dream. How do I go on from here? There will be no help from Heaven. God has left me, and so has Gabriel, why does that destroy me? It is because I am small and pathetic without them, God is right. I look around this filthy cell, at my hands and feet, my dirty clothing. What have I become, Are you not Lucifer the Archangel, I ask myself. I do not need God, or any other, I will not let life, or God destroy me. I am better than life, and I am better than God! I will survive this and be back with Rebecca soon. I make this promise to you Rebecca, and to you David Brookes.

The lock turns in the door, and I grab the hood. "Carlos hotel is open for business," he says as the door opens and begin the normal toilet procedure. When we return to the cell, I ask him,

"Did you sleep well Carlos?"

"Very well," he replies.

"Carlos, is there any chance I could have a razor, to shave?"

The Songs of Angels

"I do not think so," he says.

"Perhaps just a trim then, you could do it."

"I will ask."

"And Carlos," I enquire, "Do you think you could get a toothbrush for me? I had one in my pack, do you think you could possibly find it?"

"Maybe tomorrow," he says, and the door closes for another day.

I remove the hood but it is not my hood. It is only the hood. I will never call it my hood again. There is some food waiting and what appears to be a cup of coffee. I have had nothing but water since day one. I drink it slowly, it is almost cold and there is no milk or sugar, but that does not matter. Also there is fruit, two bananas, slightly to ripe, some nuts, I don't know what kind, bread and mashed vegetables. A feast fit for a king.

I rerun God's words over and over in my head, trying to commit every sentence to memory, so that I can reference it later. I cannot forget a word.

He said he had been a man like me, he even reinforced the statement, what did he mean, what cryptic message was hidden in those words? Become all that you can become, how do I know what I can become? Does he mean that I could perform miracles as he did? As an Angel I had some control over the material world. I could, when allowed, appear on Earth, as God appeared to me. I could influence the weather or even physical matter itself.

It's worth a shot, I pick up the plastic water bottle and hold it. "Please turn into wine," I ask the water, feeling a little stupid. Nothing happens, as I expected. Or has nothing happened because I expected it?

"Turn into wine," I command it.

"Turn into wine now!" I almost shout, all the guards think I'm mad anyway. It still looks like water; perhaps it's white wine. I have a little sip and feel stupid. I put the water back on the shelf and sit down. Miracles, it seems, are off the menu. But, I think with a smile, I have plenty of spare time to practice. The smile overflows to laughter, as I realize that I must be going totally insane.

※

I have had all night to think about what God said. The light has just flicked on at Carlos's hotel. The question that keeps going through my mind is this, Why did he visit me? God does nothing without reason, although the reasons are often beyond anyone's understanding. He would not do it on a whim, he would not do it just to spite me. What was his objective, and what did he mean, when he said that life devours him. He was pretty mad when he said it, perhaps he exposed more of himself than he intended. How does life devour God?

I hear doors opening and shutting, the other captives doing their shithouse run. Three so far, it will be my turn soon.

Life devours me, life consumes me, life eats me? It is not a true statement, life surrenders it's soul when an animal dies, it all goes back to God, except humans. Shit, that's it! Humans devour God, and they do not surrender their souls. But why should that worry him? He is not directly responsible for every living soul, or perhaps he is. Is that how he created life, does every living thing, require God to provide it with a soul? It's a hypothesis that would explain the statement.

How many living humans are there now? Six billion if my memory serves me well, and how many in Heaven and Hell? This human mind is useless at calculations; evolution equipped it to count up to ten, with a little tuition. Ah, ten percent of all humans that ever lived are alive now, who worked that out? I cannot remember. But that gives me a rough figure of sixty billion souls on all planes, which have potentially taken a little piece of God and not returned it. How much can he take? Is that one percent of his being, or ninety percent? What if God ceases to exist tomorrow, what happens to the Earth, the universe, to the Angels? Will life seek a new source to tap? Will life then devour the Angels, or even the very universe it sprang from. Or will all new life be stillborn and grind to halt?

If this is true, then to him, it must be like a virus eating away at his body. And it will get worse, the human population is set to double by 2040, twelve billion living souls. This does not include the ones who die between now and then, how many is that? How many total human souls will there be by 2040? Assuming the population rises on a curve from six billion to twelve billion and the average human dies at three score and ten. I estimate a further eight billion humans will die. That will be around fourteen billion more souls in the next thirty-eight years. Around seventy five billion total souls.

And Hell is the bottomless pit where most end up. And they will never leave, he could never get anything back, so this cannot be correct, God would never allow it

The lock is turning, I pull on the hood, "Good morning David Brookes," Carlos says. "Please come forward," I stand and pick up the piss bucket. "Wait!" he says, "Hold out hand." I comply and he places something in my palm. "OK" he says, and we move off to the bathroom.

Once inside, I remove the hood and stare down at my toothbrush in my hand, God bless you Carlos. Brushing my teeth is a little bit of Heaven, even without toothpaste.

Once back inside my cell, I sit down in the corner, still clutching my toothbrush, and say, "Thank you Carlos." I wait for the door to close, but it does not.

"Is no problem," he replies, "I ask about haircut, maybe tomorrow." I thank him again. "You soon out of here."

"When?" I ask.

"Soon," he says. The door closes for another day. I notice that no more doors are opened. I am sure that only six of us were taken to the bathroom. I decide to double-check the next day.

❧

Three days later and Carlos leads me back to the cell. I was right, there are only six of us here now. Should I be hopeful that someone has been released? Or maybe he/she was not so lucky, and maybe another murder charge was added to the ELN's list. "Please to take of hood when in room," Carlos instructs, "and put on blindfold you find on bed."

"Why?

"Haircut day at Carlos hotel," he says, "Carlos cannot cut hair through sack."

Carlos waits outside when I enter the cell, I remove the hood, taking care not to look at the open door. A black strip of cloth, to be used as a blindfold is lying on the bed. I don and tie it at the back of my head, then tell him I am ready. He leads me back into the hall and positions me on, what I assume is a stool.

I jump at the sound of an old fashioned clipper being switched on. "No problem," Carlos says, and proceeds to remove chunks of matted hair from my head and chin. Sometimes it sticks and rips a few hairs from my head. His language is testament that he is having difficulty cutting around the blindfold, and he moves it up and down, careful that he does not reveal my eyes.

He must be nearly finished, when suddenly he catches the blindfold in the clippers. It is ripped violently from my head, and before I can even think, our eyes are locked together. He was standing directly in front of me. We both stare at each other, like rabbits that are caught in headlights. The clippers buzz in his hand, attempting to cut through the blindfold that the blades are tangled with. They will kill me now, the thought repeats in my mind. I finally just close my eyes and sit there.

Our eyes breaking contact, also breaks the spell and brings Carlos back into action, "Fuck!" he says as he turns the clippers off and struggles to release the blindfold from them. He replaces it on my head and jerks me off the stool. I stumble as he leads me back into the cell, he pushes me into a sitting position.

His breathing is erratic, and with a hand still on each of my shoulders, I hear him lean forward, and he whispers, "It did not happen, understand?" I nod. "It did not happen," he repeats, "no one else saw this."

Then I hear him retreat and he closes the door. I remove the blindfold and throw it into a corner. Do I believe he will keep our secret, or were his words a ploy to calm me? Should I be expecting them to come back and murder me?

※

Perhaps Carlos was sincere, as they did not come for me in the night. But today was different, there was no chat from him, his commands were brisk this morning. But I survive another day at lights out. All night I have thought of the look in his eyes. His face, is the only human face I have seen since that afternoon with Francisco. There was terror in his eyes, that is the only way I can describe his emotion as we stared at one another.

※

The Songs of Angels

Days pass, they all blend into each other. I have started exercising, running three steps forward and backward, press ups and squats. I did not realized how unfit I was becoming, until I started. And it passes the time, as I do not have to think so much. I run into the wall when the lights go out. I sit down in the darkness and have a drink of water. The key rattles in the door, no one has ever opened the door at this time. This is it, this is when they kill me. I decide I will go out fighting, so I get ready to spring at whoever comes through the door.

"It is Carlos," he whispers, "I have automatic weapon, do not try anything, you have hood on?"

"No, fuck you!" I shout.

"Quiet!" he hisses, "Other prisoners will hear." The door opens, I am confronted by torchlight, and it is all I can see, the light and the barrel of a gun. "Please sit down, if I wanted to kill you, I would have done it before."

I have no chance against that gun in this small cell. I can fight him and die, or I can sit down and possibly die. Either way, my life is in this mans hands. I sit, and look up at where I think his eyes should be.

He enters the cell, "Put on hood," he says.

"Why," I ask, "I have seen your face."

"Quiet please, put on hood, I do not want to see your face." I pull on the hood. If he is going to shoot me, I can do nothing so it does not matter. And if he is not, there's no point making him mad.

"What do you want?" I ask.

He pauses for a second, and then says, "Since I cut your hair, I have question. Always someone else around before now, so I could not ask. Tonight Carlos only guard."

He is alone here, if I could get past him, then I would be free. But he still holds the gun and I am sitting in the dark, with a bag on my head. "What question?"

"Who are you?" he asks.

He knows who I am, "You know my name is David Brookes," I answer puzzled by his question, but relieved that he hopefully not about to shoot me.

"That is your name," he says, "Who are you?"

"I don't understand the question Carlos."

"What are you?" He asks.

"I'm a reporter with Channel Three," I reply.

"Who are you?" he repeats.

"I don't know what you want me to say," I admit, fear beginning to rebuild.

The light disappears, and I hear the door lock, then his retreating footsteps. I start to shake. Tonight, when the door opened I expected to die. And he asks stupid fucking questions. I wish I knew what that was all about. I wish I was in Rebecca's arms, far away from here.

***

Four days have passed without any instances. Then once again, a few minutes after lights out, the door opens. This time I put the hood on straight away, and sit waiting for him to enter. It is the same question that he asks, as he shines the torch into my hooded face. Who am I?

"What do you want me to say Carlos?" I ask.

"The truth."

"OK," I say, "I'm the fucking president of the United States, no I'm not, I'm Father Christmas. I was bringing your presents, when you kidnapped me."

"¡No soy un estúpido!" *I am not stupid!* he screams, I hear him stand, "Who are you?"

"I no longer know or care Carlos, go away."

The blow is savage, he hits me in the stomach with the but of his rifle, then again and again, he rains blows down on me one after another, his mind has snapped. I scream for him to stop and blindly try to block him with my arms, but he does not stop. I am slipping away, I am going to die. I can hear someone screaming and realize it is me. When he finally tires, he falls back against the wall. I can hear crying, it is not me this time, I do not have enough energy or sense of mind, it is Carlos crying.

I am dimly aware that he has stood back up, he moves to the door, but before he leaves, he says through his sobs, "Lo siento, pero usted no deberia estar aqui." *You should not be here, I am sorry.*

***

The Songs of Angels

I wake in a half dream, someone is in the room and the light is on. They talk in Spanish.

"Jesus Carlos, what did he do?"

"He screamed and shouted, and when I came in, he tried to escape."

"Get the doctor. You should have called last night. Francisco will not be happy if he dies."

I feel reality slip away again.

※

I am awake, lying on my back and in a real bed, my eyes are still covered. I try to move my arms, but they are strapped to the side of the bed. "Welcome back," someone says, I do not know the voice. I can feel a breeze on my right shoulder.

"Where am I," I ask, "In Hospital?"

"No, but you will be alright."

"Are you a doctor?"

"Yes," he says, "We have kept you sedated for a couple of days, while you heal."

"Am I still with the ELN?"

"Yes," Francisco answers my question and then addresses the doctor, "¿Puede regresar a su celda, doctor?" *Can he go back to his cell Doctor?*

"No lo recomiendo," the doctor says. *I would not advise it.*

"¿Va a estar bien? No se va a morir, ¿cierto?" *But he will be OK now? He will not die?*

"No, no morirá." the doctor replies, "Debe tomar mucho líquido." *No, he will not die. He should have plenty of fluids*

"Carlos," Francisco calls, "Take him back downstairs."

"Doctor," I call out, "Why do you help these people?"

"I help the sick and injured," he says, "I help you to stay alive despite what these people do."

"And for that I thank you doctor," I say as I am untied and lifted by two people, there is still a lot of pain, "I should not judge you." They carry me back to my cell, where I am laid down.

"There is food for you David Brookes," Carlos says, I do not answer. "Call if you need anything."

"A 4x4," I whisper through the agony.

"What?" he asks, I think you heard, I hear his breathing as he puts his face close to mine and he whispers, "Perdóneme." *Forgive me.*

※

Two days later, and I can walk with difficulty, more of a shuffle really. I am told that I was sedated for a further two days. That's four days in total, there was four days between Carlos's first and second night visit. I think they take it in turns to stay here at night, and every fourth day, Carlos is the lone guard. If I am correct, then that means he will be alone tonight. I am dreading another visit from him. I don't think he will harm me again, how would he justify it. He could not tell them that I tried to escape again, because I am not capable. I just do not wish to see him.

At lights out, I sit waiting to hear his footsteps outside. They do not come. I still haven't figured out why he beat me so savagely. I was sarcastic, yes, but that warranted maybe a kick, or a single blow, not what he did to me. A few weeks ago, I would have said that nothing could warrant one human being striking another. Now after a few beatings, I am justifying his brutality by my own actions. How quickly we accept the intolerable as normal.

The lights are still out when I wake to the sound of the lock turning. Carlos opens the door before I have time to don the hood. I am holding it in my hand as the torchlight plays across my face. He sits against the opposite wall, an automatic weapon cradled in his lap, "Forget the hood," he says. I let it drop, he puts the torch down on the floor, pointing towards me, but I can make out his face. He is probably only four or five years older than I. We stare at each other and say nothing. I will not speak to him.

I do not know how long we sit there, finally his gaze drops to his lap and he starts to talk, in a low whisper. I just sit there and watch him, giving no encouragement or any sign that I am interested. Occasionally he switches to Spanish, I don't think he knows he is doing it. He tells me about his parents, how they worked their farm all of their lives, and died in poverty, That he took control of the smallholding at the age of eighteen, as his elder brother had already left to join the rebels. How he met and married his wife and had a son called Jose. How in 1997 the AUC raided his farm, probably looking for his brother. Fortunately, or unfortunately, it depends how you look at it, he had been in the fields. They killed his wife and son, and then burnt down his house, while he hid in the forest, frozen with fear for his own life. Jose was three years old.

How he joined the rebels expecting to be part of the struggle against the government, to be a freedom fighter, how he searched for his brother and never found him. And how he now hated, what the ELN had become. And how he had nowhere else to go.

I sit in silence for the hour, or so, that he goes on, reminding myself that this is the man who tried to beat me to death a few days ago, and that I should not feel sorry for him, I should hate him. Finally he is silent, staring into his lap. He rises and makes for the door, as he closes it I say, "None of this can excuse what you did to me Carlos."

"I know," he replies as he locks the door.

※

My strength has mostly returned in the last few days and I have started exercising again. Not as much as I did before, but it is a start. After Carlos's confession, and that is what I realize it was now, I can feel the turmoil that he has been through. He is more prisoner here, than I am. Eventually, and hopefully, I will get out of here, but Carlos never will. All of the guards are prisoners of their own making, prisoners of their circumstances and this sad country. I cannot hate them any longer.

Every forth night, Carlos comes to my cell and we talk, usually about nothing. But sometimes the conversations spill over into politics or religion. They are all Roman Catholics, all the guards consider themselves as good Roman Catholics. It was a surprise to me. He is due tonight, and although I cannot forgive what he did, I now look forward to our chats. It breaks the monotony. Sometimes he brings Coca-Cola, which he shares.

I realized that he felt so guilty about the beating he gave me, now he wants to make friends. I could never be his friend, I will never fully be at ease with him. The lights go out, he will be here in the next twenty minutes.

When the door opens, Carlos just stands there looking at me.

"What's wrong?" I ask. There is no reply, "Carlos, what is it?" He takes one step forward and lets out a sigh.

"Put boots on," he instructs, as he looks over his shoulder, into the darkness, "We leave now."

"I am being released?" I ask, hope springing into my heart.

"No, Carlos take you out of here."

"What?" Is this a trick, is they're someone waiting to cut me down as I run through the door?

"No time to waste," he says, "Put boots on!"

"Why would you do that?"

"Please David," he says. He means it, he means to let me go.

I scramble for my boots, in the torchlight and then stop, "I cannot go, if I do, they will kill Sean!"

"What?" Carlos asks.

"Sean Peters, the man who was taken with me, Francisco said he would be killed if I escaped. I cannot go."

"He has gone, two weeks ago, he has gone home. Please we waste time."

"How come he has gone home and I have not?"

"We have to go now!" he says. I pull my second boot on and follow Carlos out into the other room. He grabs my hand and almost drags me up the stairs. In the upstairs room, the lights are off. This is the room where I spoke to Francisco. He stops at the front door, and then beckons me forward. We run across a clearing and then into the bushes besides the road, his torch pointing at the ground directly in front of him. My boots, without laces are flapping and slowing me down.

Carlos stops and I run into the back of him, "Grab." He whispers.

"Grab what?" I ask, staring out into the darkness.

"Grab netting, help me," he says. Then I see it in the dark, he has a car, covered by camouflage netting. We remove it and force it into the boot. Once inside the car, he throws a revolver on the back seat, starts the engine and skids onto the track. "Boot laces for you, take." He hands me the laces and continues to drive in the dark. I look back, though the window at my prison as it disappears. All I can make out, is the silhouette of the roof in the moonlight.

"Why are you helping me Carlos," I ask.

The Songs of Angels

"Because you do not belong here, because people are getting worried that your ransom will not be paid, and your death has been talked about."

"Why would they pay Sean's ransom and not mine."

"They ask much more for you than your friend, his ransom was negotiated quickly." He says.

"You negotiate the ransom demand?"

"Yes," he says, skidding around a corner, "It is how it works, we ask five times more than we expect to get, it is like barter. When we agree demand, you are let go. But it seems TV channel, do not think you worth as much as ELN think."

"They will kill you, if we are captured."

"Ha," he replies, "They will not catch me, I get you to safe place, then I go to mountains or stay in Venezuela, or even America."

"I still don't understand why you are helping me, you are risking a lot." I say.

"Trust Carlos, he has nothing left with ELN. You do me favour, making me leave."

"Where are we going?" I ask.

"We go east to Cúcuta, then follow the highway to Caracas, there you can find help to get home."

"How far is that?"

"About two hundred kilometres to Cúcuta, it will take about five hours, and another seven hundred to Caracas. but we will be on highway all the way."

"When will I be missed?" I ask.

"No one will come to house until about eight tomorrow, we will be in Venezuela by then," he turns and smiles. And it sinks in, I could be home in a couple of days, with Rebecca. I sit back and start to thread my laces, I'm going home.

࿔

"Why are you stopping?" I ask, Carlos is pulling over to the side of the road. We have been travelling for around three hours.

"Fill tank," he says, he jumps out of the car and opens the boot, "Get out, on the back seat there is change of clothes for you." For the first time, I notice that he has normal clothes on, he must have changed at the house. I grab the bag and remove the contents. Then strip of my dirty and worn attire, and replace it with the shirt and jeans that were in the bag. Carlos fills the tank from the jerry can, which he had stashed in the boot. He then discards the empty can, into the bushes besides the road.

I am pulling my boots back on, as he jumps back into the drivers seat. The car lurches forward, sliding back onto the road. "I have to use headlights here," he says, "This road is no longer familiar to me." He drives, intermittently switching the headlights on, when he is unsure of the road, and off if there is a straight stretch, or if the foliage around us does not obscure the moonlight.

I do not know how, but I am very tired, my eyelids will not stay open. How can I sleep at this time I wonder. I wake with a start, the dashboard clock tells me I have been asleep for over an hour. It says 2:10am. We are on a high pass, the moonlight illuminates the valley besides me. I can see two bright lights, one above the other, dead in front of us. For some reason they appear to be getting brighter. The lights streak over the roof of the car, Tracers! It is my last thought before the windshield explodes. Carlos shouts something, and pitches the car off the road. We bounce down a bank and wedge against a tree. Steam from a ruptured radiator billows from beneath the engine hood. "Out," Carlos says, "Get away from the car, they may come to see what they hit."

I open my door and scramble a few feet down the bank, then turn to wait for Carlos. He is rooting around on the back seat. His door will not open, so he shuffles across and gets out of my door. "Go!" he shouts. I have no idea where to go, so I wait as he stumbles down the bank, "Come on," he says and pulls me behind him. He seems to be having trouble keeping his feet.

"Are you OK?" I whisper. He beckons me on with his hand. We reach the bottom of the hill where he stumbles and falls flat on his face. I turn to help him up, but he does not move. "Carlos," I whisper, "Get up." There is no response, so I kneel down besides him and roll his body over. In the moonlight I can see blood pumping from his chest, I have it all over my hands.

He opens his eyes and says, "Go!"

The Songs of Angels

"No," I say, "I will not leave you."

"Please get away," Carlos rasps, I can hear air escaping from his lungs as he tries to breathe, "Leave me, I am not important, you are."

"Why do you think I am so fucking important."

"I know who you are now," he replies, "I saw it in your eyes."

I can hear a car engine in the distance. He coughs and blood speckles his chin.

"Who do you think I am Carlos?" I reluctantly ask, dreading what he thinks he has seen in my eyes, and through his own.

"You are Jesus," I stare at him, "Please go," he softly says, "If they catch you, Carlos will not be a hero." He coughs again and a fountain of blood is ejected from his mouth. "Perdóneme," Carlos whispers, and then he is still. *Forgive me.*"

The engine noise is getting closer. "I forgive you Carlos," I tell him, "And I thank you. Please Lord, if you have any compassion, please take this man to Heaven." The car has stopped, I have to go. I creep away through the bushes, trying to make as little noise as possible. I can hear men crashing down the hill towards the car. I wriggle under the largest and thickest bush I can find and stay there, trying not to move, trying not to breathe.

I can just about hear them on the wind, one says there is no one in the car, and another tells him to come back. I do not move, someone laughs. Eventually I hear their engine rev, as they drive away. I have to move, they are gone, they would not leave anyone behind would they? I have to go back to Carlos, he has money hopefully, and the gun. I creep back to his body, I cannot see anyone else around. "I am sorry," I whisper as I take his wallet and his watch, the gun is by his side where he dropped it. I tuck it into my waistband and back away. A thought goes through my mind, I have never seen his face in daylight.

I pick my way through the bushes, but I have no idea where I am going, just away from here will do. The moon is still bright as I trudge around hills and bushes, walking into the night. I have no food and water. I am sure that I can trust no one in Colombia. We travelled for about four hours, and Carlos said it would take five to reach Cúcuta, which was east. That puts me somewhere between thirty and sixty miles from the border. On this terrain, and assuming I am going in the right direction. It will take me three to six days, if I walk all night and sleep all day. Even if I don't walk over a cliff, there is no way I will make it. My body has been beaten and locked in a room, for God knows how long. I am in no condition for this.

I check Carlos's watch in the moonlight. Four am, sunrise at this latitude is always around six am. I need to find somewhere to hide before then. I walk for a further hour, and fatigue is already taking over. So I find the thickest bush I can, it has a small rocky outcrop behind it. I squeeze underneath and rest my back against the rock, and try to sleep.

Sleep does not come, only tears for Carlos, and for myself. He did not go to Heaven. He was too consumed with guilt over the beating he gave me. Over his life, and that his wife and child died. God would not take him, no matter that I pleaded. He thought I was Jesus, how ironic. I am glad that he did know the truth. But if he saw something when he first looked into my eyes, why did he beat me half to death? I remember the terror in his eyes, what went through his mind from that point? Did he punish me, because he did not want to believe, what he thought he had witnessed? What ever it was, he finally took me out of that place. Even if I die out here, I will never forget you Carlos. And when I am back in Hell, I will see you again.

Through the leaves, I watch the sunrise. It is a beautiful sight to behold, as it rushes to climb above the distant landmass. That is the way I must go, east. I can make out snow capped mountain peaks to the north and west, and I am glad I am not going that way. There are no visible signs of habitation in any direction. Carlos's wallet contains around ten thousand pesos, I cannot remember what that is worth, I do not think it is much, but I have nowhere to spend it anyway. I also find a faded black and white photograph, of a woman and child, which must have been his wife and son. I should not have taken it away from him, they should have stayed together. I lie down and close my eyes.

※

When I wake, it is evening, the sun will dip behind the mountains soon. I will have to move before the night is full, because I have to find water. In the twilight I crawl from my sanctuary, keeping to the thickest foliage I can find. I head for a eastward gully, that I spotted earlier, I figure if I am to find water, I have to go down hill. As I descend, it gets darker, and I cannot see the horizon where the sun rose this morning. I do not know which way I am going anymore. To my relief, I can hear a stream and I home in on the noise. When I get there, I am in total darkness because of the trees, but it sounds like it is running fast, so should be safe to drink.

I cup my hands and take a sip, the water is tangy, which is hopefully just the infusion of leaf litter. I have no choice anyway, I have to quench my thirst. I take my fill from the stream and then wade through it, climbing up what is hopefully, the eastern side of the gully. At the top, I can make out the last rays of the sun, so I walk with my back to them.

I estimate I have walked half of a kilometre, when the sunlight fades completely. I push on into the darkness, there is no moon yet, but the stars give some light. But not enough to walk with confidence, so I feel out every footstep and my pace is slow. My original estimate of three, to six days, was bullshit. At this pace I will be lucky to cover five kilometres a night, never mind ten. I have no idea if I am going east anymore. I decide to get my bearings, the sky is clear, so all I have to do, is find the North Star. What latitude will the North Star be at, in Colombia? It has to be nearly on the horizon. I climb a small hill to get a view, find Ursa Major, the outside two stars line up with the polestar. I scan the horizon, and find it. But I cannot see Ursa Minor or the polestar, then I realize I am looking at the mountains on the horizon. I can just make out the darker regions. The polestar is behind the mountains.

The polestar must be at a point on the horizon, below Ursa Major If I keep these two stars on my left shoulder, I am going east. I set of in the direction I hope is east. Around ten O'clock the moon comes up in front of me, and I can see more. As it climbs into the night sky, my pace improves.

It's four O'clock, I am moving on automatic, every muscle in my body hurts, the moon is directly above head and Ursa Major has dropped below the mountains. I look for Vaga in Lyra. Vaga should be the brightest visible star, I scan the sky and find it. So the next bright star, to its right and below, has to be Deneb, in the constellation of Cygnus. The Draco constellation is below it, and Ursa Minor will be beneath. Now I have two new stars, too keep on my left side.

I'm starving, thirsty again and tired beyond belief. The wise men only had to follow one star, I have to cross reference four fuckers just to stay in a semi-straight line. Oh stars of wonder, stars of might, guide me to thy perfect light, or Venezuela, or even a banana tree would do.

※

Daylight and I welcome the sun, and the heat it brings. I must be climbing, as the vegetation has thinned out, and the temperature has dropped. I found a small river around five am, so I am not thirsty anymore. And this is where I stopped. My camp is around thirty yards from it, at least when I set out tonight, I will get a drink before I go. Again I will set out while there is still some light, so I can ford the river in relative safety. I still haven't found anything, which I can eat. There are various fruits on the trees and bushes, but none that are edible for humans. And I figure, that if I eat something that makes me sick, I will almost certainly die out here, so I go without. I rest my head on the ground and must instantly fall asleep.

I wake to the sound of a dog barking. Where there are dogs, there are humans. Carlos's watch tells me it is two pm. What am I to do? I can hide here until dark and blunder on into the night, or go and investigate my neighbours. I suppose that I have to look, I could walk straight onto a farm, or into an army base in the night. I run and crawl in the direction of the barking dog, trying to stay close to the bushes and below any crests. At the base of a low hill, the barking sounds very near, so I crawl to the top and slowly peep over the top.

In front of me is a small village, possibly fifty dwellings, around a small river, the same river probably, it must have looped back on itself. My barking dog, is chained to a post behind one of the closest dilapidated houses. He barks at nothing in particular, a woman's voice repeatedly calls for him to be quiet. I shuffle back down the hill and contemplate my options. I could wait until dark and skirt around the village, then continue east with no food. Or head into the town, possibly steal some food and a car, though I did not see any vehicles. It's a risk, the town could be rebel controlled, possibly the FARC, or worse, the AUC who are known

The Songs of Angels

to murder journalists. But I could find out where I am.

Balls to it, if I am careful I may be able to check out the town. If it looks dangerous, I can always retrace my steps and carry on with plan A. And I have the gun if worst comes to worst. Then again everyone else, in Colombia, seems to have a gun. I decide to go around the hill and approach the village through the tall grass that I saw from there. Keeping low and moving slowly, I make my way along the row of houses, until I get to the last one, closest to the river. It appears empty as I creep into the back yard, and peer through the window. I try the back door, there is no lock, I let it swing open still staying outside, waiting to hear voices. None come so I step inside, letting my eyes become accustomed to the gloom.

I walk through the room and peep through the front door, at the dirt road that is outside. A lone woman walks away and down the street, carrying a basket. I wonder if I could pass as a native if I just stepped out the door and strolled up the road.

"Are you robbing me?" A voice asks in Spanish behind me. I jump and turn around. How could I have missed her, lying on the bed amongst crumpled covers.

"No," I answer, also speaking Spanish, "I am not robbing you, please do not scream or shout."

"I am to old to scream and shout," she says, as she throws the bedclothes off, and rests her feet on the floor, "If you are not robbing me, why are you in my home?"

"I am sorry, I thought the house was empty, and I wanted a look at the main street. I will not hurt you."

"But you have a gun tucked in your pants," she says as she stands with difficulty, and shuffles over towards me.

"I do not know how to use it," I admit.

"You are not Colombian," she states.

"No," I say, "I am a journalist."

"Ha," She says, "You look in worse condition that I am. Why would a journalist be here?"

"I have no idea where here is," I tell her, "I was being held hostage, but escaped. Who controls this village?"

"You are in Colombia, Mr. Journalist. No one controls anything in Colombia. If you are asking who rides shotgun over the village, then it is the FARC." She stands in front of me and asks, "So what are you going to do now, shoot me, tie me up. My Son will be home soon, what will you do then?"

"I do not know, but I will not tie you up or hurt you."

"No," she says, "I do not believe you will."

"The question," I ask, "Is what will you do now?"

"Let me see your face," she says, then reaches up and holding my chin, turns my face to the window. "Not the face of a robber, or murderer. But the face of a tired and hungry man." She releases me, and shuffles across the room, "What I am going to do, is make some coffee. You are welcome to join me, or sneak out the back, and be on your way."

"Thank you," I say, then ask, "How far is Cúcuta from here?"

"Around eight Kilometres north of here," She says, as she lights a gas burner connected to a bottle, and places a pot on it. I am closer to the border than I thought. "I have no love for the FARC," she says, "Or the ELN, or any of the other so called 'freedom fighters' that plague this country, or the government for that matter. They are all as bad as each other. None help ordinary people, they are all only interested in power and money. Were you held by the ELN?"

"Yes," I say.

"They have become bad people, the ELN, but you are safe in my home. Unfortunately there are others in this village, who would hand you over to the FARC in a blink of an eye. I have seen innocents treated so, I am an old woman." She hands me a cup of coffee that I sniff, just the odour of it is delicious. "Here," she adds, "Some bread, you look like you need it." She hands me a chunk of dark flat bread, which I tear into. My stomach protesting as it has to digest food for the first time in days.

"Thank you," I say again, "Thank you for helping me."

"If you get back home, you can say that not all Colombians are bad. Some are God-fearing Christians. Now, what am I to do with you now? What is your plan when you reach Cúcuta?"

"I do not have one, somehow cross the border and get to Caracas."

"There are better places to cross the border, I will ask my son to take you when he comes home."

"He will do that?" I ask, "I can trust him?"

"If I tell him to do it," she says, "He will do it. I am his Mother."

We spend the next forty-five minutes talking about how I was captured and held by the ELN. How Carlos rescued me and died trying to help me. I do not tell her that he thought I was Jesus. She produces biscuits and nuts, which are welcome. Her name is Eva and she is sixty-three years old, but she insists I call her Mother.

When her son comes home, she meets him at the door and explains who I am. He enters and eyes me with caution. He seems to be in his forties. Eva introduces him as Gabriel, which makes me smile. After a few minutes of arguing with his Mother, he agrees to take me over the border. Gabriel has a motor scooter. At dusk he fetches it. Eva wraps a blanket around my shoulders and says, "My God go with you David."

I reply, "And you Mother, I will never be able to thank you enough. God bless you." I kiss her forehead and then go outside to Gabriel, and sit behind him, he shoots up the road on the little scooter like a man possessed. We are out into the country in seconds and on our way. The suspension bottoms out on every rut, it feels like the bike will fall apart at any second, and I hold on for dear life. I am reminded of Steve McQueen, trying to escape from the Nazi's on his motorbike in the Great Escape. Here I am, on the back of a battered Honda C50. I would smile if my teeth were not jammed together. After about fifteen minutes, which feel like fifteen hours, he drives into some bushes and cuts the engine.

"OK," he whispers, "Come with me," We get off the scooter and descend a bank. At the bottom we come to a railway track. Gabriel explains that this track runs all the way to Caracas. The trains pass this spot slowly, and I can easily jump onto a freight train and hide. I do not know how to thank him, I end up shaking his hand and giving him most of Carlos's money. "Good Luck," he says as he crashes back up the bank. I hear his scooter start and listen to the engine fading into the distance, as I sit in the bushes, waiting for my train.

A few hours later, I hear the track tingling and then see the lights of the tractor approaching. I shrink back as the driver passes, and then make sure it is a freight train, it is, as there are no lights on the carriages. I run along the side of the train, which although slow, is still moving faster than I am. I manage to grab a ladder, which feels like it will pull my arm off. The blanket slips away and flutters down the track but I hang on, and haul the rest of my body onto it. So far so good, but what now? The train is picking up speed. Go up I suppose, there is not much choice, and I cannot hang onto this ladder all the way to Caracas. Slowly I climb the ladder in the dark, and pull myself onto the roof.

On my belly, I inch across the roof and find a skylight. Opening it against the wind is hard work, I poke my head inside, then my arms and reach out. It would be careless at this stage, to fall into an empty carriage and break my neck. With my arms outstretched, I feel sacks below me, so I lower myself headfirst, feeling out their positions. The carriage is stacked three quarters full. I let myself fall, the skylight slamming shut behind my feet. And I lie there, taking giant gulps of air as the train clanks and bumps away from Colombia. I am almost home Rebecca.

※

The next thing I am aware of is that I am woken, by people pulling me from the train. I have slept through the train stopping and the carriage being unloaded. I am dragged, headfirst onto a loading platform. Four or five men are crowded around me, shouting various questions in my general direction, one is calling down the track. My gun is pulled from my waistband and handed to a new human, who has just arrived.

He wears a uniform that I am unfamiliar with, I am not sure if he is a policeman or a ticket collector. "What are you doing in there?" he asks.

"Where am I?" I reply in English, then repeat in Spanish.

"Caracas," he responds, "What were you doing in there?"

"Hiding," I say from my position on the floor. I have made it to Caracas. He pulls me up and marches me through the station, where we wait for around half a hour. A police car pulls up, I am handcuffed, despite my protests and driven to the local station. There I am interviewed, I tell them my name and that I am a reporter for Channel three, and that I was taken captive by the ELN near San Christóbel. That I escaped and walked cross-country until I stowed away on the train, where they found me. My words are taken with some scepticism. I do not tell them about Carlos, or Eva and Gabriel. I do not trust anyone yet.

Finally I am locked in a cell and given some food. Two hours later I am taken back to the interview room and left with a well-dressed man, in his thirties. As the door closes he smiles, and with an American accent he

The Songs of Angels

asks, "You are David Brookes?"

"Yes," I say.

"Well, well, you've come a long way. Can you tell me what happened?"

"Who are you?" I ask.

"Sorry," he says, reaching into his jacket and producing a wallet, which he flips open and passes to me, "Adrian Westwood, American Embassy." The identification appears genuine and I pass it back to him. Again he asks, "Can you tell me what happened?"

I figure that I have to trust some one eventually, so I go through the story again, this time I include Carlos, but not his reasons. I also tell him, how I was helped by Colombian villagers, but I will not give him names, or the name of the village. It is not worth risking their lives with small talk. He listens attentively until I have finished.

"You have had an adventure," Adrian says.

"You could call it that," I say.

"When the ransom negotiations for you broke down, the ELN told us you had killed a guard and fled into the jungle. We did not hold out much hope of finding you."

"That is not true," I tell him, "I did not kill him, I have told you what happened. They are unlikely to tell you that one of their own, turned on them"

"Yes, yes, of course I believe you, it's just this ELN man, Carlos was it?" I nod, "I have never heard of any of them doing anything like this. It is strange."

"Perhaps he saw the error of his ways," I say, "Perhaps, as he died helping me, we will never know his reasons."

"Quite," he says, "Anyway, I am arranging for your release. Once the paper work is sorted, we can go back to the embassy where I can find you fresh clothes and you can clean up. Hopefully by tomorrow, we will have you on a plane to the US." He smiles and I thank him.

We are in a car, two hours later, cutting through the streets of Caracas, heading for the American Embassy. "What's the date?" I ask.

He looks at his wristwatch, "It's the first of May, you were held for over a month as you were taken around the nineteenth of March."

"The twentieth," I correct him.

He rattles on about it not being that long, as some captives are held for six, or even twelve months, and how lucky I was to get away. "Forty days," I say. "It's been forty days."

We land at Miami airport, it's a media circus. I am shepherded through the mass of flashing bulbs and shouted questions. I do not want to be interviewed, all I want to see are the faces of the two people, who I am told will be here to meet me. My Mother and Rebecca. In a small reception room they are waiting for me. I don't know what to say to them as I enter.

So we say nothing, we just hold each other for ten minutes, and cry tears of joy and relief. When all the tears are spent Rebecca just says, "Lets go home."

Its two days later, I am at home with my Mother and Rebecca. Neither of them has pushed me to tell them what happened. I suppose it will come out at the right time. I have spoken to Sean on the phone, I feel so guilty that I took him there and have told him so. But I don't think he blames me. He said his captivity was not too bad, but his voice betrayed his real feelings. We have promised to get together soon and get drunk. My story has been reported on the television and in the papers, although I have not spoken to anyone, except the authorities. I suppose I will have to do the interview for Channel Three, as I still work for them. Then I will give them notice, my reporting days are over.

I was held for forty days, forty days in the wilderness. I tell myself that it is a coincidence, it means nothing. After all, it was not my choice to be there. But the question nags at the back of my mind, is it too much of a coincidence? Am I controlling my own destiny, or are strings being pulled from afar? Carlos thought I was Jesus, reincarnated. He was wrong, very wrong. In a way, Jesus and I, have the same father, but we are from different moulds, and we are not the same. I am the Archangel Lucifer, and we are very different people.

PART TWO

CHAPTER 6

(Thirteen years later)
Year thirty-six: April

"It is an absolute fact that we are all born of stars. We may have been recycled a few times but all the elements of planets, and our planet, were formed in stars. And that includes you and I. The nuclear reaction of hydrogen into helium in a new star is finite. When the core runs out of hydrogen it goes to work on helium. Transmuting helium into lithium and so on, working its way through the periodic table including carbon, oxygen and all the elements up to iron.

Once the core of the star is iron, then the star is in trouble. Iron is the most stable of elements. To make iron into a heavier element requires more energy than it produces. The stars core therefore cannot sustain enough nuclear pressure, to equal the gravitational pressure that the stars own outer layers are exerting upon it. It is crushed, the core pressure rises and rises, and fusion starts again. For a brief period it can equalize. This is the catalyst that forges the heavier elements, the alchemist turning lead to gold. If the big bang was God's first attempt at cookery, then stars are his Cordon bleu range.

In this flash of runaway nuclear activity, all the heavier elements are formed. Every new element produced, puts more pressure on the core. The phenomenal pressure building and building, fabricating heavier and heavier elements every time it runs out of the last. When it can go no further, the star is so unstable, it explodes off its outer layers to achieve equilibrium, casting its stash of elements into space."

"This is all very interesting. But the life and formation of a star, was not the question. Are you suggesting we should worship the stars Mr. Brookes?"

"No Reverend Banks," I reply, "Just that the truth is every bit as captivating as the stories you believe."

"You refer to Genesis as just a story. That is typical of your bravado!"

"Please Reverend Banks," our host, Al Whelan says, "There is no need to lose your temper, I am sure Mr. Brookes meant no disrespect." He looks my way and raises his eyebrows.

"No I did not," I say, "I believe that the majority of the Old Testament, is a factual account of the history of the Hebrew nation, from Abraham onwards. But there are myths, exaggerations and tall stories mixed in with it. Genesis was not even a Hebrew belief, it was added much later and appears to be based on the Babylonian creation myth."

"A true Christian cannot pick out the sections of the Bible that please, and discard the rest. The Bible is the word of God Almighty and I truly believe every one of them. You will not sway me from this, with your talk of science." Reverend Banks continues, "You have no more proof of exploding stars, as I have for Genesis. Your big bang theory, where everything magically sprouts from nothing, requires a bigger leap of faith, than my faith in God."

"But," I ask, "You believe God sprouted from nothing?"

"God is eternal, God always was and will be forever."

"You have every right to believe whatever you wish Reverend. For the record, I do believe that God exists." Believe may be the wrong word, but I cannot declare that I know for certain that God exists. "The big bang theory is not my theory, and in my view, there is a lot of information still missing. But it is better than Genesis. My point was this; People do not have to believe every word written in the Bible, or the Quran, or any other religious book, to believe in God and in Heaven. God does not write books, people do."

"And what about your book, Mr. Brookes?" Al asks.

"I do not claim that God wrote it," I respond.

"But you claim an awful lot of other things." He says.

"My book is a collection of my thoughts. I do not mind if you don't believe it all. But if one sentence registers in your mind, and makes you a better person, then I will have achieved something."

Al Whelan produces a copy of my book and holds it up for the cameras. "Your book is called, 'Heavens gate' and it has upset a lot of people. Even the very first line is controversial, and I quote," he opens the book for effect, he does not need to, the words are scrolling up on an autocue. "'Believe me when I tell you that God exists, and believe me when I tell you that he cares nothing for you' and then In chapter three you say, 'If God created life, it was a mistake.' Can you explain what you mean?"

"You have taken two sentences from the entire book," I say, "Just for dramatic effect. If you read it all, you will know what I mean. The book is about how people should live, if they want to live and die without misgivings about themselves, and that is the only way to Heaven."

Reverent Banks interrupts, "Jesus said, the only way to Heaven, was through him."

"I don't think he meant it literally," I reply, "I don't think Muslims or Buddhists are exempt from Heaven, because they don't believe Jesus was God incarnate. He meant that the only way to Heaven was to be a good person. And that is what my book is about."

"But you believe," Al asks, "That God does not care."

"Take a look around you. Take a look at the world that we live in. Do you think a caring god would allow the senseless suffering, murdering and poverty that you see?"

"Reverend Banks?" Al asks.

"It is men that do these things, not God. The Lord does not condone these things. The struggle for good against evil will continue until the end. Then all shall be judged before God."

"The struggle for good against evil is in your head," I say. "Every human follows his own path, and knows if he is right or wrong. God does not lead men to good, any more than Satan leads them into evil. When a man blames Satan for his crimes, he just tries to shift the blame away from himself. It is just an excuse, and men know this in their hearts."

[Bravo brother!]

I almost jump out of my seat, Both Al Whelan and Reverent Banks stare at me.

Is that you Michael?

[Don't mind me, carry on with your little speeches.]

"Mr. Brookes?" Al asks, "Are you OK? You have gone a bit green. Do you want to stop?"

"No I'm fine," I say.

"Cut it!" the editor shouts. "Lets have a five minute break and then carry on." A young girl walks across and unclips the microphone from my lapel. I take a drink that is offered to me and bring it to my lips with trembling hands. I make for a private corner, where no one can see my distress. Michael?

[How are you?]

Fucking amazed that I am talking to you!

[I knew you would be glad to hear my voice.]

Does God know?

[I should think so, as far as I know, he knows everything.]

But why are you here after all this time, and where's Gabriel?

[He's still sulking, haven't seen him for ages.]

But why are you here?

[I've been your watcher, since Gabriel was jacked.]

Then why didn't you speak?

[Rules.]

And now?

[The rules have changed, I got a message a few minutes ago, saying it was OK. I don't know why.]

Jesus Michael, it's good to hear your voice, but you could have waited a while. I was in the middle of a television interview when you scared the shit out of me.

[Well that's nice! I haven't spoken to you for decades and this is how I am welcomed.]

"Mr. Brookes?" someone asks, I turn my head to find the editor, "Are

The Songs of Angels

you able to continue? You don't look well at all."

"Really, I'm fine," I say. My microphone is clipped back on, Al and I sit back down. He addresses the Reverend and me.

"Look, we may as well wrap this up. Reverend, would you like to respond to Mr. Brookes last statement?"

"I have said all that I need to," He says.

"OK," Al says, "I have one more question Mr. Brookes, is that alright?"

"Yes," I reply.

The cameras start rolling again and Al gets his cue to begin, "Mr. Brookes," he says, "I understand you were recently married. I was wondering what your wife thinks of your book?"

I smile, "My wife Rebecca, does not agree with everything I write."

"Is that because she is a devoted Catholic?"

"My wife believes in God, but she also has her own mind and understands that I have mine." Rebecca and I married last year. She has gradually, since Colombia, returned to the religion of her youth. I think she made a deal with God, that if I came back, she would believe again. She has never said this, but it is my opinion.

"Well thank you for being here."

"It's been a pleasure," I say.

"And you Reverent Banks," Al says. The Reverend nods.

Al finishes off, "I am sure this debate will continue, The book by David Brookes, 'Heavens gate' has now sold over one-hundred thousand copies and, whether the church likes it or not, will probably sell more. In the end, it is up to you to decide, if this is a ray of light on conventional thinking, as claimed by some critics. Or as the Catholic Church claim, that it is blasphemous nonsense. I'm Al Whelan and you've been watching 'The Whelan Debate'. Good night to you all."

The lights dim and the cameras go off. Our microphones are stripped off again as the lights come back up. The Reverent stands and glares in my direction. "Mr. Brookes, can I speak to you?" he asks.

I get up and move over to him, "Yes, and call me David."

"Mr. Brookes," he says quietly, "You may think me a stupid old man, who leans on God and religion, like a cripple leans on a crutch. Let me tell you I am not. The church has seen a thousand men like you, who like to stir the waters, and survived them all. The church will still stand when you are forgotten."

"You mean like Jesus?" I ask, "Didn't he rock the local religion, and didn't they help get him crucified?"

"You have the tongue of the devil, you are not as clever as you think, and you're a dangerous man. Science is not the corner stone of humanity, the belief in God is. You cannot just claim that God does not care for people, it is outrageous"

"It is how it is. Search your soul Reverend, you will find that I am correct."

He turns and walks away, shaking his head.

"Everything OK?" Al asks as he walks over.

"Yes," I say, "But I fear, the Reverend and I, will never be best friends."

"Anyway," he says, "I enjoyed your book, thanks for coming on the show. The finished version will go out next week. Thanks again," He smiles and moves off.

[I liked your book as well Lucifer.]

You read it?

[Most of Heaven has, there were many sharp intakes of imaginary breath.]

And the Boss? Did he read it?

[Lucifer, Lucifer, he was probably looking over your shoulder and reading it, while you were writing it.]

I make my way out of the studio, to the lobby. There, a driver supplied by the network, waits to take me home. He nods and opens the back door for me. I slide into the seat and fasten my seatbelt, while he climbs into the front.

The last time we were together, was in a car like this one Michael.

[That was an eventful day.]

How are things in Heaven and Hell?

[Naughty question Lucifer, you know I cannot answer.]

I don't understand Gods motives. Why are we suddenly allowed to talk again?

[I have no agenda Lucifer, no instructions from him.]

But he must think it will help him somehow. Gabriel was denied access to me, because God thought he was giving me too much information. What is to stop you doing the same?

[Nothing, like I said, I have no instructions except that non-mortal affairs are none of your business.]

The driver finally pulls out into the New York traffic, and I am on my way home. I sit back into the seat and try to figure out what this unexpected move means.

⁂

In Heaven.

God:
How did he take it?
Michael:
He was surprised.
God:
Was he wary of your intentions?
Michael:
He wants to know why you have had this sudden change of heart. And for the record, so do I.
God:
Do you trust me Michael?
Michael:
Yes Lord, but he is my brother. I will not be used against him.
God:
And I am your Father, you would pick him over me?
Michael:
No Lord. I love you both.
God:
Raphael would do anything I asked.
Michael:
Yes lord he would, but Lucifer would refuse to talk to Raphael. You had a choice of Gabriel or I. And Gabriel is still bitter about what happened in Colombia. So you were left with me.
God smiles.

God:
I would not wish for you to deceive your brother Michael. But he is lost and needs our guidance.
Michael:
I disagree Lord. For the first time, I think he now knows exactly what he is doing. His book has a deep and profound message for mankind. He may have painted you as an uncaring God, and I hope he is wrong about this.
God:
He is wrong.
Michael:
But the message of his words, to anyone who has a mind to understand, is one of love, caring and compassion towards their fellow men. Is this not what you also strived for?
God:
Yes.
Michael:
So when you say that he is lost, what do you mean Lord?
God:
Lucifer thinks that I fail him, and the rest of mankind. Everything I do Michael, is for a reason. You believe that don't you?
Michael:
I admit that I sometimes do not understand what you do Lord, but I do trust you.
God:
So help me with Lucifer.
Michael:
What would you have me do Lord?
God:
Help Lucifer find his way, let him understand what you understand. I am not his enemy. He may feel hard done by, and perhaps he is, but I am his Father and Creator, who will always love him, even when he thinks I have left him.
Michael:
I think it is too late for you and him. He will think it a deception
God:

But you will try.
Michael:
Yes Lord.
God:
Thank you, Michael.

※

"Rebecca! I'm home!" I shout as I close the front door.

"In the kitchen," she replies. I make my way through to the kitchen, and kiss her on the back of the neck. She is preparing a salad. "How was the interview?" She asks, as she turns to me.

"I think it went well," I say. "The show goes out next week, I think it will help with the book sales."

"More non-believers converted to your cause. I am surprised there isn't a mob of outraged Christians tearing down our door."

"I wouldn't be surprised," I reply, "If you were at the head of them."

"I would be," she says, with a grin, "If I didn't already know you. Your computer has been beeping steadily all afternoon, and there is another bag full of mail on your desk. Dinner will be ready in ten, if you want to check your mail first."

"OK," I say as I kiss her again, before retiring to the study. There are around twenty letters, which I start to open.

[Are they about your book?]

The ones forwarded from the publishers, yes.

[What do they say?]

It's about fifty-fifty. Half of them say how much they liked it, or your book has changed my life, and the other half are usually nasty, ranging from death threats, to letters saying I will go to Hell. At least they got that bit right.

[Does it worry you?]

Going back to Hell will be a picnic, after all this.

[No, I mean the death threats.]

Everyone dies Michael, it's in the contract you have to sign, when you shuffle onto the mortal stage. It is the only certain thing that life can offer.

[That sounds sad, coming from you.]

Don't misunderstand me, I do not want to die, I have too much to do in the time I have left. Dying is not in my plans.

[And what do you plan?]

Is that why you are here? Too see what I will do next? The boss is getting nervous, so he sends you, to find out the strategy?

[He is not your enemy Lucifer, God loves you.]

Ha! He has a strange way of showing it, as he left me to rot in Hell for two thousand years. Did he tell you to say that he loved me? Do you actually believe your words?

[I believe them, and he has spoken them.]

Michael, he is playing with my mind, and now with yours. God loves only God. The Angels, the universe and life are his amusement. Do not be taken in by his words because he is not like us. He has his own hidden agenda, and I wish I knew what it was.

[That cannot be true.]

Don't deceive yourself. Did you not see the wars that have been fought, just in my lifetime. Did you watch the twin towers come crashing down! Why would a God who cared, stand back Michael, answer me that!

[Humans do these things, not God.]

And all these humans have one thing in common, they all believe in God. The suicide bomber, and the soldiers who shoot at people they do not know, all think God is on their side. They do it for God! They expect a place in Heaven, for flying a jumbo jet into a skyscraper. Or they feel justified to fire missiles into towns full of civilians. How can this be acceptable?

[It is not acceptable.]

But they believe it is, because of God! All he has to do, is say 'Not in my name' and they would have no excuses. But he does not, he just sits there and watches it all. So my plan is this, and you can tell him. I plan to take God away from them. I plan to make them see the truth. That God does not care how they live and die. He cares nothing for their suffering and their children's suffering. I will tell them, that they are better than God, because all humans are capable of love, and God is not.

[Do not say these things Lucifer!]

Why not? It is the truth! And when humans see this, when they see

The Songs of Angels

that their actions are their own. And if you kill another human, or take any life without reason, it is your own doing, and Hell is waiting for you. Only then, will they will stop doing it. And when they know that Heaven is a real place, where they can go, if they just love one another and live in peace with their neighbours, and their own heart. Then hurting another will be alien to them. Don't you see Michael, it is their belief in God that holds them back.

[Taking God from them, will not achieve this outcome. They will love one another, no more than before. It is human nature that is at fault, not God. Did you ever really look into the hearts or humans when you were an Angel Lucifer? The truth is there, they like to be selfish, they love to trample the weaker into the ground. Life has programmed them this way. The fittest and the most ruthless get the lion's share. They tolerate other humans, as long as it does not affect their life, and as long as they can control them. Your ideal world, full of love is a pipe dream. Because one of them will always see, that it is in his interest to be selfish, to take what he wants and damn the rest.

And it is infectious, once one does this then all the rest follow, because they have to. Otherwise they are left behind. Life is 'Red in tooth and Claw'. Destroy all that get in your way because only the strong will make it.]

They do not need God anymore.

[You are wrong, they need God now, more than ever.]

Why?

[Because they know he is there.]

You are twisting everything! Why did you come here, is it God's plan, for you to change my mind?

[It is my plan Lucifer, now that I have heard your thoughts. You take your own prejudice, and lay it on all of humanity.]

That is not true.

[Rebecca believes.]

She is different, she believes in God, despite God. She does not need him to be a good person.

[Perhaps that is what you should teach the rest of them. To love God, even if he does not care. Perhaps first, you should forgive God yourself, even if he does not require your forgiveness. And if everyone loved God, and expected nothing in return, only then, would they be at peace with themselves.]

I wish you had stayed away!

[That is the human, David Brookes speaking, Lucifer would not say those words to me, because he is my brother, and I love him.]

I am human.

[No Lucifer, you always were, and will always be an Angel.]

※

Can a person love God, even when he gives nothing back? How can in individual believe without proof? But humans do, millions of them believe in a God, without verification. They love him without question or hesitation. They will never see evidence of his existence, he would not allow it. And here am I, one who knows that God exists, yet cannot believe in him. For the same reason that they do. It is the blind faith of humans that drove me to endlessly question him.

So is it a problem with me, is it me who does not see clearly?

[I do not know.]

You never stopped in Hell long enough Michael, to see the betrayal in the faces, of humans when they knew where they were. Humans who should be in Heaven, and arrived in Hell. God betrayed them and cast them into my domain. I cannot forgive him for letting humans worship him all their lives, then allowing them to go to Hell. Usually because of their own misgivings about the criteria required to get to Heaven.

[True believers do go to Heaven.]

Bullshit Michael, Hell was full of people who thought they were. A pittance gets to Heaven and I had the majority. I cannot ever forgive him for Hell. Humans would be better off without God.

The door opens and Rebecca pokes her head through the door, "David," she says, "I am going to bed, are you coming?"

"Not yet." I reply.

"Are you OK? You have been very quiet all night."

"I'm fine," I say, "Just thinking. I will be up soon."

She smiles, "See you later then. Don't stay up to late, we have a busy day tomorrow. Good night and God bless you."

"Good night sweetheart," I say. She closes the door.

[Look at Rebecca, Lucifer; can you say she is worse off with her faith in God?]

But she is not like anyone else. When we first met, she did not practice her religion. She was still the same person, still a good person. She was the first person who read my book. Do you know what she said?

[No.]

It's interesting! She read the whole book without passing comment. And when she had finished and I asked her what she thought, she said 'its interesting.' I was expecting her to beg me to burn it. I used to wonder sometimes, if it is a conflict for her being with me. But I no longer think it is, because she is so secure in her own mind. I don't think it bothers her that I can write 'God does not care'. In her mind, I am wrong and nothing I say will change that. But Rebecca would never try to change my views, or anyone else's.

As long as the message I preach is for the good, she will allow it. And that goes for anyone else, or any religious belief. Rebecca has her religion, but she can see past it. She can embrace new ideas and see every view for what it is. If I could make every human like her, I would die happy.

[But she believes in God.]

Yes, but she does not need to.

[I don't understand your reasoning.]

I thought you said you had read my book?

[I did.]

Then you did not understand it Michael. It does not matter if you believe or not. If it pleases you to believe, that's fine. And as eighty percent of humans do think there is a creator, of some kind, it obviously does please most humans. But it is also fine if you do not believe. It will not stop you entering Heaven.

What you must believe in is life, what you must have faith in is your own self. You are the one, who builds your path to Heaven. God will not take you there, nor I, nor religion. And you do this by being a true human, by caring for your brothers and sisters, and that means all life, every living thing is your relative.

[Including plants?]

There is only one true species on Earth, and the species is life. All diversity and genre are branches from it.

[But creatures eat plants, and other animals.]

Unfortunately, but that is the deck of cards that evolution has dealt us. Plants use sunlight to manufacture energy; animals do the same thing by consuming plants and other animals. We effectively get our energy, by waiting for the plants to store theirs, and them stealing it from them, or from animals that have already stolen it.

[I've never thought of life in that way. You make it all sound so basic.]

Because it is, life progresses by destroying other lives. The struggle to exist is paid for, by the life of other forms.

[So you can never stop this, how can you stop humans taking the life of other species? They have to do this, or they will cease to be. So how can you say that all life is your brother?]

Of course humans have to eat, I am not saying we should all starve to death, rather than take a life. But human minds are beyond this base rule of existence. They understand the rules and can live with an understanding, and a compassion, for all other forms.

[But humans are different, humans can go to Heaven.]

Or Hell.

[Granted]

Physically humans are animals, just like any other. But mentally, they have moved onto a different plane. My point is that humans have enough mental power now to do amazing things. They have dissected the world around them. They can see atoms and even split them if they wish. They build machines that take them into space or perform complex calculations in a nanosecond. Some of the structures erected by humans are staggering. Take a walk around New York or go and study the pyramids.

Humans want to know everything, from how many stars are in the sky, to how many cells are in my body, and they want to know, what it is all for. Did you ever wonder what you were Michael? Did you ever try to examine what you are?

[I am myself.]

And what is that?

[I've never thought about it.]

Neither did I, until I was human.

[And your analysis?]

The Songs of Angels

What, of Angels? I still have no idea. Some kind of supernatural, conscious energy form, which is related to matter. It must be related, as we can manipulate it, and therefore it must produce an effect on us.

[I am an Angel Lucifer, matter does not effect me.]

Have a look in a mirror, you choose to appear in the form of a human, as do most of us, and even God, you have a house in Heaven, that is very similar to the houses that men build. Yet you think matter does not effect you?

[Those are just illusions, I can click my fingers, and it would all be gone. I could take the form of a warthog if I wished.]

Warthogs are matter also, and you do not actually possess fingers, you copied them from humans. Can you take the form of Michael? The Michael before matter existed.

[I do not remember having a form.]

Neither do I, but we did exist, and must have had some form. Matter has demanded our attention since it's creation. Life now, and especially humans, dominates us totally. I do not know any longer, if humans are like us, or if we have become like humans.

But back to the point of this discussion, if humans were the same stuff as Angels, they would be on their way to understanding what they were made from.

[Your point is that humans are inquisitive?]

That's a slight understatement! Humans are vastly more complex than Angels. They are capable of more radical and pure thought, they have more vision and more hunger than any Angel in Heaven could imagine!

[Then they obviously don't need you at all.]

There is a price to pay for their extravagances, they are also capable of the complete opposite.

[Destructive, apathetic, evil, callous, vicious, jealous, arrogant and spiteful. Shall I go on?]

I don't think you need to.

[So you will tell them that God does not care about them, and everything will be better.]

I will tell them to care for themselves, and each other, and everything will be better. Enough of this now, I'm tired and I need some sleep. You can report back to the boss, tell him what you wish. Goodnight

Michael.

[Goodnight Lucifer.]

※

It's a dream, I know it is only a dream. But I am standing at the gates of Hell and I cannot get in. Hell is finally full, the demons are closing the gates and the souls are all around them, pushing and screaming. I turn around and can see the crowds of the recent dead building behind me. They stop and stare at me, unsure of what to do, as more and more appear behind them.

"Where do we go?" one asks me. I have no answer for her. The closest are being pushed forward as more and more souls materialize at the rear. Closer and closer, they are forced towards me and I press my back into the iron gates. "Where do we go?" they cry in chorus. Screams now as some are knocked to the floor and trampled. And then they are pushed into me and my back scrapes on the railings.

The souls begin to cry as they are crushed onto me. I cannot breathe! I cannot breathe! Someone help me!

"David!"

I awake, sweat pours from me as I take ragged gulps of air, "David! Wake up!" Rebecca shouts.

"I'm awake," I say, "I must have been having a nightmare."

"You shouted 'God help me.' It must have been a pretty awful one."

"Just a dream, I am OK now." I say, "Go back to sleep."

"Hold me David," Rebecca says as she nestles her body closer.

※

Rebecca and I are driving to a book signing in Manhattan. This is my first engagement in New York, and I am a little apprehensive. We had to call off the one in Washington, because of threats towards me. I still wanted to do it, unfortunately the bookstore would not. But this is New York.

We park our car behind the store, a young woman leads us through the back door, and introduces us to the manager. "It is a pleasure to meet you Mr. Brookes, and Mrs. Brookes. Can I get you coffee?" he asks.

The Songs of Angels

"Please," I say, and Rebecca also.

"Carol," he calls, to the woman who led us in, "Three coffees."

"Yes Mr. Pratt," Carol replies, then inquires about milk and sugar. When she has departed to the back of the shop, Mr. Pratt turns and says,

"We've had lots of interest, so we expect quite a crowd."

"Good," I reply.

"Have you any security?" Rebecca asks.

"Sure do," he says, "There will be no trouble Mrs. Brookes. Ah, here's our coffee."

"Thank you Carol," I say, and receive a smile. They have a desk set up for me at the back of the shop, along with a few dozen boxes containing copies of my book. We make our way over to it and perch on the end, while we sip our coffee. Carol begins to unpack the boxes and stacks books along side us.

"We open in about fifteen minutes," Pratt says, as he looks at his wristwatch, "If you don't mind me saying so Mr. Brookes, I expected you to be older."

"Most people do and please call me David," I say.

"Thank you, and my name is Colin," he replies, "If you will excuse me, I have a few things to attend to." He wonders away through the shelves.

"Mr. Brookes," Carol says, from behind me, I turn to her.

"Yes?" I ask.

"Would you mind signing a copy for me, before the crowds come in?" She asks, holding out a book she has just taken out of a box.

"Certainly," I respond, and take the book from her. "Anything particular that you would like me to write?"

"Just 'to Carol from David Brookes' if that's alright." I sign the book and hand it over to her, she smiles and thanks me, then goes out the back, probably to her car.

"It's a good job I came along," Rebecca says, with a grin "That's the first one you've signed, and you're already flirting."

"I was not!" I defend myself.

"No, but she was. She will probably go home tonight and read the entire book, then fall in love with you."

"I can't help it, if I've got animal magnetism."

"You've got something, I can never quite put my finger on it, but it's not animal magnetism."

[Astral magnetism?]

Colin Pratt strolls back over, "Doors open in two minutes," he says, "We have quite a crowd building."

"Thanks," I reply, and start to get myself comfortable behind the desk. Rebecca wanders away, her eyes fixed on the main doors. I think she came along, to be an additional security guard. Then the doors are opened and a queue quickly forms in front of me. "Hi," I say to the first one, "What would you like me to write?"

※

The morning has passed without any disasters, most of the people who are purchasing, a signed copy of my book this morning, have been civil. From the questions some have been asking, many appear to have read the book already.

"Hello," I say, to the next woman in the queue.

"I've read Heavens Gate, I wanted to see the person who wrote it," she says.

"Did you like it?" I ask, I am not sure where this is going.

"I would say that it has changed my life, but it hasn't. It's changed my death." She stares at me for an instant, as if she expects a comment. I stare back and hold my tongue, wondering where this is going. Eventually she blinks and continues. "I have a genetic disorder that will kill me soon." She must read my pained expression, because she smiles and continues, "I don't need your sympathy. Reading your words turned me from a self-pitying recluse, who was fast becoming an alcoholic, back to a human being. You painted a picture of the world with your words, which brought me back to life. All I need you to do now, is tell me that it is all true."

"You already know if it is true, or not," I reply, "You do not need me to tell you."

"It's true, I see it in your eyes" she says.

"What would you like me to write?"

"I do not need another copy, I already have one," she says, "I have what I came for. Thank you preacher."

"I am not a preacher."

"Yes you are," she says.

"What is your name?" I ask.

"Mary," she replies, and holds out her hand. I take it and a shiver runs through me. Suddenly she grips my hand tightly as a pained expression crosses her face. I feel like my hair is standing on end and Mary is shaking violently. I think she is going to pass out.

"Hold her!" I shout to the person standing behind, but he is too late. Her hand is wrenched from mine as she crumples to the floor. She is convulsing madly, "Someone please call an ambulance!" I scream, as I rush around the desk. Rebecca is there before me, holding her head.

"I need something to hold her tongue down," she says. Carol appears ten seconds later, with a teaspoon, which she must have collected from the staff room. Rebecca inserts it into Mary's mouth. The convulsions seem to be subsiding.

Colin Pratt comes over and says to me, "The ambulance is on the way," then he addresses everyone else, "Folks, we need to clear the store. If you could please make your way to the exits, as we have a medical emergency." People start to slowly move out of the shop, looking back over their shoulders as they go. Mary has stopped shaking now.

Michael, is she going to die?

[I do not know, but she is breathing normally now.]

The ambulance arrives with sirens blazing, and the paramedics have her hooked up to monitors in seconds. "She has a genetic disorder," I inform them, "But I don't know what."

"No problem," the paramedic says, "She appears stable." He turns to his colleague and adds, "We may as well get her straight back to be checked out." They lift her onto a trolley and wheel her to the waiting ambulance. Two minutes later the sirens are sounding, and they disappear down the street.

Rebecca puts her arms around me and I hold her tightly. I am still shaking. "Lets get ourselves home," she says. I nod. We say our goodbyes to the store staff, and Rebecca drives us back.

"Hello" I say to the telephone, "Look, I'm trying to find out the condition of a lady who was picked up from Barnes and Noble bookstore, on Lexington north of Eighty-sixth Street in Manhattan, around two pm today."

"What hospital was she taken to sir?" the bored operator asks.

"I do not know," I reply.

"What name sir?"

"I only know her first name is Mary."

"Then you're not her kin sir?"

"No," I say.

"It's not our policy to give out information, unless you are a relative sir."

"There must be someone, who can give me some information." I plead.

"I will have to put you on hold," She says, "Please wait sir."

"I've been on hold for thirty minutes already." I say, as the music starts again. This is pointless, I don't think they will tell me anything so I hang up. You could find out for me Michael.

[Yes I could, but I don't think it will be allowed. Hang on Lucifer, while I ask.]

He is asking for permission, which will be denied.

[Sorry brother.]

Well there's more than one way to skin a cat. I pick up the phone again and dial. It rings for a few seconds, "Please be in!" I say.

"Hi," a mechanical voice answers, "Your talking to Sean Peters, as you have probably realized, I'm not in at the moment, but if you leave a message, I will call you back when I can. Thank you." The beep sounds.

"Sean, It's David Brookes. Look, I need a bit of a favour, can you call me as soon as possible."

"David?" Sean says. "I'm here, how are you buddy?"

"Sean, thanks for picking up. Look, I need a favour." I explain what happened at the bookstore, "Could you use any of your contacts, to find out if she is OK?"

"Yes," he replies, "I will do my best. We have a few friends at the local hospitals, but I probably wont be able to get back to you tonight. Leave it with me."

"Thanks Sean," I say, "I will owe you one."
"It's nice to hear from you David, we don't get together often enough."
"We will have to change that." I say, "You will phone me tomorrow?"
"Yes," he replies, "I will call you. Bye David."
"Thanks Sean." He hangs up.
[What will you do if she died?]
What can I do? I just want to know.
[It was not your fault.]
You don't know that. Did you feel it, when I touched her hand?
[Feel what?.]
Something happened.
[Like what?]
I wish I knew.

※

The phone is ringing, Jesus what time is it? I reach across Rebecca and pick it up. The bedside clock tells me it is ten past seven, in the morning.
"Hello," I say, still half asleep.
"David, it's Sean. Sorry if I woke you up, but you need to hear this. First of all, Mary is fine. Her full name is Mary Kirkland and she was taken to Bellevue hospital, where she regained consciousness around midnight. The doctor I spoke to said, and this was off the record, that there was nothing wrong with her."
"That's good." I say.
"No, you're not listening to me, there is nothing at all wrong with her!"
"But she told me she had a genetic disorder that was killing her, are you telling me that she was lying?"
"Not at all, she wasn't lying, she had an incurable genetic thing, I can't remember the name of it, and now she hasn't! Look, the reason I phoned you, is because the circus has taken over. We have already interviewed her, and you will not believe what she is saying! The hospital is still keeping things close to its chest. There is no official statement yet, I don't think they know what to say."
"I don't understand." I admit.

"Watch the eight O'clock news, we are running with whatever we have, and her interview will be part of it." Sean says.

"What has she said?" I ask.

"Watch the news," he replies, "You will be getting some phone calls, but we want the first interview with you. You said you owed me one, deal?"

"Yes, but I still don't understand."

"Watch the news. Shit! I have to go, the hospital are making a statement. See you later," he hangs up.

Rebecca is awake and staring at me, she asks, "What's going on?"

"We have to watch the eight O'clock news," I reply, as I lie back into the pillow.

꼭

The news starts with the current crisis in Israel and Palestine, full scale fighting is erupting again. The US has threatened to intervene if it cannot be sorted out internally. The UN and neighbouring Muslim countries have retaliated, by telling America to keep out. After the fiasco in Iraq, a few years ago, they are probably correct. The report is followed by a few domestic stories.

The anchorman in the studio then passes over to Rob Bright, he is the reporter who followed in my footsteps, on Sean's crew. The sign behind him, informs us that he is outside the Bellevue hospital centre, in Manhattan. He begins to speak, "Thanks Bill," he says, acknowledging the anchorman, "You join us outside the Bellevue hospital centre in Manhattan. Yesterday an unconscious woman by the name of Mary Kirkland was admitted." He stresses her name, as reporters do, "She was apparently taken ill while at a Manhattan bookstore, where the controversial author, David Brookes, was signing copies of his book, Heavens Gate. The Doctors here at Bellevue, have been carrying out tests, since she was admitted, to assess the cause of her blackout. What they found was, that she was perfectly healthy.

What is amazing about Mary's good health, is that the Doctors expected the cause to be a genetic disorder that Mary had been diagnosed as having, over three years ago. In fact Doctors in Maine, had given Mary only a ten percent chance of living for a further three months! Earlier I

The Songs of Angels

spoke to Dr. Mark Sands to explain."

The scene shifts to the inside of the hospital. Bob Bright has his microphone under the nose of a middle-aged man in white. "Dr. Sands," he asks, "Would you please explain Mary Kirkland's disorder."

"Amyotrophic Lateral Sclerosis is an inherited genetic disorder, usually abbreviated to ALS, that manifests itself, in middle or old age. It paralyzes the patients muscles, eventually shutting down the heart and lungs, which ultimately leads to the death of the subject."

"And how do you treat it," Bob asks.

"We can control it to some degree with drugs, but ultimately there is no known cure."

"And have you ever known anyone recover from ALS?"

"No." the Doctor replies.

"But you agree that Mary Kirkland no longer has this disorder."

"Look, conditions like ALS are not like a common cold. They are caused by rogue genes, which the subject inherits from its parents at birth. These cannot be altered, so a patient does not recover. It is my opinion that Mary Kirkland was misdiagnosed, and never had this condition. We are waiting for Ms. Kirkland's Doctors to send through her case files, and will continue to do tests, before making decisions."

The shot cuts back to the live feed, in front of the building. "Mary, on the other hand," Bob says, "Has a different interpretation of what happened, we spoke to her earlier this morning."

The camera cut to the pre-recorded interview. Mary is sitting up in a hospital bed, a smile spread across her face. "Ms. Kirkland," Bob says, "How are you?"

"Stunned," she replies, "Yesterday I had three months to live, and today, I have the same chance as everyone else."

"The doctors here at Bellevue, can't believe you ever had ALS."

"I've lived with Amyotrophic Lateral Sclerosis for a long time. I've been tested and prodded by doctors and I know I had it. I could feel it taking over my body. There is no doubt, and when the doctors here speak to my doctor, they will know."

"They also tell me, that there is no cure for ALS, so how do you think you were cured?"

"David Brookes cured me," she says. Rebecca takes a sharp intake of breath.

"Could you explain?"

"Yes," she replies, and continues, "I read his book and went to see him, at Barnes and Noble bookstore where he was signing copies. I shook his hand, and I am told that I passed out. But something happened when I touched him, something wonderful. I think I saw heaven," She begins to cry, "It was beautiful, and I thought, well this is it, now I die. But I didn't, I awoke here and I knew I was better, even before the doctors did."

"What do you mean, when you say you saw heaven?"

"I cannot put it into words, which would adequately describe it. All I can tell you is heaven is the most beautiful place. It's more a feeling than an image. I sound crazy don't I?"

"It's OK," Bob says.

"I'm not crazy. I'm cured." She looks into the camera, "Thank you for my life David, thank you Preacher." The report cuts back to Bob Bright, outside the hospital.

"Astonishing words, from a very happy lady, here at Bellevue. More on this story later, when we hope to speak to David Brookes. But for now, back to you Bill."

"Thanks Bob," Bill replies, "Keep tuned to Channel Three, for reaction to this story. In other news this morning…" He continues talking but I am not listening anymore.

"Shit!" Rebecca says.

[I could not have put it better myself.]

"David?" she says, "What's going on?"

"I have no idea," I admit.

The phone rings, and we both jump. I pick it up and say hello. It's a reporter who wants to speak to me, I tell her that I will not, and hang up. It rings again instantly and Rebecca grabs it, "I'll get rid of them." She says, she puts the receiver to her ear, "It's Sean," she adds, and holds out the phone.

I take it and tell him, "Sean you Bastard, you could have hinted, at what she was going to say!"

"And spoil the surprise?" he replies, "What sort of fun would that be?"

"Bastard," I say, as I pace across the room.

"Don't be like that, when can we interview you?" he asks.

"Never." I say.

"David, you promised. You have to do it, we have already got a Cardinal on tape, who says this is all a hoax, engineered by you, to promote your book. If you stay quiet, people will believe it. Well?"

"Bastard," I say again.

"Anyway, it's your fault. You asked me to find her."

"I asked you to find her as a personal favour! I did not ask you to put her on TV, spouting on about Heaven and me." I cover the microphone and address Rebecca, "They want to do an interview, what do you think?"

"Tell him you will phone him back," she instructs. I tell him and he gives me a mobile phone number, where I can reach him. "Sit down and tell me the truth," Rebecca says.

"What?"

"Sit down David, and tell me what is going on."

"What do you mean?" I ask.

"A woman you have never met before walks into your book signing, with a fatal disease. Then hey presto, she is cured and then you tip off your old buddy, to go and find her. The next minute she is in television, saying that you miraculously cured her."

"You think I set this up?"

"Well your book sales are going to go through the roof." She says.

"I cannot believe you think I would fabricate something like this, just to sell my book. The bloody book tells people that God does not care! The last thing I want people to believe, is that God has started doing fucking miracles again."

"If you tell me, that you did not, then I believe you." She says. "But could someone else have set this up?"

"I don't know," I reply, "All I know is I did not."

"Do the interview then." She says.

[Lucifer, I am being instructed to attend an emergency meeting. I will speak with you later.]

In Heaven.

God:
Ah Michael, you're here. What is going on?
Michael:
I thought you might tell me Lord.
God:
Raphael, this woman, is she telling the truth?
Raphael:
So far, our investigations tell us she is. There is a woman called Mary Kirkland living in Portland, Maine. She has this genetic disorder, records show there is no doubting that. And the woman in New York appears to be her.
God:
Thank you Raphael.
Raphael:
Lord, may I ask a question?
God:
Certainly.
Raphael:
When you sent him there, you told him he would have no special powers.
God:
That is true Raphael. We have not ruled out all other options yet. It may not have been Lucifer, who cured her.
Gabriel enters.
Gabriel:
It was. We have just had conformation. Mary Kirkland had Amyotrophic Lateral Sclerosis, and now she does not. Lucifer unconsciously rewrote her DNA, and recoded the genes that cause ALS, the instant he touched her.
Raphael:
How is that possible Lord! You said he could have no powers!
God:
He asked me what powers he would have as a mortal, and I replied that as a mortal, he would have none. But he is not just a mortal, he is an

Archangel.
Gabriel:
So he can perform miracles on Earth, as you did?
God:
That is how it appears.
Gabriel:
And you knew this could happen Lord?
God:
It was a possibility.
Gabriel:
Then Lord, you should have told him this, before he went!
God:
Why? I did not know before I descended. I had to learn while I was there. Why should he be any different?
Michael:
He did this unconsciously, is Lucifer capable of unconsciously hurting someone?
Raphael:
Or worse, hurting everyone?
God:
It is possible.
Raphael:
Then we have to stop this now Lord. He is twisted. You cannot leave him on Earth with this sort of power. He will use it unwisely.
God:
Lucifer loves humans, he will not hurt them.
Michael:
But we have to tell him, of what he is capable.
God:
Yes, you will have to. He has to control himself.
Gabriel starts to laugh.
God:
What is so funny Gabriel?
Gabriel:
He will hate you even more for this Lord. Even more than he did before. He will believe that you lied to him.

God:
I did not.
Gabriel:
You did not exactly tell him the truth either.
Michael:
That will do Gabriel. Lord, do I have permission to go back to him.
God:
Yes, yes, we are finished here. In fact you may all leave. I have no wish to discuss this further at this time.

The telephone is off the hook, it would not stop ringing. There are television vans parked on the road, and cameras pointing at our house. Sean and Bob Bright are on the way. I have no idea what I will tell them when they get here.

[Lucifer!]

Well, what was said?

[It was you, you who cured her.]

I know, something passed between us when we touched.

[There is more. You could potentially do the opposite, you could kill someone so you have to control it.]

Control it! I don't even know how I fucking did it! How am I supposed to control it!

[You have to.]

He hinted this to me, when I was held captive in Colombia. He said I was a man just like he had been. Bastard, God knew this could happen! I spend all my time on Earth, trying to convince humans that God will not help them, and he arranges for a little miracle to happen. And sticks me right in the middle of it.

[It was you, God did not have anything to do with it. He was not even sure if it was possible.]

Bullshit, he knows everything. He is using us for his own designs. We are pawns in his games.

[That's not true Lucifer.]

Are you sure?

The Songs of Angels 161

[Yes.]

Oh shit! Oh shit! My father! Why could I not have saved him Michael? I held his hand for two days and watched him die. Now I hate you Lord! Are you listening to me! Could I have saved him Michael? Could I?

[I do not know.]

How do I control it Michael? Shall I never touch another human?

[Again I do not know, but we will work it out.]

Perhaps I have already killed hundreds, without knowing.

[Perhaps you have already saved hundreds, without you, or them knowing.]

"David," Rebecca calls, from the hall, "Sean is here, shall I let him in?"

"Give me two minutes," I say. This is a disaster.

[No it is not. This is what you wanted, you have the tools to do anything you wish. Learn to control them, and then use them.]

There is a knock at the door, Rebecca pokes her head in, "Ready?" she says. I nod, and she comes in, followed by Bob and Sean. Bob offers his hand, and I involuntarily back away.

A puzzled look crosses his features, but then he smiles, "I think the back lawn would be the best place."

"OK," I reply. I follow them through the house, and out into the garden. It is quite private out here. Sean sets up his camera and takes a light reading, then gives Bob a thumbs up. "Before we start," I say, "Who else have you spoken to this morning?"

"A Cardinal and an Evangelist, Mary's Doctor in Portland and another expert on ALS." Bob replies.

"And what questions will you be asking?"

"Just your slant on what happened." Bob replies, "Jesus David, you're the star of the show. Relax."

"I'm ready," Sean says.

"OK?" Bob asks me, I nod and he turns to address the camera. "After the interview with Mary Kirkland, which I am sure you have all seen by now, David Brookes, the author of 'Heavens Gate' and the man who Ms. Kirkland claims cured her of a terminal genetic disorder, has granted channel three, his first interview." He turns to me and says, "Good morning Mr. Brookes."

"Good morning." I say nervously.

"Mr. Brookes, you have obviously heard Mary Kirkland's claim, that you cured her of Amyotrophic Lateral Sclerosis?"

"Yes," I reply.

"And your thoughts?"

"I am glad she is better." I say.

"Your thoughts on the claim, that it was you who cured her?" he asks again.

"I'm not a doctor, I have no idea why she suddenly recovered. How would I know? I only met Mary yesterday at my book signing. When she collapsed, we were all very worried for her."

"How would you explain this?"

"I cannot," I say, "As I said, I am not a doctor and know nothing about this disorder."

"It has been suggested that this is a hoax, set up by you, to help your book sales."

"The very thought of that, repulses me. And the people who 'suggest' this, repulse me more."

"So you are sure this is a miracle?" he says.

"I don't remember saying that Bob. A miracle is something that has no explanation. The doctors will have an explanation, or they will not, when they have finished their tests."

"Some doctors, unofficially of course, have already said this to me."

"They do not know yet, and will have to wait for proof. Only when all the possible causes, are proved impossible, can the impossible be probable. And even then, just because we can find no cause, it may just mean that we have not considered, or do not know, what is possible. We will have to wait for that conclusion."

"Then you consider Ms. Kirkland is deluding herself?" he asks.

"Once again Bob, I do not know," I reply.

"And you had nothing to do with it," he says.

"It is improbable," I say, "that I had anything to do with her recovery."

"Then if it was a miracle," he adds, "It must have been God."

"My views on God, are for all to read in my book. I would sooner believe that the human spirit, Mary's spirit, has more to do with miracles, than God."

The Songs of Angels

"One last thing," he asks, "Why does she call you a preacher?"

"She called me that in the store, I told her that I was not a preacher."

"Thank you for talking to us Mr. Brookes," he turns back to the camera, "This is Bob Bright for Channel Three." He does a cutting mime across his neck, and Sean lowers the camera. "That was great," he says, turning to me, "We should have the next batch of interviews on TV this afternoon. I know this is rude, but we have to go now, if we are going to get this on air."

"Don't let me stop you," I say.

"See you soon David," Sean says, "And you Rebecca." They are out of the door in thirty seconds. Rebecca walks up behind me and puts her arms around me. I nearly pull away, but check myself.

"You're jumpy," she says, "I suppose a lot has happened, so I forgive you."

"How do you think that went?" I ask.

"They will cut the bits they want out of it, you used to. I would not worry about it too much." She kisses my neck. A shiver passes through me. "You will have to go and see her, to find out what she really believes."

"Yes," I reply, and we go back inside.

※

The afternoon news devotes about fifteen minutes to the story, which for a news story, is a long time. The Cardinal is the one who tries to discredit me, saying that I have fabricated the whole thing, and that only the Holy Roman Catholic Church, can sanction a miracle. He concludes that the church is conducting their own investigation. I wish them luck.

The Evangelist is a pretty oily character, but he is all for the miracle option. He sees it as proof, that faith healers work. And that God can work miracles, even through a blasphemous sinner like me. They reshow Mary's interview, and insert the clip of her thanking me, throughout the slot.

Mary's doctor, in Portland, insists that she had ALS, and there is no cure. The other ALS expert, a Dr. Briggs, confirms that he has compared Mary Kirkland's DNA scans from Portland, with a new test carried out this morning. The tests confirm that she is the same person, that I did not switch her with a doppelganger. And that her genetic makeup has changed, that she no longer carries the gene that causes ALS. He can offer no explanation, and concludes that more tests are required.

My interview is shown in full, as far as I can tell. Bob concludes that whatever the cause of Mary's recovery, be it a miracle or a natural phenomenal, that medical science has not detected yet, a miracle still happened to Mary Kirkland. The slot finishes with a close and grainy shot, of Mary's face. She says *"David Brookes cured me."* And then the other cut when she said, *"I think I saw heaven."* Then it cuts to me saying, *"Only when all the possible causes, are proved impossible, can the impossible be probable."*

※

"How are you feeling?" I ask.

"Never better," Mary replies, with a grin. She is still in the hospital. I had to sneak in the back door, after driving all over Manhattan, trying and succeeding, to shake off a reporter who followed me from the house. Mary looks well, she is sparkling, "Thank you," she whispers. I sit in the armchair, besides the bed.

"How long do you have to stay here?" I ask.

"I think they would like to keep me forever, but I have told them to finish their tests, because I am off in the morning. Back to Maine to restart my life." She looks down at the bedclothes, and continues to talk, "I assume you have been watching the news." I say that I have, "I'm sorry if I have caused you and your wife discomfort, but I had to tell the truth. I had to tell the world, how wonderful you are."

"I did not do anything." I state. "Why would you think that I had anything to do with your recovery?"

"You can say that to the TV, but not to me. You know that is untrue. Didn't you feel anything when we touched?"

"No," I lie.

"If that is true," Mary says, "Then take my hand. Nothing will happen." She reaches out towards me and I mechanically pull my arms to my chest. "What's the matter? Take my hand."

"There is no need," I say, "It will confirm nothing."

"Then there is no reason why you should not, is there?"

"I would prefer not to."

"You have just proved, beyond a doubt in my mind, that you know the truth. But it has frightened you, hasn't it? You fear to touch me. Do you think I might pass out again, and wake up with ALS once more?" She stares at me, her hand still held out, in front of her. "Take my hand David Brookes, I'm willing to take that chance."

"I don't know what will happen," I admit. She reaches further towards me.

[Chances are, that nothing will happen. After all, you have touched hundreds of people, in your lifetime, and nothing like this has happened.]

As far as we know.

I reach out and grasp her hand. There is no tingle, no shaking, just the warmth of Mary's hand in mine. I allow her to pull me towards her, she places her other hand on my cheek, and whispers, "I will never be able to thank you, but I am better now. You do not have to be here anymore. You have an amazing gift and there are many people, here in this hospital and elsewhere, who you could be helping."

"I don't know how it works," I softly say.

"But you have to try," she replies, "Follow your heart David Brookes. It is good, and it will not let you down." She releases me and sits back. We stare at one another for a second, silently saying our farewells. I stand to leave, but then turn back to her, and ask,

"Do you think you could stop telling everyone that it was me, who cured you?"

She laughs, and replies, "Sorry, but I will be telling every person I meet, until the day I die. And then I will tell all of Heaven about you." I nod, then depart, and aimlessly stroll the hospital corridors, with no destination in mind. What if I walk into another room, and touch a sick child? Do you think I should?

[I do not know, ultimately, it is your choice Lucifer.]

Will I unconsciously do what is best for them? What if they are so sick, that the best thing for them would be death, would my touch kill them? What right do I have, to experiment with the lives of humans Michael, can you tell me?

[What is your objective, here on Earth?]

To try to steer humanity into a better way of life, and keep them from Hell.

[Then you are already experimenting with the lives of humans.]

I stop in the corridor, and stare through a glass panelled door. Inside a child lies prone on a bed, tubes running from his, or her, nose. Drips plugged into a frail arm and monitors steadily bleeping.

What will be the criteria, to warrant my attention. Why this child and not the one next door, or the one in the next hospital. How about the ones in Texas or Africa? I cannot get to them all, and if I did, is it the right thing to do? Earth has to many people now. If I save this child, I add to the problem, and to the problems of the future. For every person that I potentially pull from the brink of death, I add countless generations, who will speed humanity to its final conclusion.

[Which is?]

This planet has finite resources. If the human population continues to grow, as it has done, the consequences are dire. First humans will displace all other species, and this has already started Michael. There will not be enough room for other forms. Then when the human population reaches the maximum that the Earth can support, the balance will be tipped, and nature will step in to repair the damage.

[How?]

Nature will cull them, most of humanity will starve to death.

[So saving this child, is the wrong thing to do?]

I want to.

[Of course you do, it is human nature, and your nature.]

I don't think there is anything natural about what I would be doing.

[Why is it not natural? You move and operate in a natural world. You are a human being, and an Angel. Did you not tell me that both must be natural, or they could not exist? Therefore, your 'talent' must be natural. How could it be anything else?]

It breaks the laws of nature.

[Then the rules are wrong, or misunderstood.]

But do I walk into this room now, and try to do something for this child?

[I cannot answer that, it is your decision.]

Lets go inside and have a look.

I push the door open, there is no one else inside, and walk to the foot of the bed. The child is asleep, or unconscious. I pick up the charts hanging from the bedstead and read them. The child is a boy of ten years old, he has leukaemia. I walk to his side, and look down at his sleeping form. Then softly, almost without thought, I lay my hand over his.

"Excuse me?" someone says. I turn to find a nurse regarding me. "What are you doing in here?" she asks, as she walks over.

"Nothing," I reply, "Just visiting."

"I'm afraid you must leave," she instructs, "This is not visiting time, and anyway, Peter is very ill and prone to infections."

"I'm sorry," I say, "I will go now." I head for the door, as the nurse fusses over the child, rearranging blankets and viewing the monitors.

[Well, what happened?]

Nothing, nothing at all happened. It did not work.

※

Two days later.

Letters, hundreds of letters, forwarded to me from my publishers. Some ask for me to visit their loved ones, and lay may hands on them, please save my husband, please pray for my child, please heal my brother. We read them all, Rebecca and myself, we have done virtually nothing else for forty-eight hours. It is heartbreaking, and I am describing the kind letters, we have another pile, which are not nice. In these, I am a fraud, God will judge me, I will die for my sins, I am Satan. And I cannot help any of them; it does not work, when I want it to.

[You have only had one failure, so you must try again.]

How many times should I fail, before I give up? Would one in ten be a good return? How about one in a hundred, or a thousand?

[One in a million, would still be a triumph.]

You would not have to look into their eyes, and tell them that you cannot help.

[All that God, or anyone else can ask, is that you do what you can. And if it never happens again, no one can judge you. No one can say that Lucifer did not try.]

We are silent for a few seconds, and then I change the subject.

They have run out of my books you know, all over the country. Every single one has been sold. The publishers have advance orders for two hundred thousand copies. They cannot print them fast enough.

[I know.]

If all this had been a fraud, I could not have planned it any better.

[But you did not.]

I will give all my royalties to charity, and just keep enough to live on.

[That would be very generous.]

I will give some to genetic research; I have set them back ten years with my little stunt, after all. They are all trying to figure how something like this could happen. So am I.

[You must have patience. Only time will tell.]

Time my brother, is a limited resource here on Earth.

※

CHAPTER 7

In an apartment in Queens

"Mind if I have one of your beers man?" John Pollack asks, he moves into the kitchen and opens the refrigerator. The man sitting on the sofa, does not answer, he vacantly stares at the ceiling, because he does not see, nor does he hear anything. He is dead; John Pollack murdered him, no more that five minutes ago.

Pollack returns from the kitchen, and sits besides the dead man. "Thanks man," he says, as he pulls the tab on the can and takes a gulp of beer. The television shows a news report, about Mary Kirkland. It is the interview with her in the hospital, followed by David Brookes at home. Pollack watches as he sips his beverage. "Shit," he says, to the corpse, "Wonder if he could cure my asthma?" He turns to the dead man, "Don't think he could help you Mickey, Don't think any fucker could." He finds this amusing, and falls into fits of laughter. The laughter turns to fits of coughing, he takes an inhaler from his pocket and uses it.

The Songs of Angels

"Well," Pollack says, "I can't stay here chatting with you all day. No hard feelings man, but you can't have drugs from Freddy, and not pay for them." Pollack removes a combat knife from the dead mans neck, wipes the blood onto the ex addicts T-shirt, and conceals it inside his jacket. He lets himself out of the apartment and makes his way to the street below. He lobs the half empty beer can towards a litter bin, it misses but he ignores this. The can clatters into the street and rolls away.

Pollack is thirty-three years old. Michael Sebastian was his twenty-ninth homicide victim, but he would not care to remember that. It would not cross his mind to care about this small fact. It is normal now for him to kill people for money. He walks a block, and gets into the passenger side of a dark saloon.

"It is done?" the driver asks.

"No problem man, when have I ever let you down?" Pollack replies, "Where's my money?" The driver passes him an envelope, which Pollack rips open and begins to count.

"You don't trust me," the driver asks, "After all this time?"

"Course I do man," he replies, "Just making sure you ain't miscounted."

"It's all there," the driver says.

"Sure is," he answers, "Pleasure doing business with you." He lets himself out of the car, and walks away into the night. The driver makes a call on a cell phone, and then drives slowly away.

John Pollack's first victim was his stepfather. This was the only murder that he ever committed for no gain, and the only one he was ever caught for. At the age of fourteen, and after his stepfather had beaten his Mother, Pollack followed him from a bar and crushed his scull with a baseball bat. His lawyer eventually persuaded him to take a plea, so he served ten years in juvenile facilities and prison.

His mother died of an overdose, four years into his incarceration. When he was finally released, the only other people he knew were criminals. For a fee, he discovered that he quite enjoyed helping to beat and maim the occasional lowlife. Eight months after leaving prison, for five hundred dollars, he committed his second murder. Since then he has never looked back. His fees have steadily increased, as his reputation as a killer grew. At Thirty-three years of age, he makes a steady living, does a minimal of hours and has a job he enjoys.

Washington D.C.

The tobacco smoke drifts lazily through the light shining from the projector. It causes the image on the wall to waver slightly. Two men sit in the darkness, looking up at the projection. The only other light in the room is an illuminated sign, which instructs that no smoking is allowed. The slide on the wall shows a black and white photograph of David Brookes.

Smoking man flicks through a folder, which he balances on his lap. He turns to his companion, "Is this all we have on him?"

"Yes," the other man replies, "We only started taking notice of him, when he released his book. There is a short description on how he was kidnapped in Colombia. But at the time, he was just another dumb reporter, who was in the wrong place at the wrong time."

"You've read the book?" the first man says, as he stubs his cigar, "Do you think he's a communist?"

"The book is pretty strange in places, but at this time, we are not sure of his political motives." The slide changes to a picture of Rebecca, "That's his wife, Rebecca Brookes. We have nothing on her at all, not even a parking ticket."

"And this woman with the disease, have our people had a chance to look at her medical records?" He clips off another cigar and lights it.

The second man clicks a switch and the slide changes to a picture of Mary Kirkland. "They have looked, yes. But they do not believe any of it. The doctors assure us that the records are true. But our people say it is impossible. We are investigating if the records could have been fabricated."

"There's a lot we do not know," the first man blows a cloud of blue smoke into the air, "And you know I don't like that. I want to know all about this joker, when he shits, when he sleeps, who his friends are and what the fuck he's after. Put an agent on him full time from now on."

"Consider it done Sir."

May

[How many is that now?]

Fifteen, and no successes, I will be arrested for loitering around hospitals soon. I sneak around like a thief.

[We are missing something. Why could you cure Mary and no one since?]

That's the sixty four thousand dollar question. Do you think I haven't already gone through this in my mind?

[Go through how you felt again, when she touched you.]

I felt strange, I shook and my hair stood on end. Afterwards I felt drained.

[And your thoughts.]

It was all over in a second, I don't remember thinking anything except that she was going to fall. I shouted for someone to save her.

[No you did not, you called out 'hold her']

Did I?

[Yes.]

Do you think it is significant?

[Perhaps you thought 'Save her' and that is what you did.]

But that is what I am thinking now as I hold their hands, and the connection with Mary was already made before I said anything.

[Perhaps that's it, everyone you have tried to help, since Mary, has been unconscious or asleep. Perhaps the connection was made when you spoke with her.]

Oh super, so anyone I help, has to be conscious and will know what I have done. I don't need another human seeing visions of Heaven and calling the press.

[If Mary truly saw Heaven, then she extracted the thought from your mind. You gave her that information from your memory.]

Not intentionally.

[No, subconsciously. You could learn to suppress that information.]

How?

[Close that part of your mind.]

How?

[I do not know.]

Thanks, you're a great help. Ask God how he did it.

[Even if he told me, I would not be allowed to tell you. So I will not do that.]

Come on then, lets go and find some person who is awake. I will engage them in conversation, and then I will casually touch them while keeping my memories hidden and curing them of all sorts of ailments.

[You're being sarcastic.]

You're sharp today Michael.

I go back into the hospital, scanning the rooms as I walk by, looking for my prey, my lab rat. Eventually I stop at a door.

This is the one.

[Why?]

Why not?

I walk into the room, the patient looks up at me and I smile. "Hello," he says.

"Hi," I answer, "I wonder if you can help me? I work for the hospital radio station, and we are doing a survey on what the patients like to listen to."

"I don't listen to the radio. Hospital radio's are usually boring."

"That's why we are doing the survey," I say with a smile.

[He has a tumour on his liver. The hospital are treating it with chemotherapy.]

"I usually just read while I am here," he says. I notice he has an open book in his lap.

"What are you reading?" I ask

"It's called 'Heavens Gate', I've only just started it." He holds up a copy of my book, so that I can see the cover.

[His name is James. He is not responding to the treatment well.]

I know his name, it's written above his bed.

"Any good?" I ask

"Weird," he says.

"Well," I say, "I can see you are busy, so I will leave you to it." I tap him on his hand, but my hand does not come away. It is bonded to his. Then the shakes start, me, not him. He just stares at me unmoving.

Michael! It's happening.

There is no reply.

Michael!

Still there is no reply. My hand feels like it is super glued to his. Still he does not move, in fact he is too still, not even his eyes flicker. I look around the room, and the wall clock looms into view. The second hand has stopped, so I crane my head, over my hand and look at my wristwatch. It is frozen on ten seconds past the minute. Well, this is different, what do I do now?

Michael! Say something.

He is not there, what have I done? Frozen time? I spot a minuscule fly, suspended in the air, directly in front of me, so I move my head towards it. And I notice that it's wings are moving, but It must take about two minutes to travel from the apex of their stoke, to the termination. So what have I done, slowed time to a fraction of its normal running speed? What is the normal running speed of time? I am not sure if there is one, is time not relative to the observer. Perhaps I have changed my perception of time, and everything around me is still running normally, except that I am thinking at an inconceivably rapid speed.

A hum starts in my mind, and continues. What on Earth is that? And then I understand, it is Michael, he is talking to me. To my mind, his words are trapped, on the first letter of the sentence. How will this help me cure James? I look into his eyes, not sure what I expect to find. I ask, "Who are you James?" and his life floods into my mind, running backwards in a blur, in seconds he is a child, them an infant in his Mothers arms.

"Stop!" I scream, and it does stop, at the start of his life, when he was only a few cells in his Mothers womb. I am trapped in this vision, nothing is moving. The hospital no longer registers in my mind. But I know I am still there, I can feel my weight on my legs, which tremble so much, I think I may fall down.

Be calm, I instruct myself. Take a breath and relax, there must be a reason for all this. Michael told me I changed Mary Kirkland's DNA, is this how I did it, by going back to her conception and changing the very coding of her life? I find that I can zoom in on every individual cell, which grows before me. This amazing, microscopic package of chemical reactions is revealed to me. What I thought was frozen and immobile, is not entirely the case, things are happening in the cell even in this expanded time frame, the cell is active. A thousand unexplained reactions progress before my eyes, I cannot keep up with the scale of activity. This tiny living cell is more industrious, that the entire macroscopic chemical industry. How can I ever hope to understand any of it?

Maybe I do not need to understand every detail. Can I reach out and find out what is wrong? I try, but nothing flags up in my mind. Possibly the cause of his tumour, was not a genetic defect. Perhaps it came later in his life.

As soon as the thought crosses my consciousness, the cells in my vision, are initiated into a blur of motion. They grow into a foetus; I witness his birth and first steps, his first kiss and his first love. All this time I scan his structure, looking for defects, and finding none. His life progresses to his marriage and the births of his sons and daughter. It feels as if I have stood here for hours, witnessing his life, and still I find nothing.

And then I feel the change in him, and can see the creation of this cancer. "Stop," I instruct, "Go back." The vision back tracks, and I zoom in on the tumour, as it slowly shrinks down to the size of a single cell. "Stop," I say again. This one cell is the cause of his suffering. What can I do to it? It is one of his cells, with the same DNA, but it has somehow broken away from his control. It no longer acts in the interest of the whole being, it is only interested in it's own life, and it's own reproduction. Almost akin to a separate creature, which blindly uses a host like a parasite, never considering that the hosts death will also be its own.

Although the tumour has one advantage over an outside parasitic party, it is part of the host, made from the same flesh, and therefore the host's immune system does not recognize the threat. But what if it did? What happens if I mark some of these rogue cells, which grow before me, so that his immune system, recognizes and destroys them?

I look at my wristwatch again, the second hand is now half way between ten and eleven seconds, but to my mind, hours have passed.

I try to understand these few cells, to see their composition. I have to be careful, I have to mark that these are wrong, without setting his immune system against his whole body. I imagine a change in these cells that will be observed, and attacked.

[NNNNNNNNNNNNNNNNNNNNNNNNNNo one that the hospital…… What was that? Your whole body went out of focus for an

The Songs of Angels

instant.]

My hand leaves his, and I stagger back.

"Shit!" James shouts, as he jumps, "You gave me an electric shock, did you feel it?"

"Yes I did, I am sorry." I respond, and then ask, "Are you OK?"

"Yes, it's alright" he says, rubbing his hand, "Goodbye then."

"Goodbye," I say and start to drag my now exhausted body towards the door.

How long have we been here?

[It happened didn't it?]

How long?

[A few minutes, what did you do?]

I need to sit down; I 'm too tired to explain yet.

I collapse onto a chair in the corridor and close my eyes.

[He still has the tumour]

Yes I know, but not for much longer.

In Heaven.

Raphael:
So he has done it again, but the outcome could have been very different. He used this human as an experimental laboratory rat, what if he had killed him Lord, answer me that.

God:
Humans die all of the time, it would not have changed anything.

Raphael looks away.

God:
And he knew what he did Michael?

Michael:
He thinks he knows. Lucifer's explanation was, that he experienced a heightened reality, where he could see the entire life of the subject. See into his very body and modify the construction of cells. Although, quite how he did this, is still a mystery to him. Is this how you did it Lord?

God:

The question is immaterial to this discussion. It does not matter what I did. Do you think he can control it now?
Michael:
To a degree Lord, yes I think he will.
God:
And the subject has no idea it was Lucifer?
Michael:
As far as I can tell. He is making a full recovery, and did not even know who was in the room with him.
God:
That is good, but do not encourage him any further. It is his choice what he does now.
Michael:
I was following your instructions Lord.
God:
Yes I know. I am not reprimanding you Michael. We needed him to experience the act again, so that he would understand it more. But now that he has, he can find his own way.
Michael:
Yes Lord.
God:
Is there anything else?
Michael:
Yes Lord, two things I would like to discuss.
God:
Continue.
Michael:
Mary Kirkland, she has done countless interviews and articles. Each one is more descript, and more exaggerated than the last. I am worried where this will lead. I thinks she is trying to elevate him to the status of a god.
God:
What do you think I should do about it?
Michael:
I do not know Lord.
God:
There is nothing to be done. People will believe her, or not. Your second

concern?
Michael:
Lucifer is being followed. The FBI have taken an interest in him. I do not know what their objectives are, but someone is always observing him. I am concerned that they will see things that they should not see. I want your permission to tell him.
God:
Why do you think he should be aware of this?
Michael:
As I have stated.
God:
Denied, he finds out for himself, or he does not. Anything else?
Michael:
No Lord.

Washington D.C.

There is a blue pin board in the corner of the room, which is dedicated to David Brookes. There are pictures of him: a recent snap, of his shoulders and head as he leaves his house, One taken at his graduation day, a scan of a newspaper photograph, showing a child sitting in a shallow moat, staring into the face of an enormous bear. Surrounding these are shots of Mary Kirkland, Rebecca Brookes, Sean Peters and Carrie Brookes.

Agent Adam Whiteside stands up and approaches the board. Next to the picture of Mary Kirkland, he pins another, this one shows a middle-aged man. He writes underneath it, 'James Bathgate-54- Recovered suddenly from a tumour'

His phone rings, and he returns to his desk to answer it, "Hello." There is a pause, while he listens then he says, "Yes Sir, I will be here Sir." He replaces the receiver, sits down and starts writing in a file. A few seconds later the door opens. The man who enters carries the scent of stale cigar smoke. He sits opposite Agent Whiteside and takes a cigar from his top pocket.

"This is a no smoking building Sir," Agent Whiteside informs his superior.

"Yea, thanks. I already know that." He says, as he lights up. He slaps a thin manila foolscap file on the desk, and asks, "What the fuck are you trying to get me to believe Whiteside?"

"Sir?"

"This report, what am I supposed to make of it?"

"Whatever you wish, you requested that we tail this man. You requested a weekly report. You have that in front of you. The facts inside are what we observed," Agent Whiteside pauses, then adds, "Sir."

"So, all the creep does, is sit at home. Occasionally he goes to hospitals and visits people he does not know."

"He went to three hospitals in Manhattan, and one in Brooklyn. In Manhattan he visited two patients in the first, four in the second and one in the third. All were comatose. He stands by them for a few seconds each, and then he leaves. In Brooklyn he visited only one person, who he spoke briefly to. It is all in the report Sir."

"James Bathgate, fifty-four years old, dying of cancer, but he walks out of hospital three days later, in remission, full of the joys of spring."

"Yes Sir," Agent Whiteside replies.

"Don't you find this a bit odd Whiteside?"

"Yes Sir, is that not why he is under investigation?"

"What I do not understand is this, why would Brookes set up another Mary Kirkland fucking miracle, without any publicity? I could understand the first one; with the sales of his book, the guy will be a millionaire in a few months. But your report says that this Bathgate fellow, did not even know that it was David Brookes visiting him!"

"That's what he said."

"Agent Whiteside, you know how I hate it, when I don't know all the facts. You will find out what the fuck is going on here. I smell a scam, and I want to know what it is." He stands up and offers his cigar nub to the agent. "Get rid if this for me Whiteside."

"Yes Sir," Agent Whiteside replies, taking the half smoked cigar from his senior, who makes his way from the office, slamming the door behind him. Agent Whiteside opens the window, and tosses the butt to the streets below. He sits back down at his desk and opens the left hand drawer. "You're an Asshole Brent," he mutters to himself, under his breath. From the drawer, he takes a copy of 'Heavens Gate', flicks through the pages until he find the one that has it's corner folded down, and continues to read.

᎒

June.

It's not free. Each one takes something from me.

[I know, I have seen you afterwards, you are always washed out.]

I do not mean, the lack of energy and tiredness, it takes more than that. On the last one, I thought that I was not going to finish it. I assumed that it would get easier, but it does not. It seems to be getting harder.

[But you think you have mastered the process?]

Yes, I think so. Although I still do not understand it entirely.

[You deserve a break anyway, what is your score now?]

Eight, including Mary Kirkland. I think you are right, I should stop for a while, and regain my strength.

I received a royalty cheque from my publishers this morning. Six hundred and forty thousand dollars, and he tells me that predicted sales, for this month are set to double.

[That is good news. I know that your first objective, when you wrote the book, was not money, but you should not feel guilty about it. Fine, if you want to, give a chunk to charity. But make sure you leave yourself enough to function. Money is power in this world, it allows you the luxury of choice, to follow your own path.]

I suppose so.

I get up and walk to the window, scanning the road for no particular reason, and notice something strange.

There he is again!

[Who?]

About fifty yards down the street, that man in the blue car, just sitting there.

[I see him.]

This is the third time in a week that I have noticed him. Do you think he is a reporter?

[I do not know.]

Well, I am going to find out.

I pull on my shoes and go out of the front door. As I approach him, he looks directly at me and I see his lips move. He is talking to someone, although he is alone in his car. The car engine fires up as I draw level with the passenger door. "Excuse me," I say, leaning down and knocking on the side window. He gives me a sideways glance, and without responding, slowly pulls away. "Hey!" I shout, as I watch the back of the car disappearing down the road. Shit, I should have taken his number plate.

What do you think all that was about?

[I have no idea.]

※

Washington D.C.

Agent Adam Whiteside pins another picture to his board. There are now eight pictures along the left hand side, below each one is a brief description, these read:

'Mary Kirkland-41- Amyotrophic Lateral Sclerosis cured?'
'James Bathgate-54- Recovered suddenly from a tumour'
'Paul Barry-7- Leukaemia in recession'
'Janet Hall-26- Awoke from trauma induced coma after nine months'
'Henry Castillo-67- Brain tumour disappeared overnight'
'Martin Hutchingson-29- AIDS virus no longer detectable'
'Helen Goldberg-33- Heart defect repaired itself'

He pulls a marker from his shirt pocket, and writes underneath the last photograph:

'Daniel Bolton-16- Sickle cell anaemia cured?'

Agent Whiteside stand and studies his board for a minute, then sits down at his desk. He opens a file, inside are photocopies of Daniel Bolton's medical records. He rests his chin on his hand and tries to decipher the medical jargon. The ringing of the telephone breaks his concentration. He picks it up, brings it to his ear and says, "Whiteside."

His brow creases as he listens, then he shakes his head and snarls, "Fucking amateurs!" he listens for a further few second, then tells the person on the line. "No, if he's been compromised, take him off the job and find me someone who can actually do surveillance."

He hangs up and returns to his file, after a while he rubs his eyes and then stretches. Agent Whiteside looks to his pin board, and addresses the photograph of David Brookes, "Who are you David Brookes, who are you?"

※

I am getting paranoid, two or three times this week, I have sensed people who I thought were watching me. I just catch them in the corner of my eye, and I know that they observe me. But as soon as I take notice of them, they disappear into the background. Michael just says that he does not know who they are. He has not offered to find out, so I have not asked him to. Perhaps it is nothing, just my imagination. Then again, maybe Michael does know whom they are, and is not permitted to tell me. That would be the normal form for Heaven.

I feel that I am becoming a self-sentenced prisoner in my own home. I have hardly left the house for days, except when Rebecca is at work, for my trips to the hospitals. And when I do go out, I sneak around so reporters cannot trail me. It has to stop, balls to them. Let them follow me around if they wish.

I put on a light jacket and walk out of the front door, breathing in the air, and set off on foot. I hear a car door gently close behind me, but ignore it. At a brisk pace, I head for Central Park, it is a nice day for a walk, even if there is still a chill in the air.

[Where are we going?]

For a walk in the park.

At the street junction, before crossing, I look back at the way I came. A man strolls casually in my direction. I do not think I have ever seen him before. I cross the street and turn left, still walking at a good pace. At the top of the road, I pretend that I am looking in a shop window. Actually I have a good reflection of the pavement behind me, and check to see if he is still there, he is. As he gets closer, he looks straight at my reflection, then turns his head away and crosses the road. Now he is in front of me, so I continue walking, while watching him on the other side of the road and ensuring I do not catch him up. He does not slow or turn around.

Two minutes further on, he hails a cab going in the other direction, briefly talks to the driver, and gets in the back. I watch him sitting in the back, as the cab cruises by. He does not even look up. I feel a little stupid now as I watch the taxi drive away, I am paranoid.

Fifteen minutes earlier.

"What are we doing here?" Agent Joe Hasselbank asks. He sits in the back of a plain box van, his eyes fixed on a monitor. The screen is linked to a closed circuit camera, which sits innocently on the dashboard, and shows the front of David Brookes house.

"Surveillance," his partner, Cody Davenport says.

"Who is this guy, anyway?" Hasselbank enquires.

"A writer."

"Shit," Hasselbank says, looking up "Is that illegal as well now?"

"If the boss wants him watched, we watch," Davenport's eyes flick to the screen. "Hello," he says, "We have movement, looks like he's going out." They watch David Brookes walk down his path and start up the street.

"Your turn to be the tail," Hasselbank says.

"No way," Davenport replies, "You're the new guy, get your ass out of this van, before we lose him." He puts on some headphones, "Check your radio."

"Shit-head," Hasselbank says.

"Working perfectly," he replies, "See you later." He clicks a button on the console, "Stand by," he says into the radio.

Agent Hasselbank steps out of the side door of the van, and quietly closes the door. He trots a few steps along the street, until he is the correct distance away from the target, and then begins to walk. Brookes stops at the top of the street and looks back, checking for traffic. He then crosses over. "He's going left," Hasselbank says into a concealed microphone, his lips hardly moving. The trick to successfully tailing someone, Hasselbank thinks to himself, is not to take any notice of the target, without appearing not to take any notice. "He has stopped," he reports, "Shit, he has spotted me, I am sure."

"What!" The speaker hidden inside his ear shouts, "What did you do?"

"Fuck all, but he looked straight at me. I have had to go in front of him. Fucker's following me now."

"Get out of there," Davenport instructs through the earpiece. "Jill, take over."

"In position," a woman's voice replies. Agent Jill Taylor is dropped off behind the target, she throws a scarf around her neck, and begins to walk, as Agent Hasselbank goes by in the taxi. "Target definitely spotted Hasselbank," she says, "He watched him go by in the cab."

"Keep your distance," Davenport says.

"Understood."

Brookes continues walking and she casually follows.

Back at the van where Agent Davenport sits, another car pulls up behind. A man steps from the car, he is dressed in overalls and around his waist he wears a tool belt. He opens the van door and gets inside. "Do we go?" he asks.

"Yes," Davenport replies, without looking around, "Keep your frequency open, just in case he should return quickly." The man leaves, and signals another agent from the car. They both head for David Brookes home, bypassing the front door and heading for the back.

"Target is entering Central Park," Taylor says through Davenport's earphones.

※

Well, here we are.

[Yes.]

What shall we do now?

[You could visit the Charles A. Dana Discovery centre, the Conservatory Garden, maybe Belverdere Castle? Or you could sit in the sun. It is up to you Lucifer.]

I think I will sit here for a while.

I sit down on a bench, watching people walking their dogs, skateboarders whizzing by and joggers trundling past.

Michael, that man who I thought was following me, why would he walk all along the street, then get in a cab and go back the way he came?

[Perhaps the cab turned around, or maybe he forgot something.]

It's a possibility. Do you think I am seeing things?

[No.]

So you agree that people are observing me.

[It's a possibility.]

Yet you do not offer to find out whom they are, do you?

[No I do not, you have not asked me.]

And if I do ask you, will you find out?

[It will not be permitted.]

How can you be so sure, unless you have already asked? That's it isn't it. Shit, you know who they are and you are not allowed to tell me.

[I cannot confirm that.]

It's a fact.

[I cannot continue this conversation.]

Fine.

[Sorry.]

Don't be, I know it is not your desire to keep information from me. It's all part of the fucking game that God and I play. I am indifferent to his bullshit now, and I will find out myself. These people are not reporters, that's one thing I am certain about. Reporters don't act like this.

"I know you!" someone shouts, to my left, I turn my head to see who, "I know you!" he repeats, pointing his finger at me as he gets closer. The individual stops and stares at me, he wears dirty and soiled clothes and has an unkempt mass of hair.

I stand and reply, "Then you have me at a disadvantage, because I do not know you."

"No you don't," he says, grinning and showing his yellow teeth, "But I know you."

[He is drunk, just walk away.]

"I see you!" he cries, "Why do you come here!" He starts to laugh, "Do you think you can save us? Ha!" I start to walk towards him, and he backs away. "Don't touch me!" he spits out. People are stopping to see what is taking place.

"Can I help you?" I ask.

The Songs of Angels

"I am beyond your help, unless you have some whisky," he says.

"That's that writer," one of the spectators says, "David Brookes. I saw him on TV."

"That's what he calls himself," the drunk says to her, "But it is not his name. I know you, I know your name." A shiver runs through down my spine, it is impossible, that he could know anything about me.

"What do you think my name is?" I ask.

"No, no, no," he says, shaking his head, "I will not say it, I will not. She knows!" he cries, pointing to a woman at the back of the crowd. I turn to look at her, she is in her thirties, and wears a red scarf around her neck.

"I'm just taking a walk," she says, looking away.

"Ha," the drunk shouts, and then rushes to my side, "Don't touch me!" he says again.

I hold my hands up, "I wont," I reply.

He whispers, "She knows you, be careful preacher man. Be very careful. They will try to stop you, they will betray you."

"Who will?" I ask.

"All of them, all of them at the end." His lip wobbles, "You would not hurt me, would you?"

"No, of course not."

A youth in the crowd shouts, "Smack the dumb fucker in the mouth!" I turn and stare at him; he averts his gaze and shuts up. When I turn back, the bum has walked away. I let him go and start heading back for home. I look up and down the path, but there is no sign of the woman with the red scarf.

※

"Did you hear all that?" Agent Taylor asks.

"All on tape, though the end is a bit fuzzy," Davenport says. "Any idea what it was about?"

"No," she replies. "He's on his way back I think."

"That's OK, we are finished this end."

"Are you going to pick up the drunk?" Agent Taylor asks.

"Already done."

※

Washington D.C.
24 hours later.

"He's on to us, he knows that someone is watching him," Agent Whiteside says, to the assembled team.

"Do you think he is surveillance trained?" The man at the head of the table asks.

"Improbable Sir," Whiteside replies, "We have now compiled a detailed history, of David Brookes life. There is no suggestion that he ever worked for any government agency."

"But he keeps detecting your agents."

"Yes Sir."

Another man, sitting to Whiteside's right, speaks, "Your report is extraordinary Agent Whiteside, all these people recovered, some time after a visit from Brookes. Do you have any idea how?"

"No Sir," Whiteside admits. "Nor do the various hospitals, where they were receiving treatment."

"Could he be secretly administering drugs to them?" he asks. The woman opposite him snorts, "You wish to make a comment Dr. Catcher?"

"Well, yes I do," she replies, "Are you suggesting that this Brookes fellow, has a cure for AIDS and cancer? But he does not tell the World, he just secretly treats a few people? Do you have any idea what a drug like that would be worth?"

"I can imagine," he replies.

"And there are no drugs that can cure Amyotrophic Lateral Sclerosis, or Sickle cell anaemia." She adds.

"That we know of." Whiteside says.

Dr. Catcher looks at him, "That the best medical minds on Earth know of."

"OK," the man at the head of the table says, "On to the incident yesterday in Central Park. You have all read the transcript of the conversation that took place. Have we had any luck, with the end of it?"

"No," Whiteside says, "The bum was whispering, and our agent was too far away. The only word that we can pick out is 'Preacher'. The bum called him preacher."

"Didn't that woman call him preacher, in the interview with Channel

Three?" the Doctor asks.

"Yes," Whiteside confirms, "Mary Kirkland also called him that."

"He could have seen the interview on television," the man on the right offers.

"With respect, it is unlikely Sir," Whiteside says, "The bum lives in a cardboard box, I don't think he owns a TV."

"What did he have to say, when you picked him up?" The top man asks.

"I have it here sir," Agent Whiteside picks up a compact disc, "You can listen to it now."

"Please."

"I'm afraid Andrew, that's the bums name, is not entirely lucid." He takes the compact disc from its case, and inserts it into a recorder-player built into the table. It begins to play:

> 'Why am I here?'
> 'You're not in trouble Andrew, we just want to ask you a few questions. Is that OK?"
> 'Yes.'
> 'The man you spoke to in the park, do you know who he is?'
> 'Yes.'
> 'Can you tell me?'
> 'No.'
> 'Why not?'
> *Silence*
> 'Have you met him before?'
> 'No. Can I have a drink?'
> 'Yes, what would you like?'
> 'Whisky.'
> 'We don't allow alcohol in this building Andrew, but if you answer our questions, we can get you something. Deal?'
> *Silence*
> 'Maybe a whole bottle.'
> 'No, no, no. You try to tempt me, but you do not believe.'
> 'Believe what?'
> 'Do you promise?'

'Promise what?'
'A whole bottle you said.'
'If you answer my questions.'
'OK.'
'The mans name is David Brookes, did you know that before you spoke to him?'
'Someone called him that.'
'But you think he has another name?'
'Yes."
"Can you tell me?'
Silence
"Why did you speak to him in the park, if you have never met him? Why did you say those things Andrew?"
'I heard him speaking to someone.'
'Who?'
'I could not see it, I only heard them talking'
'On a telephone?'
'You cannot speak with an angel on the telephone.'
'You heard him talking to an Angel?'
'Sort of.'
'Can you explain?'
'No.'
'Why did you call him preacher, he isn't a preacher.'
'I got scared. I am a bad person and I did not want him to hurt me.'
'Why would he hurt you?'
'He can.'
'How Andrew?'
'He is powerful.'
'In what way?'
'Can I have my whiskey now?'
'Soon. When you tell me who he is.'
'I cannot, you do not believe.'
'Then I cannot get you any whisky.'
'But you promised.'
'If you tell me his name.'

'He is a messenger, he has a message for the dead.'
'Do you mean, from the dead?'
'No, for the dead. For when you're dead. I don't want to die.'
'Have you read his book Andrew?'
'What book?'
'He wrote a book.'
'I'm no good at words. I want a drink.'
'We had a deal Andrew.'
'I don't really know who he is, but I know what he is.'
'And what is that?'
'Do I get my drink?'
'Yes.'
'He's an Angel as well.'
'What do you mean?'
'I ain't saying anything else, get me my drink.'
'What do you mean Andrew?'
Silence.
'What do you mean Andrew?'
Silence.

Agent Whiteside turns off the player, and looks around the table.

"That would explain a lot," Dr. Catcher says, with a nervous laugh. No one else finds this funny.

"Any suggestions, on where we go from here?" The man at the head of the table asks. No one answers, "Well the facts are, David Brookes hasn't broken any laws. I agree this is all very strange, but does that give us the right to spy on him and bug his house?"

He looks straight at the last person at the table, who has not yet spoken. The man has an unlit cigar clamped between his teeth. The man speaks, "Sir," he says, "This Brookes fellow is up to something. I request that we keep investigating."

"Do you realize how all much this surveillance costs?" he looks at the faces around the table, "Very well, you have one more week to turn something up. Thank you Gentlemen, and Ladies" he adds, acknowledging The Doctor.

Portland, Maine

"I'm trying to contact David Brookes," Mary Kirkland says into the telephone. "Listen, can you please get a message to him? Tell him Mary Kirkland needs to talk to him, can you do that?" She waits for an answer, and then gives her telephone number, "Thank you, and tell him it may be important." She hangs up.

"You didn't reach him," her son Paul asks, as he enters the room.

"No," Mary replies, "I have left a message, for him to call me."

"Who do you think they were?" he asks.

"They weren't reporters, something is going on."

"Well, you have done what you can," he replies, "I would love to meet this man, who you talk about all the time."

"Perhaps you will, if I can persuade him to speak about his book at the convention," Mary says, "Have you read it yet?"

"No," he says, "You know what I'm like with books."

"Please read it Paul, for me."

"I will Ma," he says, "I'm off out, see you later."

"Be careful," Mary shouts after him.

"I'm twenty one!" he calls back as he leaves.

The home of Agent Marcus Brent.

In almost total darkness, Marcus Brent sits and stares out at nothing in particular; he holds a glass of bourbon in one hand. With the other, he brings a light to another of his obligatory cigars. He is alone now in this big house, which he built for her. As soon as his children finally fled the nest, his wife followed. She said that she had only stopped with him, for the sake of the children. And that he loved his job more than her. That was all six years ago. She was probably right. Marcus does love his job; he has had to up to now, because it was all he had.

That was true until last month, and then everything changed. Something

The Songs of Angels

amazing happened. Now he has a goal in life, a quest.

-So how did it go?-

Marcus Jumps, and spills a drop of bourbon, "Lord," he says, "I only have a week to find something, then they will close the investigation."

-You do not have to speak out loud, I have told you before. Just think what you want me to hear.-

Sorry Lord, I don't think I will be able to convince them to continue.

-It is of no concern, you will help me Marcus, that is why I chose you.-

Yes Lord.

-Because we have to stop him, is that not true?-

It is true Lord.

-He will destroy everything.-

We will not allow that Lord!

-Because we know who he is.-

He is the Devil Lord.

-Yes Marcus, he is the Devil, and we must stop him.-

ॐ

Portland, Maine.
The next day.

The phone is ringing as Mary walks in, she drops her bags on a chair, and picks up the receiver, "Hello," she says.

"Mary, It's David Brookes. I'm sorry I never called you yesterday, but I only got the message this morning. Are you alright?"

"Yes, yes," she says, "I'm fine. Look this may be nothing, but two gentlemen visited me at the weekend. They said they were reporters, but I don't think they were. They asked a lot of questions about you, and to be frank, they put me on edge a little."

"They did not hurt you did they?"

"No nothing like that, but the questions were more the sort of thing a policeman, or a private investigator, would ask."

"This may sound odd," David says, "But have you noticed anyone following you?"

"Should I have?" she says, with shock in her voice.

"Probably not. Sorry, I did not mean to frighten you. The fact is, that some agency has me under surveillance. So I shouldn't be surprised, that they would want to talk to you."

"Who?" Mary asks.

"I do not know, but don't worry yourself about it."

"As long as you're OK."

"No problem, thanks for letting me know," he says.

"One more thing," Mary asks, "Would you be interested in being a guest speaker, at a convention here in Maine. I have been pushing your book for weeks, and there is a lot of interest."

"Let me think about it Mary, I've got your number and I will let you know" he replies. "Goodbye for now."

"Goodbye David," she says, and replaces the receiver.

❧

"You should do it," Rebecca says, "We both could do with a change, and a trip to Maine sounds like a good idea to me."

"You want to come with me?" I ask.

"Yes, of course I do, I am owed a couple of days off work."

"You don't need to be working anymore," I say, "With the money coming in from the book, you can stop anytime you wish."

"I still enjoy my job, I don't want to quit yet," she replies.

"But if you want to, you can."

"How much are you worth now?" She asks.

"You have not looked?"

"No," she says.

"We have over one million dollars in the bank," I tell her.

"Jesus," Rebecca replies.

"If it is OK with you, I want to donate a substantial amount to charities," I say.

"That's very noble of you, but you do not need my permission. It's your money."

"It's our money," I say.

"So, are we going to Maine?" She asks.

"Yes, I will phone Mary and find out exactly what she wants me to do."

One Week later.
Washington D.C.

Agent Adam Whiteside returns to his office, he sits at his desk and swivels his chair to look out of the window. He has just returned from the last meeting about David Brookes. In the meeting, his superiors informed the team, that the investigation was over. There was no evidence that Brookes was breaking the law, in any form. And although it was noted that there were many unanswered questions surrounding Brookes, the surveillance was to stop. Agent Whiteside stands up and walks to his pin board, he methodically starts to take down the pictures, printouts and notes, and packs them into a box. Then he adds all his own related information, but stops short of putting the book inside. He looks at the cover for a second, and then puts it in his jacket pocket, Finally he seals the box, and places an adhesive label on the side. The label has a case number and the word 'ARCHIVE' printed on it.

Although he never saw David Brookes in the flesh, over the course of the investigation, he feels that he has come to like the man. He promises himself, that he will read the book one more time.

In the meeting, he watched his immediate superior Marcus Brent. All through it, Brent's face became steadily sterner and he never uttered a word. Whiteside has noticed a change in his boss, over the last few weeks. The man has progressively become transfixed by this case, as if nothing else was important. Not that it matters anymore, because his transfer came through. In one weeks time, Adam Whiteside will be working at the Whitehouse.

He returns to his computer, and types out an order for the team working on the Brookes investigation. All agents are to cease surveillance, all listening devices are to be removed from the house, as soon as feasibly possible. With the click of a button, the order is sent into the heart of the FBI mainframe. He picks up the box and walks to the elevator. Five minutes later and he hands it over to be filed, along with thousands of other boxes, in the basement of the building.

※

"Fucking assholes," Marcus Brent mutters to himself, "They don't know shit." He slams his file down on his desk. He will have to be careful now, although he has no intention of leaving David Brookes alone, he will have to use outsiders to gather evidence against Brookes. There are enough lowlifes out there, who owe Marcus Brent, all favours are due, and will be called in.

-So they called off the investigation.-

Yes.

-But we will not give up, will we Marcus.-

No Lord.

-You do not sound convinced Marcus? Is something troubling you?-

It's just that he has not really done anything bad.

-What about that book, you have read it.-

Yes Lord I did, and it is blasphemous, how can he say those things about you Lord? But the people he has saved, how can that be wrong?

-Yes he did save them, but it is an act, a sham. They say that the Devil is a charming man Marcus, and this is the truth. He will play the part of the righteous man, until he can make a play for power. And then you will see who he really is. And at that time Marcus, he will find that we are prepared for him. And we will send him back to Hell where he belongs. You believe this Marcus, do you not?-

I believe you my Lord. I truly believe you.

-You are my champion Marcus, I chose you well.-

※

CHAPTER 8

Year thirty-six: July 16th
Portland, Maine.

"And now David Brookes will take the stand and answer any questions you may have," The chairman of the book review hands me a microphone, "Mr. Brookes," he says.

Most of the audience gives me respectful applause; I notice that many do not. We are in a marquee, on a field in Portland. There are perhaps eighty chairs set out, but it appears that the organizers have misjudged the attendance, at least the same amount of people are standing around the sides.

"Good Afternoon," I say into the microphone. No one seems to want to ask the first question, and the audience and I, stare at each other for a few seconds, "Don't all rush," I say, to which a few people nervously laugh. Then a woman on the front row raises her hand. "Yes," I say, pointing to her.

"Mr. Brookes," She says, "I'm a close friend of Mary, she tells everyone that you miraculously cured her sickness. My question is, do you make that claim, or do you think Mary is as crazy as we all do?"

The crowd laughs, I smile and say, "I could not make that claim, whatever the reason for Mary's recovery, we should all just be grateful that she is still with us. I like to think that Mary cured herself."

"After reading your book?" she asks.

"That would be nice, yes. But aren't we are supposed to be talking about my book?" A few more hands are raised. I point to another woman in about the fourth row.

"Mr. Brookes," she says.

"Wait!" I say, "Could you all please call me David."

"David," she says self consciously, looking to her left and right, "In your book, you said that we should not believe in God."

I cut her off and say, "No! I did not ever say that, the words I wrote were these. Believing in God will not grant you a place in Heaven. You can believe or not believe. It does not matter to God. What you must believe in, is yourself. What you must be, is content with your own life, and sure that you lead the best life that you can. That does not mean that you have to win the Nobel peace prize, just that you can stand up at the end of your life, and say. I tried to be the best person I could. And if your religion helps you do this, then by all means believe."

A man stands up, and I await his comment. He begins, "You tell us God does not care, I am a God fearing man Mr. Brookes. I find that offensive."

"What is it about God, that you fear?"

"I'm sorry?" he says.

"You said that you feared God." I reply.

"It's just an expression."

"Is it?" I ask. "But it must have some roots. Why would people say that they fear God? Do you think he will strike you down if you are not afraid of him? Why does God not strike down murderers and child molesters, they obviously do not fear the wrath of God. Let me answer that question for you. God is not interested in individuals. God does not care if you go to Heaven, and he does not care if you go to Hell."

A woman stands up, "These are just your opinions, why should we believe you?"

"You do not have to," I reply, "What is true in your heart is true. Make your own mind up."

"But you trip up your own argument," another man says, "If you believe something without question, aren't you exactly the same as all the other beliefs?"

"Yes," I reply, "You are speaking about dogma. The absolute belief that you are correct. Unfortunately people are good at declaring absolute truths. The world is flat and held up by four turtles, well of course the earth is flat, look out your window, and there must be something holding it up, or it would fall down. The sun revolves around the earth because it does. It comes up over there and moves across the sky in an arc, and then it disappears over there. We're not sure where it goes at night, but if you pray to God, it will come back in the morning.

The point I'm trying to make is that none of this was made up for a laugh, all these writers, were using the information they had at hand, and trying to make sense of what they saw. I can only poke fun at this now because I think I know better. However I cannot say whether the things I think I know, are correct. In fact we must always assume that we will never have all the information available. Hopefully in a thousand years time, someone will hear this, rip it to bits and inject another view of the absolute truth.. But my point is, never close your mind, always be ready to adjust your point of view, when information is available that may change your belief. It can only ever be the truth, as far as you, or I, know."

The same man replies, "But still you think yourself correct."

"With the information I possess, these are my views. Einstein imagined the theory of relativity, without proof, but it was true from the beginning. You all know what is true, what is correct. A jury imagines what has taken place, and then uses it's judgment to come to a conclusion. And the judgment is based on what they feel is correct. I ask you to do the same. Forget what you have learnt, and grasp what you know."

"Weren't the Nazi's following a path, dictated by what they believed to be the truth?" he asks.

"There is always a danger, that individuals will twist what you say, for their own ends. This has happened with every piece of literature ever penned. But overall, the truth will always prevail. It is imagination that drives us, and mans imagination has elevated us from the trees to the present day, and will continue to move us. It has built and crushed empires and religions, races and species. We can visualize and build a wheel, or take a man to the moon and eventually the stars. We learn from our mistakes and from our predecessors. The person who designed the Saturn rocket applied the same skills as the man who used a stick instead of his hand, to dig out furrows for his seeds, the man who added the blade, the man who attached his plough to a horse or oxen, the man who added and engine. All did the same thing, they saw something and added their ideas. We may think of ourselves as civilized, but put a twenty first century man in a situation, in which he has never seen a wheel and he is unlikely to invent a motorcar. The reason we 'know so much' is because it is passed down to us. The sum of all known human knowledge is there for us at birth to build on. Unfortunately this fact also holds us back. We are fed all this information as we grow. We are told this is the truth because this is the sum of all understanding at this time.

But never be frightened to question the truth, and never be afraid to refine your view. When you stagnate then your beliefs are dogma, and any view that contradicts yours, can envision misplaced justification for your actions. Ask the Nazis if they were justified to murder Jews, Ask the Israelis if they are justified to murder Palestinians."

A murmur goes around the crowd, and I wait for the next speaker, scanning the multitude for a response.

"David," a woman stands, and asks, "I think that most of the people here, have read your book. The problem I have, is this: You did not write your book, saying that 'this is my view', you wrote it as though it was a fact."

How do I answer this without revealing myself? "I believe that which I wrote to be true."

"But," She says, "You do not know, you have no proof."

"No," I respond, "It is the sum of my knowledge, and I am open to suggestions that may refine this view." A few people chuckle. "Look," I say, "The book is about living with yourself, I do not wish, or aspire, to knock your God or your religion. I want you to understand that your life is paramount. You are more important than your beliefs, or than your God."

There is total silence for a few seconds, and then one man stands and asks, "Will you tell God this, when you finally stand before him? Or will you beg for his forgiveness?"

"I will tell him," I reply, "He already knows my views."

"And if there is no God, or Heaven?" someone calls out.

"Then it does not matter what I write or say," I reply, "And it does not matter what you do, or omit to do. Because when you die, you will cease to be. Do you believe there is no God?" I ask him.

"I see no proof that God exists," he answers, "I cannot believe in something that has no evidence of existence. Why, if God exists, does he not show himself?"

"Do you believe that Pluto exists? I mean the planet, not the Walt Disney character."

He smiles, and says, "Yes."

"Been there?" I ask.

"No," he replies, "But I could find evidence that Pluto exists. I could bring you a photograph."

"And I could bring you evidence that God exists, I could bring you a bible."

"It's not quite the same." He says, "A photograph is solid evidence, the bible is a story book." The crowd mumbles at this statement.

I hold my hand up, "Everyone here is entitled to his or her own opinions," I say. "But I bet you that every picture that you found, and held up as evidence would be an artists impression or a computer model. Even the best telescopes, only see a blob of light when they are trained on Pluto."

"So you doubt that Pluto is actually there?" he asks.

"On the contrary, I am positive that Pluto is there. But before 1930, when Clyde Tombaugh finally found it, I could not have proved it. That did not mean that Pluto did not exist before 1930. The Planet has been there since the birth of the solar system, and if the human race had failed to detect it, then it would still be out there. You cannot disprove God, by saying there is no evidence. You can only say that you have failed to find God."

He shakes his head, "But if you search and find nothing, it usually means, there is nothing to find."

"Or," I say, "That which you search for is difficult to find, or in my view concerning God, that he chooses not to present any evidence. Because, as my book points out, God is indifferent to your search. He does not need you to find him."

I point to another person holding up his hand, he says, "I have found God, I know God exists. I don't need to see proof of his existence. God is in my heart and mind."

"I hope this makes you a better person than you were. I'm glad that you need no evidence of his existence, because you will never find it on Earth. But if you think that will grant you a place in Heaven, then I think you are wrong. It is not enough to believe in God, you must truly believe in your own self."

A voice from behind me asks, "What if you find God through the actions of another."

I turn to Mary, and ask her, "What do you mean?"

"I have found him through you David, your actions convinced me that there is a God. And it saddens me to hear you say, that God does not care about us."

"It would be wonderful if he did, but believing that he does, will only lead to disappointment. If you have to believe, then you have to see that God will never be there for you. Your life is what you make it, through your own actions. If parts of the bible are true, and God once took an active interest in human affairs, then he has changed his game plan. There is no such thing anymore, as divine intervention from God."

The chairman walks over and I hand back the mike. He says, "I am sure you would all like to join me, in thanking David Brookes for coming here and sharing his views with us." The applause is more enthusiastic than when we started. He continues, "Unfortunately we have overrun our time slot for now. But David Brookes will be giving his time up again this evening, when hopefully we will find a few more chairs, and you will have another chance to put your questions to him."

I thank him, and shake his hand. He starts to introduce another author, as I spot Rebecca, and make for the exit. Mary sadly smiles in my direction as I pass. We leave the venue and start back for the hotel for a couple of hours.

"How did that go?" I ask her, as we get to the car.

"You don't know?" she replies.

"I want your opinion," I say.

"When you consider that a lot of the people there didn't agree with what you say, no one really tried to put you down. No one shouted scripture at you or called you the antichrist."

"You expected that?" I ask.

"Perhaps," Rebecca says, "I was watching them watching you. When you are in front of a crowd, you change. You demand attention, and somehow you get it."

"Is that bad?" I ask.

"It depends on what you tell them. Do you ever think, that what you say and write, might make people worse than they were?"

"I have considered it. If I thought that was the case, I would not say anything. Ultimately I think if I can make people care more about each other, then maybe I will save a few of them."

"I hope you are right," she says, "I really do."

"I am."

"And David Brookes, who is going to save him?"

"He was saved," I say, "Along time ago, when he met you."

The Songs of Angels

A few seconds later she asks, "Did you know that Mary had you videoed?"

"Yes," I reply, "She asked me if it was OK, and I told her I did not mind."

"But what does she want it for?" She asks, and I shrug, "Let's not go back to the hotel," Rebecca says, "Let's find somewhere to stop and watch the world go by for a few hours."

"Fine with me," I say, as I start the engine and pull away.

※

We arrive back, at about eight-thirty, and Mary walks over to meet us, "Well," she says, "We found some more chairs at the local community centre, but we still have a problem."

"What?" I ask.

"The marquee is too small," she says. "So we have taken the sides off and borrowed some speakers to put outside."

"How many people have turned up?" I ask, as we turn the corner.

"I don't know," she replies, "How many do you think there are?"

The marquee is dwarfed by the mass of people, all around it, "Jesus," I say, "There must be three thousand people here."

"More like five," Mary replies.

※

Marcus Brent watches the marquee, he listens to the words which David Brookes speaks, and the words in his head. At no time does he say a word. His eyes are just fixed on the figure at the head of the stage, his ears only tuned to the speaker on his right. The humans around him discuss some of the things Brookes says, sometimes they express amusement, and sometimes they are shocked. Marcus shows no emotions, but beneath this outward show, he rages.

How dare he say that, about you Lord!

- Do not despair Marcus, for you see through his lies, you know how much I care.-

But these people here do not! They hang on his every word. I think they actually believe him Lord. How can you endure this? Strike him down!

- Patience Marcus, if we end this here, mankind will never see that which he really is. We will wait until he reveals his true nature for all to witness. Then Marcus, then we will destroy him, and cast him back into the hell, in which he belongs.-

Marcus continues to listen to the voice of David Brookes. He waffles on about the creation of life, claiming that life on Earth was an accident, a fluke in the makeup of matter. And that God was uninterested then, and indifferent now.

- Take it all in Marcus, know your enemy as you would know yourself. See how he plays on their fears, their dreams. See his strengths and his weaknesses. Remember his every word, for in his words, is his annihilation. Every wrong he does his maker, does consign him to Hell.-

Brent stays until the end, Brookes talks for over a hour, even then people are still shouting questions at him. Craving for a response, as if his every answer is a true statement. Brent watches him leave with his wife, the perfect Rebecca, who claims to believe in God. How could she, he thinks, when she fornicates with the Devil?

He walks back to his rental, and sets off for the airport. As he pulls away, his cell phone rings. Marcus flicks a button on the dash, and a male voice rings through the vehicles interior.

"Marcus?" the anonymous voice asks.

"Yes," he replies.

"You want us to still keep tabs on him?" the man asks.

"Of course," Marcus says, "That's what I'm paying your boss for."

The voice laughs, "Bribing him more like. Spooks don't pay for fuck all."

"That is none of your concern, just do as you are told." Marcus instructs, slightly perturbed that this nobody has the audacity, to speak to him in this manner. An FBI agent would just do as he or she was told.

"Yeah OK," the man replies, "If Freddy says so then you're the boss, for now."

The line is disconnected.

The Songs of Angels

July 17th 6:15pm. Local TV news report.

"Yesterday in Portland," The female reporter says to the camera, "Organizers of a book review, failed to anticipate the interest they had stirred up, when over four thousand people turned up for a question and answer session with David Brookes. David Brookes is the author of the controversial book, Heavens Gate, in which he claims that God is not interested in human affairs." The director cuts to a video recording, of David walking outside his home, then back to the reporter.

"This reporter has obtained an amateur video of the crowds that gathered here yesterday evening." The video shows a panoramic view of the field, and the gathered people around the marquee. David Brookes' voice is muffled through the inadequate pick up on the recorder. The reporter talks over the video, "Just why so many people turned up here last night is a mystery, so we have found a couple of eyewitnesses."

The camera returns to the reporter, and then pans to another young woman who was just out of shot before. The reporter asks her, "Can you explain why you, and so many other people came here last night to see David Brookes?"

"Every one was talking about him, about what he had said that morning. So we came along to see what it was all about."

"And what was it?"

"He talked about life, and Heaven. I did not understand all of it, but he has a nice voice."

"Have you read his book?" The reporter asks.

"No," the woman replies, "But my friend said she would borrow it to me. So I will now."

The reporter moves on to a man, "And you sir," she says, "Why did you come?"

The man replies, "I did read David Brookes book, but I thought most of it was nonsense. So I came here to tell him that."

"And did you get a chance to?"

"No," he says, "There were too many people here. And by the end of it, what he said seemed to make more sense."

She moves to the last man in the line. He says, "It was terrible, I could hardly hear anything. The queues for the toilets went on forever and the burger bar ran out of buns."

"Earlier," the reporter says, "I spoke to Mary Kirkland, who was one of the organizers." The camera cuts to Mary's home.

"Mary," She says, "Were you shocked at the interest David Brookes inspired?"

"We were amazed," she says with a smile, "We never dreamt that so many people would come to see him."

"You claim that you were cured of an illness, when you read his book?"

"No, I was cured when I met him," Mary says.

"And you have no explanation for this?"

"Ask David Brookes, he knows what happened. Him and possibly God. For anyone else who is interested in seeing footage of David, a group of us have set up the David Brookes website. You will be able to log on and view the video of yesterday's discussions. There are also comments about his book, and you can put questions to David."

The editor cuts back to the live feed. The picture shows the reporter talking but the sound is missing. She gesticulates for a few seconds and is then cut of. The studio takes over and the display shows two men sitting side by side.

"That was Jenny Small, who we appear to have lost. Our apologies for that. Jenny was reporting from Portland," The first one says. He looks to his co-host and raises his eyebrows.

The other turns to him and shakes his head, "Shocking stuff Dennis, in a modern world, how could any decent snack bar run out of buns. In other news today, the President's trip to Portland, which was scheduled for next week, has been cancelled. A Whitehouse spokesman said that he is suffering from mild exhaustion, due to his hectic workload but stressed, that there is no cause for alarm. And finally, Six year old Bobby Harper, from Augusta, had a miraculous escape, when he……………"

July 18th.

Mary walks from the kitchen, with two cups of coffee. She offers a cup to Rebecca, who takes it, and then sits down herself.

"Thank you," Rebecca says.

Mary smiles, "You're welcome," she says, "So, are you going to tell me what this visit is about? I am sure you are not here for a coffee and chinwag."

"I'm not quite sure how to put this," Rebecca replies.

"Then let me tell you," Mary says, "You want to know what my intentions are. You do not quite trust me."

Rebecca stares down at the coffee cup held in her hands, "Basically, yes."

"Rebecca, there is nothing for you to fear. My intentions are honourable. I just want the world to know what a wonderful man your husband is."

"What do you hope to gain from it?" Rebecca asks.

"Gain?" Mary asks, "Nothing more. I have already gained my life from him. I want the world to gain, by knowing him."

"He is just a man Mary, but you seem to be trying to make David into something else, and that frightens me."

"You believe David is just a man?" Mary asks. "I'm sorry if I scare you with my actions, but David is more than that. You of all people should see this."

"I see my husband, being manipulated by others."

"I see a man, who could change the attitude of America." Mary says, "I see a man who will lead mankind. Did you feel that crowd? The way they hung on his every word, the way they adored him."

"But you cannot tell me, that you believe him totally. When he talks about God. You believe in a caring God, as I do."

"I did," Mary says, "Before I read his book, and before I met David. But now I'm not so sure. When David preaches, his words have a certainty about them. I think he believes them so much, that he infects the audience with the blinding truth."

"He is not a preacher," Rebecca says, standing up.

"Please Rebecca," Mary asks, "Sit down. I am not your enemy. I was hopeful that you would join us."

"Us?" Rebecca enquires.

"I wont lie to you Rebecca, please sit down," she replies. Rebecca retakes her seat. "Yes us," Mary says, "There is a group of us now, from all over the north. We get together and discuss David's book, and his words."

"How many people does 'us' signify?" Rebecca asks.

"A few hundred, don't look so shocked. We are not a secret society. Everyone is welcome at our meetings, you especially." Mary says. Rebecca does not answer. "Just come to one discussion Rebecca, and meet the people that David has touched. Then you will see that there are no hidden agendas. I promise you that there is nothing that you need to concern yourself over." Rebecca still does not reply. "Come as a sceptic, come as devils advocate if you wish, and I promise you will join us."

"Why don't I see what you see?" Rebecca asks, "All I see is my husband. You would raise him to sainthood over this bloody book. I wish he had never wrote it."

"It's not just the book Rebecca, It's the man behind the book that I wish to project into the hearts and minds of America, and then the world."

"You really are trying to make him a saint," Rebecca says, in disbelief, "You're crazy."

"For the first time in my life," Mary states, "I am absolutely sane. Come to one of the meetings."

"Yes I will." Rebecca replies, "Someone has to keep an eye on you."

Mary laughs, "Well that's a start anyway," she says.

※

Section extracted from the seraphim records: Meeting 10,113,596,307 of the council of Heaven.

Michael:
Is our Lord not attending?
Uriel:
Our Lord sends his apologies, he says that he has too much to do in Hell, and has therefore asked if I will chair this meeting. He has asked for a full report.

Raphael:
He spends more time in Hell, than in Heaven. It is not fitting.
Gabriel:
You question God's morality Raphael? Do you think he is incorrect, to finally take an interest in the affairs of Hell, do you question his judgment?
Raphael:
I did not say that Gabriel.
Uriel:
Thank you, may I remind you that this report will be submitted to our Lord. I am sure he will not want it to be records of your bickering.
Gabriel:
Please accept my apology.
Uriel:
Onto your report Michael.
Michael:
Well, you have all seen Lucifer's escapades in Maine by now. He is getting numerous requests from TV and Radio, to be interviewed or just to talk. He has not accepted any yet, but I am sure he will. Mary Kirkland's band of followers grows daily, and the website has had more hits than Elvis Presley.
Uriel:
Why do you think Mary Kirkland is doing this?
Michael:
Because she is fascinated by him. She thinks Lucifer can change the world.
Raphael:
Hopefully for the better. Do you think Lucifer has influenced her in any way?
Michael:
If you mean, has Lucifer influenced her with his words and actions, then yes, of course he has. If you mean to imply that is forcing her will, by some other means, then the answer is emphatically no.
Uriel:
Raphael, if you have to slip a snide remark in, with every question, then I would prefer you to keep silent. Lucifer was given free reign, by God,

to go to Earth. And as much as you, or I, may think it a poor decision, it has happened. So get over your prejudices and either get on the team, or get off.
Raphael:
Forgive me.
Uriel:
Is there anything else Michael?
Michael:
One more thing, the FBI closed their investigation, but there are still people covertly observing him.
Gabriel:
Who?
Michael:
They do not appear to be a government agency. At this time, I really do not know.
Uriel:
The church?
Michael:
Definitely not. The church were investigating Mary Kirkland's recovery, but that has now ceased.
Gabriel:
What did they find?
Michael:
The same as everyone else, there is no possible way that she could be cured. So they will not release their findings, even internally. The church does not want a man who preaches 'God does not care', linked to a miracle cure.
Uriel:
You will make every effort to find out whom these people are?
Michael:
Yes I will.
Uriel:
Then this meeting is closed my brothers.

The Songs of Angels

The assembled Archangels file out of the boardroom. As Michael walks away, Raphael calls, "Michael! A word please."

Michael turns back to him and replies, "Yes?"

"These people following Lucifer around," he asks, "You truly do not know their identity?"

Michael gives him a quizzical look, "Do you think I would lie?"

"No, no," Raphael responds, "I am sure that they are just other random humans, who are interested in Lucifer."

"I fear there is something more going on, but I will find out."

"Yes, I am sure you will Michael. I'm sorry to have kept you, I know you are busy, so I will let you get on. Good day Brother"

"Goodbye Raphael," Michael replies, and they go their separate ways.

❃

August.

"What are you staring at," I ask Rebecca, without looking up.

"My beautiful husband," she replies.

I laugh and turn to her, "You do not look at me, the way you used to."

"I don't know what you mean, I look at you and see the man I love. That is how I have always seen you," she says, "How would you like me to look at you?"

"I'm sorry," I say, "I love you too, more than life."

She rests her head on my shoulder, and says, "Talking of life, I think it is time that we went to see a doctor. It might not be you, it may be a problem with me, but it's not happening is it?"

"Give it time, it will happen, God willing."

She chuckles, "I cannot believe you said 'God willing'. We will wait a few more months and then I will have to put my foot down. Agreed?"

"Agreed," I reply.

[There may be trouble ahead.] Michael sings into my mind.

Shut up!

"You're on TV in fifteen minutes," Rebecca says, "Are you going to watch it?"

"No," I reply, "I know what I said."

"Well I am," She says, "Then I'm off to meet Mary."

"You two are as thick as thieves lately, what are you planning for my life now?"

"I could tell you, but then I'd have to kill you," she jokes, "But it might cost you a lot of money."

"Now I'm worried."

"We will talk about it tomorrow," she says, and stands up, "I'll go in the back room and watch you, if you want."

"No, stay here," I say, "I'll go to the study." I kiss her forehead, and retire to the study.

There is nothing wrong with Rebecca is there?

[No, it's you who's sterile]

I am not sterile, sterile implies that I can never have a child. If I can chose not to impregnate Rebecca at this time, then why should I not take that option?

[Through tampering with your own body.]

You disapprove?

[I disapprove that you are deceiving Rebecca. She wants a child, your child]

How can I bring a child into this world Michael?

[How can you deceive Rebecca any longer?]

Tell me again, what a child of mine, would be.

[You know all this already. A child does not inherit memories from its parents. A baby born of you would be the child of David Brookes, the human, and not the child of Lucifer the Angel. It would be a normal person.]

So what do I do?

[What you think is right.]

You're always such a great help Michael.

[Sarcasm Lucifer, is the lowest form of wit.]

I could get away with it with Gabriel, but you are sharper than he was.

[Don't ever tell him that.]

It scares me to think of raising a child in this world.

[It scares normal people.]

The next day.

Rebecca outlines the plan, which she and Mary cooked up last night. The plan is to buy airtime on television to reach more people. The cost is astounding.

"I do not want to be a television evangelist," I tell her.

"It wouldn't be like that," She states, "We would not allow it to be."

"Then what?" I ask.

"Mary thinks it should be based around your book. People could send in their questions and we would answer them."

"I don't want to be an agony aunt either," I say.

"We will include current affairs also, you can give your views on everything. Just think of the audience you could reach."

[She is correct. Your aim was to influence as many humans as possible. What better way is there, than television?]

"I definitely do not want to be involved in politics." I say.

"You already are David."

I pick up the figures that Rebecca and Mary have come up with, "Even with the money we have now, we would soon be broke, if we have to spend this much on every programme."

"We start with a pilot programme, and see where it goes. If we get good audiences, then the station will cover the costs."

"You have spoken with them?" I ask.

"Mary has," she responds and then asks, "What are you afraid of?"

"Turning all which I have done so far, into a farce," I say, "TV has a way of doing that."

She sits beside me, "We will not allow that to happen. Will you think about doing this?"

"I already am," I reply, "If you and Mary can come up with a decent format, I will do it."

"Consider it done," Rebecca says and plants a kiss on my lips. "Right," she says, as she stands up, "I'm going to phone Mary and get the ball rolling." She smiles and leaves the room. A few seconds later, I can just about hear her, talking on the phone.

[I believe this will be a good move.]
We will see.

In Heaven.

Gabriel:
Michael! Wait!
Michael turns, and waits for Gabriel to catch him up.
Gabriel:
How is he brother?
Michael:
He is fine.
Gabriel:
Are you sure? Your face tells a different story.
Michael:
Yes, Lucifer is fine. But something else is worrying me.
Gabriel:
What brother, tell me.
Michael:
You remember our last meeting, when I told you that Lucifer was still being watched? Well they are no longer watching him. Or maybe they are being much more careful, and I have not noticed them.
Gabriel:
What are you trying to say?
Michael:
It just seems an extraordinary coincidence that they backed off, immediately after the last meeting. If I did not know better, I would say that they knew I was onto them.
Gabriel:
That is impossible.
Michael:
I know, and that is why it worries me.
Gabriel: *he moves closer and whispers,*
Unless, unless someone here is interfering, here in Heaven. But who

The Songs of Angels

would do such a thing? This is unthinkable.
Michael:
Half of Heaven sees my reports, but who would actively go against God's directives?
Gabriel:
No Angel would go against God, except Lucifer maybe, and he has an alibi.
Michael:
This is also what I have contemplated. No Angel, so who does that leave?
Gabriel:
No Michael, no! You think God is deceiving us? Deceiving Lucifer, but why?
Michael:
He did not want to send anyone in the first place. He did not let you help Lucifer and he ties my hands now.
Gabriel:
But he picked Lucifer to go, once the vote went against him.
Michael:
But why did he pick Lucifer, was it because he expected him to fail? And what if he is looking at Lucifer now, and doubts that he will fail. Could he then have a plan to make sure he falters?
Gabriel:
This cannot be!
Michael:
What else can I think? Tell me a better theory.
Gabriel:
I have none brother. What if God hears our words, what if he listens now? What will he do?
Michael:
It's too late to worry about that now, I have said what I have said, and if he listens we will know soon enough. But although he likes everyone to think that God knows everything, I do not think it so. Why would he need reports about Earth from his Angels, if that were the case?
Gabriel:
What will you do now?

Michael:
Nothing Gabriel. Lucifer is all but finished if I am correct and confront God. So I will play it by ear for a while, and see what else turns up.
Gabriel:
I wish I had not stopped you today.
Michael:
I am sorry to burden you with my problems brother.
Gabriel:
That is what brothers are for. You will let me know what else you find?
Michael:
Yes, but next time, we will find somewhere more private than this hallway. I will see you soon.
Michael walks away; Gabriel watches him for a second, shakes his head, then turns and goes in the opposite direction.

CHAPTER 9

Year thirty-six: September 4th

Plans for the TV programme are coming together; Rebecca is out with Mary again. I sit at home and watch a news report on the Middle East. Once again fighting between Israel and Palestine is reaching a point of no return. The US has troops waiting on standby in the Mediterranean and the Gulf. The only reason that they do not proceed, is that Israel has indicated they will consider any US involvement, an act of war. And as the US outlook is tightly linked to the Israeli, they sit and wait. Even though Israel massacres thousands of Palestinians.

I am not sure whether sending US troops would ease the situation. They would be reluctant to come to blows with the Israeli forces over the Palestinians. After all, the Palestinians hate America as much as they hate Israel. And when has force ever proved the correct course? America

The Songs of Angels

has a long history of sticking its nose into the affairs of other countries. The fiasco that happened in Iraq should be ringing alarm bells. America's President needs to review his nations history. If any force is to try and keep peace in the Middle East, then it should be a UN force. But as usual, the UN is too busy shouting at, or vetoing each other, to make an actual decision. A US force would probably fuel the fire rather than douse it.

The telephone rings and I pick it up, "Hello," I say.

"David Brookes," A mans voice states.

"Yes?" I ask.

"Mr. Brookes, you do not know me."

"If I don't know you," I say, "How did you get this number? It's not listed."

"Mr. Brookes," he says, "I need to talk to you, I'm sending a car for you now."

"What is this about?" I ask, realizing that this person has my address, as well as my phone number.

"I thought it courteous to ring you, I don't want you to panic. You could do your country a great favour." He says.

"What if I do not wish to meet you? Tell me what you want first."

"Not on the phone," he replies. The doorbell rings, and I jump. "That's the car, you will come to no harm," he says, and hangs up. I stand with the dead telephone in my hand and stare at the front door. The doorbell rings again.

Michael?

[I believe that they are FBI agents.]

I have done nothing! What do they want?

[I do not have that information Lucifer.]

What should I do?

[Answer the door, I do not think they are here to harm you.]

How can you be sure?

[It does not appear to be their intention.]

The doorbell rings again, and someone calls my name.

I walk to the door and open it. On the step are two men, dressed in the usual black suit and sunglasses that the movies stereotype.

"David Brookes?" the nearest asks.

"Yes," I say.

"FBI," he says, holding up his identification card, "I'm Agent Morwood. Will you please accompany us sir," he indicates the car parked in front of the gate.

"Am I under arrest?" I ask.

"No sir," he says.

"And if I refuse to go with you, will you arrest me?" I ask.

Agent Morwood just stares at me for a few seconds, and then repeats, "Will you accompany us please sir."

They have instructions to take me, whatever I say.

[I still do not think they mean you any harm.]

"The car sir," Morwood says. I grab a jacket, close the door behind me, and walk down the path with the two of them. The second man, whose name I do not know, whispers quietly into his shirt collar. I am ushered onto the back seat, they sit either side of me and slam the doors. The driver, who I cannot see through a smoked partition, pulls the car away.

We head out of Manhattan, taking the tunnel under the East river and into Queens. "Where are we going?" I ask. No one seems in a talkative mood, so I repeat the question.

"The Airport," Morwood replies.

"Why?" I ask, and get no response.

Some time later, we arrive at La Gaurdia airport, and take a back door into the complex, Morwood flashing his I.D. at the security checks, no one asks for mine. Eventually he stops at a door and knocks, a voice from inside grants him permission to enter. Morwood opens the door and indicates that I should go in.

"Just me then," I say, "You're not coming."

He nods, and says, "That is correct sir."

I step into the gloom of the office as the door closes behind me. I can just make out two men, one sits on the side of a plain table, the other approaches me. "What is all this shit about!" I shout. The man who was nearing me stops.

"Quiet please," the one sitting on the table says, and indicates that the other man should continue. He holds a sort of paddle, like a long table tennis bat, which he sweeps around me, finishing at my feet. He stands and puts his finger to his lips, indicating that I should not speak. He then walks to the first man and whispers something. The first man walks the few steps back to me, and mimes taking off his shoe, then taps my left leg.

"You're crazy," I say, "What is this? Am I joining the fucking Masons?"

"Please," he whispers. I remove my shoe and he holds out his hand to take it. I pass it to him and they both retire to the table. A desk lamp is switched on and they converse in hushed tones for around a minute. I cannot see what they are doing as they have their backs to me, so I stand in my one shoe feeling foolish.

"OK," the second man says, at normal volume, "It's not a vocal transmitter, it's a tracker so you can talk."

"Whose is it?" man one asks.

"Excuse me," I say, "Could someone please tell me what on earth is going on."

"Don't know," man two says, ignoring my question, "Anyone can pick these up. I could buy one on the Internet."

The main light flickers into life, and I squint, "Mr. Brookes," the first man says, "Sorry for all this, but we had to be sure that no one else could hear us." He holds out his hand, in the palm is a tiny flat plastic disc, "This is a tracking device that we took out of your shoe. But it could have been a vocal transmitter."

"My wife bought me those shoes," I say.

"And someone likes to know where you are."

"Who?" I ask.

He shrugs and passes the cube to the second man who asks, "Do you want me to destroy it?"

"No James," The first man replies, "Have a stroll around the departures lounge and drop it into the pocket of someone who is flying a long way off. That should have them scratching their heads for a few days."

James smiles and says, "Understood." He leaves the room and closes the door behind him.

"Please sit down Mr. Brookes," man one says, pointing to a chair, as he takes one himself. "My name is Adam Whiteside, I work for the FBI." He passes my shoe back to me, "Sorry, we had to cut the heel."

"Forget the shoe," I say, peering a the cut in the heel, "Why would someone want to track my movements?"

"I do not know, but you are becoming a public figure, and you upset a lot of people when you talk."

"And you're telling me that it is not the FBI?"

He holds his hands up, "Not that I know of, and that does not mean it positively is not. The FBI is a vast organization. Another department maybe, but I doubt it. That tracker, as James said, can be bought by anyone. So it's more likely a private detective or non-government group."

Michael, did you know that this was in my shoe?

[No I did not know about it, but I was not looking for tracking machines.]

"So what do you want?" I ask. "What is so important, that you feel the need to sweep me for bugs?"

Whiteside replies, "In May and June I was in charge of a FBI surveillance team, who were observing you."

"That was you," I say, instantly defensive. I lean back in the chair and fold my arms. "Well I knew someone was. The question is why?"

"I do not know for sure," he says, "If orders say 'Watch David Brookes.' That is what we do. But it was as your book came out, and when that woman claimed that you cured her illness."

"Nothing illegal." I state.

"We investigate a lot of people Mr. Brookes, if we considered your actions to be illegal, we would have arrested you. As it was, the case was dropped."

"So why tell me all this now?" I ask.

"I know someone who is extremely ill." He says, "I want you to look at him."

"Why?" I ask.

"David," he says, "We tracked your movements for two months. At no time were you unobserved. I was in charge of putting all the information and reports together."

"And?" I ask.

"I have their names written down," he opens a file and withdraws a piece of paper, "Do you want me to read them out?"

"I don't know what you mean," I lie.

"Bullshit," he says, "Mary Kirkland, Amyotrophic Lateral Sclerosis cured; James Bathgate, recovered from a tumour; Paul Barry, Leukaemia cured; Janet Hall, awoke from coma; Henry Castillo, brain tumour disappeared; Martin Hutchingson, AIDS virus disappears; Helen Goldberg, Heart defect repaired; Daniel Bolton, Sickle cell anaemia cured." He looks up, "All these things happened after a visit from you." I just look at him, "We stopped the investigation then," he says, "So I do not know how many more should be added to this list."

"What are you implying?" I ask.

"You said it yourself in one of your interviews, when the probable is impossible, then the impossible is probable. And I am sure that I have eliminated all the possible, so all I have left, is the impossible. You had a hand in the recovery off all these people. Eight people are cured after a visit from you. Are you going to tell me that this is a coincidence? Do you know what the odds are against that?" He stands and walks away, then turns and says, "I don't care how you do it, and I really don't want to know. I honestly do not care if you inject them with a super drug, or if you are a fucking miracle worker. Just take a look at this man. If you can do nothing, then so be it. I will feel stupid and you can go home."

"And if I want to walk away now?"

"Then you can," he says.

"You said I would be helping my country, how will your friends recovery help the country?"

"He is not my friend, he is my boss. I am head of security at the Whitehouse."

"Your FBI boss?" I ask.

He sits back down and places his hands on the table. For the longest time he just stares and I wait for a response. Then he lets out a deep sigh and looks to the ceiling. "I suppose that I will have to trust you, if I am to expect your help. So perhaps I should rephrase my last statement." He pauses again, "He is not only my boss, he is 'THE' boss, work it out."

It takes a second for the penny to drop. "The President?" I whisper.

"You cannot tell anyone, if the papers or a hostile nation should receive this information," he leans over me, "It could compromise US stability. I really could not let that happen."

"I understand," I say, "What is the matter with him?"

"He has a brain tumour," Whiteside says, as he slumps back down in the chair, "It has begun to send him incoherent at times. We have had to cancel all live engagements. We have to edit out the pauses and the swearing when he does TV broadcasts. He can no longer function as the President of the United States."

"Shit," I say, "What about the doctors?"

"They walk around shaking their heads, they tell me that they have tried everything they can." He says, and holds his head in his hands.

"I cannot promise anything," I say.

He looks up, "You will try?" he says, and I nod, "I have a plane waiting to take us to Washington. Do you need anything?"

"Like what?" I ask.

"I don't know, tools, a vial of super drugs or a fucking Ouiga board."

"No," I say, "Nothing, but I would like to phone my wife. She may be wondering where I am."

"You can do it on the plane," Whiteside says, "Lets go."

※

On the plane, I read through all of the Presidents medical records. The tumour was only diagnosed six months ago, how it was missed when he came to power is a mystery. It occupies a part of the brain that cannot be operated on without causing permanent damage. The doctors have been feeding him a cocktail of drugs, whose names go straight over my head. A car is waiting for us when we land at Washington National airport.

As Whiteside drives the car across the Potomac River, I look down on the Jefferson memorial and we head for the heart of Washington D.C. "Where is he being treated?" I ask.

Whiteside turns and looks at me, before focusing back on the road, "At the Whitehouse, do you think we could keep this under wraps if we admitted him into the local hospital?"

"I have no idea what you can do." I say.

"I've registered you as a Doctor from California, but I will try to keep you away from the other quacks. Your I.D. will be waiting for you at security."

"Are you telling me that you have arranged a pass, with my photograph on it? In the time it has taken to fly here?" I ask.

"Not quite," he says, "I anticipated that you would want to help. Dr.

Alan Walker, has been registered to arrive today, for two weeks. I have one more confession."

"Then you had better tell me."

"No one else knows about this," he says.

"Except the FBI," I say.

"No," he responds, "I have not told anyone else, only me and you know. Even the agents who picked you up did not know why."

"This is fucking great," I say, "What if someone recognizes me?"

"What did you think? That I would stand up in front of the Whitehouse staff and say, 'Hey guys, I know this author who does voodoo, why don't we let him have a look at the President!' They would have booted me out of the gate, and locked it."

"I don't do voodoo," I protest.

"Like I said, I don't care," he says, "I care about this country. Whatever you do, if it helps him, it will help America."

I ask, "Who is Alan Walker?"

"I made him up," he says, and I groan, "Everything is in order, don't worry yourself about it. If anyone cares to look, they will find that Alan Walker is a brilliant neurosurgeon, with an impeccable career in California."

"Your people in the Whitehouse, they don't know either do they?"

"No," he says, "But I am head of security, they work for me and therefore, will give you no trouble. OK, we are here, try to look confident."

How does a confident doctor look?

[Like everything is beneath him. Try to look like God.]

A gate guard pokes his head through the window, "Evening Sir," he says to Agent Whiteside.

"Evening Brian," Whiteside replies, as he shows his I.D. "This is Dr. Walker, I believe that you have a pass for him in the gatehouse. He looks me over, and I pay no attention to him.

"We do sir," he says, and goes back to his hut. A few seconds later, he returns holding an I.D. badge. He scrutinizes the picture, his eyes flicking repeatedly from my face to the photograph. "OK gents," he finally says, as he hands the pass over.

"Thanks Brian," Whiteside shouts, as the electronic gate opens. He guns the engine and proceeds up the drive. We park the car and walk to a side entrance. Whiteside swipes his I.D. and I hear the door click open.

"Does mine do that?" I ask.

"No," he laughs, "You have to be escorted on, or off the premises. You do not get in or out without me." We make our way through a labyrinth of corridors, and finally arrive at Whiteside's office. "Do you want coffee?" he asks.

"Water please," I say. He presses an intercom and asks for a coffee and a glass of water.

"In the restroom, there is a set of clothes for you, they should fit." He says.

"You have a white coat for me?" I ask.

"No, a suit," he replies, "You don't look much like a doctor, in jeans and sweat shirt."

I look down at my attire, and say, "Well I was not expecting to visit the President when you dragged me from my home." Whiteside smiles and indicates that I should go and get changed. In the restroom an expensive two piece and a shirt hang. On the floor are leather shoes. I would not wear leather normally, but in this instance, I make an exception. I would look odd in this suit, with my casual shoes. I change quickly, amused that the FBI knows my neck size and I don't, or should that worry me?

[You are beginning to treat this as an adventure. That should worry you.]

After you assured me I was in no danger, your comments are noted with a pinch of salt.

[I never said you were in no danger, I said that it was not Agent Morwood's intention to harm you.]

I step back into the office. Whiteside is sipping coffee. On the desk is a glass of water, which I take and rapidly drink. Whiteside says, "You will just about pass, if no one looks at you too closely."

"What now?" I ask.

"Let's go and see the patient," he replies, "By the way, can you impersonate a Californian accent?"

"No," I say.

"Then try not to say anything if anyone stops us, let me do the talking."

We leave the office and once again wonder through the maze of offices

The Songs of Angels

and corridors. In time we come to the place where the President resides. It is an intensive care unit, which would not be rivalled in the very best hospitals. I marvel how they could get all of this equipment and staff, into one of the most watched building in Earth, without raising suspicions.

"Dr. Walker?" a voice calls.

"Whiteside nudges me, and whispers, "That's you."

A tall balding man bears down on us with his hand outstretched, a huge smile on his face, I shake his hand, I do not think he will ever let go. "We have been expecting you. I read your paper on oncolytic viruses when I heard you were coming, very exciting, very radical."

What's he talking about?

[Beats me.]

Whiteside interrupts, "Dr. Walker, this is Dr. Francis, he heads the team here."

"Pleased to make your acquaintance," I say.

"Would you like to go over our diagnosis?" He asks, "See if you agree?"

I look to Whiteside for help. "Dr. Walker is already up to date with all the Presidents records. I was just taking him to see the patient." He says.

"That's right," I say.

"Excellent," Francis says, "I will come with you."

"No," Whiteside almost shouts. The doctor looks quite shocked.

"I do not want to appear rude," I say, "But as I explained to Mr. Whiteside, I prefer to meet the patient on a one to one basis, before coming to any decisions."

"Yes!" Whiteside exclaims. I give him a wide-eyed look, trying to instil some calm in him.

"Very well," Dr. Francis says, "We will talk later, I have some interesting questions about your paper that you will want to answer." He wags his free finger at me.

"Marvellous," I say with a forced smile, "If I could have my hand back Doctor?" He looks down and realizing that he still holds my hand, releases it.

I follow Whiteside into a larger room. A bed stands in the middle and in it the President of the United States lies. He appears to be sleeping. "What's this paper?" I ask Whiteside.

"I assigned some recent medical papers that looked fitting, to Dr. Walker."

"And you have no idea what they are about?"

"I'm not a doctor," Whiteside says.

"This gets better every minute," I reply before walking to the side of the Presidents bed, and looking down at his gaunt face. I address Whiteside, "He's at deaths door, I'm not sure if this will work."

"I ain't dead yet," the President whispers. His eyes open and they stare unfocused in my direction. "Who the fuck are you?" he asks.

"Mr. President," Whiteside interrupts, "This is Dr. Walker. He has come to help you."

"I don't need no more fanny ass quack doctors, poking me with fucking needles and experimenting on me," he shouts.

"Shush," I say, intending to calm him.

"Don't you tell me to shush, I'm the fucking President. How old are you son? They're sending fucking students now!" Dribble escapes from his mouth, "Did I tell you I'm the President?"

"Yes Sir," I say.

"You may as well leave, you cannot help me. Only God can help me now. Do you believe in Heaven son?" he asks.

"Yes Sir, I do," I reply.

"Well I ain't going there," he says, "Do you know what you have to do, when you're a President? I used to be President, did you know?"

"Yes," I say.

"Questionable things son, things that God may not forgive you for." He closes his eyes for a minute, and then opens them and looks straight through me, "Who the fuck are you?" he asks, and then his eyes shut.

We both stand there for a second, and then Whiteside quietly asks, "Can you do anything?"

"I don't know," I say, as I take the Presidents hand. The stream of saliva on the side of his chin stops its downward journey. I look around at Whiteside who stares at me, but sees nothing. We are bonded and I am in. I look deep into the Presidents mind; the tumour spreads across his brain, like a hand crushing a ripe melon. No wonder he has no idea what he says, it must be agony.

Lets go back: time spirals backwards and the tumour shrinks and I find

The Songs of Angels

the very first cell. Tag it like before, so his immune system can deal with it, and then I can get out of here. Done.

Not done? Still here, still suspended, Whiteside still stares at me.

Forward: I watch the tumour grow again unchecked.

Back again: Ah, I missed that on the first rewind, there are two tumours, growing independently of each other, competing for space and resources. When I dealt with the first one, the second was allowed to monopolize. A second tag should do it.

Still stuck here, what is going on? I'm getting very tired now. Forward again, there is the third one, and the fourth. Jesus, there are eight more to deal with. I cannot do it. I am too tired and I want to go back now.

Nothing happens, I am still here, this is too much, I can't do it!

And then the reality of the situation dawns on me, there is no getting out, unless I cure him. Why did I not realize this? Maybe it is because I have never been bonded and failed before.

So what happens now? I am stuck in this time frame and stuck to this dying man. How long has it been so far? It feels like about four hours, maybe five to track and neutralize the first two. Perhaps another twenty hours to finish the rest, if I can stay awake. It's too long, and what if it does not work? Will Whiteside see me dehydrate and die in a few seconds, while I wait here for a week?

Stop panicking and concentrate on a solution. It is over when he is cured, and not before; so find another way to tackle this. Why should he have multiple tumours? What would trigger them and how do they get there? Check the rest of him, ignore his mind and find the source. I home in on the rest of his body, there are hundreds of tumours sprouting up in every conceivable place. I start to panic, I cannot deal with all of them. But there must have been a start to this. One tumour has spread throughout his body. Concentrate on the whole body and go back again.

I am so weary, that I miss it. When I concentrate again, I am passed the starting point, and there are no tumours present. Painstakingly I move time slower and slower, homing in by trail and error, cutting the time sweep down with every pass. Finally I stop and observe the start of it all.

Got you, you bastard! After what feels like ten hours, I home in on this single cell and flag it for destruction.

"Anything at all," Whiteside says, as saliva dribbles of the Presidents cheek and stains the pillow. My hand parts from his, and I stagger back, "Shit, are you alright?" Whiteside asks as he rushes around the bed and supports me. "Can I do anything?" he asks.

"A drink of water would be nice," I say. Whiteside sits me on the visitor's chair, and fetches a glass of water from the sink. I greedily gulp it down

"If you're feeling better, can we get back to the task in hand." He says.

I laugh, "It's done," I say, "Well I think it's done, no I'm sure it is."

"What!" he says, "But we have only been here fifteen seconds, and you didn't do anything."

"I'm sorry that it was not more spectacular, but trust me when I say that I have done all that I can. Now I just have to close my eyes for a second."

"You cannot go to sleep here!" Whiteside exclaims.

"Just for a minute," I say, "Just five minutes."

❧

I awake; I can hear a conversation so I open my eyes. Whiteside and the President are talking. I listen for a few seconds. The President sounds sane.

"Look here Adam," the President says, "Our young Doctor is back with us." Whiteside turns his head in my direction. The President continues, "It comes to something, when my personal Doctors are worked so hard, that they fall asleep in front of me."

"Excuse me," I say.

"Are you alright?" Whiteside asks.

"Yes," I reply, "Just exhausted." I stand and stretch my aching body. Then step over to stand besides Adam and the President. "How are you feeling Sir?" I ask him.

"Better than I have for a long time son," he says.

"You should sleep as much as possible," I tell him.

"Adam tells me, that you are from California Doctor," the President says, "You don't have a Californian accent, and I usually know when someone is lying Mr. Brookes." I look at Whiteside and he looks at me, we both look back at the President. "Shit Adam," he says, "Did you think I would not recognize him, it's my job to know who stirs the shit in this

The Songs of Angels

neck of the woods. So who is going to tell me what has occurred here?"

"Mr. President," Whiteside says, "This is my doing, I persuaded David to come and see you. I smuggled him into the Whitehouse using a fake identity."

"I agreed to come," I add.

"Why?"

"David has a talent sir," Whiteside says, "He can help people with illnesses, he has helped you sir."

The President stares at me, "I know something has happened, I can feel it. I trust Adam Mr. Brookes."

"You should," I say.

"Have you helped me Son?"

"I hope so Sir."

"And what was your diagnosis Mr. Brookes?" he asks.

"I think you might make a full recovery." I say.

"Then Adam better get you out of here, before anyone else recognizes you," the President says, "And Adam," he asks, "You have broken all the security rules in the book. You have managed to get a total stranger into the Whitehouse, and within striking distance of the President of the United States."

"Yes Sir," Whiteside says, "Do you want me to resign?"

"No Adam," he says, "I want you to conduct a full review of Whitehouse security. If you can do it, what is to stop anyone else? Now get out of here and let me sleep."

Whiteside grabs my arm and pulls me from the room. Doctor Francis has been waiting for us, he jumps up as we approach, "Well?" he says, "I am sure that you realize, that there is no hope for the….." He stops in mid sentence, "You look awful Dr. Walker."

"It's the shock," Whiteside says, "Of seeing him like that."

"Oh dear," Francis says, "Can I get you anything, a sedative? Some water?"

"No," Whiteside replies, "I forgot to complete some security forms. I'm afraid I need Dr. Walker for a while. You can see him later."

"Very well," Dr. Francis says to our backs, as Whiteside virtually drags me from the room. We head back to the office. Whiteside grabs the car keys and we are off again. We have no problem getting out of the

Whitehouse grounds.

On the road back to the airport, he asks, "What did you do in there?"

"I thought you didn't want to know?" I reply.

"Was it the same as the others," he asks.

"I do not quite understand what happens, all I know is that I can sometimes help people."

"There are more, aren't there. More than I know of."

"Yes," I say, "Many more, but that was the hardest ever. I thought I would fail at one point."

"But you didn't," he states.

"No," I say, "But if I ever do, I think it will kill me."

He looks at me, "Then I'm sorry that I put you through this."

"Watch the road," I tell him.

"Shit," he says as he corrects the steering. "What you can do is a miracle. Why do you hide your talents? Why not tell the world?"

"Why? Because people would not believe it, or would turn me into a lab rat, trying to find out how it works. You must promise to keep this to yourself. We both have a secret that the world does not need to know."

"If that is what you wish," he replies, and then adds, "My reports on you last year, they were read by many people at the FBI. Someone may come to the same conclusions as I did."

"That cannot be helped now," I say.

We arrive at the airport, skirting security and stopping next to the FBI Gulf Stream jet. "The jet will take you back to La Gaudia. I will arrange a pick up, to take you home from there."

"You're not coming?" I ask.

"No," he says, "So goodbye for now David Brookes, and thank you."

I nod and get out of the car, as I walk to the steps, Whiteside calls for me to wait, gets out of the car and starts to run over, "I forgot to tell you," he says, "The tracker that we found, in my experience, it will not be the only one. Check your home, your clothes, your car."

"You think there are more?"

"I would put money on it. On second thoughts, I will send someone over to do a sweep, it's the least I can do."

"Thank you Adam," I say.

"No, thank you David," he says, and holds out his hand. I shake his

The Songs of Angels

hand, bid him goodbye and then board the jet. Five minutes later we are in the air.

Can you check the house Michael?

[I'm on it.]

Before we land, Michael reports back.

[There are sixteen devices in your home, including six digital cameras. Your car has two, a tracking device and a recorder, and so does Rebecca's. All your shoes contain GPS trackers. Your overcoat has a miniature transmitter sown into the collar.]

The question is, who put them there?

[That is what I will try to find out next.]

※

As Adam Whiteside drives back to the Whitehouse, he decides to find out if it is the FBI who are monitoring David. He promises himself, that he will make discreet enquiries.

※

September 19th.

[So you made the decision.]

What?

[Are you telling me that you have not noticed the change?]

What are you talking about?

[Rebecca, you really have not noticed yet?]

Will you stop talking in riddles, and say what you mean.

[She is pregnant. I hope you did make the decision. It is yours isn't it?]

Rebecca's pregnant?

[Yes. I hope I have not put my foot in it.]

What? Of cause it is mine, but it has happened so quickly.

[Congratulations Lucifer, you are going to be a Father. Or more accurately, congratulations David.]

"Rebecca!" I call.

"Yes!" she shouts from another room.

"Are you OK?" I ask.

She comes through the door, "Fine," she says, "Why?"

"Nothing, just checking," I say, trying to stop the smile from spreading over my face. She looks at me inquisitively. Thankfully the doorbell rings before I am coerced into answering the question that was probably building in her mind. With her attention momentary diverted, she goes to answers it.

"David!" she calls, a few seconds later, "There is a man at the door who thinks we have an insect problem."

"Oh," I say, "I called them to check the house, nothing to worry about."

"Thanks for telling me," she shouts, sarcasm evident in her manner, then adds as she passes me by, "I hope he will not be spraying anything."

"No," I reply, "Just a survey." I walk to the door.

The man who Whiteside called James stands on my doorstep. He wears a white boiler suit, hair net and goggles. The insignia over the pocket reads 'Fumigators, for Bugs & Insects'

He smiles and says, "FBI sir, insects don't stand a chance."

I look down the path and discover that he has pulled up in a van, decorated with cartoon bugs. The letters FBI wrote straight across the middle. "You cannot be serious," I say.

"Insects are no joking matter Sir," James says. He hands me a clipboard, with the company logo on, and a load of junk about bugs. On the bottom, wrote in pencil are the words, 'You do not know me, play along for the audience.' He says, "If you could just sign at the bottom Sir," and hands me a pen.

I scribble in the spot indicated and hand it back to him. "Shouldn't you be called the FFBAI?"

"Doesn't have the same impact," James replies. "Shall I start in the living room?"

"Go wherever you please," I tell him.

I let James get on with his work, and join Rebecca in the garden. "Since when have we ever had an insect problem?" She asks.

"You cannot be too careful, termites could be eating our floorboards as we speak."

"In New York?" she asks.

"There's a new strain that migrate here in the summer, and go home in winter." I say. "Big buggers."

"Crap." She replies.

"I'll tell you about them later," I say.

It takes James about an hour to sweep the whole house. Finally he appears in the garden. "Would you like your report Sir?" he asks.

"Please," I say, and follow him into the house.

"Well Sir," he says, "You seem to have a mini infestation. I could destroy all the ones in the house if you wish, but I cannot promise that they will not come back."

"What do you suggest?"

"We could try to track them to their source. That way we may be able to stop them dead," he says.

"Find the nest and take out the Queen?" I suggest.

"Exactly Sir," James says, "Of course, sometimes we fail to find the nest, sometimes there is no visible connection."

"I don't like the thought of them in my home," I tell him, "I think I would like them all exterminated."

"No problem Sir," he replies, "This should not take long. I need to go back to the van and get some equipment."

"Fine," I say. He disappears for a few minutes and returns with a small flight case. I leave him to it and once again retire to the garden. Rebecca is pottering about at the bottom. When James appears again, he has removed the hairnet and goggles.

"All done," he says, "Your friends are blind for a while. I have removed sixteen devices from around your house. I'm afraid that you need to buy some new shoes, and I have taken some of your clothes away."

"What will they think?" I ask.

He shrugs his shoulders; "They will get the message that you are onto them, when the trackers in your shoes, all arrive at the FBI headquarters at the same time. If that does not scare them off we are probably dealing with the CIA, or a foreign agency."

"And they will replant them?" I ask.

"It's possible, but I have a couple of presents for you. Courtesy of Adam and the FBI." He opens the flight case and passes me an electrical device that looks like a miniature digital radio, "This will pick up any new bugs, anything that is transmitting." He demonstrates how to use it, "Walk around your house every couple of days, if this light flashes, then you have a bug. You can home in on it by triangulating the signal. Your clothes and car are most at risk, so sweep them every time you come home. And finally," he says, "This is for you." He passes me a cellular phone.

"I have one," I say.

"Not like this one," James replies, "You can talk to anyone normally with this phone, but if you phone another like this, it will be a secure line and no one can listen in. Adam instructed me to put his number in it, if you ever need him for anything."

"Thanks," I say, not sure if it is for me to contact Adam, or for Adam to contact me. "Tell him that I appreciate all of this."

"And the best part about it is, no one will ever send you a bill for it." He smiles, and says, "If you will just give me yours and Mrs. Brookes car keys, I can finish up and be on my way."

I had forgotten about the cars, "Yes of course," I reply, and fetch the keys from the rack. James takes a few minutes to clear the cars, and then goes on his way.

[He found them all, the house is clear.]

Good. Although I still cannot understand why anyone would go to these lengths, to keep tabs on me. Have you had any luck, finding out who is behind this?

[No. It is harder than I thought, and I do not understand all this technological stuff. I'm afraid that I am still in the dark ages, when it comes to human gadgets.]

Well, they know that we know now, maybe they will have to crawl out of the woodwork.

[Yes maybe.]

꽃

As James O'Hare drives away from David Brookes home, he punches a number into his own cell phone, and waits for an answer.

"Hello," his car speaker says.

"Hi Adam, it's James."

"How did it go," Whiteside asks.

"You were right, the place was buzzing with surveillance equipment. I have removed six cameras, plus various trackers and transmitters. They are all safely locked up in the back."

"Any idea whose they are?" Whiteside asks.

"It was definitely an amateur set up, but a good one. Except for three of the transmitters in the house."

"What about them?"

"They're ours," James says, "FBI issue, but last years model."

"What?" Whiteside says, "They must be from the original surveillance and categorically should not be there. I processed the order for their removal myself."

"Then someone overruled you."

"If someone overruled my order," Whiteside says, "they will have left a trail. Thanks James."

"This wasn't an official assignment was it?" James asks.

"No James, I owe you one."

"I'm just freaking out a bit," he says, "If it was a FBI operation, they may have seen, and heard me. They will know our bug van. And that will lead them to me, so I need you to watch my back."

"If it comes to it," Whiteside says, "I will take the flack, as far as you are concerned, it was official."

"Thanks," James says, "Bye then."

"See you soon."

※

Adam Whiteside hangs up the phone, and logs on to his computer. He searches out the original investigation and enters his password. Everything that was committed to the FBI mainframe is presented before him. He bypasses most of it, and finds his final order to terminate the case. It is the last entry.

Puzzled, he conducts a search, for any related orders or entries. In another database, he finds a report saying that all the surveillance equipment was removed two weeks after he issued the order. But it was not, he thinks to himself, could these three bugs have been overlooked? Whiteside pulls up the inventory of what was installed, and what was removed. They match exactly. So someone falsified the report. He notes the agent I.D.

number on the report and starts another search.

A few minutes later, a name is displayed on his screen. It says 'Cody Davenport'

Cody was one of his guys, before he moved to Washington. But Whiteside cannot imagine Cody falsifying a report; it would not be his style.

He switches his computer window over and calls up his contacts list, scrolls down to D, and dials Cody Davenport's number.

"Davenport," his speakerphone says.

Whiteside picks up the receiver and says, "Cody, its Adam Whiteside. How are you?"

"Fine Sir," Davenport replies, "How are things at the big house?"

"Can't complain," Whiteside says, "Cody, do you remember the last case we did, when we were watching that author in Manhattan?"

"Yes," Davenport replies.

"I have just read the log, saying that you removed the equipment from the Brookes house. Did you file that?"

"Yes Sir," he says.

"But I know that three transmitters were left in there."

"That is correct Sir." Davenport says.

"I'm confused now Cody," Whiteside says, "Are you telling me that you knowingly entered a false report?"

"Yes but hang on Sir, I received a counter order instructing me to do exactly that."

"Who from?" Whiteside asks.

"You Sir." He replies.

"Me!" Whiteside exclaims,

"It came through about a week after you transferred," Davenport adds.

"But there is no order from me, or anyone else on the mainframe."

"It has to be there Sir," he says, "It was official."

"I've checked Cody," Whiteside says.

"Hang on Sir," Davenport says, "It was a secure E-mail, and I always save all my orders, so I should be able to find it." The line goes quiet for a moment, "OK," he says, "I'm looking at it now."

"Cody," Whiteside asks, "Can you E-mail me a copy of that order."

The Songs of Angels

"Yes Sir, I will have it sent in five minutes. Are you saying that you did not send this order Sir?"

"Yes Cody, but I will find out who did."

"Will I be in any trouble Sir?" Davenport asks.

"I might be calling you to an inquiry, if I track down the bastard who issued a command and used my name," Whiteside replies.

"Very well Sir," Cody Davenport says.

"Cody, don't mention this to anyone else," Whiteside instructs, "Until I find out what is going on, I don't want to alert anyone." His screen beeps, and tells Adam that he has mail. He opens it and checks the heading. "OK Cody, I have your E-mail. I will contact you later."

"Goodbye then Sir."

Whiteside hangs up, and turns his attention to the file that Cody has sent him. He reads through it and notes that Cody did as he was commanded. He notes his own identification marker and name as the originator of the order. "Bastard," he whispers to the screen. Then he checks back to the sender of the order, and sees his own I.D. But there is more, the order was routed through his old computer and the I.D. behind it is not his. He makes a note of the I.D. and returns to the mainframe.

"Got you now," he says as he enters the code. Seconds later the words 'Confidential information-Access denied' pop up in front of his eyes. "Shit," he says. The person who used his name must have had a higher rank than he.

"Fuck this," he says, and dials another number, "Mr. President," he says, "How are you feeling?"

"Good son, but these quack doctors wont let me out of bed yet. What can I do for you?"

Whiteside replies, "I need a tiny favour Sir."

❧

"We were being watched?" Rebecca asks, "By who?"

"That's the question," I say.

"So who was that man?"

"Someone I know from the FBI." I reply.

She looks worried, "How do you know people who work for the FBI?"

"Just an acquaintance," I say, "Whoever was monitoring us, may try to replace this equipment again. So we have to be cautious. Not that we have anything to hide, but I don't want anymore crap in our house."

"Yes of course," she says.

※

Twenty minutes later, Adam Whiteside's phone rings, "Adam?"

"Mr. President," he replies.

"Son, you would not believe the shit I have had to go through to get this name." The President says. "

"I'm sorry to be a nuisance Sir," Whiteside replies

"Is it important Adam?"

"It could be Sir," Whiteside says.

"Well I know I can trust you Adam," the President says, "The I.D. belongs to someone called Marcus Brent. Do you know him? Does that help you Son?"

"Oh I know him Sir, but I still don't understand what is going on."

"Well, once you do know, you will let me know what all this is about. Understood?"

"Yes Sir," Whiteside says, and the President hangs up.

Marcus Brent, his old boss. What are you up to Brent, Whiteside wonders. What possible reason could he have, to run illegal taps, and risk his career over David Brookes?

※

September 20th.

He has people in my own organization helping him.

-The agents of darkness take on many forms Marcus.-

But we are blind Lord, he can work his evil and we cannot see or hear him. I have people watching the house again, but they are worse than useless, untrained amateurs.

-You will overcome this problem Marcus.-

How Lord? I need professionals.

-Then perhaps it is time that you looked further a field. The battle of

The Songs of Angels

Good verses Evil has begun Marcus. It will be fought on Earth as prophesized. Through cunning and trickery, the Devils human manifestation draws his minions to his evil. And as the hand of God Marcus, you must bring your allies to the light, so we are ready when Satan makes his move.-

It will be done Lord.

September 23rd.

[You are quiet today.]

I'm just doing a lot of thinking. Suddenly everything is gathering momentum.

[Which is what you wanted.]

Yes I know, but I keep going over everything in my head. Is it all going the way I want it to? The TV broadcast goes out this evening. I think it has turned out satisfactory, but how can I be sure that the message is getting through?

[Lucifer, the message is loud and clear, and people are listening to it in there millions. Your book is being held up as the most shocking piece of literature since Darwin wrote 'The Origin of Species'.]

Mary worries me, I know she means well but the media are calling her movement a new cult.

[It is not her movement it is yours. She only organizes it, and people join her because of what you say.]

I do not want to be the head of a cult. I have people sending me money and donating meeting halls. I have fifty-seven 'churches' scattered across the northeast, and another twelve across the country. This is not what I had in mind.

[Then you have to control it.]

I cannot be everywhere, how do I control it all.

[Push the money back into the movement; sign the properties over to the people who use them. Set up rules for the meetings and delegate the responsibility to the people who run them.]

What do I do with the humans that jump on the bandwagon, because they see a few bucks in it for themselves?

[You underestimate the awe these people have for you; I do not think it will happen. And if it does then you will have to deal with it.]

Perhaps I could set up an independent, none profit making trust, shared between all who make up the movement. I will speak to Mary about it.

A still of the President on the TV snatches my attention, so I turn the sound up. In the studio the newsreader says, "In other news, the President made his first public appearance in over six weeks. He attended the opening of a new science and technology park in Texas. A Whitehouse spokesperson said that the President had been suffering from exhaustion but is now fit and well. These pictures from Dallas Texas,"

The report shows the President walking down the steps of Air force one, the reporter says, "On his visit today to Dallas, the president showed no signs of the illness that has kept him from public duties during the last few weeks. He came to Dallas to open a new science and technology park……."

※

September 29th.

My phone is ringing. The phone Adam gave me.

[Perhaps you should answer it?]

I pick it up, Adam Whiteside's number is displayed in the screen. I punch the button and say, "Hello."

"David, its Adam. How are you?"

"Fine," I reply, "What can I do for you?"

"Are you clear to talk?" he asks.

"The gadget you sent me has a green light on it," I tell him.

"Good," he says, "Then I will get straight to the point. The President wants to meet with you."

"Why?" I ask.

"He did not share that information with me, but I assume he wants a conversation with the man who saved his life. He has invited you to Camp David for the weekend."

"When?" I enquire.

"This weekend."

"How can I refuse?" I reply.

"Excellent, I will phone you tomorrow and sort out the details. Obviously this is hush hush. What will you tell Rebecca?"

"She is away until the middle of next week, doing work for the TV show in England."

"Yes, I watched your first show."

"And?" I ask.

"Lets say that I was intrigued. Anyway I will call tomorrow."

"OK, speak to you then." I say as the call is terminated.

Saturday.

The black Chrysler MPV has the darkest windows I have ever seen, I can barely see out of them. Not surprisingly, the President does not want any other parties knowing that I am visiting him. I sit alone in the back, cut off from the driver by a screen, which is just as black.

The driver's intercom crackles, and she says, "We will arrive in two minutes Sir," then cuts off. I have no clue how to reply, so I do not. She pulls the MPV of the main road and stops at a checkpoint. I can see her talking to a secret service agent, but no one looks in the back, and then we continue on our way. We pull into a covered garage and stop, the roller door squeaks as it closes and locks us in.

The side door opens, and a face I know looks back at me. "Adam," I say, "Nice to see you."

"And you," he replies, "Follow me." I get out of the car and follow him into a side corridor, "Are you sure you are clean?" he asks, as we walk.

"Behind my ears and everything," I say.

"No, I mean from bugs," he says, and turns to me, but I am already holding up the detector for him to see. The green light blinks at him and I flash a smile. "Come on funny man," he says, and leads me into a reception room. "Take a seat. The President will see you in about half an hour. I hope you are hungry, because you are having lunch with him."

"Fine," I say, "How is he?"

"He is a different person, he actually went out riding this morning."

"That's good," I reply.

"Good?" Adam says, "It's a fucking miracle!" He smiles, "Those doctors," he adds, "They are all still scratching their heads. Dr. Francis was pestering me, to get hold of you, he was a little upset when I told him that you shipped out to an Alaskan Institute."

"Do you think he will buy that?" I ask.

"Doesn't really matter. All the medical stuff is being removed from the Whitehouse, along with him and his team. I don't think he will follow it up, and if he did, he will find a Dr. Walker registered there. If he does persist, we will slap the secrets act with his signature on it, back in front of him, and tell him to stop."

"The US does not have an official secrets act," I reply.

"Of all things I thought you were, naïve was not on my list," he says, as he places a form in front of me and offers a pen, "You have to sign up before we go any further."

"I'm not about to tell anyone what I have done," I say.

"I understand that," he replies, "But you're about to have a private conversation with the President of the United States. You cannot ever repeat what is said here today, or that I smuggled you into the Whitehouse. This will protect your secrets as well as ours. It is for all our peace of mind."

I take the pen and sign my name. "Anything else?" I ask.

"Nope," Adam says, "Lets go and see the President."

"If I had not signed my name," I ask, "What would you have done?"

He smiles and says, "Well for a start, you'd be back in the car by now."

He leads me from the room, and into another. "Come in son, come in, welcome to Shangri-La," the President says, and turns to Adam, "Everything sorted out Adam," he asks.

"Yes, Mr. President," Adam replies.

"Then you may leave us Adam," He says. From the look on his face, I don't think Adam expected to be excused.

"Yes Sir," he replies, and turns on his heels. As Adam is closing the door, the President calls me to the table.

"Help yourself son," he says, "I was told you are a vegetarian, so I had the cook whip up some rabbit food for you."

There is enough food in front of me to feed ten people, "Thank you Mr. President," I reply, and we both sit down.

"Well eat up son, and we can have a chat. Adam tells me, that I owe you my life," he states.

"You do not owe me anything Sir," I say.

"You don't have to add Sir or Mr. President to every sentence, while there is no one else here." he corrects me.

"You do not owe me anything," I repeat.

"Well since my recovery, I have paid a lot of attention to you David. I've read and seen every scrap of information I can find on you. I know more about you than you do, and it's fascinating stuff."

[You do not know everything, I assure you Mr. President.]

"Is that what you wanted to tell me?" I ask.

"No," he replies, "I want to tell you that I have come to the same conclusion as Adam. It seems you can work miracles son. How do you do it?"

"I do not know," I say.

"Adam says that it hurts you."

"No," I reply, "Not physically, there is no pain, but there are associated dangers."

"Like what?" he asks.

"I'm not sure, but I think I could become trapped in my own world, or in my own mind. And if I were stuck long enough, it would mean the end of my life."

"Then why do it?" he says.

"Because I can," I tell him. "How could I tell other people to be all that they can be, if I was frightened to use my own gift?"

"Well I can only thank you, for what ever you did for me," he says, "You have given me my life back, and I intend to use the time I have left wisely. Adam is correct, and I do owe my life to you. I know I would not be here now if it were not for you. I thank you again. I see something in you son, you have an aura about you that makes people listen to your words. I have watched some recordings of your speeches, and I can only admire the way you make people believe what you say. You should have gone into politics. But you are going to make many enemies with your talk about God, when you say he is uncaring. This is why I brought you here in secret. I cannot be associated with you, because it could ruin me. So how am I going to repay you?"

"I do not ask for any reward," I say.

"If you could only retract your statements about God," he says.

"I could not, and even if I could then I would not, because I believe my statements to be true." I reply

"Truth never meant shit. How can you say that anyway? Surely what you can do is a gift from God."

How can I answer this? As I was created and was sent here by God, then technically, it is a gift from God. "You may be partly correct, but not in the way you think yourself correct," I answer, "God did not appear in a vision before me, and bestow this gift upon me. The truth is quite the opposite. Although I do not understand how this works, it does not mean it is beyond explanation. One day in the future, scientists will work out what is going on."

[Do you believe that?]

No, not really. But I have to tell him something.

"Whatever you did son," he says, "I personally thank you here and now, but you will never receive any recognition for this. As far as the world is concerned, I was never critically ill. You cannot ever let anyone else in on this secret."

"I never intended to," I respond, as he pours coffee and offers me a cup.

"Your book and now your TV programme," He says, "What is your objective? What do you aim to achieve?"

"I cannot say this, without sounding like Miss World," I reply, "So I will just say it. World peace, freedom of thought and an end to unnecessary suffering."

"You know these things are not achievable."

"But should that stop us reaching for them?" I ask, "Maybe we will not see it, but if we set the ball rolling, perhaps our grandchildren will, or their grandchildren."

"Pipe dreams David, in your book you talk about population control, you say there are too many people on Earth. Then you say every life is sacred, that it should be cherished and saved. How do you propose to limit the population, if no one dies? Do you expect governments to pass laws, limiting the number of offspring people are allowed?"

"No," I say, "It would not work. What I expect is for people to eventually reach that conclusion themselves. Eventually this message has to sink in. The consequences are too awful to contemplate. Because they are mass starvation for the human race, and total extinction for the majority of other species."

"Son, the truth is that most people cannot see past their next meal, or their next pay slip."

"I think you are wrong Sir, people just need to know the truth."

"The truth son? When you get to my age, the truth blurs a little," he says. "What you wrote about space exploration, surely you cannot ever think that will happen?"

"It has to happen, if the human race can outlive this planet, and that is a long shot, we have to make plans to live somewhere else. Not in one place, but hundreds and thousands of places. We have to start now, even if it takes a hundred years for the first humans to leave."

He looks at me as if I am insane, "I'm the President of the richest country on Earth, and I cannot get funding for a five year space mission, never mind a hundred years."

"Yet you manage to find enough money to send warships to the Gulf." I say.

"You made your point about our soldiers being sent into Israel quite clear on your programme. Do you really think I want our boys out there?" he asks.

"Then pull them out," I say, "Let the UN be the force it is supposed to be."

"The UN will do nothing," he replies.

"You are the President of the richest country on Earth, make them do something." I say.

"The enthusiasm of the young. Everything is black and white to you isn't it?" He smiles, "Don't you ever run for President son, I'd be out of a job."

"I won't," I say.

"If you have finished eating, lets retire to the den." He leads me into the next room, and indicates a leather seat opposite his, "Sit down son," he says.

"Did you really bring me here to talk about my book?" I ask.

"Only partly," he replies, "I knew of you before the Whitehouse incident, but I never looked deeply into your character, or your words. You were just an annoying upstart, preaching and writing blasphemous words, to decent God fearing Americans. But when I was well, I asked for a copy of 'Heavens Gate', even the Whitehouse staff could not get me one, there is a waiting list."

"Yes I know," I say.

"What amazed me was, fourteen people at the Whitehouse offered to lend me their copy, and now I have just finished your book, Adam kindly lent me his. But more than the book, what I saw when I watched a recording of your speeches really got my attention. You are magnetic when you stand up in front of a crowd, and although most of what you ask people to believe, will never be achievable, they believe it."

"Why is it not achievable?" I ask.

"Human nature," he replies, "God himself could not aspire to the level that you want normal people to achieve."

"People are better than God," I respond.

"Yes, so you have said. It does not say much for God."

"I'm sorry if you are uncomfortable with that," I say.

"I'm not," he replies, "But my voters would be if they heard me say it. What I am leading to is this; I think a lot of what you call for is just not possible. But a portion may just benefit this country, and therefore I want to work with you. If between us we can swing a tiny fraction of the population, away from crime, away from hate and self pity, then we will have achieved something."

"What about the voters? Will they stand for it?"

"Unfortunately, the voters cannot know," he replies, "We would have to keep everything low key."

"You mean secret." I state.

"I always associate the word secret with underhand dealing, which this would not be, but you are correct."

"So," I ask, "You want me to be your secret advisor?"

"Confidant is a better word, it would be a two way street." He replies.

"I'm not sure what to say," I respond.

"It will not be long," he says, "before you have more followers, than I

The Songs of Angels

get votes."

"And then you will jump out of the closet, and be my best friend."

He laughs and says, "Possibly, if you could just think about it, I'm afraid we are out of time for now. As I am already five minutes late for another meeting, but talking to you has been interesting. I will call Adam who is going to give you the tour, show you the sights, and we will talk later."

"Thank you Sir, I would like that," I say. By some unknown means, Adam appears thirty seconds later. I say goodbye to the President, and leave with Adam. He chats, and digs for information about what was said, but I do not disclose anything. I figure, that if the President wanted him to know, he would not have dismissed him.

As we walk he says, "I will show you where you will be staying first. You can freshen up and then I will show you around." Then he asks, "David, have you ever met, or had any dealings with a man called Marcus Brent?"

"I've never heard of him, why do you ask?"

"Just some enquiries I've been making." He says, "Don't worry about it."

Why should I be worried? Who is Marcus Brent?

"OK," I say.

"Can you ride?" he asks, and I shake my head, "You may have to learn quickly."

"Sounds fun," I say, in jest.

Who is Marcus Brent?

[I will find out.]

ॐ

In Heaven.

Raphael:
I caught him snooping around the Human Records Library.
Michael:
I was not snooping and I certainly was not hiding anything. I was just looking someone up.
God:

Why?
Michael:
Lucifer is interested in someone on Earth.
God:
Who?
Michael:
A man named Marcus Brent.
God:
What do you know about this man, Marcus Brent?
Michael:
Well nothing yet; as Raphael virtually dragged me out of the library.
God:
I will say this one more time Michael. You are not Lucifer's private detective. You may find out what you wish about this human, but you will not divulge this information to Lucifer. On second thoughts, it may be best if you do not make any enquiries, you may be tempted to tell Lucifer something he has no right to know. Are we clear?
Michael:
Crystal clear Lord.
God:
Why do you look at me that way Michael?
Michael:
I was unaware that I looked at you any different to normal Lord.
God:
You may go Michael.
Michael leaves.
Raphael:
He presumes too much Lord, he and Lucifer are old allies.
God:
You presume too much Raphael; I will say this also, one more time. You are not Michael's overseer. He answers to me if he oversteps the mark, not you.
Raphael:
I only do your will Lord.
God:
I know you mean well Raphael. You may also leave.

I spend the rest of the afternoon in Adams company. To someone who lives in New York, this place is vast. Although you do not notice the security very much, I do not think a rabbit could get in here without someone noticing it. Late in the afternoon, we arrive in the stables.

"This is Jess," Adam says as he walks over to a bay mare and strokes her nose, "You're riding her."

"Now?" I ask.

"Why not?" he replies, he proceeds to saddle the horse and then his own, who is introduced as Thunder. "Jess will look after you," he says, "There's not a softer horse in the world."

I walk over to Jess and stroke her neck; she turns one eye in my direction and studies me. Although I have never been on a horse, I think Adam is actually telling the truth. I'm just glad I am not riding Thunder.

"You will need this," Adam says, as he places a Stetson on my head, "It's obligatory."

"I think I would be happier with a crash helmet," I say.

"This is America boy," he replies, "Saddle up!" He helps me to mount and goes through the commands that the horse will hopefully respond to. I cannot believe how high up I feel. Adam leads both animals outside and mounts his own.

[You have to relax, or the horse will sense your discomfort.]

How many horses have you ridden Michael?

[You know the answer to your question, and I was just trying to help. By the way. I have some bad news; I cannot give you any information about Marcus Brent.]

Why is that not a surprise?

We ride the horses out over the meadow and into the low hills. I am not really doing anything; Jess just follows Adams horse, which is just as well because I have forgotten most of what he told me. We amble along for around twenty minutes, before stopping at the top of a hill. Adam stops and Jess obediently comes to a halt beside him. The view, with the sun going down, is stunning.

"The President was right to call this place Shangri-La," I say.

"It's not his name for it," he says, "Where were you in history classes?

Roosevelt named it Shangri-La."

"I did not know," I reply.

"Then Eisenhower renamed it Camp David after his son," he informs me, as he looks into the distance, "But I think Shangri-La is a much better description." He turns his head towards mine, "It will be dark soon, so we best head back. Are you brave enough to have a gallop when we get back to the meadow?"

"Only if you tell me where the brakes are," I reply.

Adam sets of and Jess follows, when we reach the meadow I whisper to her, "If you're going to run, don't let me fall off. OK?" As if she understood, she immediately sets off and I hang on for grim death. Within a few seconds, Adam catches us up and overtakes. Apart from every bone in my body being jarred, I enjoy the sense of freedom I feel as Jess shoots across the meadow, although I probably look like a sack of potatoes strapped to her back. She switches to a walk as we enter the stable and stops at the doors. Adam, who has already dismounted looks up to me, and smiles.

"So you thought you could get the drop on me? Well there isn't a faster horse than Thunder around here." He says.

"I didn't tell her to go," I reply as I dismount, "Jess was driving." Adam laughs and I pat Jess's nose.

"You have a friend for life there," he jokes. "Lets get these saddles off, and then you have a few hours to yourself before the President is free again. We remove the saddles and tack, stable the horses and give them a brush down.

※

The sun has disappeared behind the hills, as I sit on the balcony of my room watching the afterglow. In ten minutes I have to go back and give the President an answer to his proposal.

[It would be good to have him on our side.]

Yes, but at what cost? Does he expect me to agree with everything he does?

[You will need to ask these questions.]

There is a knock at my door, and I shout for the caller to come in. Adam enters the room and walks through the French doors, "Ready?" he asks.

I nod and follow him through the ranch house. The President greets me from his sitting position on the porch, and offers us both a seat.

"It's good to sit here again," he says, looking out into the twilight, "Watching the world with a drink in my hand." Then he turns to us and says, "Help yourselves to a shot, both of you. Did you enjoy your afternoon?"

"Very much," I tell him, thinking about the ride we had. Adam pours two glasses of what I assume is whisky, and passes one over to me.

"Thank you," I say, and take a sniff of the alcohol in the glass. Just the smell of it makes my head spin.

"I've filled Adam in on the conversation we had this morning," the President says, "He will co-ordinate our efforts, if you are agreeable."

"In theory Sir, it would be tremendous if we could assist each other," I respond, "But I have a few questions before I agree."

"Shoot," the President says.

"Firstly," I say, "I will not be censored by you, if I think you are wrong then you will hear exactly that."

"Go on," he asks.

"Secondly, I will pull no punches with what I say on the show, or when I am speaking. Even if what I say does not put you in a good light."

"If I thought you would," he replies, "Then we would not be having this conversation. I never asked you to join my party or be a yes man. I have enough of those."

"Good," I say, "Because my next broadcast doesn't exactly paint a pretty picture, regarding this governments decisions, and I do not intend to change it."

"Yes, I know," he says. I am wondering how he knows, as the show has not been aired yet. Then again, he is the President so I should not be surprised if he has obtained a copy of it. "Listen son," he continues, "I've played this game for a long time. Being knocked comes with the territory. So are we in agreement?"

"Yes Sir," I reply, "I think we are."

"Although I would prefer you not to disagree with me, you understand. Too many people listen to you. It boils down to this: I want to help you, and I want you to help me. I cannot promise to agree with everything you say, I may be President but in politics, even the things I want are not always within my reach. But maybe if we work together we can find a middle ground, and for once do some good."

"I would like that," I say.

He raises his glass and says, "Then it is settled, we will play it by ear for a while and see how it turns out." I pick up my drink, and we seal our deal with a slug of the potent liquid. He looks out into the sky, which is now quite dark, and asks, "I've been thinking about what you said this morning, about spreading the human race across the stars. They say that there are more stars up there, than grains of sand on Earth."

"Many more," I reply.

"It kind of makes all of us seem insignificant," Adam says.

"I disagree," I say, "Of all the billions of stars and planets out there, possibly only one has given birth to life, and we are part of that life. That makes me fell very significant."

The President turns and smiles at me, "You see Adam, that is why I want this young man on my side. He sees everything from a new perspective. I have a good feeling about this." He pours himself another drink and offers the decanter to me, which I refuse as I am having trouble finishing the first one.

We sit there and talk into the early hours of the morning, on subjects ranging from foreign policy to the baseball world series. Although we disagree on many things, I can feel our respect growing for each other. Eventually we call a halt and decide to get some sleep. The President has to be back in Washington at midday, he invites Adam and I, to go out riding again at first light, but I cannot see how he will be in any fit state, judging by the amount of whisky he has consumed.

⁂

Sunday.

I am wrong about his ability to soak up alcohol, of the three of us, the President seems to be the one who is wide awake and ready to go, as we saddle the horses. Once again I am riding Jess, who appears to know the commands I intend to give her, before I do. The chat is casual this morning, and for the first time, as we ride through the chill morning air,

The Songs of Angels

I see the man, the human behind this office. And I decide that possibly between us, we may be able to accomplish something.

ॐ

5th October.

Rebecca shuts the front door, and throws her case in the hall. "Hello," she calls.

I meet her and give her a hug, "How did it go?" I ask.

"Very well," she says, "Jesus, I am so tired." I help her to remove her coat and we sit down. "Your books are going faster over there, than they did here. I've shaken more hands, and had more applause than I can count, just for being your wife. Unfortunately I have been feeling very run down. Mary has done all the work, I just followed her around."

"How do you feel now?" I ask.

"Just tired," she says and closes her eyes.

"Perhaps you should have a doctor check you over," I say.

"I just need a bath, and some sleep," Rebecca replies. "But it would not hurt. I will make an appointment tomorrow," She stretches over and plants a kiss on my forehead. "Go and run a bath for me."

"No problem," I say, and proceed to go upstairs.

[She is tired, because she is pregnant.]

I know, and the doctor will confirm that when she sees him. Then hopefully she will slow down.

I sit on the side of the bath while the water level rises.

Michael, why do you think you were forbidden to find out about Marcus Brent?

There is silence for a while, [I am not permitted to talk to you about it.]

Never mind, I should have expected this from Heaven, and it's probably nothing, but I will quiz Adam when I see him again.

[That would be your best course of action.]

I return downstairs to tell Rebecca that her bath is ready, but when I get there, she is fast asleep. So I gently carry her upstairs, and put her to bed. I rest my hand on her stomach and say out loud, but quietly so not to wake her, "This is my child growing inside her."

[Yes Lucifer.]

That's a miracle Michael: That is a real miracle.

❧

Washington D.C.

Adam Whiteside reads through the report on his desk. The report tells him that Marcus Brent is heading three cases in New York. None have any connection to David Brookes. Adam realizes that he has two major problems. The first is that Brent is a respected and powerful member of the FBI, which makes it extremely difficult to conduct any sort of enquiry without raising suspicion. The second problem is if he made public, the fact that Brent had falsified documents, he would probably never find out what Brent was actually up to.

He sits back in his chair, looks up at the ceiling, and whispers to himself, "Softly, softly on this one Adam."

❧

October 12th
The second program of the television broadcast titled 'Heavens Gate'
End speech of David Brookes.

"It will not do anymore, to be detached nations. Mankind grew from a family to a clan, from a clan to a tribe, from a tribe to a nation. Why have we stopped at this point? It is because we still think like the families who walked the savannas of Africa, all those millions of years ago. Mankind still looks to protect his territory and his family, but his territory is now his country, and his families are his countrymen.

There is one more step to take, which will finally separate you from *Homo Erectus*. To do this, we must return to the notion of the family, and that family is the family of mankind, every man or woman is your relative, your brother or your sister. And every country is a part of the greatest nation, and that nation is Earth.

Yet I watch brothers kill brothers in the holy lands, and although they have wronged each other, they do not kill because they have wronged each other, not because they are better or worse than each other, or even because one is evil and one is good. They fight because they cannot remember what it was like, not to hate each other, and each death spirals them deeper into hatred, while both believe that the same God is their private property.

If two of your children are fighting, do you send a bigger brother into their squabble? Do you tell that child to hit them both as hard as possible? Would you expect it to end the argument, or would you now see three of your children fighting. Yet the powers of this nation are poised to do just that. There will be no peace between these brothers if America alone tries to separate them. This is not a problem for America alone, this is a problem that the parents must resolve, because their brothers are all nations and their parents are all mankind. And the parents of these brothers must act together, not to punish them, but to understand them, comfort and teach them.

Only when they understand that it is their brother that they strike, and their brother that strikes them back. When they see that all the hurt that they cause, is rained back on them and that no one can ever win. Then maybe these brothers can cease to strike out at one another, forgive one another and at last, be at peace with one another."

October 13th

I let myself into the house; it seems quiet so I assume Rebecca is still out. But I find her sitting silently in the living room. "Are you alright?" I ask, and tears fill her eyes as she looks over in my direction, "What's wrong?"

She holds her arms out to me, and replies, "Nothing is wrong, everything is fine. I'm pregnant." I take her in my arms and hold her.

"Then why the tears?" I ask, "This is wonderful news."

"I just cannot believe it David," she says, "You're happy aren't you?"

"Yes, of course I am, why would you think anything else? I love you and we are going to have a child. How could anything be more perfect?"

❧

October 15th.

-He spent the weekend at Camp David, with the President. -

What! How could I not know about this? How could he do this without the FBI knowing? This is terrible news Lord.

-He has tricked his way into the Presidents confidence Marcus. –

How Lord? How could a man like the President, be fooled into believing him?

-It does not matter how; it is the Devil's first mistake Marcus. You can turn people to our goal if they know that this man, this non believer, is influencing the President of the United States. Will they not help us to stop him? –

Yes Lord, we have to get him away from the President.

-No Marcus, the more he meddles, the more harm he is seen to do, the more allies against him we will have. We will leave him there for now. –

But the President, what about him?

-What of him? –

It could harm him Lord.

- That is not my concern. If I thought the President was worthy, I would have chosen him instead of you. I did not. You will make it known to the people who will help us, that the President knows David Brookes, that Brookes conspires with him, that he influences him. -

Yes Lord.

❧

I answer the phone, expecting it to be Adam, "Hello," I say.

"David," the Presidents voice says, "How are you son?"

"Fine Sir," I reply.

"Save this number in your phone memory, I will probably never be there when you call, but just leave a message and I will always try to get back to you."

"OK," I say, "What can I do for you Sir?"

The Songs of Angels

"Stop calling me Sir," he says, and then, "Have you seen the news this morning?"

"No I haven't," I admit.

"Well you should, you may find it interesting. I will speak to you soon, got to go." He hangs up without waiting for a reply, and I press the end call button on the phone. I search around for the television remote control, when I find it I turn to CNN twenty-four hour news, it is half way through a report, but I realize what it is about instantly. It shows US warships leaving the Mediterranean and the Gulf.

The caption scrolling along the bottom of the screen reads, 'US government make U-turn in Israel crisis and order all troops to stand down. President demands that the UN must take the lead and pledges support.' The main window cuts to a Whitehouse spokesperson and she says, "While this government wishes that the conflict that continues to escalate in Israel, could be brought to a swift end, it no longer feels that an American force alone will realize this outcome. This government urges Israel to cease their aggression and demands that the United Nations acts immediately, if they do not comply.'

Have I done this?

[It appears that you may have had a hand in it.]

It was the right thing to do wasn't it? Even if I am now responsible for deaths that may have been avoided had American troops stepped in? It would have made it worse, I am sure of that.

[He would not have pulled US troops out if he did not think it the correct and right course of action. The President knew what was right, you just reminded him.]

I pick up the phone and dial; the answering machine on the other end invites me to leave a message. When it beeps, I just say, "Call me."

CHAPTER 10

Year Thirty-six: 5th December.

"He is calling it 'The Genesis Project' he has ordered an enquiry into deep space travel. NASA has been requested to formulate the following plan, first to set up a colony on the Moon, which will be the launch pad for a bigger colony on Mars. This has to be self-sufficient by the way, a complete eco system and running by 2030. If that's not enough expense, phase two will knock you over. His plan is for the Mars colony to be the prototype for ships that we will launch into outer space."

"Going where?" a man asks.

"To the two closest and suitable stars."

"This is ridiculous! Does he have any idea how long it would take a rocket to get to the nearest star?" the man asks, "The crew would be dead before they travelled a thousandth of the way."

"I don't think you grasp the scale of this enquiry. We are not talking about space shuttles. He wants to build ships as big as towns, and that is why the Mars prototype has to be self-sufficient. He knows the original crew will not see the end of the voyage. We are talking about the seventieth or eightieth generation, actually arriving at their destination. Then they would have to find a suitable planet, in an Earth type orbit and make it suitable to live on.

Get this! Best estimates that the space nerds have, suggest that each colony would have to orbit their planet for a further two thousand years, while the planet was 'terra-formed'. They would have to introduce hydrogen-guzzling bacteria to release oxygen from the seas. Working their way up to microbes and plants. So from start to finish, total 'journey' time is estimated at four and a half thousand years. All this before the first human can set foot on their mythical new Earth."

"What if there are no suitable planets, when they get to their star?"

"It doesn't matter, they're self-sufficient, they move on until they find one."

"Where did you get this information from Marcus?"

"A contact at NASA," Marcus replies, "Of course NASA are loving this, the budget just for the enquiry makes the moon landings look like chicken feed."

"The US could never afford this, how does the President intend to fund it all?"

"By selling out," Marcus replies, "This is why my contact at NASA spilled the beans to me, he's worried. The President wants the whole world to chip in, which would mean all our technology being shared with any country that contributes. Russia, China, the whole world."

"This is insane."

"I know," Marcus says, "That's why I thought you should know."

"And you think all this has something to do with this Brookes fellow?"

"I am sure Sir," Marcus replies, "I know that the President meets with him. His book is full of shit like this."

"Madness Marcus! Total madness; keep this under your hat for now. I have to make a few others aware, and then we will talk again. What else do you know about David Brookes?"

"A lot, and none of it's any good."

"Then you had better continue Marcus."

※

8th December.

Freddy Nash: Drug dealer, links to prostitution, racketeering and implicated in seven murders in the last three years. Nash owns two nightclubs in Queens, and has one conviction on drug trafficking in 1988, for which he served five years. Since then no one has touched him. There are rumours that he has friends in the local police force, but no proof. Adam reads through the file, and then returns to the field report on his desk.

Marcus Brent and Freddy Nash, meeting in a car park yesterday afternoon. There are half a dozen grainy black and white photographs, which his agent took from a distance. There are no records of what was said, just that they talked for thirty-five minutes. One photograph shows Brent passing a file, contents unknown, to Nash.

Adam wonders if Marcus could actually be on Nash's payroll? The thought sends a shiver through him because it is unthinkable, that a man in Brent's position would do such a thing. Maybe Brent is using Freddy, but why would a man with the might of the FBI behind him, feel the need to press a lowlife like Freddy Nash into his service? Unless he was doing something that he did not want the FBI to know about.

Could there be a connection to David Brookes? Adam picks up his phone and dials a number, when it is answered, he says, "Paul, can you search through your database, quietly mind. See if there is any connection between any of Brent's cases, and a known drug dealer called Freddy Nash."

"Sure Adam," agent Paul Minor replies, "What am I looking for?"

"Anything," Adam replies.

"Is this an official investigation into Brent?" he asks.

"No Paul," Adam replies, "But I might be onto something. Keep this quiet for me."

"No Problem," Minor says, "I will get back to you tomorrow."

"Cheers," Adam says, and hangs up. He returns to the file on Freddy Nash. The list of suspected crimes goes on forever, but each time he has wriggled out of danger. Through lack of evidence, witnesses disappearing or smart lawyers. He comes to a section of Freddy's known associates, Adam flicks through twenty odd photographs, he knows none of their faces, and then closes the file.

⁂

10th December.

The four men sit in a closed room, at the back of a rundown factory near the docks. Bodyguards discreetly patrol the area outside, to make sure they are not disturbed or overheard.

"Thank you all for coming," Marcus says, "I realize this is out of the ordinary, so we should get on. If you would start James."

Presidential advisor James Locke, clears his throat, "I'm not sure if I like this," he says.

"Just tell everyone what you told me," Marcus asks.

Locke looks around at the other two men and says, "I just commented to Marcus,"

"No James," Marcus interrupts, "It was not just a comment, you confided in me because you are concerned, because you are worried." He stares at Locke.

"Yes," Locke replies, "The President, he has changed since his illness, I do not know who he is anymore. He tells me nothing and he asks me nothing. It's like I am talking to a different person. It started with the Israel conflict; he ordered the withdrawal before he informed anyone else that he planned to do it. Then there is this Genesis nonsense; once again he set NASA jumping through hoops for him, before we even knew about it. I am concerned because no one at the Whitehouse knows what he will do next."

The third man, William Clarke, a Deputy Director in the CIA joins in, "Doctor," he asks the fourth man, "The Presidents illness, could it have done something undetected to him, made him unstable?"

The fourth man, Doctor Arnold Francis removes his glasses, and addresses the others, "The reason Marcus asked me here, is that you do not know the true nature of the Presidents condition."

"I know he was worse than we let on, but I understood that he responded to your treatment." Clarke says.

"That is the story that we told everyone who knew he was ill. But he was not just ill, he was dying," the Doctor states, and Clarke sits up. The Doctor continues, "Cancer was eating his body away. Unstable is not the right word for his condition at the time. Incoherent and bedridden, unresponsive and on deaths door are closer. You see, the pain was driving him insane and I did not expect him to see the week out."

"So how did you cure him?" Locke asks.

"Tell him about Brookes," Marcus says.

"I'll come to that," the Doctor says, "We were told that a new doctor was joining our team. One Alan Walker, a neurosurgeon from California. His credentials on paper were outstanding, so I was quite eager to work with him. He arrived, spent fifteen minutes with the President then disappeared. Tests the next day showed the cancers in recession. Three days later he was as fit as you and me, and I have no idea how this could happen. All we know about medical science said that the President was a dead man. Naturally I was curious about this Doctor, especially as he was rushed away so quickly, but all the enquires I made fell on deaf ears. In fact I was politely told to drop it, so I did."

"Are you telling us this mysterious doctor cured him?" Clarke asks.

"I do not know, but I know it was not my team," Francis replies, "Then the strangest thing happened. I'm watching TV and there is Dr. Walker staring out of the screen, only his name isn't Walker, it's David Brookes."

"You're sure it's the same man?" Clarke says.

"Were positive," Marcus replies, "I've checked out Dr. Walker. The paper trail is perfect, he has worked in California since graduating from university, he was on the hospital staff, and now works at an institute in Alaska. Every computer you log onto will tell you that, but no one at the hospital has ever met him and no one in Alaska has ever heard his name. Dr. Alan Walker is an invention, someone went to a lot of trouble to build this fictional character. All so they could smuggle Brookes into the Whitehouse."

"Could Brookes have fabricated this identification?" Clarke asks.

"He has money, a lot of it," Marcus replies, "But to go to the lengths that this does, it would have to be someone in the bureau, or in your department William."

"Shit," Clarke says, "So you think Brookes has some hold over the President?"

"They have met clandestinely four times to my knowledge," Marcus states, "And it seems they have a scrambled phone connection."

"That would explain a lot," Locke adds, "We were wondering who he was talking to."

"Let me get this straight," Clarke says, "You are suggesting that the President of the United States, is having his policies dictated to him by this Bible thumping author?"

"Apart from the fact that he isn't religious, Brookes seems to hate God," Marcus replies, "Then yes, that is my conclusion."

"If all this is true," Locke says, "Then we have a national security breach."

"Yes we do," Marcus states, "And it is up to us, to do something about it."

The four men are silent for some time, as each one contemplates what they have heard. Marcus's eyes sparkle as he looks at each one in turn. The Doctor looks down into his lap, unwilling to make eye contact with any off them.

-You should not have involved him this far Marcus, he has visions of assassins in his mind.-

What of the others Lord?

-The same, but they are not petrified by it.-

What should I do with him Lord?

-What ever you have to, we cannot have anyone on the side of light, who may come apart in our finest hour.-

William Clarke breaks the silence, "Get me proof Marcus, solid proof that this is true. I will give you every assistance you need, people and equipment. Do you agree James?"

"Yes," James Locke says, "Then we will decide where to go from there."

Outside as they leave, Marcus pulls the Doctor to one side, "Doc," he says, "You understand that you cannot breath a word of this conversation to anyone."

"I know," he replies, but he still will not make eye contact.

"Remember that you are bound by the official secrets act."

"Yes, but that is to protect America," he says, "But I'm not sure that the conversation I just heard is in the best interests of the America, or the President of America. I will not be part of any killing."

"What gave you that idea?" Marcus asks, "No one said anything about killing."

"Then what did you mean?" the Doctor asks.

"That we have to keep an eye on Brookes and the President. America is important, and no individual is more important."

"I wish I believed you," the Doctor says. He walks to his car and gets inside. Marcus watches him go, and then heads for his own car.

As he drives away, Marcus punches a number into his car phone. "Freddy?" he asks when it is answered.

"For fuck's sake Marcus," Freddy Nash replies, "What now? My business is going to shit, all my people are running around doing crap for you."

"If you would prefer twenty years to life, I will hang up now."

"I will kill you," Freddy threatens, "When all this is over."

"Yes, and the files I have on you will go straight to the District Attorney. Consider what you are doing for me, as your reimbursement to society. Besides, every time you help me, you help yourself."

"What do you want?" he asks.

Marcus explains what he wants.

"That's got to be worth something," Freddy says.

"Probably an arm full of files for your shredder," Marcus says, "And a few corrupt or deleted files on my computer."

"The trouble with this arrangement, is that I have no idea how much shit you have on me."

Marcus laughs, "When I ask you to do something, and have no files to give you: Then you can kill me. But then again, how will you know there is nothing left? How will you be sure?" Freddy curses something under his breath. "I promise this will all be over soon," Marcus tells him, "I will not need your people in a couple of days."

"Who else are you blackmailing?" Freddy asks.

"Don't you worry yourself about it, just do as I ask." Marcus says. He hangs up and continues to drive back to his home.

That Same night.

Doctor Arnold Francis drives his Mercedes through the quiet residential streets, almost back at his house. The thought that repeats in his mind is this: Were those three men actually talking about killing David Brookes? He tries to convince himself that they were not, but something in the back of his head will not let go, the look in Brent's eyes when he said that it was up to them to do something.

He pulls onto the drive of his home, and looks up at the empty windows in the gathering darkness. Sitting in his car, he wonders if his imagination was running riot. Finally he switches off the engine and walks to his front door. As he unlocks it and steps inside, he detects a faint and strange odour, one that is out of place in this house. He is accustomed to the smells of this house, as he lives alone. Disinfectant that the cleaning lady leaves behind or flowers that she changes every few days.

Then the odour is gone, and he dismisses it from his mind. Doctor Francis walks to his bar and pours himself a shot of Jack Daniels. The alcohol burns his throat as he drinks it in one swallow. He takes the glass to the kitchen and leaves it on the drainer, then decides to retire; it has been a long day.

On the stairs he stops and looks back, cursing as he turns and remembers that he has forgotten to lock his front door. He backtracks and throws the deadbolts on the top and bottom of the door, then sets the alarm control box that is hanging on the wall besides it. Finally he heads back upstairs.

After some time lying on his bed, sleep will not come. Every bang of the central heating system, every creak of contracting timbers, brings him wide-awake. He rolls over, sits up and switches on the lamp. Blinking as his eyes adjust to the brightness, he eventually focuses on the man standing in front of him, the man who is pointing a gun at his head.

Involuntary he jumps back, pulling the bedclothes with him, and lets out a weak screech, "Shut up or die," the gunman quietly says. The Doctor is paralyzed with fear, and does as he is instructed. The gunman continues, "Don't you ever sleep man? Fuck it, now this is going to be messy."

"Take anything," the Doctor stammers, "Anything you want."

"What I want," the gunman replies, "Is for you to shut the fuck up!"

Arnold Francis looks down at the floor, as tears fill his eyes, "Are you going to kill me?" he asks, through sobs of self-pity, and self-loathing that he is quivering in front of this man.

"Unfortunately for you," the gunman replies, "Yes I am." The Doctor breaks down, and begins to bawl, tears mix with the snot that dribbles from his nose. "Now stop that," the gunman says, "Be a fucking man about this. If you could've just gone to sleep, then you would be none the wiser, so blabbing won't do no good."

"Why?" The Doctor asks as he wipes his nose on the back of his hand.

"Nothing personal man, it's just my job. But now we have a dilemma. I had planned to pump you full of this crap," he says, holding up a fat syringe.

"What's in it?" the Doctor asks.

"Enough tranquillizers to put you to sleep forever, don't suppose you feel like obliging me do you?" The assassin enquires.

"Fuck you!" The Doctor says.

"Didn't think so," the man raises the gun.

"Wait!" Doctor Francis screams, "I know why you are here! I know things! I know why you were sent to kill me!"

"So do I," the gunman replies, "Five thousand dollars." The first bullet makes hardly any noise as it travels through the silencer, rips through the Doctor's collarbone and knocks him off the bed. The second takes him in the gut, and the third is a close up headshot that takes the Doctors life.

The assassin puts away his firearm and steps away from the body. As he turns away his breathing becomes ragged. He takes an inhaler from his pocket and pumps atomized air into his lungs. "Suppose I better make it look like a robbery now," he whispers to himself, and proceeds to turn over the house.

11th December

The message on Adams phone is from Paul Minor. In it, he says that he is sorry that it took him so long, but he could find no mention of Freddy Nash, in any of Brent's active cases. There is however, a connection dating back to 1995. Brent was on a team who investigated Nash, but no charges were ever brought against him.

The report on Adams desk is from a field agent. Brent had been followed the previous day. The agents report said that he had trailed Brent to the docks, where he met with at least three unknown men. The agent goes on to report, that he could not get near the location of the meeting, as they had muscle all around, and never saw the faces of the other men. What Adam does have from the report, is the make and registration numbers of three cars, besides Brent's.

The first two numbers draw a blank on his search. The computer will not tell him the owners. That can only mean that another agency, the CIA or the secret service, or even the bureau owns them. Then the final one makes him take a sharp intake of breath. Dr. Arnold Francis, what

The Songs of Angels

was he doing meeting with Marcus? Adam stares at the photograph of the Doctor on his monitor. Here is a link, between Brent, David Brookes, the President, and ultimately back to himself.

If Francis has blabbed about the Presidents illness, then Brent may put two and two together, which could lead him back to David. Adam thinks for a while and then decides that he has to act. He picks up the phone and calls his superior in Washington. When he finds that he is unavailable, he makes an appointment to see him the next day. Then he begins to compile all that he has amassed on his ex boss, he will present it and finish Brent off.

※

"You fucking idiot!" Brent screams down the phone at Freddy Nash.

"Calm down!" Freddy replies, "These things have a tendency to go pear shaped."

"It was supposed to look like suicide!"

"Yes, I do fucking know!" Freddy shouts, "But he took my man by surprise, so now it looks like a robbery that went wrong."

"Amateurs!" Marcus cries.

"Look Marcus, he's dead! That's what you wanted. There's no connection to you, so chill out for Christ's sake."

"But there is now a murder investigation Freddy." Marcus says, "If this ever comes anywhere near me, you are fucked! I will make sure of it."

Freddy replies, "Yea, I love you too Marcus," and slams down the phone.

※

12th December

Charles 'Chuck' Bourne flicks through the assorted papers that he has on his desk. He then looks up and sits back in his chair. "Well Adam," he says, "You are making some pretty big accusations here."

"Yes Sir," Adam says to his superior.

"You know that Marcus Brent is a respected and powerful member of the bureau." Chuck Bourne points out.

"I do not make these accusations lightly Sir, I just think that he is doing something underhand, and I cannot find out what it is on my own."

"But you have amassed some damming evidence on your own, without authorization, and using the bureaus time and manpower," Bourne says.

"I'm sorry Sir," Adam says, "But I could not think of another way of doing this, not when it involves a man like Marcus Brent."

Chuck Bourne leans forward and flicks through the file again, "Well Adam," he says, "Thank you for bringing me this information. I will deal with this from now on, you can go back to the job you should be doing at the Whitehouse."

"What will happen to Marcus?" Adam Asks.

"There will be an official investigation Adam, if this is all true, then I would expect he will be in prison soon."

"Thank you Sir," Adam replies, "If I can help with anything, you know where I am."

"Yes Adam I do," Bourne holds out his hand, and Adam shakes it, "Adam," he says, "Don't ever try to run inquires on your own again. If you have concerns, you can always come to me."

"Yes Sir," Adam says smiling. He leaves the room confident that Marcus will be dealt with.

Chuck Bourne flicks through the file as he dials a number into his telephone. "Mr. William Clarke's office," The female voice on the line says.

"Is he there?" Bourne asks.

"No Sir, can I take a message?" She asks.

"Yes, tell him to contact Chuck Bourne, tell him it's urgent and we may have a problem."

"Consider it done Sir," the woman replies.

13th December

"We now have forty thousand people, who are official members in our meeting places. That figure does not include the people who come and go, and do not register. The fact is we cannot keep up anymore." Mary says.

"How many halls does the trust have on its books?" I ask.

"One hundred and eighty, and growing at around two a week," she says, "I no longer know where half of them are. A man in Boston gave us a warehouse last month, we are upgrading it now, it will probably hold over a thousand people when it's finished."

"Do we have that much support in Boston?" I enquire.

Mary laughs, "One warehouse will not be enough in a month. People read your book, and it changes them, they want to know more, but most of all, they want to know you. Can you up your schedule and visit more places?" Mary asks.

"I'm already doing two sessions a week." I reply.

"I know," she says, "But do the maths, as the meeting places are growing by at least two every week, it means that you can never visit them all."

"I am just one man," I say.

"You are the driving force behind all this, people want to see you, and they want to put their questions to you."

"Alright," I say, "From now on, schedule three meetings a week, but I will have to slow down as Rebecca gets closer to her time."

"I'm fine," Rebecca says.

"But I won't be," I tell her, "If I'm in Texas when our baby comes."

"I have an idea," Rebecca says, "The problem is that most of the meeting places are too small. I know that you like to be up close, when you talk David, but lets face it; you will never get around to everyone. Why not have bigger gatherings."

"Where?" I ask.

"Hire conference centres, or even stadiums if the interest is there."

Mary says, "The interest is there, I think we could fill Yankee stadium."

"But could we afford to hire it?" I say.

"David, the trust has more money, than we know what to do with." Mary replies, "We are spending at an alarming rate, grants, scholarships, building upgrades. As well as throwing money at every worthwhile charity we can find. But every week I look at the figures and we have more. You could hire Yankee stadium for a year if you wished."

"Then look into it," I say, "No ticket sales though, I do not want people paying to see me. So start small and see where it goes."

"Excellent," Mary says, "One more thing, I really meant it when I said that I cannot keep up anymore, especially as Rebecca will be taking a back seat from now on. I have a lot of people giving up their time for us, but this is getting so big now. We need to hire people, professionals to run the trust full time."

"Do it," I tell her, "But I would like you to stay in overall control. Draw a salary for yourself if you wish."

"I would be happy to run this for you, but I couldn't take money out of the trust. I do not need it. Rest assured David, anyone I do pay, will be on our side. There will never be any fat cat trustees as long as I am here."

"Mary," I say, "Do what you wish, I trust you to do the right thing. If you have to hire people, I want you to pay them what they are worth."

"Definitely," she says as she stands up, "Well I have to be going, lots to do." She hugs Rebecca and I, and then says her goodbyes.

Rebecca stretches and yawns, "I think I will have a nap for a while," she says.

"You're feeling alright?" I ask.

"Stop panicking," she replies, "Just bushed, wake me in an hour or so."

"OK," I say, she kisses me and heads for the bedroom.

[Gathering momentum.]

Yes, but even forty thousand souls is still a tiny fraction of this nation.

[That is today, how many will there be next year, or the year after?]

Never enough.

[You can never hope to have everyone on your side; even Jesus could not do it.]

Christianity is the biggest religion on Earth.

[Look at it this way, you have at least forty thousand followers, and you are still alive.]

I don't understand your point.

[While God lived as Jesus, his grand total was twelve, and one of those betrayed him.]

Point taken.

20th December.

"So what happens now?" Adam asks Chuck Bourne.

Bourne stands up and paces Adams office, "Obviously we will put out a warrant for his arrest."

"And how long has he been gone?"

"Marcus failed to come to work four days ago," Bourne replies, "We went looking for him the next day, to find his house cleared of all his personal affects. His bank accounts are empty and his database at the FBI has been wiped."

"So he has gone to ground. Someone tipped him off."

"It would appear so," Bourne confirms.

"Therefore you are not just looking for Brent," Adam states, "As he must have accomplices in the FBI."

"There is no need for you to tell me my job Adam."

"Brent is dangerous Sir," Adam says, "You have to find him."

"Don't worry, we will." Bourne replies, and then says, "How is the President."

"Never better."

Bourne stares at Adam for a few seconds, "That's good," he says. "Don't panic about Marcus, we will find him."

"Yes Sir," Adam replies as Bourne sees himself out of the office. He walks back to his car and checks out of the Whitehouse grounds. As he drives away he makes a call to William Clarke at the CIA.

"Chuck," Clarke asks, "How did it go?"

"I think he is contained for a while, he trusts me."

"You are sure that we do not have a problem with Adam Whiteside?"

"He will not do anything," Bourne says.

"Marcus thinks that Whiteside has thrown his lot in with Brookes and the President."

"How is Marcus?" Bourne asks.

"Settled into a safe house in New York, we are meeting there tomorrow evening, to discuss the latest events. Will you be able to make it?"

"Yes," Bourne replies.

"I will send you the address and see you there tomorrow." Clarke says.

"See you there," Bourne says.

Adam sits at his desk and stares at the wall. His boss Charles Bourne failed to tell him something. The fact that Dr. Arnold Francis was murdered the same night he met with Marcus. The night before Adam had handed over his files, clearly stating that he was seen with Marcus and persons unknown. Adam was told about the Doctors tragic demise, by a contact in New York, and Bourne must also know. Then why would he omit to share this information?

Someone in the FBI tipped Marcus off, someone told him he was under investigation, why else would he run? Could his boss be that man? Could Adam have made a massive mistake confiding in him?

21st December.
CIA safe house. N.Y.

There are six of them who meet here in this house. Three others join William Clarke, Marcus Brent and James Locke. The new members of Marcus's group are Kirk Cope, Vice President of the US. Nathan Bolton, CIA and Chuck Bourne. All have been brought up to date, regarding the situation at the Whitehouse.

Locke finishes his statement, "Finally, the latest rumours are that he will ban compulsory religious education in all schools, and make it voluntary. But evolution theory will be made compulsory."

"There will be riots in the bible belts, they will not stand it." Bourne states.

"Not to mention the loss of votes," Kirk Cope adds.

"We do not give a fuck about your votes Kirk," Nathan Bolton replies, "What is important is the stability of America."

"Now Gents," Marcus says, "We are on the same side."

Clarke says, "Marcus is correct, you have all seen the evidence that he has presented. There can be no doubt that Brookes sways the President, and his course of action will eventually harm our country. The question is how will we stop this?"

The Songs of Angels

"Brookes has to be removed." Marcus says.

"And you think that his disappearance, will halt the Presidents present course of action?" Nathan Bolton asks. No one answers him. "What do you expect us to do with Brookes Marcus, ask him to just leave the President alone?"

"No," Marcus says, "He has to be removed permanently."

"Kill him?" Locke asks.

"It's not just the President, Brookes has to be stopped from turning good Americans from God. You have seen his TV programme, his book, and now he plans rallies all across America, feeding misinformation into the minds of our people."

"Couldn't we discredit him somehow?" Locke asks.

"I think it is too late for that James," Clarke says, "Brookes has to be dealt with, and so does the President. American stability is at stake."

Kirk Pope says, "How can the removal of the President be good for stability? Perhaps it would have been better, if he had died."

"I'm not talking about impeachment," Clarke replies, "And I agree, it will be better if he dies."

"That's not what I said, I was talking past tense," Pope says, "You are talking future."

"No one was talking about killing the President," Marcus interrupts, "Just Brookes."

-Let it go Marcus, the President is unimportant as long as the fight with Satan is victorious. -

"Do you think the President will sit by idly, if we assassinate Brookes?" Clarke asks Marcus. Marcus does not reply. "I say that they both have to go."

"Do you think the assassination of the President will bring stability to America?" Bourne asks.

"It is better than leaving a man in charge, who is clearly unstable. Besides, we may bring the people together against a common enemy, if we can find someone to blame it on."

"Islamic terrorists, everyone would believe they wished to kill Brookes, with his statements about God." Bourne offers, "And the President, after he pulled out of Palestine and left them to die."

"Unfortunately Chuck," Locke replies, "I don't think we have any suicide bombers in the CIA."

"Excuse me, but that is not quite true," Bolton says. All eyes turn to him.

Locke asks, "Are you saying that you have links with Islamic terrorists?"

"No, of course not," Bolton replies, "But we do have people," he stops for a second and then continues, "I don't quite know how to put this. There is a department who train specialists, who would die for their cause."

"We would all die for our country, but are you saying that America has it's own suicide bombers?" Locke asks.

"Yes and no," Nathan Bolton says, "No they are not American, and no, they would not die for America, because they do not know that they work for America. They believe that they are actually terrorists, and would die for Allah and their cause. Unfortunately for them, they have no links with any actual terrorist group and are controlled by the CIA. So yes, you could say that America has suicide bombers."

"They are brainwashed?" Marcus asks.

"Motivated," Bolton says.

"Fuck!" Locke replies.

※

Year thirty-seven: January 08th

Adam Whiteside enters the Oval office. The President has ordered all the staff that they should not be disturbed. "Sit down Adam, and tell me what worries you."

"Thank you for seeing me Sir, I'm sorry to take up your time," Adam says, "But I believe that David may be in danger."

"Explain," the President instructs.

"I think that a break away group, some in the FBI, are planning actions against him, I don't know what. It all centres on Marcus Brent, my old boss in New York. Since I discovered that he falsified orders, orders to keep David under surveillance, I've been keeping an eye on him, and everything I find out makes me more concerned."

"Pass it onto your superiors, if Brent falsified orders, then they have a

The Songs of Angels

case to bring him to call."

"That's another thing that worries me," Adam replies, "I did just that. I passed on all that I knew to Charles Bourne. Two weeks later Marcus disappeared. At first I thought that someone had tipped him off, that he was under investigation. Now I find that there never was any investigation. Bourne never started one, and Marcus is officially on sick leave."

"What are you saying?"

"I believe that Bourne sent him to ground, that he is part of, or knows what Marcus is up to." Adam states.

"I have known Chuck Bourne for more than ten years Adam, I cannot believe that he would be conspiring with Brent."

"Never the less," Adam says, "I cannot find another explanation."

The President sits forward, and rests his face in his hands, "Do you think they know about our contact with Brookes?"

"I do not know," Adam admits, "But another strange thing happened. Do you remember Dr. Francis?"

"Yes," the President replies, "I heard about his tragic death. He was murdered in his home by robbers."

"On the same day he met with Brent," Adam adds, "One of my men saw them."

The President is silent for a few seconds, and then asks, "What do you want to do?"

"Firstly, I do not know who to trust. Secondly, I think confiding in Bourne may have put David in more danger. So I suggest that I need to devote all of my time, finding out what is actually going on."

"Take all the time you need," the President says, "You are officially on leave from today. Megan can look after things here, we can trust Megan can't we?"

"Thank you Sir, I have no reason to distrust Megan. I will brief her on her duties before I go."

"Keep in touch, and be careful," the President urges.

"I will," Adam replies, and leaves the Oval office.

⁂

"How long will you be gone?" Megan Marshall asks Adam, as they sit together in his office.

"I have no idea," Adam replies. Megan grins, "You don't have to be this happy that I am going Meg," he says.

"I'm sorry," she says, "But this will be the first time that I will be in sole charge. I'm just looking forward to it."

"Well I trust you to look after everything, I know you're capable so don't let me down."

The grin returns to her face, "You can count on me boss."

"I will keep in touch," Adam says, as he pulls on his coat and heads for the door. He turns before he goes and adds, "Look after him."

Marshall executes a mock salute and says, "Yes Sir."

※

As Adam checks through security, his mind is on the job that he has taken on. Where to start? Marcus is the key to all of this, so he has to find him. First stop has to be the FBI headquarters in New York. See where Marcus is supposed to be on vacation, then tonight, his house.

※

The alarm system on Marcus' house is deactivated in seconds; Adam congratulates himself on remembering his field training, although he could not open the back door with his skeleton key, and ended up breaking a side window to gain entry. His trip to FBI headquarters was fruitless, although it is policy to leave a contact number, when on vacation; Marcus appears to have overlooked this protocol.

He switches on his pencil beam torch, and heads on through the kitchen, alert to any sounds around him. There are none, and he is convinced that the house is unoccupied. A brief search of the lower floor tells him that Bourne was telling the truth, when he said that Marcus had abandoned his home. The rotting food in the fridge is testament that no one has been here for some time.

Keeping the beam of his torch low, Adam locates the study and begins his search in earnest. Wading through all of Marcus' files takes some time, and gives him no clue to his whereabouts. In the upstairs floors, Adams search is also in vain, and realizing he will find no reference to

Marcus' location, he backtracks and departs.

※

January 9th.
In Heaven.

After the briefing, Michael pulls Gabriel to one side and indicates that he wishes to speak to him in private. They meet in their usual place, in the open air, near the memorial to the twin towers, the shrine that human souls erected in Heaven after the atrocity.

"What do you wish to tell me brother?" Gabriel asks.

"I missed something out of my report," Michael replies, Gabriel waits for him to speak, "Lucifer is being observed again, but these humans are the best I have encountered. It was only luck that I realized that it was happening. There is a team of them."

"Why did you not report this?" Gabriel asks.

Michael blows air down his nose, "Do you think I should notify our Lord? Tell him that I am onto him? So they can disperse like mist, as they did last time? No Gabriel, this time I will watch them closely."

"I think that we are playing a dangerous game my brother."

"That may be so," Michael replies, "But I do not see what else we may do."

※

January 14th.

Adam Whiteside sits at the bar of Freddy Nash's club, sipping a drink and watching the activity all around him. On the stage half naked, and half stoned females robotically cavort around chrome poles, but they are not what Adam is looking at, he watches the lackeys, how they come and go, looking for a way to get at Freddy, without flashing his badge in front of him.

Freddy appears at regular intervals, swaggering around the crowd, shaking hands with regulars and showing himself to other lowlifes. With smiles and greetings on the outside for other gangsters, all a show of strength, and always flanked by armed minders.

Adam decides that the club is not the place to confront him and heads outside to the car park. He sits in darkness watching Freddy's car parked under the spotlight outside the back door.

At around one-thirty the door opens and a minder steps out, Adam sinks in his seat. The minder scans the vehicles around him, and then calls someone forward. Freddy steps outside and gets into the passenger seat. Then the minder walks around the automobile and gets into the drivers side. He reverses out of the bay and heads around to the front of the building and the main road.

Adam follows, neglecting to put his lights on until he is in the flow of traffic. One minder should not be too much trouble. He edges his car until he is directly behind Freddy. As they reach the intersection, he gently drives into the back of his car, smashing the rear light and bending the rear fender. Adam gets out of his car, "Shit!" he shouts, "I'm sorry man!" He walks to the driver's window as the minder winds it down. "I can't believe I did that," he says as he approaches.

"You fucking asshole," the minder says as Adam looks through the window, "Didn't no fucker ever teach you-" His words stick in his throat as Adam presses a revolver into his eye.

"Keep calm," Adam says, "Hands on the wheel, and you Freddy, hands on the dash." Adam reaches inside and takes the minders gun from his holster. "Out," he tells the minder, who does as he is told, "Lie on the floor,"

"It's wet." The minder replies.

"Don't worry," Adam says, "A bit of water is better than blood stains, Freddy will foot the dry cleaning bill." The minder lies face down on the floor.

"No I fucking won't!" Freddy shouts, "You're fired you big ape!"

"Don't be nasty Freddy," Adam says as he eases himself into the back seat, one gun trained on the back of Freddy's head, and one on the minder in the road. "Shuffle over Freddy, let's go for a drive and keep your hands in sight."

"How the fuck can I shuffle over with my hands held up?" Freddy asks.

"You can manage, if your hands go lower than your shoulder, it won't matter anymore. Understand?"

"You aren't going to hurt me," Freddy states, "You're law enforcement, I can smell you from here." He slides over and then asks, "Where to?"

"Just drive," Adam responds, then shouts to the minder, "Look after my car ape, don't you damage it." There is no way that Adam will return for this car, but the minder does not know that fact. As Freddy pulls away Adam closes the back door and moves to the other side of the seat, so he can see more of him.

"You're fucking dead," Freddy says, "What sort of a stunt is this? I got contacts who will string you up."

"Who?"

"Fuck you," Freddy says.

"I've just got one question, and then we can all be on our way."

"I'm not telling you shit," Freddy replies, "You've got nothing on me and you won't hurt me."

"Wrong answer," Adam says, as he smacks the butt of his gun into the side of his head. Freddy swerves, and reaches for his ear. "Hands on the wheel Freddy, watch the road."

"You fucking cock sucker!" he screams, "You're a dead man!"

"All this abuse is making me nervous," Adam says, "Why can't we just have a civilized conversation?"

"You can't do that to me, you're fucking establishment." Freddy whines, "Is my ear bleeding?"

"It's just a flesh wound, turn right here." Adam instructs, and he does. "Then stop over there."

"What now?" Freddy asks.

"Out, stand by the wall." Adam tells him. Freddy does as he is told and Adam also gets out. He jams the gun into Freddy's midriff, and quickly searches him, removing an automatic and throwing it through the open car window. Adam stands back and lines his weapon up with Freddy's head. "Where is Marcus Brent?"

"Who?"

"Wrong answer, I will ask one more time, where is Marcus Brent?"

"I don't know anyone by-" Adam lowers his gun and lets off a round towards Freddy's knees. Freddy jumps up, "Jesus fucking Christ!" he cries,

"You nearly took my kneecaps off!"

"Did I miss?" Adam asks, as he retrains the gun onto his head, "Where is Marcus Brent?"

"Look, I really don't know where he is." Adam begins to lower the gun again, "Wait!" Freddy screams, "It's the truth, I swear!"

"When was the last time you saw him?" Adam asks.

"A few weeks ago."

"I just bet that he will be calling on you soon, and when he does you will be calling me Freddy," Adam takes a mobile phone from his pocket and passes it to him. "There is only one number in it, you will call it when he calls you."

"Yea, sure I will, I hate the shit head anyway."

"I wish that I believed you Freddy," Adam says, "But for some reason I don't trust you. Do you still think I'm a policeman?"

"You look like one," Freddy says.

"Maybe, but would a policeman do this?" Adam lines up his gun, and shoots Freddy through the foot. Freddy crashes to the ground screaming. "I found you once, I can find you again. If you cross me, I will kill you. Are we clear?"

"Yes," he replies through gritted teeth.

"Have a nice walk home." Adam gets into Freddy's car and leaves him on the sidewalk. He powers away down the road, about three blocks away he dumps the car and heads for the subway.

16th January.

"Rebecca?" Mary says over the telephone, "Is David there?"

"No," she replies, "He's done one of his disappearing tricks again, he gets a call and shoots out. If I didn't know him better, I would think he had another woman."

"He would not do that to you."

"Oh I know," Rebecca says, "I was just joking around. What did you want him for?"

"Tell him that I have a theatre booked, with three thousand five hundred seats, for February 16th."

"That's excellent Mary. How are we going to advertise the tickets?"

Mary laughs, "You're too late, we put it on the website yesterday, inviting people to apply for a seat. There were twenty-six thousand requests, so we're going to put all the names on the database and draw it like a raffle. I'm still talking to a few more people about bigger venues. I really think he could fill a stadium."

"I don't doubt it," Rebecca says, "I will tell him when he comes back. Is there anything else?"

"No," she says, "How are you?"

"Tired and hungry all of the time," Rebecca replies.

"Take care Rebecca."

"And you Mary, I will get David to call you."

※

20th January

Charles Bourne leaves his office and is ushered into the waiting limo by his driver. Adam watches from about three hundred yards away. This is the second full day that he has followed his boss. Adam sits in his car with two days of stubble sprouting from his chin, and the remnants of junk food wrappers strewn around his feet.

As the limo pulls away and passes him, Adam cuts across the traffic and swings into the same lane, but four or five cars behind. So far, following Bourne has drawn a blank. He has done nothing except go to work, sitting in his office and then returning to his home, while Adam catnaps in his car down the road.

What Adam cannot see, or more accurately hear, is whom he talks to, at work and at home. The limo stops outside another office block and Bourne jumps out of the car, the driver shadowing him inside. Adam knows the building, as it is a CIA front. Bourne being here is no surprise, the FBI and CIA work together on many projects, or more precisely, they tolerate each other and exchange the minimum of information. It is a game that has been played for many years; you only tell the CIA things that you think will help the FBI, and visa-versa.

Adam passes the limo and pulls up further along the road. A policeman strides over and indicates that he cannot park there. Adam flashes his badge and the policeman goes on his way. Perhaps he is wrong about Bourne, maybe he is not involved with Marcus, and everything so far is getting him nowhere. There is no word yet from Freddy Nash, but this does not really surprise him. It all depends on who Freddy is more afraid of, Marcus or himself. He closes his eyes for a second.

Adam wakes with a start and looks at his dashboard clock, he has slept for forty minutes. A glance in the rear-view mirror, informs him that Bourne has departed while he was in the land of nod. "Fuck," he curses under his breath. To top it all, there is a parking ticket on his windscreen; some bastard gave him a ticket while he was asleep in the car. He slides the window down and grabs it, then shoves it in the glove box with the others.

He will have to pick Bourne up at the office or his home. Then he reconsiders and thinks, as he has lost him, he may as well go and get some needed sleep. Adam starts the car, pulls out and heads for home. He will get a fresh start tomorrow and give Bourne one more day to lead him to Marcus.

※

January 21st.

"What happened to your foot?" Marcus asks.

"I fell," Freddy replies, "You sound like you actually give a fuck."

"No not really."

They are on top of a multi-story car park, Freddy has just hobbled over and got into Marcus' car. He had considered telling Marcus about the encounter with the man searching for him, but then decided to keep it to himself for now.

"What do you want?" Freddy asks.

"There is one more job that I need you to do. Then you can have everything and you will never see me again." Marcus explains, "You will be my back up, and hopefully your people will have nothing to do."

"And I still get everything back?"

"Yes," Marcus says.

"How can I trust you Marcus?"

"You can trust me, this is the last."

Freddy smiles, "What and when?" he asks.

"Soon Freddy soon. I will contact you when all the details are fixed."

"If you fuck with me, I will find you," Freddy threatens.

"Ditto," Marcus replies, "Now get out of my car, I will contact you soon."

Freddy limps back to his own car as Marcus pulls away, once inside he picks up a cell phone and punches a number. When it is answered he says, "It's a blue sedan, he should be coming out in about two minutes." He tells the individual the registration number, "Don't let the fucker see you, just find out where he goes." Freddy hangs up and also leaves the car park. He heads back to his club, cursing at the pain in his foot.

Around an hour later, John Pollark walks into his office, "You're supposed to knock," Freddy says.

"Yea, yea," Pollark replies.

"Well?" Freddy asks.

"That's where he's staying," he replies, dropping a scribbled address onto Freddy's desk, "What do you want me to do now?"

"Nothing." He picks up the piece of paper and reads the address. A smile creases his features as Pollark leaves. This day is turning out well he thinks, as soon as Marcus passes over all the shit he has on him, he will be receiving a visitor, and judging how the man treated him, Freddy does not think Marcus will be to thrilled to see him.

༞

11:30pm.

The lights go out in Chuck Bourne's house. Adam starts his engine and heads for home. He is no nearer to Marcus, than when he started. What can he do now? That is the question Adam asks himself. Does he continue to follow Bourne around, or is there another avenue, which Adam has not considered? Questions for tomorrow he thinks.

CHAPTER 11

February 16th

"How's the crowd looking?" I ask.

"Expectant," Mary says.

"Perhaps I should get a warm up man," I say in jest.

"Who would you suggest?" She asks, playing along, "It's a shame we didn't think of this before, we could have had jugglers and fire eaters."

"Perhaps not," I say.

[If I suddenly appear above your head, blazing light over you, do you think we would get their attention?]

Michael makes a joke! I think you may have hung around too long with me.

"Time to go David," Mary says, "Give them Hell."

"Hell is the very thing I am trying to steer them away from."

The walk to the stage takes a few moments, I can hear my name being announced, and as I walk out of the wings the volume of the applause rises. I take the microphone from the stand, feeling a bit like a stand up comedian who has forgotten all his jokes. I had rehearsed everything I would say, main points and the like, but now that I am standing here before all these people, it seems too prearranged, too planned out.

I wait for the clapping to subside, trying to decide where to start.

[Do you think you should say something?]

"Good evening," I say into the mike, a few people call back, "I was talking to a man in a bar, some time ago," I say, "By the way, this isn't the start of a joke, this actually happened. The man in question was Scottish, and we chatted and got on well for about an hour, then the conversation somehow turned to different countries, races and creeds, and he sat there and stated in a matter of fact way, that he hated all Americans.

The Songs of Angels

I was taken back by his sweeping statement, and eventually pointed out, that I was from America. He replied that he knew this, and was not referring to me. In his words, 'Not you mate; you're a sound bloke. It's all the other bastards I hate.'

Later on, I was trying to analyze his thoughts, and my theory is this: I was 'a sound bloke' because he considered that he knew me, and because I had an individual identity fixed in his mind, he could not make such an all-encompassing reference to me. So I think what he really meant to say was this; I hate all Americans who I do not know.

Now I can understand someone disliking, or even hating someone they do know, but how can you hate someone you have never seen? The answer is that you cannot. So why would anyone utter those words? Again I pondered on this and eventually it came to me, what he meant was that he hated the stereotypical American, the one who does not exist, what he hated was his perception of Americans, What he hated were his own thoughts and fears.

Since then, whenever I hear someone say, I hate Mexicans, or blacks, Jews, Christians, Texans or Muslims, I could go on but I won't. What they are actually saying is that they fear the unknown, they fear people who do not slot into their perception of what is normal, I tell them that their hatred only lives in their minds, and there is a simple way around it. Get to know them, understand them and let them understand you.

Then sometime back a horrible thought struck me, that I am the same, not with people I hope, but with God. I am often asked why I hate God so much, and I tell them that I have never wrote or spoken about hating God, and that is true, but I have thought it often.

I stand by the statement that God seems to care nothing for us, but what I do not understand is why, and by my own reckoning, how can I hate anyone I do not comprehend? The fact is, that we cannot know God and therefore cannot hate him. We must try to identify him, try to understand him, even if he is indifferent to us.

This rule then has to apply to all of human kind, if someone is abusive to you, if someone says that they hate your race or nation, tell them that you are not a race, or a nation, but a human, a person with the same fears and hopes that they have. Tell them that you cannot hate them, because you do not know them and if you did know them, then their statement could never be true.

Tell them that it is fear and ignorance that hold us apart, it is compassion and understanding that will bind the race of man together."

I look out across the sea of heads, silently fixed on me, perhaps they did not want to hear this anecdote; maybe I have sent them all to sleep. Then one man stands up and begins to clap, and almost as if it shocks them back into life, he is progressively joined by more and more, until everyone is on their feet applauding.

In the safe house.

It will take time to organize.

-He is getting ambitious; we have to end this soon. –

I could get rid of him tomorrow lord, if you tell me to.

-I do not want him shot in an alley Marcus. I want the world to see his demise. You will continue to use our allies, but push them harder.-

Like I said, it will take time to organize. The people we work with will want to cover their backs. None of them got where they are by being reckless.

-So be it.-

"…. Be all that you can be, be compassionate, be caring, be a member of life and humanity and you will be a member of Heaven."

The whole crowd stands as one, clapping and cheering. I wave to them and shake the outstretched hands in the first row. I feel a little like a pop star. Then abruptly the noise stops, I look up at the faces in the crowd and the penny drops. They are frozen in mid cheer, their arms stationary between each individual clap. So I look down at the hand I am holding, the hand that is bonded to mine, and the person attached to it.

She is not very old, probably in her late twenties. She wears a scarf around her head because she has no hair. She is thin and wasted by the disease that sucks away her life and the treatment she is receiving for it. Why has this had to happen now? I thought that I had total control over this, but I apparently have not.

Well I have to take care of her now, as there is no way out of this except to see it through. The process is just like the others, and within an hour in my time frame, I have isolated the rogue cells. These I tag and expect reality to crash back around me, but it does not. I look into her again, and can see nothing out of place.

Then I jump when I see her blink, but no one else is moving. She blinks again and creases her forehead. "Can you hear me?" I ask.

"What's happening?" She replies.

"Do not worry," I tell her, "It will be alright." Somehow she has entered my time frame. My hand is still bonded to her, and I dare not try to pull away. She looks at the frozen faces all around her, and then asks,

"What is the matter with them?"

"Nothing," I say, "It is you and I. When we touched something happened to us. It is my doing, although it has never happened like this before. We are in a different time frame. These people are not motionless, they are just moving so slow that to us, they appear stationary."

"I don't understand," she says, "Can you let go of my hand."

"No," I say, "Not yet. Tell me your name."

"Julie," she replies.

"Julie, the disease you had is gone, generally at this stage things go back to normal, but something different is happening."

"How can that be?" she asks, but I do not answer her, my attention is taken by her face, because it is changing in front of me. The dark patches that surrounded her eyes have faded, her cheeks are filling out and her colour has changed from pasty to a healthy crimson. But most apparent is the hair that is visibly growing and pushing from under her scarf. "What are you looking at?" she asks.

"Your hair," I reply. She reaches to her scarf with her free hand and slowly takes it off, feeling her head and running her fingers through the ever-lengthening brunette locks.

Tears fill her eyes and she says, "Tell me what is happening?"

"I cannot explain, but trust me, no harm will come to you. Your cancer is gone and you are beautiful again."

"This is a dream."

"You are not dreaming, you must take this gift Julie," I tell her, "You have your health back. Take it and do some good with it. You have a second chance at life, use it well." Her hair has reached shoulder length and the hollows in her cheeks have filled out. She looks around at the man standing next to her.

"He is my husband. How will I explain this to him?"

I have no idea, "He will be shocked, because he will not have seen any of this, and to him your hair will appear instantly."

The roar of the crowd after the silence is deafening. Our hands part and she falls back into a sitting position. I take a backward step and just about regain my balance.

[You went out of focus, what happened?]

It happened.

[Are you OK?]

Yes.

The people around her have not even noticed that anything has changed. Julies husband still has his attention focused on me. She looks up to me, and I move the microphone to one side and shout, "Are you alright?"

She nods, and silently mouths a thank you; I nod back and wave once more to the crowd, before departing the stage.

❦

February 19th.
In Heaven.

Michael:
The papers are full of it again. One apparent miracle, people could ignore or say that it was a freak incident, but now he has again publicly demonstrated his abilities, people cannot realistically say that he is unconnected with the phenomenon. The press was all over him, and the house was under siege until they fled.

Gabriel:
Where have they gone?

Michael:
They are at a retreat in Vermont, at a lodge, which belongs to a friend of Mary.

God:
Did Lucifer want this to happen?
Michael:
He claims that he was bonded with her without consciously seeking this, and it was different. This time she took the trip with him, and he was able to converse with her while he was in this heightened state. Were your experiences similar Lord, when you were mortal?
God:
No, what Lucifer experiences, is not the same.
Raphael:
So Lucifer is saying that he still has no control over his actions. He could still potentially hurt humans.
Michael:
Perhaps, but he has not. Twice this act has taken him by surprise, and both times he has saved the life of the recipient.
Raphael:
So far.
Gabriel:
What are you trying to infer Raphael? Every time we meet, you have to have a little snipe at Lucifer. Always it is you who points out the negative. Are you jealous that God chose him to go to Earth over you?
Raphael:
No I am not, but I feel and have always said, that he was the wrong choice for this quest.
God:
Are you suggesting that I made an incorrect decision?
Raphael:
Lord, you are incapable of fault therefore it must be I, who is not enlightened. All I do Lord, is for the good of Heaven and your glory. But Lucifer insults you on Earth Lord, how can this be proper?
God:
You are correct Raphael, when you say that you do not understand. This is why I allow you your tantrums.
God looks back to Michael.
What is Lucifer going to do now?
Michael:

I do not know Lord; he has not made his mind up.
God:
Then you should return to him, so this meeting is over gentlemen.

⁂

Vermont.

The lodge sits in thick woodland without another soul for ten miles in any one direction. The lake on our doorstep shimmers with mist on this frosty morning. I sit on the balcony in the freezing cold, a blanket wrapped around my shoulders and a mug of coffee held in both hands, as I stare out over the water and listen to the silence, which is only broken occasionally by bird calls. The trees that crowd up to the waters edge bend under the weight of the snow on their boughs. Heaven is not this beautiful.

The door opens and closes behind me, "How long have you been out here?" Rebecca asks.

"Not long," I tell her.

"Come inside," she says, "You will freeze to death."

"In a moment," I reply. Rebecca goes back into the lodge and I sit and take in the scenery. We had a long chat the other night. It was no good to lie to her any further. She would not have believed me if I had insisted that I had nothing to do with Mary and Julies recovery. It is now beyond coincidence. So I told her that I helped them, but of the process, I pleaded ignorance. She was hurt that I originally kept this information from her; I could see it in her eyes. And I told her about the others, the trips to the hospitals, the failures and eventual triumphs. Rebecca has been distant since my confession. I have betrayed her trust in me by keeping secrets from her.

I can hear a car engine approaching, so I walk to the corner of the balcony and peer around the house. The car struggles for traction on the snow packed drive. As it gets closer, I see it is Mary's car and I return to my seat. I hear the motor die and the car door slam shut, then her crunching footsteps as she walks around the side of the house. She shakes her boots as she climbs the steps, and squats down in front of me.

"How are you?" She asks.

"Fine," I reply.

"And Rebecca?"

"I told her the truth about you and the others. She thinks I deceived her."

Mary kisses my cheek and says, "I will talk to her." She enters the lodge and closes the door.

※

Rebecca is sitting in front of the log fire as Mary approaches. Mary sits opposite her and removes her scarf, then holds her hands out to the warmth of the fire. "He needs your support to continue."

"Continue what?" Rebecca asks, "His trip to sainthood?"

"Yes," Mary agrees.

"He lied to me."

"Oh come on Rebecca. Would you have believed him if he had said, 'by the way I can do miracles' No you would not. You did not believe me when I told you did you? I told everyone and everyone considered me unhinged."

"I thought I married a man," Rebecca states, "But it turns out I wed superman."

"You did marry a man, a very special man. A man with a talent for turning normal people, not just physically but mentally, into whole human beings. But still a man, a man who loves you more than anything in the world."

"They are not all normal people, did he tell you about the President?"

"No." Mary replies.

"It seems that David worked his magic on him too, this is who he talks to on his phone. They are best buddies now."

"That's good Rebecca, perhaps they will both learn something."

"But he did not tell me, and he would not have told me, if this last one had not been so public."

"You cannot blame him for this," Mary says, "David needs you by his side, and I think he would give up and hide if you asked him to. Do you love him Rebecca?"

"Yes."

"Then you have to get over this, you have to be strong for him and he has to continue what he has started."

"I know," Rebecca says.

"I'm going to talk to him now, I will see you soon." She stands and picks up her scarf. She leans over and says, "You know I love you both." Rebecca does not reply as she leaves.

※

I still sit on the balcony, as Mary comes out. "Aren't you cold?" she asks.

"Yes," I say, "Frozen actually."

"Then go inside and sit with your wife."

"Yes I will," I reply, "How are things in Maine?"

"Manic. I have reporters camped on my front lawn. I must have given ten interviews yesterday. The only way I could escape was to slip out the back in the middle of the night, and come up here to see you."

"I'm sorry about all this."

"Sorry?" she says, "Don't be, this is amazing. More and more people are looking to you for inspiration. Julie Benson's recovery is the icing on the cake. Now they have to believe you, how can they not?"

"Some will still doubt me. Some will still think it a trick, or a hoax."

"Then they are stupid," she states, "Stay here for as long as you need, but come back to us David. The world needs you."

"Rebecca is my first concern, especially in her condition." I say.

"Yes I know," Mary says, as she kisses me on the forehead, "God bless you David."

She stares at me for a moment, and then smiles. "What does a woman have to do, to get a cup of coffee around here?" she asks, "I don't know, I drove all night to see you two."

I have to return her smile, "Help yourself," I tell her, "The pot should still be warm."

She pushes her car keys into my hand, "Be a love and fetch my bag from the car." She goes back inside and I pull the blanket tightly around my shoulders, as I listen to her footsteps sounding through the lodge.

[What are you going to do?]

The Songs of Angels

Stay here with my wife, for as long as she wishes.

[For how long?]

I think we are due a break, so I do not know for how long. Until the press finds us, I should think.

[And then what?]

Continue what I have started.

I make for the car, to retrieve Mary's overnight bag, and then turn around towards the door and the warmth.

༜

February 21st.

Adam walks into his Whitehouse office and throws his bag on the desk. He is still no closer to finding anything about Marcus plans. After trailing Charles Bourne for a few more days, and getting nowhere, he switched his attentions back to Freddy Nash.

This also proved fruitless, and Adam conceded that Freddy was not going to tell him, or truly did not know where Marcus was. He then shadowed a few of Bourne's subordinates, hoping that one of them was the go between, and still had no success.

There is a knock at his door, and Megan pokes her head around, "So you're back," she says.

"Temporarily," Adam answers, "Come in and bring me up to speed."

Megan enters the office and sits opposite him. "You look rough," she observes.

"Thanks, too many late nights," he replies.

"So how did your business go?" she asks.

"I've drawn a blank at the moment, so I will stick around for a while until I come up with another plan of action."

"Well everything here has gone great, no problems," she says, with a smile.

The phone rings and Adam picks it up, "Hello," he says, and then, "Yes Sir." He turns to Meg as he replaces the receiver, "I've been here five minutes and I'm summoned already."

"Duty calls, I'll get out of your way," she says. Adam leaves the office and makes his way to the Presidents private accommodation. The President ushers him inside and sits him down.

"What do you think?" he asks.

Adam stare at him, unsure what he is talking about, "About what?" he asks.

"What happened to David of course."

"What's happened?"

The President takes his turn to stare at Adam, "You don't know? Where have you been, the moon?"

"Sitting in my car mainly. Is he alright?" Adam asks.

"Yes he's fine," the President picks up a newspaper and passes it to Adam. The front page has a picture of a young woman with brunette hair, inserted below it is a picture of David. Above her head is a single word. It just says 'Miracle?' "Look at her and then turn to page two," The President instructs. Adam turns the page, on it is another picture of a woman, he starts to read the editorial, "There's no need to read it all now, look closely at the pictures; it's the same woman."

"What?" Adam says, flicking back to the front page to stare at the image.

"She went to one of David's talks. She went in looking like that," he says, pointing at the second picture, "And came out cured of cancer, six pounds heavier and with a full head of hair."

"Jesus," Adam answers.

"All in front of thousands of people, and caught on video. Someone was filming him from backstage. They had it on the news last night, on normal speed you hardly notice her, as he shakes her hand, but they slowed the film down as slow as it would go. It's grainy and slightly blurred but you can actually see her hair growing."

"It's a miracle," Adam says. "The whole world will notice him now. Have you spoken to him?"

"Yes a few times, he's gone to ground for a while, hiding from the press."

"Where?" Adam asks.

"Somewhere in Vermont, but he said he was coming back soon."

"He might do better to stay there," Adam says. "He will be hounded if he goes back to New York."

"He'll be back."

"I want to assign some protection for him when he does. You never know what sort of crazies are going to pop out of the woodwork now."

"I agree," The President replies. "Take the paper with you Adam, I've got something else on now."

"Thank you," he says. As he leaves the room, he passes Charles Bourne, who is waiting to see the President. "Good morning Sir," he says, "Is there any news on Marcus Brent?"

"No Adam," Bourne replies, "He has vanished, probably out of the country by now, but we will continue to search."

I bet you will, Adam thinks, "Very well Sir," he says.

❧

March 13th.

We returned to New York yesterday, not to our home, but to the house of another follower and friend of Mary. They are away in Europe, but did not hesitate to lend us their home when she asked. I know the press will find us soon, so I have made a pre-emptive strike. I have contacted the major networks and offered to do an interview if they will give us some space. We are still waiting for their replies.

Rebecca is visibly getting bigger now, with our child. Pregnancy suits her and she has never looked more radiant. I think she has come to terms with me now, I do not know what Mary told her, but it seems to have helped.

Mary has arranged minders for us. At first I refused but she eventually convinced me that it was needed, it is sad that I will need minders now when I go out in public. First to keep the press at arms length, and secondly to stop me being mobbed by the very people who believe in me. I asked Rebecca if she wanted to stay somewhere else, with her parents until the baby is born at least, but she will not leave me.

The television stations have interviewed everyone I have ever met, schoolmates, my Mother, whom I have now had to move to a safe place. Even Sean has been on the other side of the camera, talking about our time in Colombia. Adam has two FBI goons shadowing me, just in case of emergencies he said. The press has the list that Adam had. The first people I helped, he does not know how they got it, but someone in the FBI must have given, or more likely sold it to them.

We have another show, should I call it a show? Another mass meeting planned for mid April, this time we have eight thousand seats and they are all taken. The press is officially banned, but we expect a few to get in. The six shows we did for the TV are being re-aired, and this time the networks are paying for them, paying the trust anyway.

And finally, Mary is ninety percent certain that I will be in Yankee stadium in June. There will be over fifty thousand people in one place, and all listening to me.

[Exciting times.]

You could say that.

[You have what you set out to achieve, the ears of the world.]

Just as long as they listen.

[They are listening Lucifer, they are listening.]

March 15th.

"Mr. Brookes, Brian Kennedy of CNN. Mr. Brookes, can you give us a straight answer about Julie Benson and Mary Kirkland. Did you miraculously cure them?"

We are live on national television and I lean into the microphone and say, "No I cannot give you a straight answer. What do you think?"

"That it would be a miracle if you were present at two miracles and had nothing to do with them." He says.

"Yes," I reply, "That is true."

"So you are saying you were part of it?"

"If you are prepared to believe in miracles," I tell him, "Then you must believe that there is a possibility that I had nothing to do with it, and it was just a miracle that I was present."

"But I could also believe the opposite, that you did it."

"It is your option to believe or not. If I sat here and took credit for these phenomena's, then you would ask me how it was possible. As I cannot prove that I did these things, and I cannot prove that I did not, you have the choice of believing it or not."

"Mr. Brookes, Bob Bright, Channel three."

"How are you Bob?" I ask.

"Fine," he says, "I have a list here, a list of names that the FBI collected. All were mysteriously cured around the same time as Mary Kirkland, all in the New York area. Did you cure these people Mr. Brookes?"

"Have any of these people claimed that I did?"

"Well no," he replies.

"And have the FBI said that the list is genuine?"

"No, they deny it came from them," Bob states.

"Then put it away Bob, you're a journalist, and should know better than stating facts with no back up."

"You get away with it," he says, which gets a few sniggers, "You wrote a whole book of so called facts which you cannot back up."

"But I wrote Heavens gate, to enrich peoples lives Bob, hopefully to show them a way forward, and not to fill a five minute slot with one of your little stories."

"That's unfair," he says.

"I apologize, but the truth needs no back up. It is blatantly obvious when you see it."

Another woman stands up, "Joyce Parker from CBS," she announces, "Your wife gives birth to your first child soon Mr. Brookes. Do you think he will be a miracle worker also?"

"First of all," I say, "He could be a she, we don't know yet, and I would prefer sensible questions."

She smiles, "Some of your followers claim you have a direct line to God."

"I'm not sure if this is a sensible question Miss Parker," I say, "If it were true, I am sure he would not answer it."

"How about the direct line to the President? Does he answer it?"

Shit, that stopped me in my tracks, how do I play this one?

[Lie or tell the truth.]

"If you read the papers, you will find I converse with God, Aliens, the Devil, Albert Einstein and Marilyn Monroe. So you should not be surprised if someone told you I have a direct line to the President, but I can confirm that I speak to the Archangel Michael."

Everyone laughs, which was the reaction I wanted.

"It was from a reliable source," she says.

"I am sure they all are," I respond, and get another laugh. "Last question." I point to a man holding his hand up and he stands.

"Jack Jarvis, BBC," he states, "What is your aim Mr. Brookes, what do you expect to get out of all this, apart from the money your trust makes."

"The trust is none profit making," I state, "I do not control it or take money from it. All the donations and profits are ploughed back into the communities that contribute to it. You are welcome to inspect the books Mr. Jarvis.

What I expect to get out of all this has to be evident, even to you. I want the human race to grow up, I want a united species of man to go forward arm in arm and build a future fit for its children." I stand up and say, "I want you all to seek Heaven, not just when you leave this mortal life, but while you live it."

Five or six of them shout out further questions, so I say, "That was the last question for now, thank you for your time."

I am whisked back outside, through the reporters who could not get in, or were not invited. My phone is vibrating already in my pocket.

[When I told you to lie or tell the truth, I did not expect so much information.]

I did not lie.

[But you knew they would not believe it, so you technically lied.]

I cannot be held responsible for the way in which my words are understood. I did tell the truth, they chose to disbelieve it.

[If someone else said that to you, then you would not accept it as a satisfactory answer.]

I know he is right, but do not tell him this, as I get into the car and answer my phone.

"Shit David, I said you should have taken up politics, I nearly fell off my chair when she asked you that."

"You weren't the only one, but it means you have a leak in the Whitehouse Sir."

"This place creaks under the weight of the crap that seeps through it," he says, "I'm surprised the roof keeps the rain out sometimes."

"Never the less, you don't want to be mixed up with this."

"Remember when we talked about how I would jump out of the closet, when you had more followers that I have voters? I think you are almost there son. Got to dash, speak to you soon."

"Goodbye Sir," I say and he hangs up.

ಝ

April 17th.
(Section extracted from the seraphim records: Meeting 10,640,071,112 of the council of Heaven)

Michael:
It was magnificent, he had the whole place spell bound. When he talks people hardly dare to breath, least they miss a word. The whole thing was broadcast live across the continent.
God:
I listened to him.
Michael:
And?
God:
Do you want me to say that he is right to tell humans that I do not care for them?
Michael:
No Lord, but his message for them, is it not good?
God:
Yes Michael, the underlying message is good. The delivery is questionable
Raphael:
He twists the truth.
Gabriel:
The proof of the pudding is this; will those who listen to him get to Heaven Lord?
God:
Only time will tell.

Uriel:
I was against sending him, but now I see that your choice was, as always the correct one Lord. Maybe he has a chance, and maybe Heaven will be more crowded in the future.
God:
I hope it is so. What else Michael?
Michael:
Only that he has confirmed a day for the Yankee stadium rally. It will take place on the sixth of June, in front of approximately fifty thousand people.
God:
Very well, we look forward to it. Thank you gentlemen.

Outside.

"Michael wait!" Gabriel calls, "Walk with me brother." They set off for the square, "Are you well?"

"Yes," Michael answers.

"Are you still worried?"

"I think that when our Lord speaks as he just did, how can I doubt him? Sometimes I am sure he would not lie to us, and others? Oh I do not know."

"Is Lucifer still being observed?" Gabriel asks.

"Yes, but by everyone. People sit outside his house, and crowds gather if there is even a hint that he will appear somewhere. I cannot tell who is who any longer."

"This is worrying."

Michael sighs, "But if Lucifer wants the attention, he must endure it."

"Keep me informed brother,"

"I will," Michael replies.

May 1st.

"I have the plan, we can achieve both objectives, at the same time. It will look like a co-ordinated terrorist attack," Bolton says.

William Clarke takes the notes from his co-conspirator and reads through them, when he is finished he looks up and says, "It has potential. I will call a meeting with the others and we can thrash out the details." He hands the papers back and says, "Did you hear about their public meeting?"

"No," Bolton says.

"They chatted at a charity dinner in Boston last night, in clear view of the world press, acting like they had just met. You will see more of this; they will be hugging soon and best buddies for the cameras. The fact that Brookes slates God does not worry our illustrious leader anymore. He may loose a few hardened Christian votes, but he will gain more now, by getting into bed with Brookes. That's if he runs again, or perhaps the plan is that Brookes is put forward as the next candidate."

"Over my dead body," Bolton replies.

"The dead body won't be yours Nathan."

May 29th.
At a house owned by the Brookes Foundation.

"I would shit myself if I had to stand up there" Adam says.

I laugh, "I probably will, I've never been very nervous, even on the TV, but this is bigger than anything else."

"Sixty six thousand people, including those on the baseball field," Rebecca says.

"Are you going?" Adam asks her.

"Try to keep me away." She replies.

"I was just thinking about your condition Rebecca, all that excitement," he says with a smile, "We don't want baby Brookes arriving early."

She returns him a wry smile, "I have a while to go yet."

"Seriously," he says, "I know you have your own stewards and crowd control, but we are putting a dozen agents in there with you."

"It's appreciated Adam," I say. "Why don't you come along?"

"I would, but I have other duties that night. I am in New York with the President at a benefit, and he has asked if you will both come along to join him, as his personal guests, as soon as you finish at the stadium."

"Wow," I say, "That closet door is swinging wide open."

"What does that mean?" Rebecca asks.

"Just something I told the President, when we first met." I tell her, and then to Adam I say, "Tell him we would be delighted to join him, as long as you feel up to it Rebecca."

"Don't worry about me," She says, "It's you who will need uppers to stay awake."

"Good," Adam replies. "I will see you there. Right, who's for another drink?"

"I don't know why you're asking me," Rebecca says, "But you can fetch an orange juice for me."

"You know where it is Adam," I say.

June 3rd.

"This will be our last meeting, once this final job is complete, I will be off your back forever," Marcus states.

"Somehow, I still do not trust you," Freddy replies.

"Lack of trust makes the best sense in our business, but this time I swear to God that you can. Everything I have on you will be returned; a solicitor will hold all the evidence that I have put to one side. They will have instructions to deliver it to you on the day after the job, unless I contact them and tell them otherwise. You will never see me after today."

"Where are you going?" Freddy asks, "I will miss you, and once you have no hold over me, I would love to send one of the boys around, with a present."

"You will not find me Freddy," Marcus says, "Just do as I ask and then we can forget each other."

"So tell me what I have to do."

Marcus explains Freddy's part in the plan, omitting any reference to the President.

"So my people will be back up only. You must really hate this guy to go to this much trouble."

"It is not a question of hate," Marcus says, "You will be doing your country a service, you may be doing the world a favour."

"I don't give a shit, you just send me all my junk," he replies.

"Goodbye Freddy," Marcus says, "I would say it's been a pleasure knowing you, but we both know it would be bullshit."

"Yea, fuck you too Marcus," Freddy shouts as Marcus gets out of the car and heads for his own. Freddy sits there and watches him leave, pondering what to do. He would not put it past the bastard to send all his stuff to the authorities, even if he goes along with the plan. If Marcus has actually told him the truth, then by the time his evidence is returned, Marcus will be long gone.

"I promised I would kill you Marcus," he says to himself. "I don't like broken promises." Then he smiles, he has one thing up his sleeve, he knows where Marcus is, if he goes along with the plan, he can hit Marcus at the last minute. How can Marcus instruct his solicitors not to send the information back, if he is dead? And if Marcus intends to double cross him, at least Freddy will have vengeance, because Marcus will be dead, and if he does not, then he will still be dead. "You're fucked Marcus, I know where you live," he mutters as he starts his engine.

June 4th.
The safe house.

"All the details are arranged," William Clarke tells the five men present, "We just have to give the go ahead and the operation is on." He looks at each of them, one at a time and then says, "What we plan is for the good of America, sometimes you have to get dirty to preserve what you believe in. When we leave this room there will be no turning back, so before we go, I want to make sure we are all of one mind."

"We have to do it," Marcus says.

James Locke looks around nervously, and Clarke addresses him, "James, are we all of one mind?"

"It's just that we are actually doing this," he says, "When we were just talking, it did not seem real. But now we are taking about reality. We are ordering the deaths of real human beings."

"Would you prefer to wait until Brookes is running the Whitehouse? Or until the President starts to carry out his plans?" Nathan Bolton asks.

"No," Locke states, "I'm with the programme."

"Kirk?" Clarke asks.

"Let's do it," he says.

Nathan Bolton sniggers, "I think Kirk has other things, besides what is best for America on his mind."

"What does that mean?" Kirk Cope enquires.

"Looking forward to being President?" Bolton asks.

"That's enough Nathan," Charles Bourne says, "Kirk knows how important this is, and I am sure that American stability is foremost in his thoughts. Besides we will be right behind you Kirk, and always on hand to help you."

"You will all be rewarded, when I am in control," Cope says, "I promise you that."

"Charles?" Clarke asks.

"I have known the President for a long time, but the man I knew and respected has gone," he says, "I'm for a go."

"Nathan?"

"Go."

"Very well," Clarke concludes, "We will meet here on the afternoon of June the sixth; just to ensure everything is in order." He turns to Marcus and says, "When are you leaving?"

"When it is over," Marcus replies.

"It may be easier if you go before. The airports will be on full alert."

"No," Marcus says, "When I hear that Brookes is no longer a threat, I will go."

"Fine, I will see you all on Saturday."

Queens.

Freddy packs the last of his personal affects, and scans the office one last time as John Pollark walks in. "Everything set John?" he asks.

"No problem, I cased the joint myself. So you're off then."

"Yes," Freddy says, "And I advise you to steer clear of this place for a few days. I think we should assume that Brent will try to pull a fast one."

"What are you going to do about Brent?" Pollark asks.

"I will make a call when I am safely away, and let the foot shooter have him."

"And what if this guy doesn't want him dead?"

"I don't think that's the case," Freddy says, "But have someone watching the house. If it looks like Marcus isn't going to meet his maker, kill them both."

"I'll do it," Pollark says.

"No," Freddy says, "I want you at the main event. Give it to someone else."

"And even if he does kill Marcus, I'll have your foot shooter blown away."

"If he kills Brent, let him walk," Freddy instructs.

"He shot you in the fucking foot," Pollark says, "You can't let him get away with that Freddy."

"Being shot in the foot is a small price to pay, if he gets the bastard. You will let him walk if he does the business. There will be other times when we will catch up with him."

"You're going soft."

"Freddy laughs, "That's why I employ people like you John."

"So, once Marcus is dead, do you still want us at the stadium?"

"Unless you hear different, stick to the plan. If Marcus has double-crossed us and this place is unsafe, join me as soon as you can. Otherwise I will see you in two weeks."

"Sure boss, don't worry about it." Pollark says.

Freddy nods and says, "I'm not." He picks up his effects and heads for his car. The driver pulls away, heading for JFK international and Argentina. Freddy looks back at his club. If it all goes tits up he will lose his clubs, but everything else is accounted for, all his assets are hidden away, and besides, at the very worst, there is always room for another gangster in South America.

※

June 6th 3.00pm

I sit in the dressing room, Rebecca and I stood on the makeshift stage ten minutes ago, and we looked up at the rows upon rows of seats, they seemed to touch the sky. In a few hours this monument to sport, will be filled with humans, who want to listen to my words.

[You have come along way.]

The path goes on for a while yet.

Rebecca looks around at me, then comes over to sits at my side, and wrap her arms around me, "Is this what you wanted?" she asks.

"What do you mean?"

"All of this, is this what you planned your life to be."

"I'm not sure, I trust that I am doing something good. What else can anyone hope for?"

"What else?" she whispers, as she kisses me.

※

June 6th 4.45pm

Adams heart jumps as the cell phone on his desk rings. Only one person has this cell phone number, Freddy Nash. He presses the receive call button and holds it to his ear. "Hello."

"Do you know who this is?" Freddy asks, the line crackles, like this is a long distance call.

"I'm guessing," Adam says, "But is that hop along Cassidy?"

"Very fucking funny. I have an address for you." Freddy says, "But I need to know something first. Are you going to do him in?"

"Give me the address," Adam asks.

"I'll make you a deal, if you kill the bastard, I won't hunt you down for the rest of your life."

"If you don't give me the address, I might do some hunting myself," Adam says.

"Very well, have you got a pen?"

Adam scribbles the address down on the back of a file and cuts the connection. As he grabs his car keys, he dials another number. The phone is answered as he leaves his hotel.

"Meg," he asks.

"Yes," she replies.

"I'm not going to be coming to the benefit, you will have to look after everything."

"OK," she says, "May I ask why?"

"No," he says, as he gets into his car, "If the President asks where I am, tell him I have a lead on the situation I've been following."

"Will do," she answers.

"Look after him, and I will join you as soon as I can," Adam says, then hangs up. He pockets the phone and punches the address into his navigation system, and then he is on his way.

The journey takes around fifteen minutes. Once there, he cruises past the address, noticing at least five minders, who sit in various cars along the road. Surely they cannot all be there for Marcus. He parks along the road, where he can keep the house in view, hopefully without being spotted himself. He removes a gun from the compartment in the glove box and checks to make sure it is fully loaded.

Donning his jacket, with the gun tucked into a pocket, he leaves the car and walks up the road. This time he counts eight minders, possibly agents, trying not to be noticed. He concludes that if Marcus is in the house, he is not alone; something is going on. Adam walks into a coffee bar and sits at the window, where he watches the house and orders an espresso. He decides to wait it out and see what happens.

An hour later and nothing has changed; the thought of another cup of coffee makes him cringe, so he decides to return to his car. He walks along the opposite sidewalk and as he draws level with the house, the door opens and he catches sight of Charles Bourne leaving. "Fuck!" he hisses under his breath, if Bourne spots him, it's all over.

He continues to walk at the same pace, tilting his head away, trying not to do anything that would bring attention to himself. At his car he looks back, to find that no one is looking in his direction, thankfully Bourne did not see him, and is entering his own car. The car pulls away, taking two of the agents with it.

Adam gets into his own vehicle and waits.

CHAPTER 12

**Yankee Stadium.
Year thirty-seven: June 06th. 7.30pm**

I cannot believe the size of this crowd that fills the tiers and the playing field before me, the mass of expectant faces all looking to me. I begin:

"Jesus said that the only way into the Lords house was through him. I say that the only way to Heaven is through you! You may scream that life is unfair, or that your sins are not your fault, You can cry to God for forgiveness, but he has neither the desire, or the power to allocate it to you, You may confess your sins to a priest, and think it is all you need to cleanse your soul, but it will never give you forgiveness in your own heart. The right or wrong of your life cannot be confessed away, or found in a book, be it a holy book or a book of law. The right and wrong is in your own hearts and your own minds. And ultimately, it is you who will make the choice of Heaven or Hell and no other.

Those of you, who have made it this far, to this place, may no longer need to hear my words of encouragement. Fore I see before me a crowd of people, who have come together for a reason, and the reason is this, you want to be more than you are. I see a thousand people who need just one final push, who have come here for that push. I see each of you before me, and I no longer see the baseness of the human species, I no longer see the beasts that you were, I see the Angels that you will make of yourself, and the promise of the divinity that your children can become through you.

We are the human race, the family of man, and man has transgressed the matter that he sprung from. Nature has equipped you with a mind that can rationalize, it has handed you the power of reason, and with that reason you can surpass nature itself, but reason is a two edged sword. You can decide to live a life of deceit and selfishness, which will probably see you through your days, it may even make your life comfortable, it could possibly even make you powerful, you may even be happy.

Or you can decide to be part of the human arena, to be part of the array of life. If you decide to help your brothers, to give without taking, to have mercy when none is returned, to love without the need to be loved, to turn from the primal side of your nature and embrace all that is beautiful and perfect about you and around you. Then your life may not always be a comfortable, and you may not be as powerful as the man who turns from humanity.

But you will have something he has not, the knowledge that you never turned away from someone who needed your help, you will have the conviction in your heart, that you were all that you could be, and that is the passageway to happiness and contentment. Then the comfort and power of the selfish man will be nothing, when compared with what you will possess. For in your hands you will hold the keys to Heaven.

A famous man once said;

Ask not what your country can do for you; ask what you can do for your country. Well I'm not interested in your country, I am interested in the nation of Earth and in humanity, in life itself, and I ask this:

Ask not what you can do for your country,

But ask what you can do for your brother,

Ask what you can do for your sister, for that is the beginning,

Then ask what you can do for your species, and for this nation of Earth.

Ask yourself if you can stand, without delusion and without pride, and say that I am better than my nature, I am more than the sum of the particles of matter with which I am built. I am a true human being and I am worthy of your Heaven Lord. I am worthy of Heaven."

The safe house.
7.40pm

The last person leaves the house, there are no more minders. If Marcus is in there, he is alone now, Adam Whiteside checks his watch, seven-forty PM, and then quietly gets out of his car. He approaches the house from the right, careful that he keeps to the shadows and that he does not show himself at any of the windows. He slips along the side alley and silently climbs the small gate, dropping down into the rear garden, and there he squats down and listens for any sign that he has been noticed.

Satisfied that nothing is out of the ordinary, he slowly edges his way along the brickwork and turns the corner. There are a pair of French windows about six feet in front of him, he creeps forward and peers into the dusk lit room. Still there are no signs of life, no sign of Marcus. Just the faintest glow of a light bulb beyond the partly open and adjacent door.

He removes the revolver from its pocket inside his jacket and holds it before him. Softly he tries the door handle, which begins to turn in his hand. The latch makes the faintest of clicks as it disengages from the stopper plate, he waits again for a few seconds, with his eyes shut, letting them adjust to the gloom. He takes one more glance to check the way is clear, and then swiftly enters the room, gently closing the door behind him. Stale cigar smoke invades his nostrils; it is a smell he remembers.

Moving rapidly to the far door, he leans with his back to the wall, his gun pointing at the ceiling and once again he listens and hears nothing. Crouching down, he slips one finger through the gap between the door and frame, and opens it a further inch. The light comes from the kitchen at the end of the hall. Slowly he pulls the door open, praying that it does not squeak or stick.

Edging through the door, he hugs the wall and then freezes as he hears the click of a firearm being primed in the shadows behind him. "Put the gun down," he is instructed. Adam slowly releases his hold on his revolver, knowing that he could never turn in time to get a shot off, and leaning down, he places it on the floor.

"Marcus," Adam says, as he straightens up with his hands held out. "How are you?"

"Who the fuck is that?" Marcus asks, flicking the light on, "Turn around." He instructs. Adam slowly revolves and faces his former boss, "Your approach was shoddy Adam, you made more noise than a rampaging bull, and you walked through a door without checking your back. I guess they don't train them like they used to."

"I thought that I did quite well, but I'm more at home behind a desk these days," he replies.

"Are you alone?" Marcus asks.

"As I no longer trust anyone in the bureau," Adam says, "I took it upon myself to come and arrest you."

Marcus laughs, "Go back in there and sit down, walk slowly. You know I will have no hesitation in shooting you, so be sensible." Adam walks back into the room that he came from, and seats himself. Marcus follows him, switches on the light and stands near the door. "So how did you find me?" he asks.

"Does it matter Marcus?" Adam replies, "You have the gun and I assume you don't intend to let me leave here alive."

"Your assumptions are correct."

"Then before you do, can you answer me this, why would a man in your position throw everything away? How old are you Marcus? How long was it before you could have retired on a fat pension? Yet you squander it and join up with a drug dealer. Why would you do that Marcus? How stupid are you?"

"You don't know anything." Marcus spits.

"I know that I never liked you, I know what an arrogant bastard you were to work for, I know you blackmailed Freddy Nash and have a grudge against David Brookes. I know that you are being used by certain individuals to achieve their goals."

"You really don't know anything do you," Marcus says, "No one is using me, I am using them. They do my will," he grins and moves a step closer, "So you think I have a grudge against Brookes? I don't have a grudge against him, I'm going to kill him."

"Why?" Adam asks shocked.

- Kill him Marcus. -

"Why?" Marcus shouts, "Because he is the Devil!"

"You are insane," Adam says.

- Just shoot him now! -

"I have never been more sane, David Brookes is Satan."

"How did you arrive at this conclusion Marcus," Adam laughs, "How could anyone outside of a lunatic asylum ever think this?"

- He is trying to provoke you, shoot him.-

"Fuck you Adam," Marcus cries, "I was not taken in by Satan's lies as you were, and God picked me, God told me who he was, and what he was!"

"Was it a vision Marcus?" Adam sarcastically says, "Did he come to you in a cloud of smoke? Or does he give you instructions as you go along?"

- Shoot him! -

"You can laugh all you like Adam," Marcus spits, "But it will not change anything, it's to late. Brookes is probably dead already, and his friend." Marcus grins and Adam gives him a puzzled look, "Yes Adam his friend! It's probably best that I am about to kill you, because you would have to resign in the morning. Did you think America wouldn't notice, that the President is licking the Devils backside?"

"You are truly insane," Adam whispers.

- For the love of God Marcus! Stop this bullshit and shoot him! -

Adam watches as Marcus' eyes glaze for a second, and as they do, the gun he still points wavers off target. He takes his chance and springs out of the seat, his intention to get inside Marcus's aim. Marcus jumps back and lets of a shot, the bullet whistles past Adams ear and deafens him. Adam grabs for his arm and feels his head make contact with the bone of Marcus's nose. They crash against the wall and fall in a heap to the floor.

While Adam holds Marcus' gun hand with both of his, Marcus regains his wits, and starts to punch Adam with his free hand, all the while screaming abuse at him. Adam tries to ignore the blows he is receiving while struggling to release the gun from his hand. Marcus has a grip like iron; he will not let go and pushes with all his strength, trying to bring the gun level with Adams head.

So Adam uses Marcus's strength and lets his arm rise, he pulls his head down as the gun arks past his face. Marcus lets another shot go and Adam feels the rush of air as it sweeps his hair. He jams his knee against Marcus's elbow and pushes his arm down until the gun is forced into Marcus's throat.

Marcus realizes what Adams intention is and uses his free hand to tear at Adams eyes. Adam curls his thumb around Marcus's trigger finger as Marcus scratches lumps of skin from his face.

Marcus, comprehending that he is unable to stop the pressure from being applied to his finger, feels the trigger move and begins to scream. He reaches over with his free hand and scrambles at Adams finger, temporarily stopping the trigger from being pulled.

"Give up Marcus," Adam says through clenched teeth, "It's a matter of time, you give up or eventually this gun goes off."

"Fuck you!" Marcus whimpers.

-You should have shot him when I told you to!-

"Help me Lord!" Marcus screams.

"It's just me and you Marcus," Adam whispers.

-You cannot give up.-

"Help me Lord!" Marcus screams again.

- You must not be taken! You have already blabbed enough. He cannot know the details or he will destroy everything.-

I have to give in! He will shoot me!

-Yes give in Marcus, pull the trigger.-

"What!" Marcus shouts.

-It is for the best. I am your God and I demand your life! Pull the trigger!-

The bullet enters under his jaw, and takes the back of his head off. Adam falls back as Marcus goes limp and looks at his blood soaked hands; the gun is still clasped in Marcus' dead grip. He wipes the blood from his face and sits on the floor, drawing ragged gasps of air into his overworked lungs. "Shit!" he shouts, he took his own life. "Shit!" Adam says again as he realizes that has no idea how they intend to carry out their plan.

He pulls his phone from his pocket and flips it open, only to find a dead screen staring back at him. Vainly he punches the buttons and puts it to his ear, but it must have been broken in the struggle. "Fuck!" he shouts as he throws his useless phone into the corner, and wobbles to his feet. Adam looks around the room for a landline and does not find one. He makes his way into the hall and retrieves his own gun, still searching for a phone, but finally accepts that there is not one installed. He then quickly searches Marcus, looking for any reference to the assassination attempt or a cell phone. He finds neither.

Finally in desperation he races out of the front door and back to his car, starts the engine and guns it up the road, the wheels spinning wildly. At the end of the block, he makes a left, looking for a payphone, and forces a pick up of the road. Just along the road he screeches to a halt in front of a phone and jumps out of the car.

He dials, and when it is answered, he says, "Where's the President?"

"Is that you Adam?" the recipient of the call asks.

"Where's the fucking President Megan!" Adam screeches.

"On Fifth Avenue, in the car in front," Megan replies, "Were on the way to the benefit."

"Don't go!" Adam says, "There's going to be an attempt on his life, but I don't know from where or who. Get off the route we planned, go anywhere. Get the President out of his car and into yours."

"Are you sure?" Megan asks.

"I've just killed one of the conspirators, so yes I'm fucking sure. Do it now Meg!"

"Understood," she says.

Adam cuts the call and dials another number; it rings a few times and switches to voice mail. "Shit!" he says, realizing that David is at the stadium and will not have his phone near him. "David!" he says to the recorder, "You're in danger! Get away from the stadium, someone is trying to kill you."

He runs back to his car and dives inside; he has a choice what to do next, and decides instantly. He is only a few minutes from Fifth Avenue and the President is his first responsibility.

As he speeds along the road, he hears an explosion a few blocks away.

※

Two Minutes earlier.

Agent Megan Marshall radios the President's car and explains Adams warning. The procession pulls up and Agents pour out of the cars. She runs to the President, who is leaving his vehicle, surrounded by bodies.

"Do you think there's a bomb in my car?" he asks.

"We don't know Mr. President," she replies, "But Adam would not panic us unless he was concerned." She gets the President into the back of her car and rushes around to the drivers seat, pushing another agent out of the way while declaring, "Move! I'm driving." The agent runs to the front car and gets inside at the same time as Megan slams shut her door. She sees the truck swerve out of the oncoming traffic as the front cars pull away.

She watches the lead car's brake lights flash on as the truck glances off the van in front of it. She slams her vehicle into reverse and throws the steering wheel over, clipping the car behind as she mounts the pavement and straightens up, flooring the accelerator and tearing backward along the sidewalk. All her attention is on the back window, so she does not see the truck cut through the lead car and spin it off the road, then plough into the Presidents car and pin it against another.

The explosion rips the truck apart, debris rains all around, and every window shatters for five hundred yards in each direction. Megan's car is pushed along the sidewalk like a toy, but stays on its tyres. As the dust clears she spins the car around and tears off along the Avenue.

She almost hits Adams car as he screeches out of a side road, recognizing him she slams on the brakes. "I have him!" She shouts through the shattered side window.

"Get to safety!" he shouts back, "Go!" She nods and speeds off along the road. Adam takes in the burning wreckage, the Presidents car folded in two on the sidewalk. Many of his personnel, many of his friends will be dead and tangled in that carnage, but he has another friend, whose life he may be able to save. He throws the car into a handbrake turn and heads for Yankee stadium.

※

At the gates of Hell.

Marcus looks in wonder at the lines of humans stretching out all around him, He looks up at the grey and featureless sky, He looks down at the dusty grey earth beneath his feet, but mainly he looks at the huge gates on the horizon, which appear to pierce the heavens.

Lord! Where am I?

There is no reply.

Lord answer your servants call!

There is silence in his mind, he begins to panic, his God has abandoned him because he has failed, because he is dead.

But I haven't failed Lord! The plan will still go ahead without me!

Silence.

Finally he taps the shoulder of the man directly in front of him and when he turns, Marcus asks, "Please tell me, what is this place?"

"I've been here about the same time as you buddy," he replies, "But I know I died this evening, and I'm pretty sure this isn't Heaven, so why don't you try to work it out." He turns away and Marcus spins him back around.

"Do you mean all these people are dead?" he asks.

"You should have been a policeman," the soul replies.

"And this is Hell?"

"No," he replies, "This isn't Hell, but I'm fucking sure that is." He points to the gates that have suddenly become much closer.

"This cannot be," whispers Marcus, his eyes fixed on the gates, "This is a mistake." Then he shouts, "I should not be here!"

A voice at his back replies, "Yea, you and every other one of us."

The gates are so close now, that he cannot crane his neck high enough to see where they end. As he looks forward, a scream builds in his mind and involuntary begins to seep from his mouth. His eyes are fixed on the apparition who stands at the gate, and the scream gets louder and louder. The demon at the gate is sixteen feet high, from the tip of his horns, to the floor and his cloven feet, and this monstrous vision bends down and addresses him, "Name?"

Marcus continues to scream, "Your name sir?" the demon repeats. The scream that Marcus vocally utters dies out, but in his mind it continues. The demon reaches out and casually picks Marcus out of the line, he turns and calls a trustee soul, "This one has flipped, take him to the hold and try to get some sense out of him." The trustee takes Marcus's hand and leads him through the gates.

"You are in level five of Hell," the trustee informs him, "There is nothing that you can do about it, you may as well accept your fate. Can you tell me your name?"

Marcus regains some of his wits, "Why was I sent here?"

"No one sent you here, this is where you believe you belong."

"No! This cannot be correct!" Marcus shouts, "I should be in Heaven!"

"If you were worthy of Heaven you would be there," the trustee replies.

"No!" Marcus screams, "I am Gods chosen one! There has been a mistake! I helped the Lord on Earth, I was helping him defeat Satan on Earth!" The trustee regards him with pity, believing Marcus to be deranged.

"These are delusions," he says, "Or you would not be here."

"Fuck you!" Marcus cries, and pushes the trustee away from him. "This cannot be happening!"

"What occurs here?" An Angelic voice enquires. Marcus turns and beholds the most beautiful creature that he has ever set eyes upon. He falls to his knees and grabs the Angels robe.

"You are an Angel!" he cries.

"I am Sariel," the Archangel replies, "What occurs here?"

"Oh thank you Lord," Marcus says, "Oh thank you," The trustee, who still sits where he fell, puts his finger to his head, and makes the international sign for insanity, by rotating it at his temple. Marcus continues to talk, "The Lord has sent an Angel to transport his servant to Heaven. Everything will be alright now, thank you Lord."

Sariel picks Marcus up and tells him, "I am not here to take you to Heaven. This is level five of Hell, and no one on level five goes to Heaven."

"What is this?" Marcus whimpers, "Then why are you here?"

"Hell is in my charge at this time," Sariel says.

"But I'm Marcus Brent."

The Angel regards him with a puzzled expression, "And you think your name should mean something to me?"

"Yes!" Marcus screams, "Marcus Brent! Gods chosen one on Earth, in the fight against evil, against Satan himself! If you are truly an Angel, then you would know my name."

"I am truly an Angel," Sariel says, "But I do not know your name."

"Then tell God that I am here! Tell him we will still win!"

"I'm sorry, but God does not make mistakes, none of this is true Marcus.

It cannot be true because there is no way that you could be here, if it were so. These are delusions Marcus. You have to accept this." Sariel turns to the trustee, "Please take him away, there are many souls that require my attention this night."

Marcus pulls away from the trustee and clings to the Angel, "Tell God that I did not fail him, because Lucifer still dies tonight!" The Angel pulls his arm from the grip of Marcus.

"You are making it worse for yourself," he says as four or five trustees and demons restrain Marcus, and begin to drag him away. Sariel starts to leave, but is stopped dead in his tracks, by the half heard ranting of Marcus. "Wait!" he calls to the demons, and he rushes back to their side, "What did you say!" He demands of Marcus.

"That the Devil dies tonight," he replies through his tears.

"And you said Lucifer's name?" Sariel says, "What did you call him?"

"Tell God that the Devil, who walks the Earth in the man known as David Brookes, tell him that I have not failed him, tell God that we will win, and Brookes will die this night."

Sariel stares at him for an instant, and then turn to the trustees and demons. "Take him to the offices, lock him up somewhere. No one talks to him." The trustees, unsure what is happening, do not move. "Now," Sariel shouts, and they sprint away with Marcus in tow.

༄

In Heaven.

An Angel running through Heaven is almost unheard of, so as Sariel passes, all faces turn in his direction. He races into Michael's quarters and falls before him. Michael stands up from his desk, distressed to see his brother so agitated, "What is it?" He asks.

"You have to come to Hell now!" Sariel says through gritted teeth, "I will explain on the way."

"What is it?" Michael asks again.

"Come on!" Sariel shouts, as he pulls Michael from the room.

༄

The Songs of Angels

As Michael strides back into Heaven, all Angels and human souls feel the anger that radiates from him, all give him a wide berth and watch as he passes. The seraphim at the door of the boardroom, raises his hand to stop his progress.

"Get out of my way!" Michael shouts, and forces the Angel back, he throws open the doors and storms into the room, where he walks over to his God and stands before him, his anger visible for all to see.

God turns his face to him and says, "I am in a conference Michael, what is the meaning of this outrage?"

"You!" Michael shouts, his words knot in his fury, "You betray us all!"

"What nonsense is this?" God asks.

"You plot Lucifer's end behind our backs, you betray him as you betray Heaven and Earth!" Michael screams.

"How dare you," God whispers, "how dare you say that to me."

"I dare Lord, because it is true!"

God turns to the others who are listening in stunned silence, "Leave us, all of you."

"No!" Michael shouts, "Let them stay, let them hear the explanation for your actions."

"Who are you, who I made from my own being! Who are you to countermand your makers instructions, and say what I should do!" Gods own anger now rising, "I could take your life back in the blink of an eye."

"You may as well do it," Michael cries, "Do you think I wish to stay here any longer, do you think I will continue to serve you?"

"Michael!" God says, "What could bring on an outburst like this?"

"As if you do not know, do you want me to tell them what you have done?"

"I would like to know what you accuse me of."

"Treason Lord," Michael says, "Marcus Brent is dead, he is in Hell and has blabbed out all the details, all the betrayal."

"I still do not now what you are talking about."

"You are denying this lord?" Michael asks, shocked that God would still be lying to him, "You deny knowing Marcus Brent?"

God looks into the distance, "Marcus Brent, I remember that you were trying to obtain information about him for Lucifer, and I forbade it. That is the only time I have ever heard this name."

"Yes, you forbade it Lord, and with your help, Brent has planned and plotted Lucifer's death."

The look that crosses Gods face is a new one, which Michael cannot recall ever seeing before, it is shock at these words, "It is not I," he says.

"Marcus claims that he was guided by God himself."

"Then he lies," God says.

"But he knows things Lord, things that only Heaven could tell him."

"Michael, look at me," God instructs, as he takes Michaels face in his hands, "Look at me when I tell you that I do not lie to you, and know that it is the truth."

Michael looks at the face of his God, and it dawns on him, that he is wrong, and that his Lord was not controlling Brent. He falls to his knees, "Lord please forgive me," he cries, "But there was no other conclusion that I could make."

"There has to be Michael, bring this man to Heaven, let him stand before me and every Angel, and let us find the truth."

"Yes Lord," Michael replies, "What of Lucifer Lord?"

"What about him?"

"May I warn him?" Michael asks.

"Yes you must," God replies, "Go now, let him know what you know, tell him to make every effort to protect himself, and then bring Marcus Brent before me."

※

Yankee Stadium
8.15pm

"When all is said and done, when I am departed from this place, and my words are just memories in your mind. Then you must leave this place and go out into the world, go back to your homes and jobs, to your husbands and wives, your children, your lives. Go back and decide for yourselves, did he stand up there, and did he speak the truth?

What else can the truth be, but what we believe at this moment, this instant. Truth, it is in the eye of the beholder, what you see may not be clear to your brother; it may not be real to your brother. I believe that which I tell you, is the truth, but I beg you. No! I demand that you continue to search. For when you stagnate, when you believe that there is nothing else to find, then you cease to be.

The truth is the sum of our knowledge, not the sum of all knowledge. Strive to find more, struggle to refine your every view. Endeavour to jump onto the giant's shoulder, and reach higher than he ever thought he could. For you are humans, and as humans you may climb to the gates of Heaven, you may demand entrance while you still live, and God could not deny it. You can have all that you care to dream, Heaven on Earth is yours to claim, because you never left the Garden of Eden, this Earth is your garden, and all you have to do is cultivate it, believe it, dream it and construct it.

One day, I believe that Heaven itself, will look down at this Earth, and the Angels will be envious of what you have made. I believe in you, your goodness and your beauty. One day soon, what I have said will become the truth, if you believe in truth now, if you fight for all this now. The pathway to Heaven will be before you; I hope I have opened the gate.

As every journey starts with a single step, when you set out upon that path, make your first step the step away from hate, from pride and pettiness. Make your first step, the first step towards truth, and then you can start your journey to Heaven."

The sound that accosts my ears, almost takes me from my feet, thousands of human voices are raised as one, in fever pitch, and I believe that in this instant, this very moment, that this beautiful living mass of people want this! They see the truth, and each one will leave here altered, dissimilar and superior to how they arrived.

[Lucifer! There is danger, and you must leave!]

What danger? How can I leave now? Look at them Michael.

[You are betrayed, Heaven betrays you.]

God?

[No, we do not know who, but leave now!]

How can I? I have to see this through.

[Be careful, I have to go back. Please finish this my brother, get away from here.]

Very well.

I scan the crowd and lift my arms up high, basking in the applause.

Loving every one of them, connected to them. A woman breaks forward, through the reaching arms of the stewards, and dives onto the platform. She runs forward and throws her arms around me, "We will do this for you Teacher," she says.

"I know you will, but do it for yourself," I whisper to her, and as I look over her shoulder, at the corner of the stage, I hear a scream and see stewards grappling with a man who is also trying to break through onto the stage. My eyes lock with his, but there is no love in his eyes; his eyes only hold pure hate, and although I cannot hear what he says as his lips move, the words are clear in my mind. He says 'For Allah', For God.

The noise of the explosion does not reach me instantly, first I see his body ripped into a thousand pieces, then the people nearest to him are cut apart like rag dolls, and around him the crowd is flattened. The noise hits like a hammer and blows us off our feet, this woman whom I hold, this woman who I do not know. We crash back into a tower of speakers and my head bursts in multiple colours of pain as it connects.

I think that I pass out, but it can only be for a few seconds, because when I open my eyes, litter and debris still float down from the sky, and cries of pain or terror assault my ears.

The woman I was holding still lies across me, but she makes no noise. I am looking over her shoulder, and down her back, I can see the wooden stake that was propelled through her, the stake that would have cut through me, if she had not run onto the stage. My eyes lose focus for an instant, and I feel that I am about to throw up.

I watch the crowds trample each other, in their haste to escape this place, I see a young girl go down, she tries to rise but every time she makes it to her knees, she is pushed and kicked down again. "Help her!" I shout, as I lose sight of her. After all I have said, I watch these humans climbing over one another in a frenzy to save their own skins, climbing over the dead, the wounded, oblivious to anything except their own survival.

A group of men to my right are beating another to death. The victim has Arab features, he screams and pleads, but their blood is up and already they want their revenge, it does not matter that he is terrified and has nothing to do with the act that was carried out here, moments ago.

How could I ever think that I could change them? How arrogant I must be, how wrapped up in my own delusions of grandeur. More screams and shouts from my left, I turn my head. There was more than one attacker, but the crowd is holding this one back, and they do not run away, a wall of people stand between him and me, pushing him back, surrounding him and protecting me, shielding me.

The second human bomb does not sound like the first one; it is more of a dull thud. Maybe it is because my ears are damaged, or perhaps because so many people were pressed in so closely to him, people who have just died to save me. I have caused all this; all of these people have died because of me.

"David!" I turn to see Rebecca forcing her way onto the stage, "Tell me you are not hurt," she says as she kneels besides me.

"I have to help these people," I say.

"We have to get out of here!" she replies

Two familiar faces follow Rebecca; two of Adams men are with her, I don't know their names. Rebecca says, "We have to go, there are more of them."

"No," I say, "Look at the mess I've made, I have to help."

"Mr. Brookes," one of the agents says, as he rolls the dead woman away from me, "I have lost two men already, there are armed men on the loose and we have to leave." He pulls me to my feet without asking, and virtually drags me through the back of the stage. Under the seating the screams echo wildly, we shuffle forward, dodging running people and my legs start to feel like they may support my weight.

The sound of the shot reverberates back and forth; the agent in front of us does a pirouette and falls to one knee. Before us a man begins to aim his gun towards me. The shot that comes from behind us disintegrates his head.

"Fuck," the kneeling agent says, holding his side as blood drips through his fingers. "Get them out of here John," he says, with laboured breath.

"Understood," the second agent, John replies, "This way." He leads us along a passageway, as we make a right turn another shot is fired. John pushes us around the corner and returns fire. Rebecca huddles against the wall as more shots embed themselves into the far wall. John fumbles something into my hand as he lets of another round. I look down to find a set of car keys, "Go," he says, "There is a fire escape at the end of this passage, and a blue Range Rover outside, fifty feet to the left."

"What about you?" I ask.

"We won't all make the door if I come with you, and they will cut us down. I will hold them here and give you a head start," he says, "No more questions, Go now."

All I can do is nod my thanks to him, but he is not even looking in my direction. "Lets go," I say to Rebecca and we stagger along the endless corridor, the sound of gunfire behind us. When we finally reach the door, Rebecca hesitates.

"What if they are outside?" she asks.

"We have no choice," I reply, I look back to see John still firing around the corner, and then watch as he is smashed back against the wall, his gun clattering to the floor.

"Go!" I shout, as I see the first man turning the corner.

In Heaven.

Once again the Great Hall dominates the centre of Heaven, and as Michael enters with the soul of Marcus Brent, every tier fills with all the Angels of Heaven. Michael approaches God and bows before him, "My Lord," he asks, "I need your permission to leave, it has started and Lucifer is in mortal danger. I should be with him."

God says, "Go with my blessing Michael," and Michael hurries away. God looks down at the soul of Marcus Brent, who kneels before him. "Do you know who I am Marcus?" he asks.

"You are my Lord God Almighty." Marcus replies.

"You will tell this assembly, of the events that have unfolded on Earth. You will start with your first contact with your God."

Marcus begins his story, explaining every detail and every conversation with God, of the plan to kill Lucifer and the President of the United States, and of his death and time in Hell. When he has finished, God asks him,

"Do you believe that you conversed with me Marcus?"

"Yes Lord," he replies, his eyes directed at his feet.

"Marcus, lift your face and look at me," God instructs, "And tell me again; do you believe that you conversed with me?"

"Yes Lord," he replies a second time.

"Is there any doubt in your mind, that I am your God and that I stand here before you?"

"No Lord," he says.

"So when I tell you that it was not I, then you must believe me."

Marcus begins to cry, "But it has to be you Lord, it has to be you."

"Think about it Marcus," God says, "Why would I ever have chosen you? Your life was evil before all this. You only cling to the belief, that God controlled your actions, because if you do not, then you must face up to the fact that your crimes were committed without the mandate of Heaven. Do you really think that I would instruct you to commit murder?" Marcus continues to cry.

"You were used Marcus, by someone who saw what kind of a human you were. They saw the evil in you, and knew that they could turn you to their will, I should pity you, I should have mercy for you but I do not. When we finish here, you will return to Hell where you belong."

God walks towards him, "But first we must find out who used your pathetic life for his own purposes, because it has to be someone in this hall." He scans the room slowly, looking far up into the tiers, "So all these Angels will now stand before you Marcus, and they will stand before me, and they will tell us that it was not their doing. And if their heart is true, then they may leave."

He turns to the Seraphims, and invites the first of many, to stand before their God and be acquitted, one by one they approach their lord, and one by one they deny any transgressions. When they have spoken, God nods to each of them and they leave the hall. Marcus watches the proceedings in silence. Soon all the Seraphims have departed and God turns to the Thrones, where the exercise is repeated. On he goes, working his way through the choirs of Angels, the Cherubum, the Virtues and Powers, then the Dominations and Principalities. Then he turns to the last of them, he turns to the six remaining Archangels and with tangible sadness in his voice, he says, "I wish that this were not so, and I wish that I did not see you all sitting before me. I wish this because one or more of you have betrayed Heaven, and interfered with the will if God."

"Seated before me are my most trusted Angels, my first Angels, and my closest Angels. Whom I gave life before matter existed, how can I believe that one of you has betrayed me?"

Uriel stands and walks towards his God, when he stands before him he says, "It was not I Lord." God nods to him and he leaves. Sariel and Jerahiel follow, and declare the same. God lets them walk from the hall.

Raphael walks to his God and says, "I have not betrayed you Lord." Marcus lets out a pitiful moan, and God turns to him.

He states, "You know this voice Marcus, is that not so?" Marcus looks to the floor and says nothing.

"I have not betrayed you Lord!" Raphael repeats.

God turns to the seated Angels and says, "You may leave us now, and take this soul with you." The two remaining, Gabriel and Raguel, collect Marcus and make their way from the hall. "Raphael," God asks, "You would lie to me?"

"It is not a lie," Raphael replies, "I have not betrayed you, I did what you willed. I did what you wanted."

"How could you think that?" God asks, "How could you ever assume to know the will of your God!"

"But Lord," Raphael cries, "I did it for you! I know Lucifer with his trickery and dissent. You did not want him to go Lord! You voted against this, and all his time on Earth, he has turned humanity from you. It is Lucifer who betrays you again Lord, with his words and actions. He had to be stopped; surely you must see this Lord! He has to be stopped and sent back to Hell where he belongs." Raphael defiantly stares God in the face and declares once more, "I have not betrayed you Lord!"

"Close your foul mouth Raphael!" God bellows, and the light of God floods the Great Hall, "How could you do this?" Raphael falls to his knees, "I trusted you Raphael, and I loved you! Yet you conspire behind my back, you deceive Heaven and your brothers."

"I did it for you!" Raphael says between his tears, "It was wrong to send him."

"Lucifer's betrayal was nothing," God states, "It was nothing compared to what you have done!"

"Please Lord!" Raphael whimpers, "I love you!"

"Go from my sight," God whispers, "Speak to no other until I can decide what I am to do with you."

"Please Lord!"
"Go!" God thunders, and all of Heaven shakes.

※

Outside Yankee stadium.
8.40pm

[Go Lucifer, it is clear.]

We burst out of the stadium doors, and stumble headlong through the rain that has begun, I stumble because of the blow to my head, I still cannot see straight. Rebecca stumbles, because she struggles to move any faster, with the burden of our child inside her. The thought going through my mind, even though we are running for our lives, is that she should not run in her condition.

"Give me the keys," Rebecca shouts, "You cannot drive." I pass her the keys, and we continue to run. We scramble into the Range Rover and slam the doors shut to keep the rain outside. Rebecca starts the engine with one shaking hand, while brushing wet hair from her face with the other.

"Jesus Christ," she exclaims, as she forces the gear stick into reverse and floors the accelerator.

"Calm down!" I shout, as we fly backward across the car park, struggling to find first gear before the car comes to a stop.

"Can you see anyone?" she asks.

"No," I reply, as I crane my head around. Then the tyres are screeching and we are away through the rain and on to the main road. I am still scanning the road behind for signs of pursuit, but can see no one. "I think we have lost them," I say hopefully, as the windshield explodes into a multitude of fragments, shards of glass digging into the back of my neck. The whole car bucks violently and my head is thrown against the passenger door. I can feel blood running down the side of my face and into my eyes. I try to clear my vision, as the car piles into a wall or shop front, lurching to a halt. I am slammed into the dashboard and think I feel some of my ribs breaking. A few seconds of silence pass

"David, help me please," Rebecca quietly moans, I cannot see her through the blood obscuring my vision.

"I'm coming," I say, the door will not open so I ram it with my shoulder, pain coursing through my body. The door finally gives and I roll out on to the wet pavement. I stagger around the back of the car, pain shooting through my body, and open the driver's door, Rebecca falls into my arms and we both sink down to the road where my world falls apart.

Her chest is a mass of blood, Michael what has happened?

[She was shot!] I can hear the trembling of his voice, [Dear God! No!]

I cradle her head in my lap as a trickle of blood escapes her mouth, and spoils her beautiful face; "Hang on Rebecca," I beg, "Stay with me!"

Rebecca opens her eyes and says, "David,"

I reply, "I am here," and then a frown crosses her face.

"Where is David?" she asks,

"I am here," I repeat, "holding you my love."

A faint echo of footsteps on the cobbled road behind me.

"Is David dead? Have you taken him?" she asks. I do not understand what she means.

"Rebecca, look at me!" I cry, "It's me David."

"No! No!" She screams as more blood froths up into her mouth, "I see you, I see you, you're not my David, I see you, I see you!"

"Please Rebecca, look at me!" I scream, "It's David who loves you!"

Her eyes clear for an instant and she cries out, "What are you David! Why do you deceive me?" Oh God, she sees my soul, she can see past the mortal to the fallen Angel.

"Rebecca Please! See that this is me David, and that I love you!"

Her eyes turn hard, there is hate in them as they bore into mine, "Get away from me!" she coughs and her body goes into spasms, I can save her, all I have to do is concentrate, hold her hand and concentrate. Freeze time and mend the wound cell by cell. Please God! Please let me save her!

"Why isn't this working!" I scream through my sobs, as one final shudder passes through her body and she is still. God must hear my torment as I scream and cry my pain to Heaven.

[She has passed brother, and you must stand up now.]

The sound of footsteps on the road behind me.

[Lucifer you must go, get up and run away Lucifer.]

Why?

[The gunman is coming. Run away now!]
What is the point? She is dead.
I can hear footsteps casually walking towards me.
[Lucifer, if you want a chance at living, you have to go now!]
It does not matter anymore, nothing matters.
The footsteps stop.
I turn my head to see highly polished cowboy boots, which are splattered by rain and mud. I let my gaze rise to take in the man that murdered my Rebecca. I scan his face. He is just a man, there is nothing special about him, except the gun pointing at my chest.

"Say goodnight Christian," he says, "Sorry about your bitch, wasn't aiming for her. Thought you'd be driving, what sort of shit lets his pregnant wife drive when people are trying to kill him? And now I've had to come out into the fucking rain to finish you off."

He lifts the gun, ready to fire and I ask him, "Can the condemned man know the name of his executioner?"

"Don't suppose it can hurt," he replies, "Pollark, my name is John Pollark. Time to die now."

"I will see you in Hell John Pollark," I say, as I look deep into his eyes, trying to figure out what sort of man he is. What difference is there between him and a million other humans?

He lets out a little laugh as he fires, the bullet rips through my broken ribs and left lung, shattering my backbone as it exits, "You can count on that preacher man," he replies. My body slumps over backward, there is no pain, only cold, but I am not dead yet. I can still feel the rain falling on my face and feel Rebecca's cold and damp body beneath mine. My head next to the rise of her belly, he has murdered my child also. I watch as he starts to put his gun away, into a holster concealed under his jacket.

"Hey, John Pollark," I croak out. "I have to tell you something."

"Shit," he hisses, "Aren't you ever going to fucking die? Two fucking bombs, a car crash and a fucking bullet." he fumbles the gun back out and aims for my head.

"God will not forgive you John, but I do, for you do not know what you have done."

"Fuck you," he snarls, as the gun is pressed to my head. I do not even hear the shot. I Just feel the darkness closing around me.

8.47pm

Adam Whiteside's car screeches around the corner, He takes in the motor wreckage and notes the man standing in the road, then he witnesses a muzzle flash and takes out his own gun. The figure in the road looks around at the approaching vehicle, and then takes off down the street.

Adam slams the brakes on and leans out of the window, he lets off all his remaining bullets, but does not see the man fall. He jumps from the car and races over to the prone bodies in the road, knowing he is too late. Methodically he checks for signs of life and finds none, then his composure slips and he falls to his knees. "I'm so sorry," he says, as tears fill his eyes, "I had to make a choice, I had to make a choice."

He reaches out and lays his hands on his friend's ruined face, which lies on Rebecca's stomach, as another car pulls up behind him. And then his eyes widen as he notices something.

"What a fucking mess," the agent behind him says.

"Help me with her!" Adam shouts, as he grabs Rebecca's limp body, pulling her from underneath David. "Help me get her in the car!"

"She's dead," the agent says.

"Fucking do it!" Adam screams, as he hauls her limp and lifeless body onto his lap, "Get to the hospital as fast as possible," he tells the agent, "Run every fucking light!"

"She's dead," the man says, as he gets in the front.

"She was pregnant," Adam replies, "I felt her belly move."

The car screeches away, Adam holding the cold, wet and lifeless form of Rebecca, and leaving the body of David Brookes alone in the road. The rain beats down relentlessly. In the droplets lights flicker and dance, and the light condenses into a million points of brilliance. It forms the outline of a man, a man with wings towering above his angelic head.

Michael reaches out one hand and rests it on the empty shell, the mortal remains of the man, whom he watched grow as a human.

"Well we tried brother," he says, "I will not forget you David Brookes, believe me when I tell you, that someone will pay for this." Michael rises, and notices for the first time, the young girl who stares at him from a doorway. He holds her gaze for a second, and in a flash of lightning, the girl watches this figure of light flare to blinding magnitude and she has to avert her eyes. She looks back as the thunder booms to find that the manifestation has vanished, and the rain once again falls to the earth where he stood.

ॐ

**9:15pm
Channel 3 news report.**

"Suicide bombers have targeted New York once again, and once again America weeps under the dark cloud that is International Terrorism. In a co-ordinated attack earlier this evening, an attempt was made on the Presidents life. It was only the courage and dedication of security staff that ensured that he came to no harm. Sadly we are informed that it cost at least nine secret service agents their lives, when a suicide attack was made on the Presidential motorcade as it travelled along Fifth Avenue. I repeat that the President is reported to have escaped without injury.

Minutes later at least two devices were triggered at a rally in Yankee Stadium. Reports are still sketchy, but it is believed that these were also suicide attacks. There is no conformation at this time, but the death toll is estimated as 'in the hundreds'. Rescue teams are still at the scene. Unofficial reports coming in, say that the author and public speaker, David Brookes, who was hosting the event, has been killed in the atrocity.

I am told that we can now go live now, to Fifth Avenue and the scene of the first attack......"

ॐ

June 7th.

"It's true that we have an official statement from 'Al Quida', saying that they carried out the attack," Adam walks to the window, and then turns, "We also have a verified statement saying that it was nothing to do with them."

"What do you think?" the President asks.

"That the first statement is bullshit, unless Marcus Brent was working with them, and that is impossible to believe. He may have been deranged but I think he believed that he worked in the best interests of America. Or maybe he may not have known that he worked with terrorists, but someone knew, and from what he said, I know that he did not do it alone."

The President rubs his temples, "How deep do you think this goes?"

"Very. The terrorist acts were a cover to assassinate David and yourself. They murdered hundreds of people, so that there would be someone to blame. David was not killed in the blast; he was gunned down with Rebecca, in the streets while trying to escape. We lost six agents in gun battles after the explosions."

"None of this can go further than this room," the President instructs, "The world and America does not need to hear any more conspiracy theories. As far as the official story goes, Islamic extremists, with no American connections, carried out the attacks."

"And unofficially?"

"Unofficially you have a new job, answering only to me. When I finish my term of office in a year you will be out of work, because whatever happens, I will not run again, and I fear you will make some new enemies in the next few months. So are you willing to hand pick a team and get the bastards for me?"

"I was going to do it anyway, for David and with or without your approval."

"Understand Adam, no one can go to court or to prison over this."

"I understand sir," Adam replies. He has a face etched into his memory, a face that looked at him through the rain outside Yankee stadium, before running away. And a name to go with that face, remembered from a photograph collection showing Freddy Nash's known associates.

The Songs of Angels

June 9th.
Channel 3 news report

"I will not ask you your feelings at this time Mary. I hope you realize that all of America share in your grief at this time."

"Thank you," she replies as she looks into the camera. "I just want to say, that the events that unfolded yesterday have left another scar on the face of humanity. The deaths caused by the erroneous passions of normal people will fuel the fire of further aggression. To the people who sent those adolescent young men, draped in explosives, on a misguided quest for martyrdom. I wish to tell them that if they are not already languishing in their own private hell, then hell awaits them.

The deaths of all these innocents, is a tragedy, and the death of David Brookes is a catastrophe, with which we may never see equal."

"David Brookes, in a round about way, preached love, tolerance and understanding," the reporter says, "If he could speak to the architects of this act, what do you think he would say?"

"He was the most wonderful human individual whom I ever knew," She turns her eyes from the camera, "He would do something that I cannot do, he would forgive them."

"And what will you do now Mary?"

She looks back up, "What else can I do?. How could I not go on? I will continue to spread David's words to the world. He had a dream for the human race, and it is a dream I still believe and cherish. No one will ever replace him, all we can do is to try and emulate him."

CHAPTER 13

Nowhere in time.

So that was that, it is all over, all a waste of time. Total failure. I'm dead and must be in the shadow lands. And what now, do I die as a man or an Angel? Do I go to Heaven or Hell, obviously Hell, he once said that I was not worthy of Heaven and I think I have managed to prove it.

Ah, the mists are clearing and I'm not in Heaven or Hell. What is this place?

"This is nowhere Lucifer," I turn to see God approaching, and I back away, I cannot look at him. Has he come to tell me how useless I am? To gloat? "Hold Lucifer, come sit and talk to me."

< What is this place Lord? >

"A place where we can talk"

<Talk? There is nothing to talk about. I will just go back to Hell and I will not bother you anymore. No more nagging, I have no right because I know no better. >

"Lucifer please, come sit down and talk to me for a while," So I sit with him. "Look at me Lucifer, I am not here to tell you where you went wrong, that is for you to decide. I do not think you failed me. If anything I have let you down you, because I failed to see what was happening under my nose, and I let Heaven fail you to."

< I was not interested in failing or pleasing you Lord, and I care nothing for Heaven anymore, > I want to ask him about her, about Rebecca, about where she is, because I know she went to Hell, but I can not yet bring myself to ask, < I failed humanity, that is what hurts.>

"No my son, humanity failed you. They failed you as they failed me. Do you think I planned my demise on Earth? I did not. I wanted to stay and teach them all the way to Heaven. But it was not to be, they are not yet ready."

< But you thought they were ready, why else would you let me go back? >

"No Lucifer, they are still not ready, I let you go back so you could experience what I found out about the human race two thousand years ago. That they are still in a state of flux. That there is good and evil in all of them. But which wins the fight for their hearts and minds? I cannot decide. But I still wish to give them the chance for their minds to advance into something closer to perfection. And then we will open Heaven to them all."

< So you knew all along, that I would fail? >

"No child, I did not know you would fail. But yes, I expected it."

< But what about her, how can you not hate me for betraying her? >

"Rebecca?"

< Yes Rebecca, I looked into her eyes as she died, and she knew me Lord! She knew on her deathbed that she looked into the eyes of Satan. And she thought I had tricked her. She saw me Lord and she hated me for letting her believe in me! > I start to cry, <And as she died she hated herself, so Heaven is closed to her, she will go to Hell because of me. > And now tears streaming from my eyes, < She is in Hell, the only human I met, who was surely to go to Heaven, I sent to Hell. >

God stands and holds me in his arms, as my tears stain him, "Oh Lucifer, my beautiful fallen Angel, my son. Rebecca did come to Hell where I was waiting to embrace her and take her to Heaven."

< And my child? >

"No Lucifer, your child did not die. Your son is alive on Earth."

<Alive? >

"Yes, the humans saved him."

<But I watched them die. >

"He is alive Lucifer."

I stare at him, my son is alive, he lives!

<And alone! > I realize and cry, <Abandoned with no Mother or Father. I will never know him. >

"You can watch him grow, you will know him."

<But he will never know me Lord. >

"He will know of you, he will know what kind of people his parents were."

< And you took Rebecca to Heaven? >

"It is more complicated than that, I have to start at the beginning. I have to tell you all." He begins, and his eyes never leave mine. "I must tell you what I have told no other, and you will have to be patient." He looks deep into my eyes, into my soul and continues, "First there was the word, and the word was God. And there was nothing else and I was restless. So I made you Lucifer. You were the first of the Angels, though quite why you turned out as you did utterly baffles me. Then the rest of the Angels, all are a part of me, all took some of me to create. I loved all, and all loved me. Matter was the last of my creations; Matter is my unfinished symphony.

Although the universe is vast, by human standards, it was a fraction of me, a blink of an eye, Even if every atom you see on Earth, and in the heavens, took a fraction of my light to create, it was little to me. But it was a beautiful show, and I was very proud of it. And all the Angels loved it. Except you of course, you just asked endless questions."

<That is unfair, I did love it, > I reply, <I just did not understand it. But enough about me, what of life. >

"Life Lucifer was like a bomb going off. I have come to think of it as the real birth of matter. I hardly noticed it at first, but something was pulling at my being. Something was taking from me without asking. So I searched for the cause, and found it on this little planet, in the corner of nowhere. And I was shocked, and a little frightened. Matter had somehow organized itself into little units, which could copy themselves. Each new one demanded a piece of me, each had to seize a little of God into its being, to animate itself."

<Why didn't you stop it? >

"Because it was incredible Lucifer! These little pieces of matter had their own will! They wanted to live, and to my relief, when they perished they released their life back to me. But more than that Lucifer, I got more back than I put in. Can you imagine that? They added to me, they made me more than I was before."

<You are describing a soul.> I say.

"Yes, of course I am. And then to my amazement, life grew into millions of different things, and you watched this also. Each variation of life demanded a different portion of my being. It was like a high interest account, I had to put a lot into it, but the benefits were phenomenal!"

<And then humans came along, > I continue the story, <And everything changed. >

"Yes everything changed when humans became self aware, and to my horror, these puny little animals gave nothing back. They kept my light! They robbed me Lucifer, even when their bodies perished, they were still alive, with part of my being. And each one that was born tore another piece from me. The human bomb, gaining momentum like a nuclear explosion"
<So you tried to end it, you tried to drown them. >
For the first time he looks away for a moment. "In hindsight it was a rash decision."
<But why save some of them? > I ask.
"Oh Lucifer, it was not my intention for any to survive, but Life finds a way. The will of life is astounding. It still surprises me now."
<So some survived, > I say, <Why did you not continue to destroy them? >
"I saw something Lucifer, I saw what they really were. What matter had made. They were something like me! With their own will even after death. But they are imperfect copies. Unfortunately, the will of some, was not for the good of the living. But what was I to do with them? All these souls wondering the Earth, interfering with mortal decisions."
<You created the void. > I state.
"I had to do something, please understand this," he says, "They are imperfect, but they are still part of me. Humans on Earth, and in Heaven, and in Hell, own a part of me. More than all the effort, which I invested into the Angels and the universe combined."
<So why do you let it continue? Eventually they will take it all. How long can you last? >
"I do not know Lucifer, I do not know where I begin, or where I end. That is what I meant, when I said that life is devouring me, all those years ago in Columbia"
<And where will this all end? > I ask, <What outcome are you looking for? >
"I should think it obvious, perfect human souls. When they are perfect, they will be Gods like me, like you. And when they are Gods, when they are perfect, they can return to me, and together we will be more than our sum."
<We were never perfect Lord. > I hang my head and he takes my soiled chin in his hand, and lifts my head.

"Lucifer, do not underestimate yourself."

<The souls in Heaven, > I ask, <Are they not perfect? >

"No Lucifer," he responds, "They are the closest, and some are very close."

<I am beginning to understand now, why you did the things you did. With the children of Israel, and your trip as Jesus Christ. You were trying to nudge them closer to perfection. >

"Yes," God says.

<But why did you stop Lord, why were we forbidden to help? >

"Lucifer," he replies, "I never stopped, when have I ever stopped? What about Mohammed, Nanak and Siddharta Gautama? Do you think humans construct their religions by themselves? And still it continues."

<How does it continue Lord? >

"Because now you have done your part."

<But I failed. > Again I ask him, <Tell me of Rebecca. >

"I have to tell you the whole story. Please be patient." He pauses and I wait for him. Eventually he continues, "When you left I was involved with the control of Hell. At first I saw only wretches, who would prefer to live like this, rather than see the light of Heaven.

Then someone came to Hell, I did not notice him at first. He was just another wretched human soul, who had lived his life with guilt and indifference. He was a soul who had murdered, and scurried in the filth of human existence. But he placed himself in level one and he seemed content with his life and his death.

To my astonishment, he gathered souls around him and he preached to them. He told them there was redemption for them all, even here in Hell. Even here in Hell Lucifer, he told them that they could be contented, they could make a decent place for themselves and be at one.

So I went to him, disguised as a human soul and asked him, what grounds he had for this? How could he tell these sinners that there was redemption for them? How could he, as a murderer on Earth, ever hope for decency and eventual peace?

And he replied that he knew God had not abandoned him, because even though his life had been wicked before he passed over, at the end God had given him purpose on Earth, and he had met Jesus Christ in the wilds of Colombia. That God had given him a chance for redemption when he gave his life to save this man."

< Carlos? >

"Is that not correct Lord? He asked as he saw through my disguise, he knew me Lucifer. And I could not answer him, I had no words to reply to his question. So I fled Hell and went back to Heaven, where I agonized over his words for days.

I came to understand that most of the souls there were just lost. And it was my fault. I had rejected them so they had turned from me. I was wrong and you were right. So I took the majority of them and offered them a choice. Of course there are some who can never leave Hell. They are too bitter and twisted, and that is probably my error as well. But to the others I gave a choice:

If they could forgive me I took them to Heaven, and thankfully most of them now sit at my side. And Heaven is a better place for this. But there were many who could not forgive, and to these I offered a further choice. They could stay in Hell, and many decided to do just that, or I offered to end their suffering.

Lucifer, you do not know how hard that was. When I created matter, it was created from me. Every star, every rock and every atom is a ray of my light. Every human soul is part of my whole, and to lose it is to lose myself."

< Along time ago, you said I had asked you to cut out your heart. >

"It was true Lucifer, and that is what it felt like to let those poor souls go. But it had to be done. If the heart is diseased, you must cut out the rot, or the whole will eventually perish. So I let them go."

< And Rebecca? >

God releases his grip on me and looks into my eyes again, as he takes my hands, "She could not forgive me. And she would not stay in Hell. I'm so sorry Lucifer, but I let her go. I had no choice."

And I fall to my knees as I hold Gods hands and weep, and I cry out, <Then I have still failed! > And the tears fall from my eyes.

"No Lucifer no, you made me see my errors, and I have put right as best as I can. No one else could have done what you have done. No one else has ever changed the will of God."

And for a long time I cry, when my sobs finally subside, I ask, < The Earth, what will you do now? >

"We will wait until they are ready. And continue to guide them, when we can"

< And what if they are never ready? >

"We will still wait, and we will always hope."

< And Hell? >

"Forget Hell, I don't want you to go back to Hell. I want you to stay in Heaven with me. You will sit at my side and another will run Hell. One who has betrayed me a thousand times worse than you ever did."

<No, I mean what of the souls in Hell. >

God stares at me and replies, "I have done all I can for them Lucifer."

< But we can do more Lord. Souls still flood into Hell, yes? >

"More now go to Heaven."

< But the ones that go to Hell, if I go back and can get them to forgive you, and forgive themselves will you accept them in Heaven? >

"But I don't want you to go back Lucifer, you have done enough. Why do you want this burden?"

< Lord please, will you accept them? >

"I can make no promises. I have already tried to take them to Heaven."

<Yet you do not say no. So I will go back Lord. Let me try. I have lost Rebecca; let us lose no more. Can I do this Lord? >

"Lucifer, Lucifer, at the end, there on Earth, I thought you had given up. But you never will give up will you? My rebel Angel who never does as I ask, although it will sadden me to see you back in that place. You may go with my blessing, if that is what you wish. And if you bring one more soul to Heaven we will rejoice"

< I will bring them all Lord. >

"I have always watched over you Lucifer, even in your darkest time in Hell and on Earth, when you thought I had forsaken you. Whenever you wish to come to Heaven, for any reason at all, you are welcome"

<Thank you my Lord, my Father. I will not disappoint you. >

The Songs of Angels

A new day in Hell

And for the first time ever, I walk into Hell without the dread that I have always felt, because there is something new in Hell, something I never had before. Hope. Hope that possibly, there is a future worth working for. And I bring hope to these lost souls, that one day, if God wills it, I will take them all to Heaven.

Sfee looks towards me, the ever present scowl in his face.

"So you are back."

< Yes. >

"I suppose I should be happy. Better the devil you know, and all that. Some of the things, which have happened while you were away were beyond my understanding. Different masters every other day, at least I know where I stand with you."

< Sfee, one of those masters was God himself. >

"Yes Sire" he says, but he does not comprehend.

< Never mind, I'm back now. >

"And we can finally get back to normal."

<No Sfee, things will never be normal again. We have a lot to do and I don't want to spend an eternity to do it. So lets get started. >

Year Thirty-eight: November 3rd.
Buenos Aires.

The hairs on the back of his neck stand, as he hears the click of the firing pin being set. His reaction is to go for his gun, but he checks himself and freezes. "Turn around John," the gun holder quietly whispers.

John Pollark slowly turns his body and stares down the barrel of the firearm, which points at his temple. A trickle of sweat runs from his hairline and into his eye, he blinks it away and looks at the man holding the weapon. "You've got me man," he admits, "I'm not going to do anything stupid."

Adam Whiteside looks over his hands holding the gun, "I anticipated that you would look different John. When I finally looked into your eyes,

I expected to see something. But all you are is another bum. You are nothing."

"Do I know you?"

"We briefly met, outside Yankee stadium," he replies, "I was the one firing bullets at you, after you murdered David Brookes and his wife."

Pollark nervously laughs, "You've got the wrong man, my name is Edward Rodriquez and I don't know anyone named John."

"You are John Pollark."

"Who the fuck are you man? You a spook? If you are, then you're out of your jurisdiction. Do you think you can march me back to the US with a fucking gun pointed at my head?"

"No John," Adam smiles, "I'm no longer with the FBI. Let's say that I am freelance now. I have no intention of taking you back to the States, and waiting twenty years while you sit on death row. We both know that a jury isn't required and I am more than happy to save the taxpayers money. I just wanted to see your face before I pulled this trigger."

"Wait!" Pollark cries, "I know things man! I can help you. You must be after Freddy, I can tell you where he is, and more!"

Adam curls his bottom lip in a parody of mock sadness, "Freddy's dead John. Didn't you hear? He was very helpful before he passed away, he even told me where to find you."

"Fuck him and you!"

"Goodbye," Adam says, as he pulls the trigger.

Hell.

I stand at the gates of Hell and view my kingdom as new inmates shuffle through. Sometimes it seems that more come in than go out. But they do leave Hell, I promised God one soul, but we have sent thousands. Earth is no better than it ever was, the wickedness is sometimes staggering. But we hope for the day, when the gates of Hell can be locked forever. The day when all of humanity, will aspire to Heaven and begin the construction of Heaven on Earth.

There is a moment some time in the future, a critical point that you will pass some day. Where the balance will finally be tipped. And the human race will travel out of the past, through this point, this final barrier, and into the future. Then the songs of Angels will not only be sung in Heaven, but will radiate outwards from the living Earth, and an empty Hell will be a curious reminder of how man once was. I know that it will be real one day; all you have to do is reach up, reach higher than you ever have.

But that day is not this day, today I watch these queues of souls sort themselves between the levels. There are six levels in Hell now, but level six only has one occupant and nothing else. No one is allowed there bar myself, I go and talk to him sometimes. I find that I cannot hate him; fore I do not understand why he did what he did. He has enough hate for himself, and not because he conspired against me, but because he has lost the love of his God.

I scan the new souls once more, wondering what they could have done to be here, and in the line for level five, I spot a face I knew, and I know what he did.

< Hold that queue Overseer!> I call out, < Bring that man to me! > I say, pointing to him. The trustee marches this new arrival over and presents him to me, < Hello John, how are you? > I ask.

"Fuck off!" he replies.

<You were murdered I see, why does that not surprise me? > Then the details of his death filter through, and I am saddened by the facts. That Adam, a friend and decent man is driven to commit these acts, that his life and chance of Heaven, will be squandered by the actions of men like the one standing in front of me. And I feel guilt that I contributed to Adams destiny by my actions.

I want to strike out at this excuse for a human. I want to end his existence, I want him to suffer, but then I would be as bad as he is. Instead I ask him, < Do you remember me John Pollark? >

"Why the fuck should I remember a shit ass like you?" he says.

< Let me help you remember, > I shift my form to the likeness of David Brookes, when this human last saw him on Earth, and recognition dawns across his face.

"Hey, I do know you, I blew you away didn't I. No hard feelings man. It was just another hit. Nothing personal."

And I shift my form again, to the horned and winged form of Satan,

< And I said you would see me in Hell, and here we are John. >

He takes a step backward and his jaw drops, "No Fucking way man! You're the Devil and I killed you on Earth?"

<Yes, >

His face moves through a range of emotions, fear is the first and then confusion. A smile finally creeps across his face and he says, "Fucking Ace! Hey, I shouldn't be here. Where's God? I should get a fucking medal for this."

< I forgive you. >

"Go fuck yourself goat boy," he shouts, "Hey everyone look at me! I rubbed out Satan!" He twirls around with his arms held high, laughing as one of the Demons strikes him and forces him to his knees.

"His name is Lucifer," the Demon snarls, "You will show respect."

<Take him away please, > I ask, and he is frog marched off to the fifth level of Hell. The volume of his hooting and laughing, slowly receding. And a thought goes through my mind, which makes me shiver. It may actually take an eternity, for that soul to aspire to Heaven.

Epilogue.

Year Thirty-eight: December 10th.

Carrie unwraps the flowers from their plastic envelope and places them on the floor. She proceeds to remove last weeks wilting flora from the urn, and begins to arrange the fresh flowers. The railings around this plot are always adorned with flowers, she does not bring them, everyone else does, but no one comes inside and changes her flowers except her.

There is always someone staring at this grave when she arrives, she cannot remember a week when she has been here, and no one was nearby. But they always move away and give her some privacy.

"How are you both?" She asks the headstone.

When she is content with her arrangement, she stands and continues to make small talk, telling them what has been happening since her last visit. Carrie stops talking and turns when she hears crying beside her.

"What's all this?" she asks the baby in the pushchair, "Are you cold?" The baby continues to cry, so she lifts him into her arms and gently rocks him, pulling the blanket around his small frame. The baby's crying subsides and he closes his eyes. "He's doing well now," she tells them, "You don't have to worry about your son."

Carrie places the child back into the stroller and straps him in, fussing over the blanket until she is satisfied with it. She pushes the child through the gap in the railings and closes the ornamental gate.

"Come on then David," she tells the child, "Let's get you back into the warm."

※

Not in Heaven, Hell or on Earth.

It's been a fiasco, hasn't it? I told you it would make no difference.

"With respect, I thought we made a great effort. And it has made some difference."

Nothing, which is worth shouting about. You're not doing very well are you?

"That's very unfair, you effectively tie my hands, and expect the impossible. I have only just begun. It will come together, I promise."

Moan, moan. We have this conversation every time I see you. The others are doing better than you are. Do you expect preferential treatment? Would you like me to hold your hand, and tell you how to do it?

"No."

How about a manual, I could colour code it, and write in big letters.

"I will achieve, what was set before me."

I cannot see it happening, I wish I had as much confidence in you, as you appear to have in yourself.

"Trust me."

Ha, trust you! I think that maybe you have your money on the wrong horse.

"If you could do it, I can do it also .I will not fail."

Do you consider yourself cleverer than I?

"No, I did not mean it, in that way."

I should think not, remember I have already done what you struggle to do. You are the proof. Do not forget that.

"How can I? You always remind me."

Ah, is my apprentice getting agitated?

"I would not be so disrespectful."

I will put in your report that you are trying, under difficult circumstances.

"Thank you Lord."

Well, what are you still doing here? You may go back to your reality.

"I will see this through, whatever it takes and whatever it takes from me."

Hope and faith will not bring this to conclusion, and under no circumstances, will I let you destroy yourself. I will end this myself, if the situation starts looking much worse, and there is nothing you could do to stop me. Do you understand?

"Yes Lord."

After all, you can always try again, it will not be held against you. So, until we meet again, I bid you farewell YHWH.

END

ISBN 1412092957